Sarah Morgan ... bestselling auth... women's fiction... copies of her books an... warmth have gained her fans across... lives with her family near London, England, where the rain frequently keeps her trapped in her office. Visit her at www.sarahmorgan.com

USA Today bestselling author **Jules Bennett** has penned more than fifty novels during her short career. She's married to her high school sweetheart, has two active girls, and is a former salon owner. Jules can be found on Twitter, Facebook (Fan Page), and her website julesbennett.com. She holds contests via these three outlets with each release and loves to hear from readers!

Andrea Laurence is an award-winning contemporary author who has been a lover of books and writing stories since she learned to read. A dedicated West Coast girl transplanted into the Deep South, she's constantly trying to develop a taste for sweet tea and grits while caring for her boyfriend and her old bulldog. You can contact Andrea at her website: http://www.andrealaurence.com

Unwrapped

SARAH MORGAN

JULES BENNETT

ANDREA LAURENCE

MILLS & BOON

First Published in Great Britain 2020
By Mills & Boon, an imprint of HarperCollins*Publishers*
1 London Bridge Street, London, SE1 9GF

UNWRAPPED © 2020 Harlequin Books S.A.

The Twelve Nights of Christmas © 2010 Sarah Morgan
Best Man Under the Mistletoe © 2017 Harlequin Books S.A.
A White Wedding Christmas © 2015 Andrea Laurence

Special thanks and acknowledgement are given to Jules Bennett for her contribution to the *Texas Cattleman's Club: Blackmail* series.

ISBN: 978-0-263-29839-0

MIX
Paper from
responsible sources
FSC® C007454

This book is produced from independently certified FSC™ paper to ensure responsible forest management.

For more information visit: www.harpercollins.co.uk/green

Printed and bound by CPI Group (UK) Ltd,
Croydon, CR0 4YY

THE TWELVE NIGHTS OF CHRISTMAS

SARAH MORGAN

To Kimberley Young: seven years
and forty-two books together.
Thank you. xx

CHAPTER ONE

'I NEVER thought this moment would come, Pietro. Let's celebrate.' Rio Zaccarelli sat back as the vintage champagne was poured into his glass. Across the table, his lawyer opened his case and handed him a sheaf of papers.

'I'm not celebrating until this one is in the bag. How did you get a table here? I've never seen so many rich, powerful people in one place.' Pietro glanced discreetly over his shoulder, his gaze skimming the other diners. His eyes widened as he focused on a man in a dark grey suit. 'Isn't that—?'

'Yes. Don't stare or you'll have security teams swarming over your lunch.' Rio flicked through the papers, scanning the contents. As he reached for his champagne he noticed that his hand shook slightly and he wrenched back his emotions, forcing himself to treat this like any other business deal. 'You haven't eaten here before?'

'I've been waiting a year to get a table at this restaurant and you do it in one phone call. There are times when I wish I had your influence.'

'Complete this deal and I'll get you a table. That's a promise.' *Complete this deal and I'll buy you the restaurant.*

'I'll hold you to that. You have to sign on the back page.' Pietro handed him a pen and Rio signed the documents with a bold scrawl.

'As usual, I owe you—for your discretion as well as your

astonishing legal brain. Order the lobster. It's sublime and you've more than earned it.'

'Thank me when it's all signed and sealed and not before. I've learned not to celebrate until the ball is in the net. It's been a hard fight and this may still not be finished.' The lawyer took the wedge of papers and slipped them into his briefcase. 'The stakes are high. They haven't stopped fighting, Rio. They don't want you to win this.'

'I'm aware of that.' A red mist of anger coloured his vision and his fingers tightened on the delicate stem of the champagne flute. The tension was like steel bands around his body. 'I want to be kept updated, Pietro. Any changes, phone my personal line.'

'Understood.' Pietro snapped his case shut. 'This deal could still blow itself apart. The most important thing is that you need to keep yourself whiter than fresh snow between now and Christmas. Don't get yourself so much as a parking ticket. Not a blemish. Not a rumour. My advice as a friend who knows you? Find an isolated ski lodge and lock yourself away. No liaisons with women, no kiss and tell stories—for the time being, sex is off the agenda.'

Rio, who hadn't gone ten days without sex since he'd lost his virginity, kept his face expressionless. 'I'll be discreet.'

'No.' Pietro leaned forward, switching from friend back to lawyer in the blink of an eye. 'If you want this deal watertight, then discretion isn't enough. I'm saying no sex, Rio. Unless it's married sex. If you happen to suddenly fall for a decent, wholesome girl whose entire objective in life is to love you and give you babies, that might actually help your case—' he gave a faint smile and spread his hands in a fatalistic gesture '—but, knowing you as I do, there's not much chance of that.'

'None at all. There's no such thing as a decent, wholesome girl and if there were she'd undergo a personality change the moment she met me,' Rio drawled. 'Within minutes she'd be thinking about prenuptial agreements and record breaking divorce settlements.'

Pietro picked up the menu. 'I don't blame you for being cynical, but—'

'I understand you. No sex. Sounds like I'm in for an exciting Christmas.' Rio thought of the Russian ballerina who was currently waiting in his apartment, lying on silk sheets, waiting for the visit he couldn't risk making.

He'd send her diamonds and give her the use of his private jet to fly home to Moscow for Christmas. They could pick up their relationship in the New Year. Or not. Realising that he wasn't bothered either way, he frowned.

Perhaps it was a good job he had an urgent business trip to make. He could work off his excess energy in other ways.

His eyes blank of expression, Rio stared out of the glass sided restaurant that had views over the centre of Rome, watching the crazy traffic fighting for space on the streets below.

There was nothing he wouldn't do to achieve the outcome he wanted. Even denying his libido for a short time.

Pietro put down the menu and picked up his glass, a hint of a smile on his face. 'I have a feeling this will be the hardest thing you've ever done. Go somewhere there are no women. I hear Antarctica is sparsely populated at this time of year.'

'I have to fly to London on business.'

'You are confronting Carlos?'

'I'm firing him,' Rio said coldly. 'His appointment was a mistake. I've had a full report from the external management consultant I put into the hotel. I need to deal with the situation before his appalling mismanagement affects the reputation of my company.'

'I don't suppose I can persuade you to wait until after the deal is signed?'

'Carlos cannot affect this deal.'

'In theory I would agree, but—' frowning, his lawyer put his glass down slowly '—this has been a difficult fight and we're not there yet. I'm uneasy.'

'That's why I'm paying you such an astronomical sum. I pay you to be uneasy, so that I can sleep.'

Pietro lifted an eyebrow. 'Since when did you start sleeping? You work harder than I do. Especially at this time of year. I assume you're planning to work right through Christmas?'

'Of course.'

The lawyer picked up the warm, crusty bread roll from his side plate and broke it in half. 'Why do you hate this time of year so much?'

A cold, sick feeling rose in his stomach. Aware that, as always, he was the focus of attention in the restaurant, Rio sat still, his features carefully composed. Catching the eye of a pretty European princess who had been gazing at him across the restaurant since he'd arrived, he gave a brief nod of acknowledgement. Desperate for distraction, he contemplated accepting her blatant invitation, but then he remembered Pietro's warning. No sex. Whiter than white.

Instead, he drained his champagne glass and formulated an answer to the question. 'Why do I hate Christmas? Because everyone uses Christmas as an excuse to stop work,' he lied smoothly, wrestling down his emotions with sheer brute force. 'And I'm a demanding boss. I hate time wasters, you know that. But I appreciate all the hours you've put into this deal and I will heed the advice. Until this deal is closed, the only person sleeping in my bed will be me.'

'It might make for a boring Christmas, but that is exactly the way it should be. I'm serious, Rio. Stay indoors. The only things you should be touching are your laptop and your phone.' Pietro looked him in the eye. 'Don't underestimate how much could still go wrong.'

'Whiter than white,' Rio purred, a faint smile touching his

mouth. 'I can do that if I really concentrate. Anyway, I'm not likely to meet a woman who interests me in London. Shall we order?'

'You can't do this to me! You can't just throw me out of my home! I can't *believe* you changed the locks when I was out. Don't you have any human feeling?' Evie grabbed the man's arm, almost slipping on the snow and ice as he shrugged her off and dropped his tools back into his bag.

'Life's tough. Blame your landlord, not me. Sorry, love.' But he didn't look sorry and Evie felt the panic rise as the enormity of the situation hit her.

'It's only twelve days until Christmas. I'll never find anything else at this short notice.'

The emotions she'd been suppressing for six stressful weeks suddenly broke through the front she'd been presenting to the world.

This was supposed to have been her wedding day. Tonight she would have been flying to a romantic hotel in the Caribbean on her honeymoon to make a baby. Instead, she was on her own in a big, cold city where no one seemed to care about anyone else. It was snowing and she was homeless.

'At least let me get my things.' Not that she had much. The few things she'd brought with her could probably fit into one rubbish bag.

Even as the thought wafted through her mind, the man gestured to a black bin liner leaning against the door.

'Those are your things.' The man snapped his bag shut. 'Good job you haven't got much stuff.'

Evie wondered what was good about not having much stuff. She'd thought moving to London would be exciting and full of opportunities. She hadn't realised how expensive it would be. Everything cost a fortune. And she hadn't realised how lonely it would be living in a city. She couldn't afford a social life. When a few of the girls at work had invited her out, she'd had to refuse.

The snow fluttered onto her head and neck and Evie huddled deeper inside her coat, her spirits as low as the temperature.

'Just let me stay here tonight, OK? I'll try and find somewhere tomorrow—' She felt as though she was holding everything together by a single fragile thread. It had been that way since the day Jeff had texted her to tell her the wedding was off. Concerned about her grandfather's distress, she'd taken refuge in the practical, returning presents with polite notes attached, cancelling the church and the venue, explaining to all the well-wishers who arrived at the house. She'd told herself that she'd shed her tears in private, but she'd discovered that cancelling a wedding was almost as much work as organising one, without any of the excitement to drive you forward. By the time she'd fallen into her bed at night she hadn't had the energy to cry. 'Please—it's going to be impossible to find somewhere else to live this close to Christmas.'

'It's a dog eat dog world, love.'

Evie recoiled. 'I love dogs. I'd *never* eat a dog! And it's supposed to be the season of goodwill.'

'I feel plenty of goodwill. Thanks to landlords like yours, I have a job.'

'Well, it's nice to know I'm supporting someone through the credit crunch—' Feeling a vibrating in her pocket, Evie dug out her phone, her anxiety doubling when she saw the number. 'Just wait there a moment and don't go anywhere because I have to answer this or he'll worry—he's very old and—Grandpa? Why are you calling in the middle of the day? Are you OK?' She prayed he hadn't had another one of his turns. It was one thing after another. Her life was unravelling faster than a pulled thread in a sweater. She'd wanted so badly to make him proud. Instead, all she was going to do was worry him.

'Just checking up on you because I saw the pictures of the snow on the news.' Her grandfather sounded frail and Evie tightened her grip on the phone, hating the fact that he was getting older.

He was the person she loved most in the world. She owed him everything. 'I'm fine, Grandpa.' She shivered as more flakes of snow found their way inside her coat. 'You know I love the snow.'

'You always did. Built any snowmen yet? You always loved building snowmen.'

Evie swallowed. 'I…I haven't had the chance yet, Grandpa. Soon, I hope. There's a huge park opposite the hotel where I'm working. It's crying out for a snowman.' She didn't tell him that no one paused to build a snowman in London. Everyone was too busy rushing from one place to another.

'Are you at work now? I don't want to bother you if you're at work, dealing with some high-powered celebrity.'

High-powered celebrity?

'Well…er…' Her face scarlet, Evie moved away from the man who had just tipped her life into a rubbish bag and wondered whether the lie she'd told about her job was about to come back to bite her. It was one thing trying to protect her grandfather, but she'd probably gone a little over the top. Or possibly more than a little. 'Grandpa—'

'I boast to everyone about you. I'm so proud of you, Evie. I told that stuffy Mrs Fitzwilliam in the room next door to mine, "My granddaughter has got herself a brilliant high-powered job. She may have been left standing at the altar—"'

Evie pressed her fingers to her aching forehead. 'It wasn't at the altar, Grandpa. No one got as far as the altar—'

'"—but she picked herself up and now she's a receptionist at the smartest hotel in London and she never would have had that opportunity if she'd married useless Jeff." He was nothing but a dreamer. And he wasn't good enough for you,

you know that, don't you? He was wet, and you don't want a man who is wet. You need a *real* man.'

'Any man would be a start,' Evie muttered under her breath, 'but fat chance of that.'

'What was that?'

'Nothing.' For once grateful for her grandfather's hearing aid, she changed the subject quickly. 'Are you OK? Are they treating you all right there?' Although he'd persuaded her he wanted to go into the same home as his closest friend, she still wasn't comfortable with the idea.

'My bones are aching in the damp weather and they make too much fuss here.'

Evie smiled. 'It will be summer soon. And I'm glad they're fussing.'

'I wish I could see you at Christmas but I know it's too far for you to come for just one day. I'm worrying about you on your own. I miss you, Evie.'

Flattened by homesickness, Evie felt a lump settle in her throat. 'I miss you, too. And I'll try and come up as soon as I can. And don't worry. I'm fine.' She pushed the words past her cold lips and then waved her hand frantically as the man loaded his tools into his van. Was he really just going to drive away and leave her here, standing on a snowy pavement in the dark? What had happened to chivalry? Her fiancé broke up with her by text and this man was about to leave a vulnerable woman alone in a big, scary city with nowhere to spend the night. Where were all the knights in shining armour when you needed them? Her grandfather was right—she needed a real man. Down with rats, wimps and cowards.

'So how's the job going?' Her grandfather used his most bracing voice. 'I told Mrs Fitzwilliam that you have Hollywood stars staying and that you'll be meeting and greeting them personally. That shut her up. Nosy old madam.'

Evie didn't know whether to laugh or cry. She was going to be struck down for lying to her grandfather. On the other hand, the alternative option was disappointing and worrying him. And she *did* 'meet and greet' guests. Sort of. If she met someone, she greeted them, didn't she? The fact that they usually ignored her didn't count. 'The job's great, Grandpa. Brilliant.' She'd been demoted and the slimy hotel manager had made a pass at her but, apart from that, it was all perfect.

The man started the engine and Evie sprinted across the pavement to stop him, her feet slithering on the ice. 'Wait—'

Her grandfather was still chatting. 'I've been watching the shares of Zaccarelli Leisure. They're soaring. You picked a winner there, Evie. At least your job is safe.'

No. No, it wasn't safe. Her entire existence was balancing on a knife edge.

Evie had a sudden urge to confess that the manager had tried it on with her, but stopped herself in time. She didn't want to upset her grandfather. And she also had a sneaking worry that he might somehow get on a train, find his way to London and deal with Carlos Bellini personally. Despite his eighty-six years, her grandfather was a real man.

'My job is…it's…well, it's great,' she said firmly. 'Really good.'

'Going to any Christmas parties? I'm sure you'll be able to have your pick of men if you do! And you won't be able to make it through the Christmas season without singing *The Twelve Days of Christmas* at the top of your voice. You know you always love doing that.'

'No parties planned. And I'm not quite ready to meet another man yet, Grandpa.' Dragging the bag behind her, Evie slithered towards the van. As she let go of it, the top gaped open and her tiny silver Christmas tree tumbled into the snow and slush. 'Don't worry about me. I'm fine.' A lump in her throat, she stared at her Christmas tree, which was now lying in a puddle. Her whole life felt as though it was sinking into a puddle.

'Don't hang around, Evie. I'm not getting any younger. Next year I want to be bouncing a great-grandchild on my knee.'

What? 'I'll do my best, Grandpa.' Wondering how on earth she was going to fulfil that particular wish when she couldn't find a man who wanted to talk to her, let alone sleep with her, Evie forced out a cheery goodbye and dropped the phone back in her pocket.

As she retrieved the dripping Christmas tree, the man drove off, showering her with slush.

It was snowing steadily and Evie was just wondering whether it was worth wading through the contents of the bag to find her umbrella when her phone rang again.

'Why am I suddenly the most popular person in the world?' Looking at the number flashing on her phone, she groaned. *Oh, no.* 'Tina? I know I'm late, but I've—' she flinched as her boss gave her a sharp lecture '—yes, I know Salvatorio Zaccarelli is arriving tomorrow and—yes, I know it's important because he's looking at the way the hotel is run and we're all under scrutiny. Yes, I know I was lucky you gave me another chance with this job when you could have fired me—' She gritted her teeth as she listened. 'I—yes, the Penthouse will be perfect, I promise—I'm lucky that Carlos wants me to do the job personally—I do know Mr Zaccarelli is the most important guest we ever have—I know he doesn't suffer fools and won't tolerate anything less than perfection—' *the guy was obviously a cold, heartless pig* '—I feel the same way,' Evie lied, making a mental note not to be anywhere near the scary, ruthless tycoon when he arrived at the hotel. The way she was feeling at the moment, she'd probably punch him. That was one 'meet and greet' that was *not* going to happen. If she saw him coming she was going to dive for cover.

Tina was still talking and Evie slithered her way towards the bus stop, the rubbish bag banging against her legs, her clothes soaked through. Snow landed on her hair and water dripped down her neck. '—Festive? Sparkling? Yes, I'm going to decorate the Christmas tree—I'll be there ever so soon, but I just need to—' she broke off; *I just need to find somewhere to sleep tonight when I come off my shift at midnight* '—catch a bus. The buses are mad because of Christmas, but I'm on my way now.' All she ever did was tell lies, Evie thought, struggling with the bag. She lied to protect her grandfather from more worry and she lied to Tyrannosaurus Tina because, until she'd found something better, she couldn't tell the woman where to stick her job. Maybe she should suggest to scary Salvatorio Zaccarelli that the first person he should fire was the manager of his flagship hotel.

As she sat on the crowded bus, jammed between stressed out Christmas shoppers, Evie wondered if she should have just told her grandfather the truth. That London was lonely. That she missed him. That she'd been demoted after just days in her new job by a boss who hated her. Apparently, she'd been too friendly.

Evie sighed, well aware that she'd probably been a little too desperate for human company. But she still didn't understand why that was a crime. As a receptionist in a hotel, how could you be too friendly? Anyway, she had no opportunity to be friendly now because, as a member of the housekeeping staff, she didn't often meet any guests. She didn't meet anyone. She'd taken to talking to herself as she cleaned bathroom mirrors.

Trying to take her mind off it, Evie picked up a discarded magazine and flicked through the pages, staring gloomily at the slender models wearing the magazine's recommendations for glittery dresses perfect for the party season. Apparently, silver was bang on trend. Absently, she picked the one she would have worn if she had money and had actually been invited to a party. Shimmering silver, she thought, with diamonds and swept up hair. Except that she'd look ridiculous dressed like that.

Face it, Evie, you're a bit of a freak.

Hearing Jeff's voice in her head, she dropped the magazine back on the seat, jumped off the bus and walked towards the back entrance of the prestigious hotel that provided a bolt-hole for the world's rich and famous. She was just wondering where she was going to hide a rubbish bag when a sleek black Mercedes drove through a puddle and muddy water sprayed over her tights and shoes.

'Oh, for—' Hopping to one side, soaking wet, Evie glared after the expensive car, imagining the warm, luxurious interior. 'Thanks a lot. Just as long as you're comfortable in your cosy, rich cocoon.' Her eyes widened in disbelief as she read the number plate. 'TYCOON.' Drenched and shivering, she wondered what it was like to live a life of luxury, filled with diamonds, shimmering silver dresses and ostentatious car accessories.

'Hi, Evie, you're late.' A colleague hurried past her in a cloud of perfume and hairspray. 'You've already missed the staff briefing. Tina said you were to go straight to the Penthouse because she doesn't have time to waste with you. The big boss is arriving tomorrow. Rumour has it that he is going to axe anyone who doesn't fit. Even Creepy Carlos is nervous. Personally, I can't wait to see Rio Zaccarelli in person. He's the most stunningly good-looking man I've ever seen.'

Chilled to the bone, Evie sneezed. 'You've never seen him.'

'I've seen him in pictures. Red-hot Rio, that's what we're calling him.'

'Ruthless Rio is what *I'm* calling him,' Evie muttered and her colleague frowned at the bag in her hand.

'Since when have you been responsible for dealing with the trash?'

'Oh, I like to be helpful. Versatile, that's me—' Evie pinned a rigid grin on her face, refusing to admit that she was carrying her home around. Like a snail, she thought, as she followed the girl through the glass door and into the plush, privileged warmth of a different life. Maybe there was a number plate that spelled out DISASTER. She could stick it on her back to warn people she was coming.

Hiding her bag in the basement behind some large pipes, Evie took refuge in the peaceful elegance of the Penthouse suite. She felt so utterly miserable that, for the first time since her aborted wedding and humiliating demotion, she was relieved that she wasn't on Reception, having to smile and be cheerful. She didn't want to meet and greet. She just wanted to curl up in a ball and not emerge until her life had improved.

The warm, spacious luxury of the top floor suite made her feel instantly calmer and Evie looked around her wistfully. Two deep white sofas faced each other across a priceless rug and flames flickered in the fireplace. Huge floor to ceiling windows gave views over Hyde Park and the elegant buildings of Knightsbridge.

Someone had put a large fir tree next to the grand piano and boxes of decorations were neatly stacked, ready for Evie to create a perfect Christmas.

A perfect Christmas for someone else.

'Imagine spending Christmas somewhere like this,' she murmured, talking to herself as she explored the Penthouse suite. 'Talk about how the other half live.'

Feeling incredibly down, Evie set to work decorating the tree, trying not to think about the times she'd done the same thing with her grandfather. Last year they'd shared a wonderful Christmas. She'd baked Christmas cake and Christmas puddings and roasted a turkey just for the two of them. They'd eaten leftovers for weeks. Turkey curry, turkey soup, turkey sandwiches—

Only a few weeks later, her grandfather had suffered a mini stroke and she'd had no choice but to agree to let him go into the home where his friends were. They'd sold his cottage to pay the exorbitant fees and now she was miles away in a city where no one spoke to anyone except to ask directions.

And she had nowhere to sleep tonight. The thought terrified her and for a moment she considered confessing to Tina and asking if she had any free rooms. Imagining the response she'd get, a hysterical laugh bubbled up from the cauldron of panic that was simmering inside her. Tina would simply remind her that one night in the cheapest room in this hotel was more than her monthly salary.

Merry Christmas, Evie.

She worked without a break, twisting lights through the branches of the enormous tree, hanging glittering silver baubles and filling vases with elaborate displays of holly. Then she started to clean the Penthouse. She was only halfway through when the door opened and Carlos, the hotel manager, strode in.

Evie was immediately on the defensive, horribly aware that she was alone with him and that her mobile phone was in her coat pocket at the other end of the room.

She'd avoided him since the day he'd tried to kiss her and she stood warily, her mind scrambling through her options. They were pitifully few. He ran the hotel and held her future in the palm of his hand. Unfortunately, he'd made it clear that he wanted to hold other bits of her in the palm of his hand, too.

His hair shone greasily under the lights and Evie shuddered, bracing herself for criticism.

Was he looking for an excuse to fire her?

'It looks perfect. Incredibly Christmassy. Just what I wanted for Rio.' Something about his smile made her uneasy.

'You're sure you like it?'

'Absolutely.' His eyes trailed over her body. 'You're wet.'

Evie stood rigid, wondering why the only man to pay her any attention had to be a total creep.

'It's snowing. I had to wait for a bus.'

'I don't want my staff catching pneumonia. Take a hot shower.'

She felt herself blush. 'I can't afford the time. I still have loads to do and my shift ends in thirty minutes.'

'You're on again first thing tomorrow morning.' Carlos frowned. 'Stay here tonight. That way, you can start work straight away. I want everything perfect.'

He was giving her permission to stay in the hotel?

Unable to believe her luck, Evie almost sobbed with relief. 'That would be helpful,' she said casually. 'Do we have a spare room?'

'No, we're full. But you can stay here. In the Penthouse.'

Evie looked at him stupidly. *'Here?'*

'Why not? Rio isn't arriving until tomorrow afternoon. Your shift ends at midnight and begins again at seven in the morning. It makes perfect sense for you to stay here. Sleep on top of the bed if it bothers you. I'll make sure you're not disturbed.'

Evie stared at him, her instincts on full alert. 'You're suggesting that I stay in the *Penthouse*?'

'Why not? It isn't doing anyone any harm and I owe you a favour.' He hesitated. 'Evie, I apologise if I came on a little strong a few weeks ago. I misread the signals.'

She hadn't given him any signals. 'I'd rather forget that.' Evie, feeling horribly awkward, was nevertheless relieved by his surprise apology. Perhaps he wasn't trying to find reasons to fire her. 'How is your finger?'

'Healing.' Carlos flexed his bandaged finger and gave a rueful smile. 'Seriously, Evie. Stay here tonight. It's in the interests of the hotel—you'll get more work done if you're here on the premises.'

What he said made sense.

So why was she hesitating? She'd have somewhere warm to stay and she could start searching for another place tomorrow. 'All right. Thanks. If you're sure.'

'Do you have any dry clothes?'

Evie thought of the bag of belongings she'd left in the basement. 'I have a…a bag downstairs.'

'I'll arrange for someone to collect it. Where did you leave it?'

Flanked by his security team, Rio Zaccarelli left his private jet under the cover of darkness and slid into the waiting car.

'No press—that's good.' Antonio, his senior bodyguard, scanned the area. 'No one knows you're coming. Do you want us to call ahead and warn the hotel? They're expecting you in the afternoon, not at four in the morning.'

'No.' Rio lounged in the back of the car, his eyes hooded as he contemplated the surprise that would no doubt accompany his unexpected arrival. 'I don't want to announce myself.'

Knowing never to question the boss, Antonio simply slammed the car door shut and slid in next to the driver. 'Shouldn't take us long to get there at this hour. No traffic. I suppose it's because it's Christmas. Lots of people have already stopped work.'

Rio didn't reply.

A cold feeling spread across his skin. A feeling that had nothing to do with the dropping temperature and the swirling snowflakes outside the car. He looked out of the window, keeping his expression blank.

Christmas.

Twenty years had passed and yet he still hated this time of year.

If he had his way, Christmas would be scrubbed from the calendar.

Blocking out the endless twinkling lights and Christmas decorations adorning the dark streets, Rio was for once grateful for the endless demands of his BlackBerry.

Anna, the ballerina, had sent him fourteen messages, each one more desperate than the last.

He read the first three, saw the word 'commitment' and deleted the rest without reading them. Christmas, commitment—why was it that his least favourite words all began with C?

The car pulled up outside the hotel and Rio sat for a moment, surveying the elegant architecture. It was the most expensive few acres of real estate in the world.

You'll never make anything of yourself, Rio. You'll amount to nothing.

Rio gave a grim smile as he surveyed 'nothing'.

He owned it. All of it. Every last brick. Not bad for someone who had once watched his life ground into the dirt.

Leaning forward, he spoke to his driver in Italian. 'Take me to the rear entrance.'

'Yes, sir.'

Rio sprang from the car and walked through the rear door of the hotel, his mouth tightening in disapproval as no one challenged him.

Antonio was right behind him. 'I'll go first.'

'No. I want you to go back downstairs and check those security cameras. And time how long it takes them to discover I'm in the building.' Rio sprinted up ten floors and reached the locked door that protected the exclusive Penthouse suite. He entered a code into the pad and the door opened. Realising that no one had changed the code, his mouth tightened and a dangerous spark lit his eyes.

Inside the luxurious suite, it was warm and peaceful.

And decorated for Christmas.

Rio froze.

He'd given strict instructions—no decorations.

His tension levels rocketing, his gaze fastened on the tall fir tree that glittered and sparkled in the elegant living room, taunting him—*reminding him.*

Turning his back on it, he prowled through the suite. His instincts, honed through years of dealing with people, were suddenly on full alert. Something didn't feel right and it wasn't just that his express instructions had been overlooked.

His firm mouth hardened and he walked purposefully towards the bedroom suite, his footsteps muffled by the thick carpet.

Pushing open the door, Rio stopped on the threshold of the room.

Lying on top of the bed was a naked woman, her glorious red hair spilling over the pillow like a spectacular sunset, her eyelashes forming a dark smudge above pale cheeks. Her mouth was a deep pink, her lower lip full and softly curved.

Rio stared at that mouth for a full minute before trailing his gaze down the rest of her body. It wasn't just her mouth that curved. The rest of her did, too, although some of the secrets of her body were concealed beneath all that glorious hair. As he studied the astonishingly vibrant colour, he felt his libido come alive. His mind computed every last detail. Eyes—green, he decided. Temper—hot. Body—*incredible.* She had the longest legs he'd ever seen and, as for the rest of her—

When she didn't stir, he strolled into the room.

Distracted by the full curve of her breasts, he sat down on the edge of the bed and slid a leisurely hand over her shoulder, brushing aside a strand of silky hair.

Unable to resist the sensual curve of her soft mouth, Rio lowered his head and kissed her. He just had time to register that she tasted as good as she looked when her eyes opened.

Deliciously groggy, she stared at him blankly. 'Oh—' Her words were slurred from sleep. 'Is it Christmas?'

If this was Christmas, then maybe it was time he re-evaluated his feelings towards the festive season. Perhaps it wasn't all bad. *Blue,* Rio thought absently, correcting his earlier assumption. Her eyes were the palest aquamarine.

Lust shot through him and he felt himself harden. Because he was staring down at her, he saw the exact moment she was gripped by the same sexual awareness. Those incredible eyes darkened. Her lips parted and he saw the moist tip of her tongue.

Unable to help himself, Rio lowered his head and was about to kiss her again when a light flashed.

He whipped round in time to see a man darting from the room, camera in hand.

Swearing under his breath in Italian, Rio moved with a speed that would have impressed an Olympic sprinter, but the man was already out of the door.

He grabbed his phone from his pocket and speed-dialled his security team but before Antonio could answer the call, Carlos came striding into the room.

'Rio? I was told there was an intruder in the Penthouse. We had no idea you were arriving this early. Reception should have notified me. How was your journey?' He held out his hand in greeting and then froze, his eyes widening as he stared over Rio's shoulder and through the open doors of the bedroom. 'I'm so sorry—I had no idea you had company— how very embarrassing. Rio, forgive me… We'll give you privacy, of course…'

Rio didn't have to look round to identify the reason for the triumphant gleam in the man's eyes. He had his lawyer's words ringing in his ears.

The most important thing is that you need to keep yourself whiter than fresh snow between now and Christmas.

He, of all people, had allowed a woman to distract him and his carelessness could have the most devastating consequences.

He'd been set up.

He'd walked right into a trap.

And now he was going to pay.

CHAPTER TWO

DIZZY from the kiss and fully aware of just how much trouble she was in, Evie scrambled frantically off the bed and then remembered she was naked. She grabbed the silk throw and covered herself, but it refused to co-operate, slipping and slithering through her fingers. Finally she managed to fasten it, sarong-style around her body. She clutched it tightly, praying that it wouldn't fall off. Hurrying through to the living room, she saw Carlos standing there, deep in conversation with a tall, broad-shouldered man. *The man who had kissed her a few moments earlier.*

Still shaken from the explosion of chemistry, a strange heat spread through her body as she took her first proper look at him and immediately her grandfather's words flew into her head—*a real man.*

He dominated the room with the sheer force of his presence, his powerful legs spread apart, his stance unmistakably commanding as he focused furious black eyes on Carlos's face.

Hearing her entrance, he transferred that terrifying gaze to Evie and she stood pinned to the spot, the simmering fury in his eyes acting like a bucket of cold water.

She went from burning to shivering in the space of a glance.

'I…I'd better get dressed,' she stammered and he made a sound in his throat that sounded ominously like a growl.

'You'll stay *exactly* where you are until I give you permission to move.'

Whatever had propelled him to kiss her, it obviously wasn't something he intended to repeat. There was no softness in his eyes. No hint of the sexual promise that had shimmered only moments earlier.

And suddenly she knew exactly who he was and that realisation came with a cold flash of horror. She'd once seen his picture in the back of the hotel brochure—read a statement from the lord and master of the Zaccarelli Leisure Group. The man who had kissed her was Salvatorio Zaccarelli—Rio to the media, who licked their lips over his taste for glamorous women and super-fast cars.

From what she'd read, Evie had already decided that he was a ruthless, cold-hearted money-making machine who didn't give a damn about the human cost of his decisions. When he took a personal interest in one of his hotels the first thing he did was to change everything he didn't like, and that included the staff. He didn't visit when things were going well. Only when they were going badly did he thunder in like an executioner wielding his sword. There was nothing gentle about him. Nothing soft. He treated women the same way as his business. He hired and fired. No one was with him for long.

Evie had planned to keep her head down and stay out of his way.

Realising that her plan had backfired in the most spectacular fashion she stared, terrified, into his smouldering black eyes. He was obviously livid that she'd spent the night in the Penthouse.

Unless Carlos would admit that he'd given her permission, her job was toast.

And so was her dignity.

Evie swallowed hard, wondering why he'd kissed her. From the firm, deliberate seduction of his mouth to the sensuous brush of his hand over her bare skin, it had been a kiss loaded with sizzling chemistry and erotic promise.

Even as she was wondering if it was usual for him to kiss the staff before firing them, a burly man she'd didn't know came sprinting through the door.

'Sorry, boss.' He stared hard at Rio Zaccarelli, as if in some silent communication. 'Lost him. He must have nipped down the back stairs. I've contacted the local police and I'm going to go through the CCTV footage with hotel security. We'll identify him. Do you want me to question the girl?'

Question her? Why would they want to question her? Her crime was straightforward enough, wasn't it?

'You don't know her?' Carlos looked shocked. 'I assumed—why else would she be in your bedroom, Rio?'

Appalled, Evie stared at him. Obviously, Carlos was going to put his own future before hers. Presumably he was worried that if he confessed to having given her permission to sleep in the Penthouse, he'd be disciplined. Feeling intensely vulnerable, she stood there, searching desperately for a way out of this mess.

'Accept my apologies, Rio.' Carlos's voice was smooth. 'We normally screen our staff very carefully but at this time of year when we're so busy—' He left the sentence hanging. 'I'm disappointed in you, Evie. You abused a position of trust.'

'She works here?' Rio Zaccarelli's voice was harsh. 'She's one of your staff?'

Everyone turned to look at her and Evie burned with humiliation. So that was that. No one was going to believe she'd slept in the Penthouse with permission. They'd believe Carlos, not a lowly member of the housekeeping team. She was nothing more than cannon fodder. Whatever happened next, she was doomed.

There was no point in defending herself.

She had no home, no job and it was less than two weeks until Christmas.

Thinking of her grandfather, Evie felt despair seep through her veins. There was no way she could tell him. Not just before Christmas. He was so proud of her new job and the way she'd picked herself up.

You're a real soldier, Evie.

After everything he'd done for her, she'd let him down.

Maybe she should just forget dignity and beg. Or maybe she should try kissing the boss again. Her eyes drifted over his handsome face and rested on his firm, sensuous mouth. *That same mouth that had taken liberties with hers only moments earlier.* Without thinking, she drew her tongue over her lower lip, tasting his kiss.

He saw the gesture and his eyes flared with anger and something else, far, far more dangerous. With a final contemptuous glance, he turned back to Carlos. 'Do you know what you've done?' His voice was thickened with emotion. 'Have you any idea how much damage you've caused?'

Confused, Evie watched as Rio Zaccarelli transferred the full force of his anger onto Carlos. Why? Had he guessed that Carlos had given her permission? Had he seen through the lies? He was rumoured to have a brain as sharp as a blade.

Hope flickered to life inside her. If Rio Zaccarelli knew Carlos had given her permission, then maybe he'd let her off this time.

He had the reputation of being an exacting boss with impossibly high standards, but, all the same—

Sweat shone on Carlos's forehead. 'What damage? I have no idea what you're talking about.'

With a growl of anger, Rio Zaccarelli crossed the room in three long strides and locked his fist in the front of Carlos's shirt. 'Have you no conscience? No sense of human decency?'

Seeing the black expression on Rio Zaccarelli's face, Evie covered her mouth with her hand.

Wasn't he going a bit overboard?

Oh, dear God, he was going to punch creepy Carlos.

And Carlos looked terrified and triumphant at the same time. Although he was undoubtedly afraid, Evie had the strangest feeling that he was enjoying seeing the other man lose control. His expression was mocking rather than apologetic, as if the outcome had exceeded his most extravagant hopes.

Trying to make sense of it and failing, she could do nothing but watch as the drama unfolded in front of her. The two men appeared to have forgotten her existence. They faced each other down like two bulls fighting for territory, but there was no doubt in her mind who was the superior, both in strength and intellect.

While Carlos blustered and bumbled, Rio's anger was cold and a thousand times more frightening.

'If you have lost me this deal—'

'Me?' His voice contradicting the look in his eyes, Carlos sounded shocked. 'You think I had anything to do with this? You seriously think—? Rio, I know you don't need this sort of publicity right now—I know you're at a delicate stage of negotiations. This could ruin everything for you.'

Evie looked on in disbelief, trying to follow the thread of the conversation. This was all about some stupid deal? That was why Ruthless Rio was so angry? What had happened to everyone's priorities? All they thought about was money, money, money.

It was only because she had her eyes fixed on his taut profile that Evie saw the flash of raw emotion cross Rio Zaccarelli's face. For a moment she thought he was going to reach out and grab Carlos by the throat.

Instead, he released him.

'*Vai al diavolo*. Get out of my sight.' His voice was

strangely robotic, his features a mask of contempt. 'From this moment on, I don't know you. You don't work for me and I don't want to hear from you or see you again. Step into one of my hotels and I'll have you removed. My lawyers will sort out the details with you. And if this causes me trouble—if I lose—' He broke off, apparently unable to finish the sentence, his voice thickened with an emotion so much deeper than anger that Evie felt real fear.

How could he be so angry about one stupid deal?

She waited for Carlos to defend himself but the other man shot through the door without looking backwards.

Which, basically, left her alone with a madman.

Evie tightened her grip on the throw. She loathed Carlos, but at least he was a familiar face. If murder was about to be committed, then it might have been useful to have a witness. Or even an alternative victim.

The burly man, who she assumed was a bodyguard, flexed his fingers threateningly. 'Do you want me to deal with him, boss? I reckon I could get the information you want out of him in less than a minute. He's a wimp.'

Another wimp, Evie thought numbly. The world was populated by wimps. Wimps and bullies.

'Don't waste your time.' Rio's tone was ice-cold. 'I know a quicker way of extracting information.'

Realising that she was the 'quicker way', Evie took a step backwards, seriously scared.

'Calm down,' she stammered. 'Take a deep breath—count to ten—or maybe a hundred—' She had absolutely no idea what was going on, but it was obvious that she was in enormous trouble for sleeping in the Penthouse. 'I don't suppose there is any point in saying sorry or trying to explain, but honestly, I don't see that it's that big a deal. I know I did wrong, but I think you're overreacting—' She gulped as Rio Zaccarelli strode towards her.

He stripped off his jacket and threw it over the back of the nearest chair. His white silk shirt moulded to his wide, muscular shoulders, hinting at the power concealed beneath and Evie found herself staring in fascinated horror as he rolled the sleeves back in a deliberate movement. He looked like a boxer preparing for a fight. And she was obviously earmarked as the opponent. She wondered whether he'd removed his screamingly expensive jacket so that he didn't end up with her blood spattered on it.

His eyes dark with fury, he came to a halt right in front of her. 'Not a big deal? Either you are the most insensitive, selfish, greedy woman I've ever met or you have no idea of the magnitude of the trouble you've just caused.'

Up close, she could see the rough shadow that framed his hard jaw. She saw that his eyelashes were thick and dark and that underneath his fierce gaze there were dangerous shadows. Other women talked about his monumental sex appeal, but Evie was too scared to feel anything other than fear. 'I'm not selfish or greedy,' she defended herself in a shaky voice, 'and I honestly don't see that spending a night in that bed is such a big deal. I shouldn't have done it, but I thought the Penthouse was empty overnight. And I didn't even dirty the sheets. I slept on top of the covers.'

'Of course you slept on top of the covers,' he gritted. 'How else could the photographer have taken his picture?' He fisted his hand in the front of the throw and pulled her hard against him. Breathing heavily, the backs of his fingers pressed into her cleavage as he held her trapped.

Evie, who rarely felt intimidated by men because of her height, was definitely intimidated now.

For once she felt dwarfed, his superior height making her feel small and insignificant and she swiftly re-evaluated her belief that it would be nice to meet a man taller than her.

Through the mist of panic, her brain finally latched on to something he'd said.

'Photographer?' Trying to breathe, she stared up at him blankly. 'What photographer?'

His eyes dropped to her mouth and that single look weakened her knees. For a moment she saw what other women saw. Raw sex appeal. She might have been attracted to him herself if she hadn't been so terrified. Wondering if she was the only one who was feeling suffocated, she gasped as he suddenly released her. Her hands shot out to balance herself and the silk throw slid to the ground.

With a squeak of embarrassment, Evie made a grab for it but not before she'd seen the sudden darkening in his eyes and heard the burly security man gulp. 'I need to get dressed!' She'd hung her wet clothes on the heated towel rail in the bathroom, but they ought to be dry by now.

With a contemptuous sound, Rio Zaccarelli turned away from her. 'It's a little late for modesty, don't you think? By tomorrow, that photograph will be all over the world.'

'What photograph?' She wrapped the throw around her as tightly as she could. 'I have no idea what you're talking about.'

Rio gave a growl of anger. 'The photograph of us kissing. I want the name of the photographer and the name of the person who put you up to this. Start giving me facts.'

Evie glanced back towards the bedroom, retracing the events of the past few minutes. 'I…someone took a picture of me?'

A muscle flickered in his jaw. 'Generally, I pride myself on my control but today I seem to be falling short of my usual high standards. If you don't want to see a first-hand demonstration of the meaning of the word angry, then don't play stupid.'

'I'm not playing stupid! I didn't see a photographer. You were in my line of vision, remember? All I saw was you.'

Deep colour highlighted his cheekbones and his eyes

burned. 'Are you seriously expecting me to believe that you didn't see the light or the man running out of the room?'

Evie thought back, but all she could think about was how amazing it had felt to be kissed by him. She remembered warmth, the most incredible excitement, flashing lights— *flashing lights?*

Appalled, she stared at him and his mouth twisted in cynical derision.

'Memory returning?' He was so arrogantly sure of himself that Evie bristled and decided that there was no way she was confessing she'd thought the lights were part of the firework display set off in her body by his incredible kiss. His monumentally overinflated ego obviously didn't need any help from her.

'I didn't see him. As I said, you were blocking my view of the room.'

'Unfortunately, I wasn't blocking his view of you. He now has a picture of us—' his expression was grim as he watched her '—together.'

As the implications of his words sank home, Evie felt her limbs weaken. 'Hold on a moment. Are you telling me that some stranger just took a picture of me, naked on the bed?' Panic and horror rushed up inside her. She hated having her picture taken, even when she was fully clothed, but naked—?

'I've already warned you—I'm not in the mood.' There was no mistaking the deadly warning in his tone or the tension in his body language. He was a man no one was likely to mess with and Evie felt her mouth dry as her gaze clashed with pitch-black eyes.

'I'm not in the mood, either,' she squeaked. 'And I'm not playing games. How did a photographer get in here? Why would he want to take a photograph of me? What's he going to do with it?' Anxiety set her tongue loose but he silenced her with a single searing glance.

'If you utter one more ingenuous question I just might drop you naked on the street outside. How much did he pay you?'

Struggling to keep up with his thought process, Evie opened her mouth and closed it again. 'You honestly think anyone would pay to take a picture of my body? Are you mad?' Her voice rose. 'Presumably, you've already noticed that I'm not exactly a supermodel! The only way anyone would be interested in looking at me naked is one of those hideous before and after photos. You know—*"and this is Evie before she went on the wonder diet and lost twenty kilos."'*

His eyes blazed dark with incredulity. 'Is that all you can think about? Whether the photographer took your good side?'

'No, because I don't have a good side! I look the same from every angle, which is why I never let anyone take my photo!' She'd never before met a man she wanted to kiss and slap at the same time and it was such a shockingly confusing sensation that her head spun. She wanted to defend herself. She wanted to protest that she wasn't superficial and that having a photograph taken of her naked was right up there with her worst nightmares. It was like being back in the playground.

Evie the elephant—

'Wh…what's he going to do with that photograph?' She tried to calm herself down with logic and reason. This wasn't the playground. 'No one is going to want to look at a picture of me naked. There is no reason anyone would want to publish a picture of me…' as she stared into his taut, handsome face, her voice faded to a horrified whisper '…but there's every reason why they'd publish a picture of *you*.' And she was in that picture. Suddenly, everything was clear. She thought of all the vile, degrading 'kiss and tell' stories she'd read. 'Oh, my God—'

Rio was watching her, his mouth tight. 'How much did he pay you?'

'Nothing! I don't know anything about this! I'm as inno-cent as you are.' But she could tell he didn't believe her and what she saw in those glittering black eyes was so terrifying that she wanted to confess everything on the spot. Because his expression was so scary, she looked at his mouth instead and suddenly all she was thinking about was that scorching kiss. *Where had he learned to kiss like that?*

'Innocent girls don't lie in wait, naked, on a guy's bed.'

'I wasn't lying in wait! How could you even think that? I've been kicked out of my flat and I had nowhere to go last night and—' Evie thought about the sequence of events. Carlos had offered her the use of the room. When she'd refused, he'd insisted. It was Carlos who had encouraged her to take a shower and dry her wet clothes on the radiator. Appalled, she looked up at Rio Zaccarelli and saw his mouth tighten as he read her mind.

'Your face is very revealing, so don't even think of telling me you have no idea what's going on.' The menacing chill in his voice confirmed just how much trouble she was in and she felt the colour drain out of her cheeks as he turned up the pressure.

'I've been set up.'

A dangerous glint shone in his eyes. 'I'm listening.'

He didn't believe her. 'Carlos gave me instructions to sleep here tonight—' Evie clutched at the silk throw, her mind racing forward with possible scenarios, all of which sickened her. No matter what she said, Rio Zaccarelli wasn't going to believe that she had nothing to do with this. 'I was really, really stupid—what are they going to do with that photograph?'

For a moment he didn't answer. He simply stared at her, as if he were making a decision about something. A slight frown touched his brows and he strolled around her, look-ing at her from the front, the back and the sides. When he finally spoke, his voice was hard. 'They're going to publish it. By tomorrow, that photograph will be plastered all over the Internet and the newspapers.'

The bodyguard cleared his throat. 'Boss—'

Rio turned on him and said something in Italian that silenced the other man immediately.

Evie felt faint with horror. *'What?'* That was by far the worst scenario on her list and she gave a low moan of horror as she contemplated exactly what that would mean. 'I thought maybe they'd just use it to blackmail you or something—'

'Is that what they told you?' His tone was dangerously soft. 'Is that what you agreed?'

'No! I didn't agree anything. I was thinking aloud—' Flustered, realising that she was digging herself deeper and deeper into a hole, Evie sank her hand into her hair, trying to think straight so that she could be more articulate. 'What I mean is, at least if it's blackmail they could be persuaded not to publish it. Of all the things they could do with that photo, publishing it would be the worst. Do you have any idea how embarrassing that would be? I'd never be able to go anywhere ever again.'

'Embarrassing? Do you think I care about being embarrassed?' The lethal cocktail of physical height and powerful personality left her shaking and intimidated but all those emotions were eclipsed by the prospect of being exposed physically to the mocking eyes of the world.

'No, you probably don't care—' Evie's voice rose '—because *you're* not the one who was lying there naked with your bottom on full view! And stop trying to scare me! This whole thing is bad enough without having to wonder whether you're going to explode any minute.' She covered her face with her free hand—the other was still clutching the throw, holding it in place. 'Oh, my God—if that photo goes in the papers— everyone I know will see it—Grandpa will see it—he'll be mortified—' Melting with embarrassment, she looked at him helplessly. 'You *have* to do something. You have to stop it.

You're completely loaded—can't you pay them or something? Do whatever it is they want you to do.' The thought of being seen naked in public was the most hideous thing that had ever happened to her. Worse than being demoted. Worse than losing her job. Worse than being dumped by Jeff.

Evie cringed with horror as she tried to work out what angle the flash had come from and remember exactly how she'd been lying.

It took her right back to the nightmare days of hiding in the corner of the girls' changing rooms trying to wriggle into her gym kit with no one noticing.

'If you genuinely care, then perhaps you should have thought of the consequences before you agreed to lie on the bed.'

Evie ground her teeth. 'I lay on the bed because I didn't have anywhere else to lie, OK? I told you—I lost my flat. I was in a fix and when Carlos made that offer—' she licked her lips '—it just seemed too good to be true. Turned out it *was* too good to be true. Look, it doesn't really matter whether you believe me or not. What's important is stopping that photograph. *Please* pay them off.'

His gaze was steady. 'They don't want money.'

'Then what do they want?'

He turned away from her but not before she'd seen the dark shadow flicker across his face. 'They want to make my life…difficult.'

'What about *my* life?'

'They're not interested in you. You've played your part. You're expendable. I'm sure you can find some lucrative way to use your five minutes of fame.'

'Do you honestly think I want to be famous for the size of my bottom?'

'If you are genuinely distressed about the idea of being pictured, why did you agree to this?'

'Are you thick or something? *I didn't agree to it!*'

There was a crashing sound as the door to the suite burst open behind him and three uniformed hotel security men pounded into the room, horribly out of breath.

Evie suddenly wished she could vanish into thin air.

Rio took a slow, deliberate look at the watch on his wrist. 'I have been in this hotel for seventeen minutes,' he said in an icy tone, 'and no one has challenged me. That is sixteen and a half minutes too long. The security code for the Penthouse hasn't been changed since the last time I stayed here as a guest, which is presumably how a complete stranger managed to access the suite. The security camera at the rear entrance is pointed away from the street. A journalist managed to get access to my suite. Is this how you protect the guests in your care?'

Evie watched as Arnold's forehead grew shiny with sweat. The security chief was one of the few people who had been kind to her since she'd arrived in London and she felt a tiny flame of anger warm her insides as she saw him squirm.

'We didn't know you were arriving in the middle of the night, sir. We were expecting you later this morning and—' His jaw dropped as he saw Evie. '*Evie?* What are you doing in the Penthouse?'

Evie tightened her grip on the silk bedspread. 'I had nowhere to sleep last night, Arnold—'

Rio's eyes narrowed. 'You know this woman?'

'Of course. Her name is Evie Anderson.' Arnold's expression softened. 'She works here as a receptionist—I mean, a member of the housekeeping staff.'

Evie was just beginning to hope that Arnold might vouch for her integrity when the door to the Penthouse opened again and a portly woman in her fifties arrived, breathless and flustered. It was obvious that she'd dressed in a hurry and her skirt was on back to front and the buttons on her shirt unaligned. Clearly woken from sleep, one half of her hair was flattened to her head and the other was in wild disarray.

Evie groaned in horror. *No.* How had Tina found out?

'Mr Zaccarelli—we were expecting you much later to-day—I'm so sorry no one was here to greet you—' Oozing deference, the woman's discomfiture was almost painful to watch. 'I'm Tina Hunter, Director of Guest Relations. We're going to do anything in our power to make sure your stay here is memorable.'

Tina's eyes widened with horror as she turned her head and saw Evie.

'Evelyn? What do you think you're doing?' She turned back to Rio, squirming with mortification. 'I'm *so* sorry. She's given us nothing but trouble, that girl—thinks she's better than the rest of us. It's my fault for giving her a second chance, but that's me all over. I've always been a soft touch. Evelyn, I want you to collect your things and go.'

Shocked by the injustice, Evie stared at her. 'You haven't even asked for my side of the story.'

Tina's cheeks turned scarlet. 'You're naked in a guest's bedroom. That's enough for me. Let me just say that I find it incredibly tacky that you would try and force yourself on a billionaire.'

'Excuse me?' Almost speechless with outrage, Evie exploded. 'Look at the guy! Even if I wanted to, I'm hardly likely to be able to force myself on him, am I? He's built like a—' Her voice tailed off and colour poured into her cheeks.

Tina was shaking with anger. 'Get your things.'

'I don't have any things. Everything I owned was in a bag and I left it in the basement. Carlos was supposed to arrange for it to be brought up here so that I could change into dry clothes. Funnily enough, it never appeared.' Evie scraped a strand of hair behind her ear with a hand that shook, afraid that this was going to be the moment that she finally lost it.

She felt tears scald the back of her eyes as she made a last-ditch attempt to extricate herself. 'Carlos ordered me to sleep here last night, not that I expect any of you to believe me.'

'Of course we don't believe you!' Tina exploded. 'Why would the Manager of this hotel give a member of the house-keeping staff permission to spend the night in the Penthouse? A room that costs twelve thousand pounds a night.'

Evie paled. 'How much? That's outrageous.'

'What's outrageous is you standing there behaving like Lady Godiva. You need to find yourself another job, young lady. Since you're so free with your body, I'm sure there are no end of options open to you if you're seeking new employment,' Tina snapped. 'And don't look so shocked. You're standing there half naked, so this "I'm an innocent girl from the country" act is wearing a little thin. You may look wholesome, but I think we all know different. Why do you think I moved you off Reception? We had such a crowd around the desk, the hotel almost ground to a standstill.'

'I was being friendly! You told me I was the public face of the hotel and I assumed you'd want that face to be smiling, not miserable! You're *so* unfair—it's Christmas and there's not a single drop of Christmas spirit or compassion in any of you. And I'm naked because my clothes were wet, not because I want a career as a porn star.'

Tina pointed towards the door. 'You're fired. Get out.'

'What, dressed like this?' Evie gaped at her. 'No way! This is the throw from the bed and I'm not giving you reason to sue me for theft on top of everything else, not to mention indecent exposure as I trail along the corridors. I think you're all vile. None of this is my fault, but I'm going to be the one who suffers. I'll get dressed and then I'll leave and I hope you all have a really Happy Christmas!' Thinking of her grandfather's reaction when he saw the photograph of her naked and kissing a stranger, Evie gave a strangled moan and shot into the only room with a lock on the door.

* * *

Wholesome—

Rio stared at the locked door, his mind moving faster than the speed of sound as he swiftly formulated a plan that could turn this situation to his advantage.

Square-jawed, purple in the face, Tina turned to the security men with the purpose of an army commander preparing for a forward push. 'She's locked herself in. Open that door and escort her off the premises. We'll do what we can to keep this out of the papers.'

Rio roused himself. Fired by the challenge, always at his best under pressure, he took control.

'Out,' he ordered harshly, striding towards the door of the suite and holding it open. 'All of you. Now.'

They all looked at each other and Rio gave a smile that shifted the atmosphere from one of tension to one of terror.

'Organise a staff meeting for one o'clock this afternoon.' Like a laser-guided weapon locking on his target, he transferred his gaze to the security chief. 'At that meeting I want the name of the person responsible for the fact that the security cameras in the street were pointing the wrong way. I want a report on how security at the hotel can be upgraded so that I have a guarantee that any intruder entering this building will be challenged within thirty seconds of entering the premises—'

'But this is a hotel, sir; people come and go—'

'If you're not up to the job, just say so, and I'll replace you with someone who is. My personal security team will assist you in preparing the report, if you wish to stay.'

Arnold quailed under that icy stare and Rio continued.

'It's your job to differentiate between guest, gawker and criminal. That's the job I pay you to perform. And you—' Rio shifted his gaze to Tina. 'You're fired.'

Tina gaped at him, her jaw slack, her unmade-up face an unflattering shade of scarlet. 'You can't just fire me—'

'I own this hotel. I can do anything I like.'

'You have no grounds—'

'Bullying and staff intimidation are grounds enough in my book,' Rio said coldly, 'and that's just the beginning. I have a full report on my desk, which includes recommendations on staffing. Your name appears on almost every page. Do you want me to go on?'

Tina gulped and opened her mouth but no sound came out.

Without a flicker of expression on his face, Rio opened the door wider. 'That's it,' he said pleasantly. 'You can go now. And on your way out ask someone to come and remove this Christmas tree. While I'm staying here, I don't want to know it's Christmas. Am I understood? No baubles, no berries, no tree, no tinsel.'

One by one, they shot past him and Tina paused, clearly panicking about her future. 'What about Evelyn? She's the cause of all this. She should be removed from the premises.'

Rio, who had been rapidly formulating a backup strategy since 'whiter than white' had exploded into the ether, sent her a look that had her scurrying out of the door.

Strolling back to the bathroom, he stared with brooding concentration at the closed door.

Wholesome.

The problem might just turn out to be the solution, he mused.

'All right, Sleeping Beauty. I've slain your dragon. You can come out now.'

CHAPTER THREE

He'd fired Tina!

With her ear pressed to the smooth wood of the door, Evie listened with her mouth open, unable to believe what she was hearing.

Afraid to make a sound in case he realised she'd been eavesdropping, she tiptoed away from the door and leaned her burning cheek against the cool marble wall of the bathroom, her knees weak and shaking.

He'd seen right through Tina and fired her on the spot. Obviously, the rumours about him being super-bright were true. All right, so he was ruthless and wasn't afraid to axe jobs, but still—maybe he wasn't so bad...

Still in shock, Evie let out a long breath. She felt as though she should feel sorry for Tina, but it was hard to feel sorry for someone who created an atmosphere of intimidation. She remembered the threats, both spoken and unspoken, the way she transformed confident staff into doubting, apologetic wrecks. Since her demotion to housekeeping, Evie had mopped up more tears than she had floors.

Had he heard the rumours? Was that what he'd meant by seeing Tina's name on every page of his report?

Who else was on his list to be fired?

Realising that she had to be right at the top, Evie closed her eyes.

There was no doubt in her mind that she was going to be next and she didn't even care any more. All she cared about was that stupid, horrid photograph. Perhaps she ought to ring Cedar Court and ask the staff to make sure that her grandfather didn't see any newspapers or television.

But her grandfather loved his newspaper. He did the crossword every day.

If they banned it, he'd just want to know why.

Hyperventilating again, Evie clutched the edge of the washbasin and forced herself to breathe steadily.

She'd thought life couldn't get much worse, but suddenly it was a million times more disastrous.

Her grandfather would panic if he knew she'd lost her job and had nowhere to live, but it was nothing to what he'd do when he saw pictures of her naked and kissing a stranger. She could just imagine what Mrs Fitzwilliam would make of that. *I hear your precious little Evie has turned into a bit of a goer—*

'You have ten seconds to come out of that bathroom.'

The deep male voice held sufficient authority to confirm all Evie's darkest suspicions about his intentions. He was obviously dealing with his problems with the brutal efficiency for which he was famed, and she was the next problem on his list. *The worst was still to come.*

She looked round desperately, searching for an escape. Apart from flushing herself down the toilet or trying to squeeze down the plughole, there was no way out of this bathroom.

Why, oh, why, had she taken up creepy Carlos's suggestion of sleeping in the Penthouse? Why hadn't she followed her initial instinct that it was a bad idea? And why had Rio Zaccarelli decided to arrive at the hotel early when the rest of London was asleep? The man obviously was a machine.

'Two seconds—' The hard, cold voice made her jump and Evie stared helplessly at the door, trying to think what to do.

She needed a plan. She needed to think what she could say that might help her situation.

While she was in here, she was safe. What could he do? He was hardly going to break the door down, was he?

There was a tremendous crash, the sound of wood splintering and Evie screamed as the door crashed open, slamming against the sleek limestone wall of the luxurious bathroom.

Rio Zaccarelli stood in the doorway rubbing his shoulder. 'What is the matter with the staff in this place? When I give you an order,' he thundered, 'I expect you to follow it. And I *don't* expect to have to demolish my hotel so that I can hold a conversation with one of my employees.'

Stunned that the door was still on its hinges, Evie gulped. 'I—you—are you *OK*? I mean—I've seen people crash through doors in the movies but I always assumed the door is made out of cardboard or something. I've never seen anyone actually do it with a real door. That must have hurt.' She looked at his powerful shoulders doubtfully, wondering whether all that muscle would act as a barrier to pain.

'*Sì*, it hurt.' He rolled his shoulder experimentally, checking for damage. 'Which is why, next time, I'd appreciate it if you'd just do as I say and open the damn door.'

Evie gave a choked laugh, clutching the silk throw against her. 'Why? So that you can fire me in person?'

'Who says I'm going to fire you?'

'You fired the tyrannosaurus.'

'Tyrannosaurus?' Still rubbing his shoulder, he frowned, his expression dark and menacing. 'I presume you're talking about that officious woman with the unfortunate hair. That's what you all call her?'

Evie froze. 'No, of course not,' she lied. 'We call her Tina.' *Or meat-eater, because she feasted on hotel staff for breakfast.*

'She didn't seem too impressed with you.'

'No.' It was impossible to argue with that. Utterly defeated,

Evie felt the last dregs of spirit drain out of her. What was the point in defending herself? It was over. 'I think it's fair to say I don't have an enormous number of supporters in high places.' Tina had demoted her. Carlos had tried to grope her and, when she'd rejected him and humiliated him, he'd set her up.

Thinking of her grandfather, Evie wondered whether it was worth begging Rio Zaccarelli to give her another chance. Gazing into those unsympathetic black eyes, she decided that it was a waste of breath. She doubted there was a gram of compassion anywhere in his muscle-packed frame.

'I have a big problem.' His deep voice slid over her nerve-endings like treacle and Evie snatched in a breath, shocked by the sudden heat that shot through her. Underneath the dangerously slippery silk throw, she was suddenly horribly conscious that she was still naked.

If ever there was a more uneven confrontation, this had to be it.

Everything about him suggested raw masculine power, from the dusky shadow of his jaw to the tiny scar that flawed the skin above his right eye.

A vision of Jeff's baby-smooth face flew into her head but Evie realised that to make comparisons between the two men would be nothing short of ridiculous. They had nothing in common. Nothing at all.

Rio Zaccarelli might have been dressed for a formal dinner, but the external trappings of sophistication didn't fool her for a moment. This man wasn't tame or civilised. He was hard and unyielding and he'd do whatever he needed to do to achieve what he wanted.

A real man.

Suffocated by the heat in the air, her limbs suddenly felt heavy and her heart hammered against her ribs. Her instincts were telling her to run, but she couldn't move.

She tried to conjure up an image of Jeff's face again but

found that she couldn't. Instead, her mind was filled with a vision of burnished skin and eyes full of sexual promise.

To make matters worse, two walls of the opulent bathroom were mirrored, which meant that his iron-hard physique was reproduced several times over, dominating her vision.

Seriously unsettled, Evie clutched at the throw. 'If you'd give me five minutes privacy, I'll get dressed.'

'You own clothes?'

'Of course I own clothes! They're drying on the—' Evie turned her head and her eyes widened. 'I left them right there—on the radiator. They're gone.' Her mind explored possible explanations and came up with only one. Feeling the panic rise again, she looked at him and he lifted an eyebrow in weary mockery.

'They walked out of the room under their own steam?'

'Forget it.' Her voice choked, Evie lifted her hand like a stop sign. 'I've had enough of this! There's no point in me saying anything because you're not going to believe me anyway.'

'Strangely enough, you're wrong.' His tone was grim. 'I'm guessing that Carlos had something to do with the mysterious disappearance of your clothes. Am I right?'

Evie lowered her hand slowly. 'H-how do you know that?'

'Because he invited you to stay in the Penthouse and I doubt he did that out of generosity of spirit.'

Relief spurted through her veins. 'I didn't think you believed me—'

'I never thought you acted alone. Now it's all slotting together—' A muscle flickered in his cheek and he muttered something in Italian under his breath.

Evie was rigid with tension. 'I didn't know what was going on. I still don't, but it doesn't really matter. I just want to get out of here. If someone could lend me some clothes, I can go.'

'You're not going anywhere.'

Her heart rate increased. 'If that whole naked photograph thing was a set up then the best thing is surely for me to get as far away from here as possible. I'll go somewhere no one can find me.'

He started to laugh, but there was no trace of humour in the rich masculine sound. It was loaded with cynicism and derision. 'Are you really that naive? The press can find anyone.'

That news shook Evie. 'But why would they want to? I'm no one.'

'Perhaps you were "no one" before you chose to lie naked on my bed with me, but now you're a person of extreme interest.'

'I wasn't *with* you.'

'Yes, you were.'

'Well, that part was your fault. You were the one who kissed me and, quite frankly, I have no idea why you did that.' And she wished he hadn't because, in the midst of this crisis, those feelings kept rushing back to torture her.

His mouth, moving over hers with erotic purpose.

'None of this is my responsibility. You were the one lying there naked.' He issued that statement with such arrogance that Evie simply gaped at him, wondering how it was possible to be terrified of someone and turned on at the same time.

'And that means what? That you kiss every naked woman you see?'

'Normally, the woman gets naked *after* I kiss her,' he drawled. 'That's the usual order of things. Despite the lengths some women go to attract my attention, no one has ever gone quite as far as stripping naked and lying on my bed. That was a first.'

'I thought we'd established that I was set up!' Evie's voice rose. 'If I'd known you were going to arrive early, do you honestly think I would have been lying there?'

'Yes. That photograph will sell for a fortune.'

'Maybe it will, but it won't be me making the fortune,' Evie snapped, stalking out of the bathroom with the throw trailing behind her like a wedding gown.

'Where do you think you're going?'

'Out of here. I'm sick of seeing your reflection in the mirrors. One of you is bad enough. Ten is more than I can take. I'm going to ring Housekeeping and get them to send up a uniform and then I'm going to go and hide somewhere even the press can't find me.'

'Running is *not* the way to handle this.'

'Well, if you can think of a different plan, I'd love to hear it. This is easy for you. You have bodyguards and you own tall buildings with fancy security. All you have to do is lock yourself in your gilded palace until the fuss dies down, but I have to live with the fact that photograph is out there. Everyone who wants a laugh can look at it. They'll probably start a Facebook page for it—*The biggest bottom in the world*.' Evie tripped on the throw and stumbled. Steadying herself, she blinked back tears. 'I have to live with the fact that my eighty-six-year-old grandfather is going to see me with my naked bottom in the air, kissing a stranger! If he has another one of his turns it will be *all* your fault.'

'Which is going to shock him most? Seeing your naked bottom, or the fact that you're kissing a stranger?'

Evie snatched the phone up. 'You're not even funny.'

'Do I look as though I'm laughing? You have *no idea* how serious this is for me. For you, it's embarrassing; for me, it's—' He broke off, his voice unsteady and Evie paused with the handset in her hand, transfixed by the raw emotion she saw in his eyes.

'For you it's what? A deal you don't want to lose? Is this an ego thing? It has to be because you clearly don't care about the embarrassment and I can't honestly believe you'd be making this much fuss about money. I mean, it's not as if you don't already have plenty!' When he didn't answer, she gave a humourless laugh. 'Oh, forget it. I don't know why I'm expecting you to care any more than Carlos cared. Why does it matter to you that one more woman's reputation is shattered? I'm just another notch on your bedpost.'

'I do not make notches on my bedpost,' he said thickly. 'I am very choosy about my relationships.'

And he wouldn't be choosing a woman like her. Evie turned scarlet and stabbed the number for Housekeeping. 'Hello? Margaret? I'm really sorry to bother you, but could you possibly deliver a fresh housekeeping uniform to the Penthouse, please. I've…spilled something…sorry?' She blushed and turned her head away, lowering her voice. 'Size twelve…I said size twelve…I'm not whispering—' She gave a gasp as the phone was removed from her fingers.

'She said size twelve,' Rio drawled, 'and, while you're at it, send some underwear and shoes. She takes a—' his gaze slid to her cleavage '—thirty-four DD and her feet are—' He lifted an eyebrow in Evie's direction.

'Forty,' she said faintly and he delivered that information in the same commanding tone and ended the call. Then he answered his mobile, which was buzzing in his pocket and spoke at length in Italian, leaving Evie standing with a scarlet face, still trying to work out how he'd been able to guess her bra size so accurately.

He was still in mid-conversation when there was another buzzing sound and he drew his BlackBerry out of a different pocket without breaking conversation.

Evie watched in disbelief as he talked into one phone while emailing from the other.

'*Sì—Sì—Ciao.*' He ended the conversation and frowned at her. 'Why are you staring?'

'How many phones do you have?'

'Three. It makes me more efficient.'

'What happens if they ring at the same time? Most men aren't that good at multi-tasking.'

He gave a cool smile. 'I'm not most men. And I'm excellent at multi-tasking.' As if to test that theory, two of his three phones rang simultaneously and Evie moved to the window as he dealt swiftly with one call and then the other.

It was still dark outside, but the roads far beneath her were already busy as cars and taxis inched their way over snowy streets.

She leaned her cheek against the glass, watching people carrying on with their lives, wishing she could swap with them. Or put the clock back. She wished she'd never spent the night in the Penthouse.

Her eyes stung with tears and she blinked rapidly, determined not to cry. It was just because she was tired, she told herself fiercely.

What should she do? She couldn't decide whether it was better to ring her grandfather and warn him that he might see some very embarrassing pictures of her in the press, or say nothing and just hope that he didn't read that page in the paper.

But someone was bound to point it out, weren't they? She never ceased to be depressed by the enjoyment some people took from watching another's misfortune.

'Move away from the windows. Your clothes have arrived—you can change in the bedroom.'

Evie turned, wondering how her colleagues in Housekeeping had managed to produce underwear and shoes so quickly. Then she looked at the elegant packaging on the boxes and realised they'd simply used the expensive store in the hotel foyer.

'I can't afford to pay for those.'

He looked at her with ill-disguised impatience. 'The price tag on your bra is surely the least of our worries at the moment.'

'To you, maybe, but that's because you don't have to worry about money,' Evie said stubbornly. 'I do. Particularly as I appear to have just lost my job.'

The phone rang in his pocket again but this time he ignored it. 'Get dressed. Consider the clothes a gift.'

'I can't accept a gift of underwear from you. It wouldn't be right.'

'In that case, think of them as an essential part of our crisis management programme. The longer you continue to walk around naked, the more likely we are to find ourselves in even hotter water.'

He had a point.

Opening one of the boxes, Evie spotted a silky leopard-print bra and panties and crushed the lid back down, her face scarlet. 'I can't wear something like that.' Hardly daring to look, she prised the lid off the other box and her eyes widened when she saw the contents. 'I can't wear those, either—'

'Why not? They're shoes. I realize they're not strictly uniform, but they will do until we can get you something else.'

'But—' She stared down at the sexy shoe with the wicked heel. It was the most beautiful, extravagant, indulgent thing she'd ever seen. 'I don't wear heels. I can't.'

'You don't have to walk far in them.'

'It isn't the walking.' Her face was almost the same shade of scarlet as the sole of the famous shoes. 'You may not have noticed, but I'm already taller than the average woman. If I wear heels, I look like a freak. Everyone will stare.'

'After last night, they're going to be staring anyway. They'll stare harder and longer if you're barefoot. Put them on.' Without giving her the opportunity to argue, he turned back to the phone, leaving Evie to stare at him in exasperation, wondering what day it was. Had December nineteenth been designated Humiliate Evie Day and someone had forgotten to tell her?

Juggling the throw with the boxes, she struggled into the master bedroom and closed the doors. At least she wouldn't be naked.

Feeling relieved to finally ditch the throw, Evie slung it back on the bed and slithered into the underwear. It fitted perfectly. Then she pushed her feet into the shoes, almost losing her balance as she teetered precariously on the vertiginous heels. She felt like a circus performer practising on stilts.

Risking a look in the mirror, she gave a moan of horror.

She *looked* like a circus performer.

She looked like a giant.

She was about to take them off when the door to the bedroom opened.

Rio's gaze swept her from head to foot.

'*Maledizione*—' His eyes went dark with shock and Evie wanted to fall through the floor as she intercepted his look of stunned astonishment.

Embarrassment got her moving. 'Get out,' she shrieked, grabbing the throw again. 'I'm getting changed.'

'Does the phrase "shutting the stable door after the horse has bolted" mean anything to you? I've already seen you naked.' Displaying not the slightest consideration for her feelings, he allowed his gaze to travel slowly down every centimetre of her body. 'I've never seen a woman who looks like you.'

For Evie, already sensitive about her looks, his comment delivered the final blow to her crumbling self-esteem.

'It's your fault for getting me those stupid shoes when anyone with half a brain could have guessed they'd make me look ridiculous. And that's before I put on the uniform. I always wear flats, OK? Ballet pumps. Court shoes with no heel. Get out of here! I'm fed up with being a laughing stock, although I suppose I ought to get used to it because it's nothing to how I'm going to feel tomorrow when that photo is published—' Pushed to the limit, she flopped onto the bed, buried her face in the pillow and sobbed her heart out.

Everyone was going to see her naked and her grandfather was going to be horribly, hideously ashamed of her. She'd wanted to make him proud, but the truth was all he really wanted was to bounce a great-grandchild on his knee and that was never going to happen.

She was a big, fat disappointment.

Lost in the nightmare of the moment, she gasped in shock as strong hands closed over her shoulders and Rio flipped her onto her back.

'Stop crying!' He sounded exasperated. 'You'll make your eyes red and that could ruin everything.'

'Ruin what? Just go away. Stop mocking me.'

Astonishment lit his dark eyes. 'When have I ever mocked you?'

'You said you'd never seen anyone who l-looked like me,' Evie hiccupped, 'and I think it's horribly mean of you to poke fun of me, even if it is partly my fault we're in this mess. We're not all supermodels and wearing supermodel labels doesn't change that. I can push my feet into designer shoes just like Kate Moss but that doesn't give me Kate Moss's legs.'

'Which is a good thing,' he drawled, 'because Kate would find it extremely hard to strut her stuff on the runway if you had her legs. For the record, I wasn't mocking you. I was complimenting you.'

Evie, who had never been complimented on her looks in her life before, looked at him through eyelashes welded together with tears. 'Pardon?'

His jaw tensed. 'I find you attractive. Why the hell do you think I kissed you in the first place?'

'Because you have an abnormal sex drive and you can't resist anyone naked?'

'I have a healthy sex drive.' His dark gaze was unmistakably sexual. 'I *definitely* don't kiss women who try and pick me up. That's a first for me.'

'I wasn't trying to pick you up—' Still struggling to accept the unlikely fact that he actually did find her attractive, Evie sat up. 'You don't think I'm too tall?'

'Too tall for what?' That silky tone turned her insides into a quivering mass.

'For…a woman.' Evie licked her lips. 'I make most men feel small and insignificant. They usually don't want to stand next to me. But I guess you're pretty tall yourself.'

'Six four,' he breathed, his eyes scanning the length of her legs. 'And I've never had a problem with a woman's height.'

That was because he was unlikely to meet a woman taller than him, Evie thought weakly. 'Most people think I'm a freak.'

Without giving her a chance to argue, he scooped her off the bed and dumped her on her feet in front of the mirror. 'Look at yourself. Tell me what you see.'

Evie closed her eyes. 'I don't see anything.'

'Look!'

Evie flinched and opened one eye cautiously. 'Evie the elephant,' she said immediately and his brows met in an impatient frown.

'If that title is a throwback to your childhood, then you'd better let it go now. You're stunning and that gives us a major problem.'

Stunning?

Evie, who couldn't even for a single moment think why being considered stunning would present a major problem to anyone, looked at him dizzily. 'Even if that was true, which it isn't, I don't see how that could be a problem. How can being stunning be a problem? People judge by appearances. I've never been a member of the "oh, it's such a bore to be beautiful" camp.'

'It's a problem because you need to look wholesome.'

Evie was about to say that she'd been trying to escape from the 'wholesome' image for most of her life, when he took her hair in his hands and twisted it, assessing the effect with narrowed eyes. 'You have good skin.'

'And freckles.'

'Freckles are good. They suggest a healthy outdoor life. Wholesome.'

Why did he keep saying wholesome?

'I'm not with you—'

'Unfortunately, you *are* with me and that is why we have a problem.'

'We wouldn't have a problem if you hadn't kissed me.'

'I'm fully aware of that fact.' He paced over to the window, keeping his back to her. 'Get dressed.'

Wriggling into the housekeeper uniform, Evie stared at his broad shoulders. 'I don't understand why you're so stressed about this. You celebrities are always in the newspapers. You may be the reason they want that photo, but it's going to damage me far more than you.'

He turned, and the expression on his face was all it took to silence her. His eyes were haunted and there was a tension in his body that was unmistakably real.

'The damage to me could be incalculable,' he said coldly and Evie thought back to the exchange he'd had earlier with Carlos.

Whatever the 'deal' was, he was obviously prepared to stop at nothing to make sure it went through. It had to be about more than money, she thought. It had to be something to do with ego. Winning. The addictive quality of power.

'And creepy Carlos did this to you on purpose and I got caught in the middle, is that right?'

'So it would seem.'

She wondered what Carlos had against Rio Zaccarelli. What was he trying to achieve with that photograph? If it hadn't been her, would he have used someone else? 'If there is no way you can stop that photograph being published then I'd better make a phone call.'

His eyes narrowed. 'You're calling a lover?'

Evie gave a hysterical laugh. 'Oh, yes—I have loads of those—' Catching the dangerous gleam in his eyes, her laughter faded. 'Not a lover. I'm calling my grandfather, if you must know.'

Bold black eyebrows met in a fierce frown. 'How old are you?'

'Twenty-three, but, like most people of his generation, he doesn't believe in public displays of affection,' Evie said wearily, 'and he absolutely doesn't believe in one-night stands. Neither do I, for that matter.' She tried to sound casual, as if talking about sex was something she did all the time, rather than something she never did.

She stared at Rio Zaccarelli, the epitome of male sophistication, and felt her face grow scarlet.

Her grandfather definitely would have classed him as a real man.

It was the ultimate irony, she thought, to have been caught naked with him.

As if—

'So you don't have a lover at the moment.' His slumberous gaze rested on her mouth. 'That's good.'

'Well, that depends on where you're standing,' Evie muttered, wishing she wasn't standing quite so close to him. She was getting hotter and hotter. 'If you must know, I was supposed to be getting married yesterday but my fiancé dumped me. If that hadn't happened I'd be in Bali now, not London. I wouldn't have lost my job and my flat and generally had a completely awful six weeks and there might have been the smallest, remotest chance that my grandfather might be bouncing a baby on his knee next Christmas. As it is, there's no chance. None. I don't expect you to understand. You look like the sort of person whose life always goes according to plan.'

'My plan,' he said tightly, 'wasn't to find a strange woman lying naked in my bed. Fortunately, I've always considered adaptability to be an asset. I can turn this situation around.'

'You can?' Evie's gaze drifted to the neck of his shirt. Dark hairs tangled at the base of his throat and disappeared inside the snowy-white shirt. She imagined the hair hazing his chest and narrowing over his abdomen, which was no doubt as muscular as the rest of him. Shocked by her own thoughts, she lifted her eyes back to his and discovered that he was watching her with an unsettling degree of sexual interest.

'*Why* did he dump you?'

'Why does it matter?' *Was she supposed to read him a list?* Evie chewed the corner of her fingernail and then gave an embarrassed shrug. 'Because he met someone more exciting. Because I'm the girl next door and he's known me since I was three years old. Because I was taller than him and I made him feel less of a man—' She stared at him with exasperation, wondering why she was having to spell this out. 'Because I'm *me*. He sent me a text, dumping me.'

His lips thinned with disapproval. 'That's bad.'

'Hypocrite. Are you seriously trying to tell me you've never dumped a woman?'

'I wouldn't use the word "dumped". I've ended plenty of relationships, but always in person. I've never sent a text. That's cowardly.'

'I suppose it's human nature to avoid a difficult conversation.'

'Difficult conversations are part of my daily existence.'

Evie had no trouble believing that. 'Jeff is nothing like you.' A wimp, her grandfather had called him. 'Perhaps he was sensible. After all the lies he told, I would have blacked his eye if he'd told me in person.'

His eyes lingered on her hair. 'A true redhead with a temper to match.'

Reminded of the embarrassing fact that he knew she was a true redhead, Evie ploughed on. 'What this boils down to is that my grandfather isn't going to be impressed to see me naked with another man. He's very old-fashioned. I don't want him to think I'm like that. I'm *not* like that! I don't flit from one man to another.'

'Unless the other man was someone important to you.' Rio spoke under his breath and she had a feeling that he was thinking aloud.

That thought was confirmed when she muttered, 'Sorry?' and received no response.

'If it was someone you'd been secretly seeing. A rebound relationship that turned into something special—' He paced the length of the bedroom and then turned to look at her, his eyes burning dark. 'Wholesome.'

'You make me sound like a breakfast cereal,' she said irritably. 'Why do you keep saying that?'

'Never mind. How long ago did you start working here?'

'I don't know…I…'

'Think!'

'Don't shout at me! I can't concentrate when people shout!'

Rio sucked in a breath. 'I'm *not* shouting. I just want an answer. When?'

'About six weeks ago. I came down after Jeff dumped me. I started as a receptionist. I thought it was my big break.'

'Six weeks—' Before the words had left his lips, his BlackBerry was in his hand and he was checking something. 'I was staying in the Penthouse six weeks ago. I spent one night here on my way to New York. I need you to find out if you were working here then.'

'I know I was because I made a point of avoiding you. So

what? What difference does that make?' Failing to follow
his train of thought, Evie looked at him blankly but he was
already dialling a number and speaking into his phone in
Italian.

He made call after call and each time Evie opened her
mouth to ask him what was going on, he simply lifted his
hand to silence her until she was ready to scream with
exasperation.

'Hello, I'm here too!' After his seventh consecutive phone
call, she waved at him. 'I need to ring my grandfather.'

'First, I want to get this announcement into the press and
arrange a photo.'

'What announcement? What photo?' Worried, irritable,
Evie snapped at him. 'Haven't we had enough photos for one
day?'

He gave a lethal smile. 'This photograph will be different.'

'Different as in I get to wear clothes? Yippee.' She didn't
know how she was still managing to joke because she'd never
felt less like joking about anything in her life.

She knew enough about the press to understand that scandal and humiliation sold better than anything else. 'Can't you
just stop them printing the photograph? Isn't there a privacy
law or something?'

'That isn't going to help us. The best thing we can do is
stop this whole thing looking sleazy.' Ruthlessly focused, he
strode towards the door of the Penthouse. 'Stay out of sight.
Whatever you do, don't emerge from the bedroom until I
come and get you. I don't want anyone to see you.'

'Why? What are you going to do?'

'Find you some proper clothes and then show the world
we didn't have a one-night stand.'

Bemused, Evie stared at him. 'How?'

'By proving that we share something special.' A triumphant gleam in his eyes, he yanked open the door and turned to look at her. 'I'm going to announce our engagement.'

SARAH MORGAN

CHAPTER FOUR

RIO gave his Director of Communications a volley of instructions over the phone and then updated his lawyers.

Listening to Pietro's dire predictions, he felt his stomach clench.

Whiter than white....

He should have anticipated this.

He should have known they'd do something to try and stop this deal going through. He'd been arrogant, allowing himself to relax and think that the whole thing was in the bag.

Sweat cooled his brow and he realised that his hand was shaking. Making a conscious effort to control his breathing, he hauled his emotions back and buried them deep. Emotions had no place in negotiation, he knew that. And this was the most complex, delicate negotiation he'd ever conducted.

'Whatever it takes,' he promised his lawyer. 'You wanted wholesome—I'm giving you wholesome.'

When the delivery arrived at the Penthouse, he dismissed the staff member and took the boxes through to the bedroom himself. He then handed them to the girl without breaking off his conversation and without risking another look at her luxuriant red hair.

Why the hell had he kissed her?

He was well aware that his own libido had catapulted him into this situation. If he'd taken one look at her and left the room, the photographer wouldn't have been able to get his shot.

As it was…

With a low growl, Rio focused his mind on the present.

Having hammered out the plan with his team in Rome, he was about to call his team in New York when he heard the bedroom door open.

The girl stood there, her eyes blazing with anger, her hair flowing like liquid fire down her back. 'Excuse me! In case you've forgotten, this affects me, too. Do you intend to discuss any of this with me or are you just going to do your own thing?'

'I don't problem solve by committee.' Congratulating himself on his brief to the stylist, Rio scanned the discreet, elegant dress with satisfaction. It was perfect. She managed to look wholesome and sexy at the same time. *This could just work*. 'I'm busy sorting out our problem right now.'

'No, Mr Zaccarelli, you're sorting out *your* problem—I'm incidental. You haven't once asked what I want to do about this mess which, by the way, is ultimately the fault of you and your stupid, slimy hotel manager, who can't keep his hands to himself.' She stalked across to him and shoved the redundant housekeeper uniform into his hands while Rio dissected that sentence into its relative parts.

'What do you mean, he "can't keep his hands to himself"? Are you saying he touched you?' Astonished by the sudden explosion of anger that was released by that unexpected revelation, Rio was suddenly glad he'd fired Carlos on the spot. His voice cold, he probed for the details. 'Did you report him for sexual harassment?'

'No. I broke his finger.'

'You *broke* his finger?'

'My grandfather taught unarmed combat during the war. He taught me self-defence.'

Distracted by that unexpected confession, Rio looked at her in a new light. 'I'll remember that.'

'You should. But, to repeat, you're not solving *our* problem, Mr Zaccarelli, you're solving *your* problem.'

'Call me Rio. I think we moved on to the first name stage about an hour ago. And, if it weren't for you, we wouldn't have a problem.' His observation appeared to act as fuel to her already happily burning temper.

'If creepy Carlos hadn't used me, then he would have used someone else and frankly I wish he had because then I wouldn't be in this mess.' She paced the room, trying to work off her stress.

Watching all that fabulous hair ripple down her back, Rio fought the urge to flatten her against the nearest hard surface and conduct in-depth research into the impact of extremely long legs on the enhancement of sexual pleasure.

He had no idea what her true role had been in what he now recognised as a final desperate attempt to stop this deal going through. Maybe she *was* innocent. Maybe she wasn't. Either way, she was the means by which he was going to extract himself from the catastrophic mess he now found himself in.

The upside of his plan was that he didn't need to struggle to keep his hands off her. In fact, the more hands the better.

He was slightly puzzled by her lack of confidence. Accustomed to women so narcissistic that they used every reflective surface to admire themselves, it came as a shock to discover one who didn't seem to spend her time in endless self-admiration. When she'd confessed that men found her too tall it had been on the tip of his tongue to point out that height was irrelevant when you were horizontal, but he'd managed not to voice that thought aloud. Rio wondered whether it would count as a charitable act to demonstrate just how well those endless legs of hers would wrap around his waist.

'You look perfect in that dress.'

'I look like a politician or something.' Keeping her back to him, she paced towards the window and Rio frowned.

'Don't go near the windows.' His clipped command earned him a challenging glance.

'Why? We're too high up for anyone to see.'

'In today's world of long lenses?' Watching her lose more colour from her face, he let the observation hang in the air. 'The next photograph they take of us will be when I'm ready and not before.'

'I don't want any more photographs taken!' But she moved away from the window, fiddling nervously with the fabric of her dress as she paced in the other direction. 'Look—this whole engagement thing is ridiculous. Can't you just stop that photo being printed?'

'No.' Rio recoiled from the sheen of tears he saw in her eyes. 'But I can stop it looking like a sleazy one-night stand. We're going to make people believe we're in a relationship— serious about each other.' Looking at her now, those high heels elongating her spectacular legs, he was even starting to believe it could work. No red-blooded male would question his interest.

'It's a really s-stupid plan.'

Rio, who had been congratulating himself on a truly genius idea, was insulted. 'It's an incredible plan.' His tone cooled. 'You're lucky I'm not currently involved with anyone.'

'Lucky?'

Rio dismissed thoughts of the Russian ballerina. 'It's unusual for me not to be in a relationship.'

'Well, I suppose that's one of the advantages of being filthy rich. Where there's money, there will always be women.'

Taken aback by that diminution of his qualities, Rio breathed deeply. 'Women are generally interested in more than my wallet.'

'How do you know? They're not going to tell you, are

they? And I don't suppose gold-diggers come with a warning hanging round their neck.'

'I can spot a gold-digger in the dark from a thousand paces.' He ignored the discordant image in his head that reminded him that on at least one occasion that statement had proven not to be true.

'Good for you.' Her slightly acidic tone matched her growing agitation. She explored the room, picking things up and putting them down again. First the vase on the table, then a notepad, then a remote control. She squinted down at it and pressed a button mindlessly and a gas fire flared to life behind a glass panel in the wall.

Swearing under his breath, Rio crossed the room and turned her to face him. 'I know you're anxious that they're going to print your photograph but, trust me, it will be fine providing people think we're together. This is the best way of dealing with it.'

'That's just your opinion.'

Rio, who had never before had his opinion dismissed, ground his teeth. 'If you have an alternative suggestion, then I'm listening.'

'No, you're not. You're pretending to listen while secretly thinking that you'll let me say my piece and then just do what you were planning to do all along, but it isn't going to work. I won't pretend to be engaged to you.'

Assuming that her reluctance was rooted in her insecurity, Rio sought to reassure her. 'By the time we've done something about your wardrobe, your nails and your hair, it will be easy to convince people that we are involved with each other.'

'Is that supposed to make me feel better?' She put the remote control down slowly and carefully, as if it were a potential murder weapon. *'You'll look fine, Evie, once I've turned you into something decent.* Is that what you're saying?'

Her tightly worded question triggered all the alarms in Rio's internal warning system.

'If this is going to be one of those, *Does my bottom look big in this?* conversations, then don't go there,' he warned, his tone thickened with frustration. The clock was ticking and her resistance was an obstacle he hadn't anticipated. Not for one moment had it entered his head that she'd be anything other than compliant. 'If you hadn't been lying naked on my bed, I would not have been tempted to kiss you,' Rio exploded with the tension that had been building since the photographer had chosen to elbow his way into his life. 'If you had worn clothes or at least slept under the covers—'

'If you had shown some self-control—'

Rio breathed deeply because that was a charge from which it was almost impossible to defend himself and that particular aspect of this whole seedy situation disturbed him far more than he was prepared to admit. He was always extremely careful with his liaisons and he never indulged in one-night stands. And yet where had his self-control been a few hours ago when he'd seen her lying on his bed? Not for the first time, he wondered what would have happened had the photographer paused before taking his photograph. *How much more revealing and incriminating would a later picture have been?*

'There is no point in dwelling on what is done,' he said tautly, 'and the truth is that a photograph of you naked in that bed was all that was needed. The rest would have been easily created from association and artistic use of Photoshop.'

'You mean they would have manufactured a photograph of the two of us together?'

'Photography software is increasingly sophisticated and you *were* in my bedroom. Stop throwing out obstacles when the solution I'm proposing is in both our interests. Your reputation stays intact. You mentioned that you have nowhere to live—I'm offering you somewhere to live. You get to stay here, in the most highly prized hotel suite in London. Anything you want, you can have. Most women in your position would be extremely excited at the prospect of an all expenses paid holiday complete with shopping.'

'Women are not a homogeneous breed, Mr Zaccarelli— we're individuals with individual tastes and needs. And why do you care so much about whether it looks like a one-night stand or something more? What is this deal you keep talking about?'

The question caught him off guard. For a brief moment he felt his control start to unravel. 'You don't need to know. Rest assured that I have a whole team of lawyers working night and day to make sure that it doesn't fall apart at the eleventh hour.'

'And if it does?'

A chill ran down his spine. 'It won't.'

'Providing I do as you say. I don't understand why this story could ruin it for you. Is this deal of yours with some old-fashioned guy who thinks you should have a blameless reputation or something?'

'Something like that.' Rio realised that his palms were sweating and he turned away from her, locking down his emotions with ruthless efficiency.

'So you'll do all this to win one deal? Money, money, money. Is that all that matters to you?' Increasingly agitated, she rubbed her hands down her arms. 'Well, I'm sorry if my decision loses you a few million, but I'm not prepared to do it.'

Back in control, Rio turned to look at her, sure that he must have misheard. 'Excuse me?'

'I won't do it. I'm just going to look more of a fool.' She covered her face with her hands and gave a moan of embarrassment. 'Every time I think about that photo being printed I just want to hide. Grandpa is never going to be able to hold his head up at senior poker ever again.'

Banking down his own frustration, Rio crossed the room. Gently, he pulled her hands away from her face. 'You are not going to hide. You are going to hold your head up high and look as though you are in love with me.' Appreciating the irony of his own words, he gave a faint smile and she instantly picked up on it.

'Don't tell me—usually you're telling women *not* to fall in love with you.'

'I'm not into serious relationships. They don't work for me. I'm not that kind of guy.' *Once, just once, and look where it had got him.*

'And I assume the public know that.'

'If you're worried that I won't be able to play my part, then don't be. I can be very convincing,' Rio assured her. 'The fact that I'm not usually serious about a woman will make this whole story all the more plausible.'

'And all the more embarrassing.'

Rio's jaw clenched and he spoke through his teeth, his patience severely tested. 'Are you saying it's embarrassing to be associated with me?'

'I'm saying it's going to be embarrassing when it ends. For all your so-called brilliant brain, you haven't thought this through. It's going to end—and then how will it look?'

'What does it matter?' Irritated to the point of explosion, Rio spread his hands in a gesture of exasperation. 'Relationships end all the time—it is a part of life. And that is surely a better option for you than having the world think you had a one night stand.'

'So basically I have two choices here—either I get to look like a big, fat slut or I get to be the only woman to be dumped twice in the space of months. Forgive me if I'm not jumping up and down with excitement at either option.'

'Relationships end. I still don't see the problem.'

Her eyes sparked. 'That's because you're only thinking

about yourself as usual. Not me. Have you ever been dumped, Mr Zaccarelli?'

'Rio.'

'Rio—' Using his name brought a flush to her cheeks. 'Has anyone ever told you they don't want to be with you any more?'

'No, of—' He caught himself and shrugged. 'No.'

'You were going to say *of course not*, weren't you?' She gave a disbelieving laugh. 'You are so monumentally arrogant and sure of yourself, but that explains why you can't understand my problem. You don't know what it's like to be rejected.'

'Given that this isn't a real relationship,' Rio said tightly, 'it wouldn't be a real rejection.'

'But if you're going to be as convincing as you say you are, then everyone is going to think it is! Six weeks ago my fiancé, a man I'd known since I was a child, called off our wedding—' She wrapped her arms around herself as if she were suddenly cold. 'Forgive me if I'm not rushing forward to embrace another public battering of my ego. It was bad enough the first time, having everyone feeling sorry for me. I couldn't even walk down the street without ten people saying they understood how hideously humiliated I must feel—this would be a thousand times worse. Only this time it wouldn't be just the village; it would be the whole world.'

'How would that be worse?' Genuinely baffled, struggling to understand, Rio stared at her. 'Why would you care what a bunch of strangers think?'

'I just would! I don't want loads of people I don't know discussing the fact that you dumped me. "Well, it's hardly surprising, is it?" she parroted. '"I mean, what would a guy like him see in a girl like her?"'

'You'd rather they thought you'd had a sleazy one-night stand with me?'

She gulped. 'No. I'd rather they weren't talking about me at all. But I especially don't want them speculating on why I always get dumped.'

Aware that the clock was ticking and that they needed to get on with this if it was going to have any chance of working, Rio rubbed his hand over the back of his neck and applied his mind to a solution. 'I'll put out an announcement telling everyone you're a wonderful woman and that I have huge respect for you.'

She cringed. 'That would make people feel even *more* sorry for me.'

'I'll say that we will always be friends.'

'Which is basically like saying our relationship fizzled because you don't find me attractive.'

Trying to conceal his mounting exasperation, Rio inhaled deeply and offered up the only other solution that presented itself. 'If it's the dumping part that really worries you, then *you* can dump *me*.'

She stared at him. 'Sorry?'

'I'll allow you to dump me,' he said tightly. 'Problem solved.'

'That wouldn't work.'

'*Now* what? Why wouldn't it work?'

'Because you're rich and handsome. No one would believe it. Why would anyone in my position dump a man like you?'

'That's easy. I'm a total bastard,' Rio said immediately, relieved to be able to deal with that obstacle so simply. 'No one who knows me will have any trouble believing you kicked me out.' His confession drew a tiny smile from her.

'You're that bad?'

Transfixed by that smile, Rio couldn't look away from her mouth. 'I'm terrible. I'm dominating, I like everything my own way—basically I'm horribly selfish, inwardly focused,

I set myself a punishing schedule and frequently work an eighteen-hour day, which usually means that all I want to do when I'm with a woman is have sex.' *And he wanted to have sex with her, right here, right now.* It exasperated him to realise that, even in this most delicate of situations, he could barely keep his hands off her.

'You manage to fit sex into your punishing working day?' Her voice was faint. 'When?'

'Whenever I feel like it—' He was intrigued by the colour in her cheeks. 'So that's settled then. I'll do something awful—'

'You mean you'll behave the way you usually behave.'

'Something like that.' He acknowledged the barely veiled insult with a dismissive shrug. 'You'll dump me and, just to make sure it looks completely authentic, I'll go round looking moody for a few weeks.'

'So you admit to being selfish, inwardly focused and a total bastard, but no woman has ever dumped you. Why? What have you got going for you?'

Rio gave a slow, confident smile. 'If we're spending the foreseeable future together then you'll have time to discover the answer to that yourself.'

'If you're talking about sex, then you can forget it. Unlike you, I think sex should be part of a relationship.'

'So do I.'

She backed away. 'Yes, but the difference is that you don't want your relationships to go anywhere, and I do. Just so that there's no misunderstanding, I'm telling you now that I'll be sleeping in the second bedroom.'

Rio, who had his own ideas about where she'd be sleeping, decided to handle that issue later. 'So you'll do it? Good. And, when the time comes, you dump me.'

'I still don't see how we can convince them that we're together.'

'By being seen together,' he said smoothly, taking her

hand and hauling her against him. 'The first thing you need is a ring, so let's go. I'm about to buy you the biggest diamond you've ever seen.'

'I've never been in a chauffeur driven car. There's masses of room.' Evie stretched her legs out in front of her, aware that Rio was watching her with amusement.

'That's the general idea.'

'Why do you need so much room? You could have a party in here.'

'Not a party, but sometimes I do conduct business meetings in the car if I'm travelling short distances.'

'What happens for long distances?'

'I use my private jet.'

Evie gave a choked laugh. 'Private jet. Of course. This year's *must have* accessory. No serious tycoon should be seen without one.'

'Not an accessory,' he drawled, 'but a practical, money-saving tool.'

'Money-saving.' Evie nodded, struggling to keep her face straight as she slid her hand over the soft leather seat. 'Of course. I find the same thing. When I'm economizing, I turn down the heating and watch my food budget but I always make sure I leave the private jet well alone. As you say, it's such a practical, money-saving tool.'

'This may surprise you, but when you spend as many hours in the air as I do, that becomes a truth.'

As the gulf in their lifestyles opened up between them, Evie's smile faltered and she flopped back against the seat. 'This is ridiculous,' she muttered. 'It's never going to work. Give me one reason why a guy like you would ever be involved with a woman like me?'

'You have incredible legs.' He moved so quickly that she didn't anticipate it. Before she had time to respond, his hand was buried in her hair and his mouth descended on hers in a kiss that sent her brain spinning. 'I love the way you taste,' he murmured huskily and she gasped against his lips.

'OK, enough, you don't have to keep kissing me—' Seriously unsettled by the way he made her feel, Evie shoved at his chest, alarmed when he didn't budge. She'd always considered herself pretty strong for a woman but her violent push had no effect on him. 'It was kissing me that got us in this mess—'

'But now we're in this "mess", as you call it, we might as well enjoy it. They'll believe it, *tesoro,* once they see you.' He showed no inclination to stop what he was doing. 'You have amazing hair, fantastic breasts—'

Evie moaned as his mouth trailed along her jaw. 'Those are all physical things. That's just sex.'

'Never underestimate the power of sex. Sex is a very important part of a relationship.' One hand slid down her back to her bottom and Evie wriggled away, mortified.

'Don't do that—'

'Why not?'

'Well, for a start because someone might see you—'

His eyes gleamed into hers. 'And that would be a problem because—?'

Evie could hardly breathe. For a moment she'd forgotten that the whole objective of this charade was for people to see them. Confused, she wondered whether he was faking the attraction. But then she remembered the kiss that had started all this...

'Unless people have X-ray vision, they're not going to be able to see your hand on my bottom,' she croaked and he gave a wicked smile as he ran his fingers through her hair.

'Any red-blooded male glancing into this car will have a pretty accurate idea of the location of my missing hand.'

'You're not funny.' She'd barely thought about sex before she'd met him. Now she was finding it hard to think about anything else. Was he going to keep kissing her? Did he think she was made of stone? Embarrassed by the burning heat between her thighs, Evie pulled away from him and this time he released her, smiling slightly as he watched her shift to the furthest corner of her seat.

His whole attitude should have been enough to make her dislike him, but instead she found herself alarmingly turned on by the electric combination of smooth sophistication and command. It was humiliating, she thought, squirming in her seat, to find a man as basic as Rio so attractive. But evidently she wasn't the only one. After all, *he'd* never been dumped...

They were driving through the upmarket streets of Knightsbridge. The windows of Harrods, the world famous store, were decorated for Christmas and everywhere she looked there were rich-looking women wearing fur and dark glasses, stepping out of expensive-looking cars.

By the time Rio's driver pulled up outside an exclusive jewellers, Evie had lost all desire to be seen in public. Even in the smart outfit and sexy shoes, she didn't fit.

Two guards stood either side of the heavy glass door and, even from the protective cocoon of Rio's car, she could see that the few pieces on display in the window would have satisfied royalty.

Thoroughly intimidated, she thought about the tiny diamond that Jeff had given her when he'd proposed. At the time she'd thought it was small because they were saving for a deposit so that they could buy their own cottage. Now she realised it had been small because he'd been spending most of their shared savings on his other girlfriend.

She'd been a total idiot. But it was partly her fault, wasn't it? She and Jeff had grown up together. Everyone had assumed that one day they'd get married. Evie had told herself that the fact she felt no spark was because she wasn't a particularly passionate person. She'd assumed Jeff was the same.

And then she'd discovered what he'd been doing with Cindy, the librarian from the next village…

She stole a sideways glance at Rio, her gaze resting on his mouth, remembering the sizzling, steamy kiss. Sparks had been shooting all over the place.

And now she was expected to pretend they were in a relationship.

'You expect me to go in there? Why can't they come to us? In the movies you just pick up the phone and loads of jewellers come running to the hotel with a selection of rings.'

'In the movies, they're not trying to attract the interest of the paparazzi.' Rio leaned across her to undo her seat belt. 'If I'd ordered them to bring the rings to the hotel, it wouldn't have been anywhere near as loud a statement.'

Flattening herself to the seat, Evie stared at him, determined not to be impressed. 'I still don't understand how this is going to work. If the whole point of this is to get the paparazzi to take a photograph of us, shouldn't someone have called them and told them we're here?'

'No need. Wherever I go, you can find photographers.' Rio's tone was bored. 'It's part of my life, which means it's now part of your life. Get used to it.' As the driver opened the door Rio gestured for her to leave the car but Evie didn't budge.

'You mean there might be someone out there with a camera? Am I supposed to smile and wave?'

'You're not the Queen,' Rio said dryly. 'Just act normally.'

'But none of this is normal for me! I wouldn't find myself in front of rows of paparazzi,' Evie said irritably. 'I don't know what I'd do. Look over my shoulder, probably, to see who they were photographing because it certainly wouldn't be me. Unless they were taking snaps for a Miss Unbelievably Big Bottom contest.'

'If you mention your bottom again, I will be forced to strip you naked and examine it in detail,' Rio promised silkily and Evie exited the car faster than rum from a bottle.

Just as he'd predicted, a flashlight immediately exploded in her face and she would have stopped if he hadn't propelled her forwards through the doors that had been opened for him as soon as he'd stepped out of the car.

'I thought you wanted to be seen,' Evie hissed under her breath and he curved his hand around her waist and guided her into the exclusive store.

'I never talk to the press,' he purred. 'I never give interviews. I have no intention of altering that pattern. We want this to look as authentic as possible, remember?'

Exasperated, Evie stared up at him. 'How are they supposed to know we're engaged if you don't tell them?' Her face cleared. 'Oh—I get it. I'm supposed to strategically flash the ring on the way out.'

'We'll leave by the back entrance so that no one will see us. In the event that there is a photographer covering the rear of the building, you hide the ring. You put your left hand in your pocket so that no one can get the shot.'

'So we're buying a ring to convince them we're engaged, but we're not going to let them see it?'

'That's right.'

'Have you banged your head or something? You're not making sense.'

'I'm making perfect sense.'

'Not to me. If we go out of the back of the building it's going to look as though we don't want them to see us.'

'Exactly right.' He smiled at the manager who was hovering discreetly. 'Franco—'

'Signor Zaccarelli—' the man oozed deference '—it's good to see you again.'

'Again? How many women have you brought here?' Evie muttered under her breath, but the only indication that Rio had heard her was his vice-like grip on her hand. 'Squeeze any tighter and you'll break my fingers and then you won't get a ring over my knuckle.'

Rio released his grip and urged her forward. 'We need a diamond, Franco.' He glanced down at Evie, a smile on his lips. 'A very special diamond for a very special woman.'

Evie was about to tell him that his smooth talk wasn't the slightest bit convincing when he lowered his mouth and kissed her.

Somewhere in the distance, through the swirling clouds of desire that descended on her brain, she heard one of the sales assistants sigh with envy.

To her, it appeared completely staged but apparently Franco was convinced because he smiled, almost convulsing with delight as he led them through to a private room. 'A very special diamond. Of course. You've come to the right place.'

Evie sat there shell-shocked from the invasive pressure of his mouth, wishing they'd had a conversation about how they were going to play this. Had he said anything about kissing? And what was she supposed to do about the ring? Was she supposed to pick the least expensive one? Or maybe that didn't matter. Presumably a man who considered a private jet to be an 'economy' wouldn't care about the price of a diamond. Or maybe he was planning to ask for a refund when this was over.

She threw Rio an agonized look but he simply smiled. The fact that he was so relaxed simply added to her growing tension.

More aware than ever of the differences between them, Evie shifted uncomfortably and was about to say something when a slender girl entered the room carrying a box.

A hush fell over the room and Evie glanced around her, wondering what was going on. Why was everyone silent?

'It's the Apoletta diamond,' Franco told them in reverent

tones, taking the box from the girl and opening it himself. 'A thing of beauty and perfection, like your love.'

Evie was about to suggest that if the ring was supposed to be a manifestation of their relationship then a small lump of coal might be more appropriate, but one look at Rio's face stopped her. He was looking at her with such intensity that for a moment she stopped breathing and, during that one intimate glance, she made the unsettling discovery that she was as vulnerable to his particular brand of sexual magnetism as all the other women in the room. Even armed with his frank admission of his long list of deficiencies, she couldn't control the explosion of excitement that held her in its grip.

Rio ignored a question from Franco, his attention entirely on her. Then he slid his hand behind her neck and slowly but deliberately kissed her mouth, his lips lingering against hers for long enough to send her heart racing frantically out of control.

'Ti amo,' he said huskily and Evie, dazed by the look as much as the kiss, wondered what it would feel like if a man looked at you like that and meant it.

Without taking his eyes from hers, Rio removed the ring from its velvet nest and slid it onto her finger with cool, confident hands and an unmistakable sense of purpose.

Evie stared down at the incredible diamond, thinking about the sunny morning a few months earlier when Jeff had done the same thing. The ring Jeff had given her had been too big for her finger, whereas this one—'It's exactly the right size.'

'Like Cinderella,' one of the girls sighed and Evie frowned, wondering what was meant by that remark. Did she look as though she'd been cleaning the cellar in rags?

'She means that it's a perfect fit,' Rio said dryly, apparently developing a sudden ability to read her mind. 'And she's right. It's a perfect fit. We won't have to have it adjusted.'

Finding the fact that it fitted slightly spooky, Evie wondered whether it was a fluke or whether Rio was as skilled at guessing the size of her finger as he was her underwear and dress size.

Good guesswork or a man experienced with women?

Another girl entered the room. 'I just thought you should know that it's a media circus out the front.' She sounded apologetic. 'I have no idea how they discovered you were here. Someone must have tipped them off.'

Rio's jaw tightened and for a moment Evie genuinely believed he was annoyed.

'Do you have another entrance?'

'Yes, sir.'

He made a swift phone call and rose to his feet, drawing Evie close to him. 'My driver will meet us out the back. That way, no one should see us.'

Evie hurried alongside him, conscious of the strength of his fingers locked with hers as they were led towards the back of the store. 'Rio—' she hissed his name '—don't we have to pay or something? I don't want to set the alarms off and have to spend Christmas in custody, if it's all the same to you.'

He didn't slacken his stride. 'It's been dealt with.'

'How? Where?'

But he simply propelled her to the back of the store. Moments later, Rio's driver was speeding through the back streets of London's most exclusive area.

Evie flopped back against the seat, twisting the ring on her finger. She tilted her hand, admiring it from every angle, watching as it sparkled and glinted. 'I still don't understand why you went to all that trouble to buy a ring if you're not going to let anyone see it. You didn't even let them see you leave the shop.'

'They know I've left. The fact that I'm being secretive will make them more interested.'

'I hope you don't have an over-inflated idea of your own

importance. Otherwise, this whole idea is going to fall flat on its face.'

Rio's response to that was to hold out his phone. 'Call your grandfather.'

'What, now?' Evie had been putting off that moment and her stomach plummeted as she anticipated what her severe, principled grandfather would say about her current situation. 'What am I supposed to say? Hi, Grandpa, you may be seeing a picture of me naked in today's papers so I just wanted to tell you that I'm not starting a career as a glamour model—'

'It won't be in today's papers. It's too late for that. There's a strong chance it will make tomorrow's editions, but it may already be up on the Internet. Call.'

'My grandfather doesn't surf the Internet. He's eighty-six,' Evie squeaked but her observation merely earned her a lift of an eyebrow.

'What does his age have to do with anything?'

'You wouldn't be asking me that if you'd been to the Cedar Court Retirement Home. They celebrated when they got a decent TV picture. They probably think high speed broadband is another type of dressing for varicose veins.'

He didn't withdraw the phone. 'Call.'

'I can't.' Evie's voice was a whisper and she shrank back against the seat as she tried to delay the inevitable. 'This is the guy who took me on my first day at school. He taught me to ride a bike. He doesn't believe in holding hands or kissing in public. I'm all he has in the world and he thinks I'm a really decent, old-fashioned girl... In fact, I *am* a decent, old fashioned girl, or I was until I met you.'

'All the more reason to call him before he hears it from someone else.'

Running out of excuses, Evie took the phone reluctantly. Her hand shook as she keyed in the number. As she waited for him to answer, she pressed her fingers to the bridge of her nose and tried not to think about how disappointed her grandfather was going to be.

After all he'd done for her, after all his love and affection, he didn't deserve this…

'Grandpa? It's Evie…how are you doing?' Her voice sounded false to her and she wondered how long it would take her grandfather to pick up on the fact that something was wrong. 'Are you staying warm there in all this snow?' Maybe that was a good link, she thought desperately as she listened to his cheerful response—*I was a bit too warm, Grandpa, so I thought I'd take my clothes off…*

'No, nothing's wrong; I just thought I'd ring you for a chat.' Aware that Rio was watching her, Evie carried on making small talk about the weather and listening to her grandfather's observations about his friends. When he mentioned that he'd been boasting about her again to Mrs Fitzwilliam, two huge tears slipped from Evie's eyes and she covered her mouth with her hand.

With a sigh, Rio removed the phone from her. 'Mr Anderson? Rio Zaccarelli here—no, we haven't met, but I know your granddaughter—yes, I'm the same Zaccarelli that owns the hotel and spa chain—' he leaned back in his seat, not looking remotely discomfited by the prospect of dealing with what could only be described as a hideously awkward situation '—yes, it's still doing well, despite the economic climate—absolutely—' he smiled '—that's how I met Evie—'

Worried that Rio might actually say something that would make things even worse, Evie gulped down her tears and tried to grab the phone but he held it out of reach, laughing at something her grandfather had just said.

'I've already learned that to my cost—yes, she is—'

Evie frowned. 'I am what? What are you saying?'

Rio ignored her. 'I know about that. Yes, she told me. But his loss is my gain.'

Were they talking about her broken engagement? Evie covered her eyes with her hands, all too able to imagine what her grandfather was saying.

'Yes, a total loser—' Rio's voice became several shades cooler '—she's better off without him… No, not too badly— that's what we rang to tell you. We're engaged. I know it seems sudden but you can blame me for that—when I see something I want, I have to have it and I've never felt like this about a woman before.'

Evie peeped through her fingers and waited for Rio to pass the phone across so that she could receive a giant telling off from her strict grandfather. Instead, she heard laughter as Rio controlled the conversation.

'We wanted to warn you that there might be some revealing photographs in the press. My fault entirely—they follow me around, I'm afraid—' Rio's voice was smooth and he gave a slight smile in response to something her grandfather said. 'I agree—I've always said the same thing—that's right. No—no, she's fine—just a bit embarrassed because she's pretty shy about that sort of stuff… Yes, I know she's modest—' he shot her an ironic glance '—well, I have my lawyers onto it but if anyone mentions it to you, you can tell them the photographer was trespassing in a private room— yes, I'll hand you over—good to talk to you—look forward to meeting you in person—' Having moulded her rock-hard war veteran grandfather into the consistency of porridge, Rio handed her the phone, a smug expression on his face. 'He's delighted. He wants to congratulate you in person.'

Evie tentatively lifted the phone to her ear. 'Grandpa—?' She was unable to get a word in edgeways as her grandfather told her how delighted he was that she'd finally met a real man and proceeded to spend the next five minutes extolling Rio's virtues, all of which appeared to centre around his ability to buck the market and grow his business, no matter what the economic challenges. The issue of the naked photograph appeared to have been absorbed along with all the other news.

Finally, her grandfather drew breath. 'Answer me one question—are you in love with him, Evie? That's all I want to know.'

Oh, dear God, how was she supposed to answer that? 'I—'

'It doesn't matter that a man is rich—what matters is whether there's strength and responsibility in his character. Rio Zaccarelli has all those qualities, but none of it matters if you don't love him.'

Talk about out of the frying pan into the fire. In order to stop her grandfather thinking she'd had a one-night stand, she'd gone along with Rio's idea but suddenly she was being sucked deeper and deeper into the charade.

Knowing her grandfather would worry, she gave the only answer she could. 'I love him, Grandpa.' She scowled as Rio raised his eyebrows, amusement shimmering in his black eyes. Doubtless he was so used to hearing besotted women say those words that he barely registered them.

Her grandfather sounded ecstatic. 'So it looks as though I might be bouncing that great-grandchild on my knee next Christmas after all.'

Great-grandchild?

Evie's mouth dropped in dismay. Somehow she'd gone from naked in bed, to engaged and then straight to pregnant!

How was she ever going to unravel this mess?

Hoping Rio hadn't overheard that particular part of the conversation, she lowered her head, allowing her hair to fall forward in a curtain, shielding her face. 'Well—let's just see how things go, Grandpa—no hurry—'

'Of course there's a hurry! I'm not getting any younger—'

'Don't say that. You know I hate it.' The thought of losing him horrified her and, when Evie finally ended the call, her hands were still shaking. Listening to her grandfather's animated voice had made her feel hideously guilty.

Oblivious to her mounting distress, Rio took the phone from her, smiling with satisfaction. 'That went well.'

She rounded on him, her eyes glistening with tears. *'That did not go well, Rio!* I just lied to my eighty-six-year-old grandfather. How do you think that makes me feel?'

'A great deal better than having to tell your eighty-six-year-old grandfather why you had a one-night stand with a man you'd never met before,' he said coldly. 'Calm down. If there happen to be any paparazzi around, I'd rather they didn't print the fact that we were having a row within ten minutes of putting the rock on your finger. Your grandfather was delighted to hear that we're together—a little surprised, perhaps, but basically pleased. I'm considered an incredible catch. You don't have anything to worry about.'

He reminded her of an armoured tank, forging forwards regardless of what was in his path. Her feelings were no more than blades of grass, easily squashed and ignored under the weight of his own driving sense of purpose.

When Rio Zaccarelli wanted something, he got it. And apparently he was willing to go to any lengths to secure this particular 'deal'.

'Why didn't I think this through? I've just raised his hopes and that's an awful thing to do.' Frantic, Evie reached for the phone again. 'I have to tell him the truth, now, before this whole thing escalates and he tells everyone I'm marrying a billionaire.'

'Leave it.'

'Rio, he thinks I'm going to get pregnant any moment! He wants to bounce his great-grandchild on his knee! I'm sorry, but I can't do this.'

But Rio had slipped the phone back into the inside pocket of his jacket. 'You agreed to the plan.'

'Because you railroaded me. I didn't have time to think it

through, but I can see now this is going to be really complicated and—'

'It's done. Too late.' With an infuriating lack of emotion, he scanned the screen of his BlackBerry. 'The switchboard at my corporate headquarters is jammed with journalists seeking confirmation that I've just become engaged. The story is out there.'

Her stomach lurched. 'And your people have confirmed it?'

'They've said "no comment", which is as good as demanding that the press print an announcement. It's too late to change your mind now. Stop panicking. Your grandfather sounded fine about the whole thing. Tell me about Jeff.'

Evie tried to ignore the throbbing pain behind her eyes. 'I don't want to talk about Jeff.'

'I'm not surprised.' Rio sprawled in his seat, texting with astonishing speed and dexterity. 'He sounds like a total loser.'

Evie stared at him in helpless disbelief. She wanted to explain how worried she was about hurting her grandfather's feelings, but she knew she was wasting her time. Rio Zaccarelli didn't care about feelings, did he? All he cared about was making sure his business proceeded unhindered.

'I really don't think I can go through with this.'

Rio watched her, a deadly gleam in his eyes. 'We made a deal.'

'Yes.' Evie croaked the word, knowing that she was trapped. If this was the only way to prevent that photograph being published, then she had no choice.

Deals, deals, deals...

She'd made a deal with the devil. And now she was going to pay.

CHAPTER FIVE

DRAGGING her aching limbs into the Penthouse suite, Evie toed off her shoes in relief and crumpled onto the rug. 'How does anyone walk in these things?' Staring up at the ceiling, she moved her toes gingerly. 'I feel as though both my legs have been chewed by a shark.'

'That is why you are lying on the floor?' Rio paused in mid-text, his eyes bright with incredulity. 'If you're tired, lie on the sofa.'

'I can't make it that far. I may never walk again.' Evie gave a long groan and flexed her sore feet. 'I bet you've never tried to squash your feet into a torture device before. Who invented heels? The Spanish Inquisition?'

Rio pocketed his phone, scooped her up and deposited her on the sofa.

'Oh—that's better.' Evie rolled on her side and closed her eyes, trying not to think about how his hands had felt on her skin. *How strong he was.*

'Most women find shopping a pleasurable pastime.'

'Yes, well, most women don't have to buy an entire wardrobe after just three hours sleep, and most women aren't shopping with *you*.' Yawning, Evie snuggled into the soft pile of cushions, twisting and turning to find a comfortable position. 'You said "no" so many times I thought that poor stylist person was going to throw herself out of the window.

I thought the objective was to have a high visibility shopping trip, not give some innocent woman a nervous breakdown.'

'I was trying to achieve a compromise between "wholesome" and "sexy", which proved to be something of a challenge.'

'Why do I have to look sexy?'

'Because it's important that you look like someone I'd date.'

Squashed flat by that comment, Evie curled up in a ball. 'Do you have any idea how insulting you are? Once in a while you could think about my feelings, otherwise I'm going to dump you long before this farce is supposed to end. And it doesn't really matter what the clothes look like, does it? It isn't as if we're going anywhere.' She glanced round the Penthouse, taking in the luxury. Something seemed different about the place, but she couldn't work out what. 'You won't even let me look out of the window in case someone takes my picture.'

'Astonishingly enough, I *am* thinking of you. It's precisely because we are going out that I expended all that time and effort in making sure you had an appropriate wardrobe,' he gritted. 'Tonight you're going to be walking down that red carpet with film stars and celebrities—I didn't want you to feel out of place.'

'Red carpet? What red carpet?' Evie shot upright. 'You didn't say anything about going out. I thought we were in hiding.'

'We were creating gossip and speculation which, by tonight, will have spread sufficiently to ensure that if that photograph appears it will be taken as confirmation that we are seriously involved.' Rio walked over to the desk and switched on his laptop. 'We have to be seen out together which, unfortunately, means that tonight we have to attend a film premiere and a charity ball.'

'Unfortunately? It's unfortunate that we have to attend a

film premiere and a charity ball?' Assuming he was joking, Evie started to laugh and then she saw the tension in his shoulders and the grim expression on his handsome face and realised that he was serious. He didn't want to go.

Her sudden excitement evaporated and she deflated like a balloon at a children's party. Her brain scanned all the possible reasons for his dark, forbidding scowl. 'You don't want to be seen with me.'

'*Obviously* I do,' he said tightly, 'given that it is the entire purpose of going.'

Evie sat with her back stiff, picking at her fingernails, telling herself that it was ridiculous to feel hurt by that comment. 'I understand that you feel you have to do it. But the reason you don't want to go is because you're embarrassed to be seen out with me.'

'I don't want to go because I'm incredibly busy at the moment.'

Something about the way he held himself told her that he was lying. Whatever was wrong, it had nothing to do with his workload. 'But we're going anyway?'

'Yes. We'll show our faces and then leave.' With a single tap of his finger, he brought a spreadsheet up on the screen. 'Wear the silver dress.'

Shimmering silver, Evie thought absently. *With swept-up hair.*

She should have felt thrilled but instead she felt the most crushing disappointment. 'What's the point of making a fuss if we're only going to stay five minutes?' The fact that he wasn't even looking at her increased her anger. 'It's hardly worth getting dressed, is it?'

'A brief visit is perfectly normal at these things. There is no point in wasting a whole evening when our purpose can be achieved in a short space of time.'

There was a tension in the room that she didn't understand. 'What if your purpose is to enjoy yourself?'

He was frowning at the screen. 'We're talking about a throng of people, none of whom have the slightest interest in anyone but themselves and their own self-advancement. As it happens, I have a very specific reason for going to this particular ball—I need to speak to Vladimir Yartsev.'

'Who is he?'

'Don't you read newspapers?'

Evie flushed. 'Sometimes. When I'm not working.'

'Vladimir Yartsev is a Russian oil oligarch. A very powerful man.'

'But not as powerful as you.'

A ghost of a smile touched his mouth. 'Different power.'

Evie curled her legs underneath her. 'Alternative energy. Like fossil fuels versus a wind farm.' Looking at the thin line of his mouth, she sighed. 'Sorry. I forgot you don't have a sense of humour. So this guy is going to be sitting at our table? I presume you want me to be extra-nice to him?'

'That won't be possible. He doesn't speak much English and I doubt his interpreter will be there.' Rio altered one of the figures on the spreadsheet. 'I'm sure if you smile at him it won't do any harm.'

His comment was so derogatory that she almost thumped him.

He made assumptions about people. Evie watched him, knowing that she was going to have the last laugh on this particular point. 'I won't need an interpreter. I'm good at communicating with people.' She was purposely vague. 'So you're hoping to meet up with this Vladimir guy—who else? Doesn't anyone just go to have fun?'

'They go to be seen. And at a charity ball they go to be seen spending money. It's a game. I go because there are a few contacts I need to make. I have no doubt it will be boring.'

'Thanks. So basically you're saying that not only do I

not look right, but I bore you. I can see we're in for a great evening.'

'I was talking about the other guests—' his tone was thickened with exasperation '—but carry on like this and I'll add you to the list. I've already told you—the reason I don't stay long is because I can't afford the time. I have work to do.'

All he did was work.

But he was taking her to a charity ball and a film premiere.

Evie felt a renewed flutter of excitement at the prospect of playing Cinderella for a night. 'So we're showing our faces at two events—but you have invites to loads more than that?'

'I have seven invitations for this evening. I've picked the two most high profile.' Showing no interest whatsoever in that fact, Rio focused on the screen. 'Normally, a hostess would do her utmost to avoid a clash, but this is Christmas so it's inevitable.'

Christmas.

Suddenly Evie realised what was different about the room. 'Someone's taken down all my decorations.' Horrified, she sprang to her feet and glanced around her. 'The tree has gone. And the holly—why would they have done that?'

'Because I gave instructions that all the decorations should be removed.'

Already bruised from his previous comments, it was hard to keep her voice steady. 'You didn't like the decorations?'

'No.'

She felt numb. 'I took *ages* getting them exactly right. I thought you'd be pleased—'

'I wasn't pleased.'

So she looked wrong, she was boring, and now he was saying she was useless at her job. It was the final straw.

Rio glanced up. 'While I'm staying here, I don't want to know it's Christmas.' His eyes were molten black and menacing. 'I don't want to see a single decoration. Is that clear?'

'Yes. It's perfectly clear.' Her voice high-pitched; deeply offended that he'd criticised her work, Evie stalked into the bedroom, yanking the doors closed behind her.

Her confidence in shreds, she leaned back against the doors.

Miserable, horrible, vile man.

Chemistry? Yes, there was chemistry—but she wished it was the sort that would result in some sort of explosive reaction that would blast him out of her life. He made her feel *small*. He made her feel useless and insignificant. Apparently she couldn't even decorate a Christmas tree to his satisfaction.

She stood for a moment, breathing deeply, horribly hurt by his dismissive comments. In a few sentences he'd shredded her fragile self-confidence.

With a sniff, she tried to tell herself that it didn't matter. Why should she care what he thought? So he hated her decorations. So what? The man was a cold hearted workaholic.

Fancy going to all this trouble just so that he didn't lose out on a stupid business deal.

He made Scrooge look like a cheerleader.

What sort of man would rather work than enjoy a night at a glittering Christmas ball? Did he think his entire business was going to fall apart or something?

Trying not to be hurt by the fact that he clearly wanted to spend as little time as possible in her company, Evie wrenched off the jacket that went with her 'wholesome' dress and flung it over the nearest chair.

Feeling miserable and unappreciated, she undressed and slipped under the covers, wanting to blot out her unhappiness with a much needed afternoon nap. As she closed her eyes she reminded herself that she was doing this so that her grandfather wouldn't be hurt and embarrassed. No other reason.

Once all the fuss had died down, she'd give Rio Zaccarelli the boot. Or should that be 'the stiletto'?

Either way, she was seriously looking forward to *that* day.

Rio fastened the sleeves of his dress shirt. Normally he relished the challenge of a difficult situation. On this occasion the stakes were too high to make the whole issue anything other than stressful. Adding an evening of Christmas celebrations into that mix simply increased the stress.

Get it over with.

There was no sound of activity from the bedroom and Rio wondered whether he should have checked on Evie. She'd been in there all day and they were supposed to be leaving in fifteen minutes. Was she still asleep?

Or was she still sulking over the Christmas decorations?

He was just walking towards the bedroom doors when they opened suddenly.

'Don't say a word. Not a word.' A dangerous glint in her blue eyes, she stalked barefoot across the carpet. A pair of silver shoes dangled from her fingers. 'Every time you open your mouth you say something nasty so, unless red eyes are the latest "must have" accessory on the celebrity circuit, then it's safer if you say nothing.'

Rio was pleased she'd instructed him to say nothing because, for once, the power of speech appeared to have deserted him. He'd been present when she'd tried on the dress—he'd approved it—but clearly he hadn't devoted his full attention to the task because he had no memory of it looking quite this good. Or maybe it was because he'd seen the dress in daylight and it was definitely designed to dazzle at night.

The fabric sparkled with every turn of her body and the effect was incredible—it was as if she were illuminated, each sensuous curve lit up and accentuated by the shimmering fabric. Her hair she'd scooped up and secured to the back of her head with silver clips, the slightly haphazard style both kooky and sexy.

'You look incredible.'

'Wholesome?'

He ignored the sarcasm in her tone. 'Sexy and wholesome. It's an intriguing combination. It would look even more effective if you could stop glaring at me.'

'I'll stop glaring at you when we're in public.' She was as prickly as a porcupine. 'Our deal doesn't include having to like each other, does it?'

Rio clenched his jaw. 'If I offended you, then I apologise.'

'If? There is no if, Rio. Of course you offended me! You criticised my work and then you criticised me. You're trying to turn me into a clone of the type of woman you date and then you get irritated when I'm not doing things right.'

'That isn't true, but—'

'No!' She lifted her hand like a policeman stopping traffic. 'Don't say anything else. You're incapable of speaking without being offensive.'

Unaccustomed to having to work so hard with a woman, Rio drew in a long, slow breath. 'It's snowing outside and that dress has no back to it. You'll need something to keep you warm—' He handed her a large flat box and she looked at him suspiciously before taking it with a frown.

'Now what? A cloak with a hood so that you can cover my face? A—oh—' she gasped, and then her face lost its colour and she dropped the box containing the snowy-white fur onto the carpet. 'I can't wear that. I won't wear fur.'

'It isn't real.' Wondering whether every interaction was going to result in confrontation, Rio stooped and retrieved it. 'It's fake.'

Evie stood with her hands behind her back. 'You're sure?'

'Positive.' He draped it around her shoulders. Her skin was warm and smooth against the backs of his fingers and he felt the immediate flash of chemistry. Her breathing was shallow and fast and for a moment she stood rigid, a faint bloom of colour lifting the pallor of her cheeks.

'Is that what you do when you offend someone? You buy them an extravagant gift rather than say sorry? Does it work?'

'You tell me. Your hair looks amazing against the white fur.' He saw the pulse beating in her throat and knew that she was feeling exactly what he was feeling.

'Don't think that just because I'm wearing this, I've forgiven you. I can't be bought.'

A woman who couldn't be bought.

Rio gave a faint smile at that concept.

'It does feel *gorgeous* against bare skin.' She wriggled her shoulders in an unconsciously seductive movement that sent his libido into overdrive.

Incredibly aroused, he drew her against him. 'You could remove the dress,' he suggested silkily, 'and just wear the fur.' Even without touching his fingers to her wrist, he knew her pulse was racing and Rio saw something in her eyes seconds before she looked away. *Desire*. Programmed to identify that look, he was about to suggest that the fur would be comfortable to lie on, when she shoved at his chest.

'You just can't help yourself, can you? We're supposed to be stopping the photo looking sleazy and all you want to do is stay in and make the whole situation even tackier. Or is this deal suddenly not important to you?'

Rio froze, horrified by the realisation that for a few precious seconds his mind had been wiped of every thought except for one and that was the erotic possibilities of fur against Evie's pale skin. 'You're right. Let's go.' Seriously disconcerted by the fact that she was so together while he was locked in the savage grip of rampaging hormones, he faced the lowering fact that, had she not stopped him, he would have tumbled her onto the rug in front of the fire and followed his instincts with no thought for anything except the demands of his own super-sized libido.

Exasperated with himself and seriously unsettled, Rio snagged his jacket from the back of the chair and urged her towards the elevator. 'The premiere starts in about fifteen minutes.'

'Great. So we'll be last.'

'That was the intention.' He pressed the button for the ground floor. 'We show ourselves in public when the crowd is at its maximum.'

'Why not? If I'm going to humiliate myself, it might as well be in a big way.'

Evie walked gingerly up the red carpet, relieved that the silver shoes were so much more comfortable than the red ones, her fingers gripping tightly to Rio's rock-hard biceps. Despite the falling snow, there was a huge crowd waiting in the hope of seeing the stars and Evie felt like a fraud as she heard the cheering.

'They're going to feel short-changed when they see me. What am I supposed to do?' She hissed the words between her teeth, her smile never faltering as what felt like a million camera lenses were pointed in her direction. 'Do I flash the ring? Do I look at you adoringly?'

'Just act normally.'

Evie felt a rush of exasperation that he had so little idea how she felt. 'I don't normally walk along red carpets in high heels pretending to be engaged to a very rich man I barely know. Some help here would be appreciated.'

'I'm by your side. That's all the help you need.' He paused to talk to a couple who seemed vaguely familiar. Relieved to see at least two friendly faces and trying to work out where she knew them from, Evie smiled and chatted, finding them surprisingly approachable. She *definitely* knew them from somewhere.

As Rio led her away into the foyer, she was still smiling. 'They were nice. I know I've met them before somewhere—I can't think where—I don't know that many people in London. Do they work at the hotel? What are their names?'

When he told her, she stared at him in mortified silence. 'Right. Both of them Hollywood stars. The reason I know their faces is because I've seen them both in the movies. *Now* I'm embarrassed. Oh, my God—they must have wondered why I was grinning at them like an idiot.'

'You were charming and not at all star-struck. And you didn't ask for their autograph, which is always refreshing.'

'That's because I didn't actually recognise them.' Evie tightened her grip on his arm. 'Do you think they realised? What if I offended them?'

'They enjoyed talking to you and the fact that you were so natural with them suggests that our relationship is an already accepted fact in some circles. You did well. There's no need to make holes in my arm.'

Evie slackened her grip. Determined not to make the same mistake again, she spent the next ten minutes glancing furtively around her, trying to put faces to names. The foyer was crammed with glamorous people, all of whom seemed completely comfortable in their equally glamorous surroundings. They looked like elegant swans, she thought gloomily, whereas she—she felt like an emu. Tall, conspicuous and horribly out of place amongst so many delicate, beautiful birds.

Watching her face, Rio sighed. 'You look as though you're about to visit the dentist. Try and relax.'

Finding the mingling in the foyer desperately stressful, Evie was relieved when they moved into the cinema for the showing of the film. Her spirits lifted still further when she discovered that it was a Christmas movie.

More comfortable in the dark, she slipped off her shoes and settled down in her seat, looking forward to a couple of hours of seasonal entertainment. Watching elves dance across the screen, she was just starting to feel Christmassy when she became aware that Rio was emailing someone on his BlackBerry.

'You're supposed to switch off your mobile.' The moment she said the words she realised how stupid she sounded. This wasn't a commercial showing. It hadn't escaped her notice that the other guests had been vying with each other in an attempt to exchange a few words with him. It was obvious that he was the most powerful, influential guest here. Who was going to tell him off?

Trying to block out the distracting sight of him ploughing through endless emails, Evie turned her attention back to the screen and soon she was lost in the film, sighing wistfully as Santa started putting presents in his sack. 'This is a lovely story,' she said dreamily, 'you really ought to watch it. It might help put you in the Christmas mood.'

The change in him was instantaneous.

Sliding his BlackBerry into the pocket of his dinner jacket, Rio rose to his feet in a purposeful movement, indifferent to the people around him trying to enjoy the film. 'Put your shoes back on. We're going.' Barely giving her time to slide her toes back into the silver shoes, Rio grabbed her hand and led her out of a door at the rear of the cinema.

'They're all looking at us—this is so embarrassing.' Breathless, Evie tried to keep up without twisting her ankle. 'Why are we leaving? I was enjoying myself.'

'I wasn't.' Talking into his phone again, he pushed open a fire door and Evie saw his limousine parked right outside.

'But I only watched about twenty minutes!'

'And that was twenty minutes too long. I can't stand sappy Christmas movies.'

'It hadn't even got going. Santa was about to be set upon by the bad guys determined to ruin Christmas,' Evie gasped, bending her head as he bundled her inside the car. 'Thanks to you, I won't ever find out how it ended.'

'How do you think it ended?' His handsome face was a mask of frustration and tension. 'Happily, of course. It's a Christmas movie. They only ever end happily.'

'I know it ended happily but I wanted to know *how* it ended happily. There's more than one route to a happy ending, you know. It's *how* they do the happy ending that makes it worth watching.'

He shot her a look of exasperation before turning his attention back to the screen of his BlackBerry. 'I would have thought you were too old to believe in happy endings—' he scanned, deleted, emailed '—especially after your recent experience.'

'Just because you haven't encountered a happy ending personally doesn't mean you stop believing in them.'

'If you go through life waiting for a happy ending then you're setting yourself up for permanent disappointment. If you're really that deluded then it's no wonder that you're currently single. No man could hope to live up to your ridiculously high levels of idealism. I almost feel sorry for Jeff.'

Digesting that cynical take on her approach to life, Evie stiffened. 'I gather you don't believe in happy endings. Just don't tell me that you don't believe in Santa or you'll completely ruin my evening.' Intercepting his incredulous glance, she gave him a mocking smile. 'You don't believe in Santa? Careful. If you don't believe, he won't come.'

Shaking his head in despair, Rio turned his head to look out of the window. 'How do you survive in the real world? I thought women like you were extinct.'

'There are some of us still flourishing in the wild.' Evie

leaned her head against the seat and closed her eyes. 'But we're an endangered species. We have to keep our distance from cynics like you who appear to have lost all hope, otherwise we become contaminated.'

'What are you hoping for?'

She kept her eyes firmly shut. There was no way he'd understand and he'd just laugh at her. 'Oh, this and that—the usual sort of stuff.'

'The usual sort of stuff being love, kids and marriage.'

'Go on—laugh. Just because I have my priorities right and all you think about is deals.'

'Trust me—there is *nothing* about love, marriage or kids that makes me want to laugh.'

'And half the world feels the same way as you.' Evie opened her eyes and turned her head to look at him. 'But I don't.'

'Why not? You were dumped six weeks ago.'

'I know.'

'You should be bitter and cynical.'

'How does that help?'

'It stops you having unrealistic expectations.'

'Or perhaps it stops you spotting love when you find it.' Evie adjusted her dress to stop it creasing. 'My grandparents were together for sixty years. I refuse to believe it isn't possible. Finding someone you can love and who loves you back might be rare, but it's not impossible.'

Rio's handsome face was devoid of expression.

Staring into his dark eyes, Evie felt the heat build in her body. 'It's probably different for you,' she said lamely. 'You're rich. Relationships must be even more complicated when you're incredibly wealthy.'

'You've already given me your opinion on the influence of wealth on personal relationships. Clearly you think no woman would entertain the idea of a relationship with me if I weren't wealthy.'

'I didn't say that. I'm sure there are women out there who like cynical men.' She told herself firmly that she wasn't one of them but, even as she gave herself a lecture, she was noticing the blue-black shadow of his hard jaw and the undeniably sexy curve of his mouth. Struggling hard not to think about sex, kissing or anything that required physical contact, Evie tried to lighten the atmosphere. 'If you haven't written your letter to Santa, how do you expect him to know what you'd like?'

'Are you intentionally winding me up?'

'Yes. Is it working?'

'Yes.' A glimmer of a smile pulled at the corners of his mouth and Evie's limbs weakened because he was even more gorgeous when he smiled and because she knew exactly what he could do with that mouth. And she couldn't stop thinking about it. She squirmed with awareness, furious with herself for being such a pushover. Rich, powerful guy—adoring girl. It was an embarrassing cliché.

As if—

'If I'm going along with this plan of yours,' she said quickly, 'there is one other thing I want at the end of it.'

'You can't renegotiate terms once they're agreed,' he said silkily, but Evie lifted her chin, refusing to let him intimidate her.

'I want a job when this is over. And, to be honest, that will look better for you, too. If I'm going to dump you and people find out I've lost my job they'll just assume you're petty and small-minded and you wouldn't want that.'

'Thanks for protecting my image.' His eyes gleamed with sardonic mockery. 'Do you have a particular job in mind? Santa's cheerleader?'

'I was employed to work on Reception,' Evie said firmly, 'and that's what I want to do. I was good at it.'

'So, if you were employed to work on Reception, why were

you working as a housekeeper when I arrived in the early hours this morning?'

'Because Tina demoted me. She said I talked too much.' Evie's eyes flashed defensively. 'But I don't see how you can talk too much as a receptionist. I was making people feel welcome. That's the job my grandfather thinks I'm doing, and that's the job I want when I finally dump you.'

'All right.'

Evie gulped. 'All right? You're saying yes? I can have my job as receptionist back?'

'I'm saying yes,' he drawled softly, 'although, if you're missing your grandfather that much, it strikes me you might be better taking a job closer to home.'

'There isn't anything. I tried that. No one needs my skills. What will happen to Carlos?'

'I have no idea.' Rio pressed a button by his seat and a panel opened. 'Do you drink champagne?'

Evie didn't want to admit she'd never tasted it. 'Of course.'

He withdrew a bottle from the fridge, popped the cork and poured the bubbling liquid into two tall slender-stemmed glasses. 'To our deal.'

Evie sipped from the glass he handed her and choked as the bubbles flew up her nose. 'Oh—that's—' she coughed '—yummy.' She took another mouthful. 'Happy Christmas. How long do we have to keep this up? When will you know if you've rescued your deal?'

He looked out of the window. 'We've arrived.'

And he hadn't answered her question.

Wondering once again what it was about this particular deal that was so important, Evie followed his gaze and gasped. 'We're at the Natural History Museum.' The famous building was illuminated against the winter night and thousands of tiny sparkling lights had been threaded through the branches of the trees. In front of the building was an ice rink and the whole place had been transformed into a winter paradise. 'I had no idea they held events here.'

'This is a very prestigious fund-raiser.'

'Can we ice skate?'

'Absolutely not.'

'But it's snowing.' Evie leaned forward, captivated by the atmosphere. 'It would be magical. Do you think we'll have a white Christmas?'

'I couldn't care less. Do you want an umbrella?'

'You don't like snow? Seriously?'

'It's useful when I'm skiing. The rest of the time it's an inconvenience.'

'When did you last make a snowman or throw a snowball?'

Rio frowned. 'We need to get out of the car, Evie.'

Evie didn't budge. 'You don't write to Santa, you hate decorations, you don't like snow, you won't ice skate—there must be *something* you like about Christmas. Turkey? Meeting up with friends? What's the best thing about Christmas for you?'

The door was opened by his security chief and a blast of cold air entered the car.

Rio stared at her for a long moment, his face unsmiling. 'The best thing about Christmas for me is when it's over,' he gritted. 'Now, get out of the car and smile.'

'So the rumours are true, Rio? You're engaged? You do realise you've just ruined every single woman's Christmas, and half the married ones, too?' Tabitha Fenton-Coyle stroked her long red fingernails over his sleeve. 'Tell me what it is about her that induced a hardened cynic like yourself into marriage.'

'You need to ask?'

'Well, she's pretty, of course, in a slightly unsophisticated way that a man might find appealing—' There was a flinty glint in Tabitha's eyes and Rio turned his head and noticed Evie laughing uninhibitedly with the two Russian billionaires, both known for their arrogant refusal to speak English at social events. They were taciturn, remote and notoriously unapproachable and yet both appeared to be listening to Evie with rapt attention.

How was she making herself understood?

From across the table, Rio tried to hear what she was saying. She was chatting non-stop, her hands moving as she illustrated her point. Occasionally she paused to sip champagne or listen to their response.

'Clever of you to find a woman who speaks Russian,' Tabitha said, 'given your business interests in that country. Is that how you met? Is she an interpreter or something?'

Evie spoke Russian?

Unable to hear her above the noise from the surrounding tables, Rio focused his gaze on her lips and realised that she was indeed speaking Russian.

His hostess was watching him. 'You didn't know, did you? Well, if she can persuade them to open their wallets when the charity auction begins, then she'll certainly get my vote.'

Where had Evie learned to speak Russian?

Why hadn't she mentioned it when he'd told her that Vladimir didn't speak good English and that she wouldn't be able to communicate without an interpreter? And then he remembered her responding that she wouldn't need an interpreter. At the time he'd assumed she'd meant that she'd be using sign language and lots of smiles—not once had it occurred to him that she spoke fluent Russian.

Coffee was served as the auction began and there was a sudden flurry of movement as people swapped seats.

Her cheeks pink with excitement, Evie swayed to her feet and found her way to the seat next to him. 'I'm having *such* a nice time. Those men are so sweet. You should have mentioned how funny they were.'

Rio tightened his grip on the glass. 'Just as you should possibly have mentioned the fact that you're fluent in Russian.'

'You were being arrogant and I thought it would be more fun to just surprise you. I thought it might teach you not to underestimate people.' Craning her neck, she looked over his shoulder towards the stage and the dance floor. 'What's happening now?'

Rio fingered the stem of his glass. 'I do *not* underestimate people.'

'Yes, you do. But you probably can't help it,' she said kindly. 'Is there going to be dancing?'

'It's the auction first. The bidding will raise money for the charity.' Rio was still watching her. 'Do you speak any other languages?'

'French, Spanish and Mandarin. So am I allowed to bid for something?'

'You speak *four* languages?'

'Five, if you count English. How much am I allowed to bid?'

'You don't speak Italian?'

'No.' She helped herself to a chocolate from the plate. 'That CD was always out of the library whenever I looked.'

Rio shot her an incredulous look. 'You taught yourself all those languages?'

'I'm good at languages. I taught myself the basics and then there was a teacher at school who helped me and I had a friend who spoke Mandarin and Russian.' She was looking across the room. 'Don't look now but there's a huge Christmas tree next to the stage—you'd better close your eyes or it will probably give you a nervous breakdown. I'm surprised you didn't phone ahead and ask them to remove it.'

Still absorbing the fact that she spoke five languages, Rio dragged his gaze to the stage and saw the Christmas tree. She was right; it was huge—a massive symbol of the unspeakable horrors of his childhood. There was a rushing sound in his ears and suddenly the voices around him seemed far away. Instead of staring at glittering baubles, he was staring into a deep, dark black hole. Memories formed pictures in his brain, taking on shapes he didn't want to see, like a gruesome kaleidoscope. That hideous morning. The discovery he'd made. The shock. And the emptiness.

Suddenly every sparkle in the room seemed to intensify the dark feelings swirling in his brain. Every silver star and rope of tinsel was a silent mockery.

Promising himself that they'd leave as soon as the auction was over, Rio sat still, ruthlessly wrestling his feelings back under control.

From inside a fog of unwelcome memories, he was dimly aware of Evie leaning across the table, coaxing the Russians into bidding enormous sums of money in the charity auction. Even Tabitha was looking impressed as Evie switched between Russian and English, extracting more money from the billionaires than they'd sucked oil from the Caspian Sea.

If the circumstances had been different, Rio would have laughed. As it was, he just wanted to leave.

They'd been seen together. The ring had been photographed. Rumours were spreading.

It was done.

Rio watched with a frown as Tabitha made sure that Evie's glass was kept topped up. She was drinking the champagne as if it were soda, and he realised that if he didn't remove her from this table quickly she was going to be drunk.

As the auction ended and a band started warming up on the stage, Rio drained his glass and turned to Evie.

'We're leaving.'

'No way! Not this time. I missed almost all of the film—I'm not missing the rest of the ball. The dancing hasn't started yet.' She started to sway in her seat in time to the music while Tabitha looked on with a mixture of condescension and amusement.

'If you can persuade Rio to dance with you, then I'm willing to believe he's in love. I've never known him to dance. If I didn't know better, I'd think he didn't have rhythm.' She gave Rio a knowing look and he saw Evie's happy smile falter as she digested the meaning behind those words.

Rio cursed silently.

She might be tipsy, but she wasn't so under the influence that she didn't recognise a barb when it was poked into her flesh.

Removing the champagne glass from her hand, he dragged her to her feet. 'You're right—we'll dance.' Without giving himself time to think about it, he led her onto the dance floor and slid his arm around her waist. 'Smile.'

'What is there to smile about? She's flaunting the fact she's had sex with you. She's *vile*. And you have no taste. No wonder you've never wanted to settle down with anyone if she's the sort of person you've been seeing.'

'I have *not* had sex with her,' Rio breathed, bending his head so that he spoke the words in her ear and couldn't be overheard. Immediately, her perfume wound itself round his senses. 'She was trying to cause trouble. Trying to hurt you. Don't let her. You're just over-emotional because you've had too much champagne. Now smile, because the whole purpose of tonight is to convince people our relationship is real.'

'Well, if this relationship were real, I would have punched her. And I'm not over-emotional, I'm justifiably emotional. That woman is a man-eater. She ought to be fenced in on a game reserve. Do you know that she's on her *fourth* husband? Evgeni and Vladimir told me that she only marries them for their money.'

Rio's tension levels rocketed up several more notches. 'You're on first name terms with the Russians?'

'I sat with them all evening, what did you expect? When I saw that awful Tabitha woman had separated us I almost had a heart attack. She put me there thinking I'd struggle, didn't she? She was trying to be unkind.'

Rio gave a faint smile. 'I think you won that round.'

'They told me that she takes men to the cleaners and lives off the settlement.'

'It's a popular career choice in certain circles.'

'Well, I think it's awful. No amount of money would make up for being married to someone I didn't love.' Evie slid her arms around his neck, her eyes slightly bleary. 'I mean, actually, when you think about it, that's not so far from prostitution, is it?'

Conscious of the shocked glances from those nearest to them, Rio smiled. 'Absolutely right,' he purred, vastly entertained by how outspoken she became when she'd had a few glasses of champagne. 'You might want to lower your voice before you cast any more aspersions on the character and profession of our illustrious hostess.'

Evie gulped. 'Oops. Do you think they heard me?'

'Definitely. They're doubtless all now engrossed in a fascinating debate as to whether our hostess is a prostitute or not.'

Evie leaned her forehead against his chest. 'Sorry. I may have drunk just a little bit too much champagne—I've never had it before and it's *delicious*.'

'You've never had champagne before?'

'Never. Last year, Grandpa and I treated ourselves to a bottle of Prosecco but it wasn't the same.'

Rio winced. 'No. It definitely isn't the same. Prosecco is excellent in a Bellini but it's not champagne.' He lifted his hand and removed a strand of fiery red hair that had somehow managed to tangle itself around his bow tie. 'I think I'd better take you home.'

'I don't want to go home. I want to dance. Anyway, I like it here and we're supposed to be seen.' Still clinging to him tightly, she swayed in time to the music and then looked up with a smile as everyone started singing *The Twelve Days of Christmas*.

'Oh, I *love* this. This used to be my party piece at school. I do all the actions. Wait till you see my Seven swans a-swimming—'

Rio inhaled deeply. 'Evie—' But she was already lifting her hands like a conductor, waving her arms and singing at the top of her voice along with everyone else.

'—partridge in a pear tree—'

'I'm taking you home.'

'No.' She dug her heels in like a stubborn horse. 'I'm not going anywhere. I've never been to a party as amazing as this one. I don't want it to end.'

Rio gritted his teeth. 'We have two more to attend tomorrow. And this time I won't make the mistake of giving you champagne beforehand.'

'I don't care about tomorrow. I want to live for today. I like *this* party.' She slid her arms around his neck and pressed herself against him, her breath warm against his neck. 'Please, Rio, dance with me. You know you want to.'

He locked his fingers around her wrists, intending to remove her arms, but then she smiled up at him and he found himself so captivated by that smile that instead of removing her arms, he slid his hands down her warm skin. Her back was bare, her skin warm and smooth and tempting and raw lust shot through him. Without thinking about what he was doing, Rio lowered his mouth towards hers.

'Four calling birds, three French hens—'

Rio froze as she started to sing again. 'Evie—'

'Two turtle doves, and a—'

'Evie!' Rio felt tension prickle down his spine.

'I like singing. If you want me to stop singing, you're going to have to gag me.'

'Good idea.' Rio closed the distance and captured her mouth with his. The chemistry was instantaneous and explosive. Because he had his hand on her bare back he could feel the tremors that shook her and he welded her closer to him, ignoring the curious looks of those around him.

After two of the most intoxicating, arousing, exciting minutes of his life, he lifted his head fractionally and tried to regain his balance. The kiss had done nothing except make him crave more. He wanted to touch and taste—he wanted to bury his face in her hair and feast on her body.

Around them, everyone was still singing but this time Evie wasn't joining in.

'When you kiss me, I don't ever want it to stop,' she murmured, her eyes slightly glazed. 'It feels incredible. Are you as good at everything else? If so, then it's no wonder every woman in the room is looking at me as if they hate me. They think we're having mad, crazy sex all the time. I wish. Maybe we should. It seems a shame to disappoint everyone.'

He cupped her face in his hands and stared down at her in exasperation. 'You're plastered. It's time I took you home.'

'I'm not plastered. And I don't want to go home. I'm having a really great time and I refuse to go home just so that you can weld yourself to your laptop again and ignore the fact it's Christmas. Kissing you, drinking champagne, dancing and singing—they're my favourite things. Honestly, Rio, you should sing too—it's fun—I'm feeling so *Christmassy*—' Her hips swayed and there was a huge smile on her face as she started to sing along again, joining in with the crowd, this time at double the volume—

When it came to *'Five gold rings'* she sang even louder, struck a dramatic pose and flashed her diamond in the air, beaming at Rio.

Before he could stop her, she flung herself towards the two Russians, kissed each of them on the cheek and then sprang onto a chair and from there onto the table.

Rio closed his eyes, cursing himself for not monitoring her champagne intake more closely. He contemplated removing her bodily but decided that she would probably make such a fuss that the best thing to do was to wait until the end of the song and hope she survived that long without falling off the table and doing herself serious injury.

Everyone was clapping and Evie was by now the centre of attention as she led the singing, her actions for *Seven swans a-swimming* causing such hilarity that Rio shook his head in disbelief.

'She's certainly the life and soul of the party,' Vladimir was suddenly beside him, speaking in slow, broken English, and beaming up at Evie, who was still mimicking a swan. 'That joint venture you wanted to explore in Moscow—we're willing to give it some consideration. Fly over in the New Year and meet with us. Evie can translate for you.'

Rio, who had given up on the usually taciturn Russians, was about to confirm the details when an overenthusiastic re-enactment of *'Three French hens'* almost sent Evie spinning off the table.

'*Scusi*—' Crossing to the table, he caught Evie as she lost her balance and she tumbled into his arms, the silver dress shimmering under the lights.

'—*Two purple doves,*' she hollered, *'and a partridge in a pear tree.'*

Wild applause surrounded them and Rio winced. 'That's your party piece?'

'One of them. I also tell a great joke about a wide mouth toad which has brilliant actions.' She eyed the microphone on the stage. 'I suppose I could—'

'No,' Rio said hastily. 'You most definitely could not.'

'I love champagne,' she said happily, leaning her head against his shoulder. 'It's the nicest, yummiest, fizziest, happiest drink I've ever tasted. Is there any more?'

'It's run out. You drank it all. Thanks to you, the global champagne market is now in meltdown.'

'Shame.' She buried her face in his neck and breathed

deeply. 'You smell so good. Why do you smell so good? Will you kiss me again? And this time don't stop. The only thing I hate about kissing you is when you stop. I just want it to go on and on and on—could you do that, do you think? You did say you were good at multi-tasking.'

Rio tensed. 'Evie—'

'You're an incredibly sexy man. If I wasn't so afraid of being rejected again, I'd try and seduce you—' she was snuggling and kissing his neck at the same time '—but I've never seduced anyone before so it's probably a bit overambitious to start with you. Like climbing a mountain and deciding to start with Everest. I ought to practice on someone small, ugly and unsuccessful first and see how I get on.'

Rio felt his entire body tighten. 'You won't be practising on anyone tonight. We're going home.'

'Not without a present from the Christmas tree,' she coaxed, lifting her head and focusing with difficulty. 'It's all in a good cause. You pay money and they give you a surprise present. The money goes to the kids. So it's sort of two presents in one. Three presents actually, because you get a warm fuzzy feeling from being generous.'

Deciding that it was going to be quicker to buy the present than argue, Rio strode towards the tree, Evie still in his arms. Around them, people were smiling indulgently.

His pulse rate doubled as he approached the tree. The smell of pine invaded his nostrils, awakening thoughts and memories long dormant.

'Which present?' he growled, adjusting the angle of his body so that she could see the tree and he couldn't. 'Tell me which one you want.' Quickly. So that he could make his escape. The past was rolling over him like a dark cloud, its creeping menace threatening to seep under the barriers of his self-control.

'The pink one with the silver bow.' Her arms tightened

around his neck and Rio felt the moist flicker of her tongue against his throat.

'That one—' His voice tight, he indicated with his head towards the pink box and one of the staff untied it from the tree and handed it to him while one of his own security team discreetly dealt with the financial aspect of the transaction.

'Thank you.' Her voice was husky, her mouth tantalizingly close to his and Rio tried to ignore the perfume that wafted from her skin.

'We're going home.'

'So that we can experiment with fur against naked flesh?'

Jaw clenched tight, he reminded himself that she dreamed of happy endings.

If there was one thing designed to kill his libido, it was a woman who dreamed of happy endings.

'So that you can sleep off the champagne.'

'Wait—' Slightly breathless, she pressed her lips against his throat. 'I want the tree. Will you buy me the tree?'

Rio stilled. 'You want me to buy every present on the tree?'

'No, I want you to buy me the *tree*. I don't think I can stand the thought of Christmas without a tree. It's like having chocolate cake with no chocolate.' Still clutching the pink box, she snuggled against him, her voice coaxing. 'That tree would look fantastic in the Penthouse. It's even bigger than the one I decorated.'

The one he'd had removed.

'I don't want a tree.'

'Why not? I know you prefer to work over Christmas, but it isn't going to stop you working just because there's a tree in the room. It cheers everything up.'

'It doesn't cheer me up.'

She frowned. 'So it wasn't my decorations in particular that you didn't like. It's Christmas trees in general. Why?

You're never too old to enjoy Christmas. Having a tree will give you happy memories.'

Rio put her down so suddenly she staggered. 'I don't have any happy memories of Christmas.'

It was the stricken look in her eyes that made him realise just how harshly he'd spoken. 'I...I'm sorry,' she stammered. 'I didn't mean—'

'Forget it. Let's get out of here.'

CHAPTER SIX

I don't have any happy memories of Christmas.

Evie sat in the middle of the enormous bed, those words reverberating around her head. She'd put her foot in it, but knowing that didn't stop her wondering and asking herself endless questions.

Why didn't he have happy memories of Christmas?

She turned her head and looked towards the double doors that lay between her and the sitting room. They remained firmly closed.

What was he doing? Had he gone to sleep in the second bedroom?

They'd driven home without speaking, Evie silenced by that one revealing phrase and Rio communicating nothing. For once, his BlackBerry was silent and he'd simply stared out of the window at the snowy streets, his handsome face an expressionless mask.

But he *was* feeling, she knew that.

Not just feeling—*hurting.*

Knowing that she was risking another rejection, Evie slid off the bed and opened the doors quietly, afraid to disturb him if he was sleeping.

The huge living room was in darkness. The flames of the fire had almost flickered to nothing and all the lights had been extinguished.

He wasn't there.

She was overreacting. He'd obviously chosen to sleep in the second bedroom.

Evie was about to turn and go back to bed when she noticed a ghostly green glow in the corner of the room and realised that it was the laptop screen.

As her eyes slowly adjusted to the darkness, she saw that Rio was seated at the table.

'It's four in the morning,' she murmured. 'You should get some sleep.'

'I'm not tired.' His voice was barely audible. 'Go back to bed, Evie. Sleep it off.'

Knowing that she was unwelcome, she was about to do just that but her feet froze to the spot as her eyes adjusted to the dim light and she managed to make out his profile. He looked like a man on the edge. A man struggling to contain an emotion bigger than him.

He was still looking at the screen, but somehow she knew that this time he wasn't reading the numbers. His eyes were bleak and empty and she knew instantly that this was about Christmas.

I don't have any happy memories of Christmas.

What sort of childhood had he had, that he hadn't retained a single happy memory of Christmas?

The sudden stillness of the room seemed loud in her ears.

Evie stood still, knowing that she was intruding on a private moment. She knew she ought to back away and return to the neutral sanctuary of the bedroom. She ought to close those big doors and leave him to his dark thoughts. She was never going to see him again once this charade was over. Why did it even matter that he wanted to shut himself away and pretend Christmas wasn't happening?

But there was something about the bleak set of his features that made it impossible for her to walk away. She never would have been able to walk away and leave another human being in so much pain, and she had no doubt that he was in pain.

She'd become intimately acquainted with the signs after her grandmother had died. Night after night, she'd seen the same look on her grandfather's face as he'd sat in her grandmother's favourite rocking chair, just staring at her photograph. She'd kept him company in the darkness, afraid to leave him alone with his grief.

What had Rio Zaccarelli lost?

What was he thinking about, as he stared sightlessly at that screen?

Evie walked across to him, knowing that she was taking a risk. She was approaching when she should have run away.

Rio lifted his head and inhaled deeply. 'I said, go back to bed.'

'My head spins when I lie down.'

'You drank too much champagne. That feeling will pass. Drink lots of water.'

'I'm not drunk.'

The barest flicker of a smile touched his mouth. 'You were dancing on the table.'

'That wasn't because I was drunk. It was because I'd lost some of my inhibitions. If I had the confidence, I would have done the same thing sober. The drink just made me less anxious.'

'In that case, remind me never to escort you when you're drunk.'

'Tell me why you hate Christmas.'

Anger flickered across his face and his swift glance was loaded with warning. 'I think you should go to bed.'

'Only if you come too.' She had no idea what had driven her to say those words. Immediately, she wanted to drag them back. *What if he said yes?* She'd never had a one-night stand in her life. Compared with his experience and sophistication, she was a complete novice.

For a moment he simply watched her, his eyes glittering in the darkness. She had the feeling that he was fighting some brutal internal battle.

'Leave,' he said thickly. 'Right now.'

'I'm not drunk.'

'That isn't why I want you to leave.'

'Then—'

'I'm fresh out of happy endings, Evie. You won't find one within a thousand kilometres of me.'

Her mouth dried and her heart was pounding in her chest. 'I know that. You could never be my happy ending. But that doesn't mean…I want to know…'

His eyes were hard and unsympathetic. He gave her no help at all. 'What do you want to know, Evie?'

She licked dry lips. 'I want to know what it would be like,' she whispered. 'If the rest of it would feel as good as the kissing part.'

'You want to know how it would feel?' He rose to his feet so suddenly that she actually took an involuntary step backwards and he registered her retreat with a sardonic smile. 'I'll tell you how it would feel, Evie. It would feel good. We've both felt the chemistry. It would be incredible. Hot and crazy. For a short time.' His voice was thickened by emotion. 'And then I'd break your heart. Like that—' He snapped his fingers in a cruel, casual gesture that made her flinch. 'Easy.'

The blood was pulsing in her ears and it was difficult to breathe. 'That's fine.'

His gaze mocked. 'You're saying it's fine for me to break your heart?'

'No. I'm saying you won't break it. To break it, I'd have to be in love with you and I'm not in love with you. I wouldn't be that stupid.'

His lids lowered, half concealing black eyes that glittered dark and dangerous. 'Perhaps I'm not in the mood for a gentle seduction.'

Evie felt a spasm of fear, intermingled with the most fierce excitement she'd ever experienced. It was like a drug, urging her on to be more and more daring. 'If you're trying to scare me, you're not succeeding.'

'Maybe you should be scared, Evie.' His voice was lethally soft and cold as the ice that had formed on the windows. 'I'm not the right man for you.'

'I know that.' They were alone in the room and yet she was whispering. 'That isn't what this is about.'

'So what is it about? What are you trying to prove to yourself? Or is this good girl seduces bad boy, just to see how it feels?'

'No! I—' Evie broke off, struggling to breathe. 'I don't know what this is. All I know is…I thought you wanted… earlier you said…'

'I know what I said. I know what I wanted.'

'So—'

'Earlier, I didn't know what I was dealing with.'

Evie flushed. 'Because I love Christmas and believe in happy endings? I said I didn't believe in happy endings with you.'

His eyes held hers. 'If you play with fire, you'll get burnt.'

'Will you tell me why you hate Christmas?'

'No. And you're making this personal. A basic female mistake.'

'All right. Nothing personal. No questions.' Part of her was shocked at herself. What was she doing?

'You think you can go to bed with a man and not make it personal?' There was a layer of humour in his voice. 'You think you can do that?'

'Yes.' *No.* She had no idea.

Rio stared at her for a long moment and then lifted his hand and took a strand of her hair in his fingers. 'You should be more careful with yourself, Evie Anderson. You could get seriously hurt.' The backs of his fingers brushed her cheek and Evie shivered, dazed by the spark of electricity that shot through her body.

Her heart pounding, she turned her head and ran her tongue along his fingers.

His response was instantaneous. With a growl, he cupped her face in his hands and brought his mouth down on hers in a punishing, possessive kiss. He'd kissed her before, but this kiss was different. This kiss demanded everything and Evie felt all her senses ignite with explosive force. Within an instant she was light-headed, her limbs weak and wobbly.

With a moan, she slid her hands up his chest, over his shoulders, feeling the firm swell of muscle beneath her hands. He'd discarded his bow tie and undone the first few buttons of his shirt and her fingers slid inside, seeking, touching, exploring. She felt the pulsing heat of his body beneath her fingertips and made a small, desperate sound deep in her throat and then he was kissing her again and his tongue was hot against hers, his relentless seduction so much more prac-tised than her own desperate offering.

The kiss seemed to last for ever and she felt her entire body stir, as if it had been waiting for this exact moment to come alive. And the feelings were so intense that it was impossible to stay silent.

When he pressed his mouth to the hollow of her throat she moaned, and when he dragged his mouth lower and toyed with the straining peak of her breast she arched her back and gasped his name. She wanted more, much more, and when he closed his hand over the hem of her nightdress she didn't stop him. There was a tearing sound as he ripped it from neck to hem and then she was naked, her body visible in the warm glow of the firelight.

If she'd thought that the semi darkness might give her some protection, she was wrong. Rio drew away from her, his breathing audible as he scanned her body, his gaze lingering on the fiery red curls that nestled at the juncture of her thighs.

'You can still change your mind.'

'No.' Emotion clogged her throat and the only thing in her head was a desperate need for this man. 'I don't want to change my mind.'

His fingers speared her hair and tightened, drawing her head back. His eyes were fierce, black and focused—focused on her.

For a few suspended seconds she didn't breathe and then he seemed to make a decision. Without speaking, he clamped his hand behind her head and claimed her mouth with ravenous hunger. It was a full on assault, his tongue in her mouth, his kiss blatantly sexual and brutally erotic and Evie went from freezing to boiling in a microsecond, her body burning up under the heat of his. She ripped at his shirt, clawing, tearing in a desperate attempt to get to the sleek male flesh beneath. Finally his shirt dangled open at the front and her hands slid inside and up to his shoulders. His body was a work of art, his muscles pumped up and hard, the dark shading on his chest accentuating strength and masculinity. Desperate to taste, Evie pushed at his chest and they rolled. Now he was the one on his back, his eyes glittering dark in the firelight as he watched her. Then his hand moved behind her head and he brought her mouth down to his, kissing her hungrily as her hair tumbled between them. Evie kissed him back, matching his hunger with her own, her hands sliding over his body as she straddled him. For a moment she paused, her hair tumbling around them, her senses reaching overload. His eyes were dark, so dark, and she felt an overwhelming thrill of excitement as she felt him, hard and ready beneath her. In that single moment, her breath caught. It was like reaching the top of a roller coaster and realising that there was no turning back.

'You're shaking—' His voice was raw and thickened

with the same passion she was feeling. 'Do you want me to stop?'

'No,' she whispered. She leaned forward so that her mouth brushed his. 'I can't stop. I want this more than anything. I want *you*.'

'Why?'

She sensed his struggle to hold back. It was visible in his eyes and in the tension of his sleek, pumped muscles.

'Does it matter?' Her mouth was against his. 'It feels right. Can't that be enough?'

He didn't answer her question. Instead, he closed his hands over her hips and lifted her, flipping her gently onto her back, once more the aggressor as he came over her. The outside world melted away. Details blurred. Dimly, Evie registered that he was now naked and that brief glimpse was enough to send nerves licking along the edges of her excitement.

He devoured her mouth and she kissed him back, every bit as hungry for him as he very clearly was for her.

The heat was shocking, an inferno of dangerous desire and carnal craving and, when he dragged his mouth from her lips to her neck, Evie sucked in air and tried to focus. But there was nothing to hold on to except him. Her whole world was tumbling around her and he was the only solid thing remaining. When his hand slid between her thighs she moaned against his mouth and he murmured something in Italian, his clever fingers sliding skilfully against delicate flesh. He knew exactly where to touch her, *how to touch her,* and Evie felt the ache in her body intensify until it was almost agonizing. She shifted her hips on the rug, whimpered his name, but Rio simply watched her, his mouth only a breath away from hers as he tormented her with merciless skill.

'Please,' Evie begged, arching towards him, 'Please, Rio—'

As if something snapped inside him, he shifted onto her.

He stroked her hair away from her face and scanned her features with eyes that were dark with secrets.

She felt the hardness of him brush against her and tensed. 'Please—' In desperation, she ran her hands down his body and her heart gave a little lurch as she touched the power of him.

He leaned his forehead against hers, holding her gaze. 'I don't want to hurt you—'

'You won't.'

There was a brief pause while he protected her and then he was inside her, hard and hot. The size of him shocked her and Evie forced herself to relax as she learned to accommodate him.

'Breathe—' His voice was husky and he lowered his mouth to hers. 'Breathe, *tesoro.*'

'Can't—' Her body was on fire and he gently brushed her mouth with his, tracing her lower lip with his tongue as he eased deeper.

She felt an agonizing flash of pain, immediately followed by excitement as he moved against sensitive flesh and she dug her nails hard into his back, feeling the tension shimmering in his powerful frame.

He was holding back. *Holding back for her.*

Her heart was pounding, her cheeks were flushed and her blood raced with every agonizingly slow stroke. Pleasure streaked through her and she cried out his name, telling him how much she wanted him, how much she needed him and he answered with his body, driving into her with controlled force, attacking her senses with a savage sensuality.

The storm inside was fierce and furious, raging through her like a wild beast, ready to burn up everything it touched. What they shared was primitive and elemental and she knew deep down in the very fibre of her being that nothing was ever going to be the same again.

She felt his fingers dig hard into the soft flesh of her thigh and then faster, harder, he built the rhythm until there was nothing in her head but a thundering roar, until everything inside and around her shattered into a million tiny fragments and she fell, spinning and tumbling, into a different world.

When she woke, she was alone in the bed. At some point during the early hours he'd transferred her to the bedroom, tucking her under the soft duvet. She had a vague recollection of pleading with him to join her and an equally vague recollection that his response to her request had been to pull away and return to the living room, making good on his earlier warning that their intimacies would be physical, not emotional. He'd returned to his laptop—to his own silent world. A world that didn't include Christmas or people.

A world that didn't include her.

Dizzy with lack of sleep, her body aching in unusual places, Evie slid out of the bed, blushing as she realised her nightdress was probably still lying in pieces on the floor of the living room.

So this was how it felt to sleep with a man you weren't in love with.

Padding across the thickly carpeted floor, she gazed in the mirror at herself, trying to see the differences. Same blue eyes. Same freckles. Same crazy morning hair.

She looked the same. Outwardly, nothing had changed. Maybe she could live a life that included sex without happy endings. Other women did it all the time. Maybe she could too.

Hearing his voice from the living room, Evie quickly pulled on a robe and followed the sound. He was on the phone, talking to someone in a time zone more alive than theirs. He'd made love to her for most of the night, but that hadn't stopped him working. Nothing stopped him working. But now she was wondering whether work was a refuge rather than a goal. A place to escape rather than a strategy for global domination.

The first thing she saw when she entered the room were newspapers stacked on the low table between the sofas.

Her stomach lurched and she felt sick with apprehension.

This was it. This was the moment she'd been dreading. This was the reason for the charade.

Had they printed that horribly revealing photograph?

Was that why he was on the telephone?

Hardly daring to look, she sank onto the sofa and stared at the newspaper on top of the pile, forcing herself to breathe slowly. It was one of the tabloids. If anyone had printed the picture of her naked, surely it would be them. Her hand shaking, she reached out and lifted it onto her lap. The headlines blurred and suddenly she didn't want to look, as if postponing the moment could alter the outcome.

'*Calma, tesoro.* It's all right.' His voice was deep and firm. 'They printed a lovely picture of you with your arms around my neck. The caption is "Tycoon tumbles" or something equally unimaginative. I expect your grandfather will be satisfied with it.'

What did he mean by that? 'So you were right.' Even though he'd reassured her, her fingers were damp with sweat as she forced herself to turn the pages. 'Because we gave them another photo opportunity and a bigger story, they used that instead. Thank you.' The relief was almost painful. 'Thank you so much.' Her eyes glistened as she looked up at him. 'I don't know what I would have done if they'd used that photograph. I'm so grateful to you.'

A muscle flickered in his jaw. 'You have no reason to be grateful to me, Evie.'

'Yes, I have. It was your idea to give them a better story. I would have tried to pay them off and that never would have worked because I suppose they would have just kept coming back for more money.'

He drew his hand over the back of his neck and she saw the muscles in his forearm flex, revealing a tension she didn't understand. 'Evie—'

'You don't have to say anything,' she said hastily. 'I do realise that this is just one day and that they could use that photograph tomorrow, but I'm not going to think about that now. We'll take it a day at a time. Maybe we can make sure they take another photograph of us tonight. Keep giving them something else to print. I promise not to dance on the table again, no matter how Christmassy I feel. What are our plans?'

He didn't answer immediately and she turned her attention back to the newspaper, turning the pages until she found the photograph. 'It's big. I had no idea they'd be that interested.' And she saw instantly why he'd made that comment about her grandfather liking the photograph. She was in Rio's arms, smiling up at him, looking completely smitten. No one looking at that picture would have questioned the authenticity of their relationship. A strange feeling twisted in the pit of her stomach. Was that really the way she'd looked at him? Had he noticed? 'We look good. They were obviously convinced.'

'Champagne certainly brings out an interesting side to you,' he drawled softly and she glanced up to find his eyes on her face.

'I really wasn't drunk.'

'But you were a virgin.'

Fire rose in her cheeks and she sat in silence for a moment, trying to find the right response. 'So what?'

'Why didn't you tell me?'

Was that the reason for his tension? Was it simply the fact that she was so much less experienced than him? 'Well, it isn't exactly something that comes up in conversation,' she said lightly, 'and I don't see that it matters. You wanted someone wholesome. If the press choose to dig around in my past they won't find anything. Isn't that what you wanted?' She kept noticing small things about him—like the bold curve of his eyebrows and the cluster of dark hairs revealed by the open neck of his shirt. Knowing what she knew now, she could easily picture the rest of his body—his chest shadowed with the same dark hair, concealing well defined muscle and breathtaking power. Knowing what she knew, everything was different. More sharply defined, more acutely felt.

The unspoken sexual component to their relationship had been there from the first moment they'd met but it had been enhanced a thousand times by the intimacies they'd shared in the flickering glow of firelight.

'You told me you were engaged.'

'I was.'

'But you didn't have a physical relationship?' His tone was incredulous.

'If you saw the house where I grew up, you wouldn't find it so surprising.' Evie pushed her hair away from her face with a hand that wasn't quite steady. 'I was all set to go to university, but after my grandmother died I couldn't bear to leave my grandfather on his own. I got a job in the village and went to night school to study languages. Jeff and I started dating because we were the only two people under fifty in the village. There was no way I was going to have sex in Grandpa's house. Even if it had been possible, it wouldn't have felt right.'

'Presumably, you didn't conduct your entire relationship with your grandfather looking on. There must have been *some* moments when you were alone.'

'Yes, I suppose there were—' Evie hesitated. 'But neither of us…we didn't really… Honestly, I think we were just friends. We should never have been anything else but I think we were swept along by the expectations of everyone around us.'

'Friends?' His dark brows locked in a puzzled frown and she smiled, thinking how much she'd learned about him in such a short time.

'I bet you've never been friends with a woman in your life, have you?'

'If by "friends" you mean no sex, then the answer is no. So you were engaged, but you never had sex.'

'I don't think either of us was in any hurry.'

'You were in a hurry last night,' he said silkily. 'Or was the champagne to blame for your sudden transformation from virgin to vamp?'

She sucked in a breath, mortified at his blatant reminder of her own desperation. 'No,' she said softly. 'It was you.'

'Let's test that theory, shall we?' He drew her to her feet and a thrill of expectation shot through her.

'Now?'

'Was it the champagne, Evie?' He murmured the words against her mouth and her eyes closed, her heart racing crazily as she rose on her toes and slid her arms around his neck. He slid his hands down her back and pressed her into him, his kiss tasting of hunger and passion.

Evie opened her mouth under his, matching his erotic demands with her own. Dimly, she registered that she shouldn't be feeling this way. They'd made love for most of the night and yet the fierce hunger inside her was as acute as if they hadn't ever touched. She was greedy for more of what they'd shared.

Rio pushed the robe down her arms with confident hands and the silky fabric slid over her hips and pooled on the floor, leaving her naked.

'It's daylight—' Evie could feel her face burning and he gave a slow smile as he tightened his hands on her shoulders and moved her away from him slightly.

'I know.'

'Stop staring at me,' she muttered. 'You've been with so many seriously beautiful women—'

'And none have excited me the way you do,' he said huskily, sweeping her into his arms and carrying her into the bedroom. 'You have the most incredible body.'

'You only think that because you're tall—and strong, which is why you can carry me without putting your back out—'

'You are extremely slender—' he lowered her onto the mattress '—most of your weight is your breasts and your astonishingly long legs and I have no complaints about either so you have no reason to be shy.' He stripped off his shirt and came down beside her in a fluid movement. 'I've never been with a woman as inexperienced as you—'

'I think I prefer the word "wholesome".' Her confidence faltered. 'Is it a problem?'

'No. It's a complete turn-on. But I'm probably going to shock you.' His dark eyes held hers for a moment and then he gently brushed away a strand of hair from her forehead with the tips of his fingers. 'I'm going to teach you everything you don't know, *tesoro*.'

The brief flicker of trepidation was swiftly transformed into breathless excitement as he kissed his way across her jaw and down her body to her exposed breasts. When he fastened his mouth over one straining peak the pleasure shafted through her and when his skilled fingers toyed with the other the torment rose to screaming pitch.

By the time he eventually pushed her thighs apart she was writhing against the sheets, the excitement ripping through her body like a vicious storm.

With no concession to the bright rays of sun spotlighting the room, Rio parted her with gentle fingers, placed his mouth against her and proceeded to subject her to the most extreme degree of erotic torture. With infinite skill, he explored her with tongue and fingers until Evie was on fire, her whole body burning in the flames he'd created. Tortured by the heat, she tried to move her hips to relieve the unbearable ache but he pinned her flat with his free hand, channelling the whole erotic experience into that one molten part of her until there was nothing in her world but him and the feelings he created.

Overwhelmed, she writhed and sobbed. 'Please—oh—how can you do those things at the same time—?'

He gave a husky laugh. 'I told you I was good at multi-tasking—'

Out of her mind with desire, Evie barely registered the fact that he was now above her before he sank into her with a single possessive thrust that filled her completely. The force and power of him stretched her sensitive flesh and she immediately shot into a climax so intense, so exquisitely agonizing, that her nails dug hard into the sleek muscle of his shoulder as her body convulsed around his.

He captured her mouth, kissing her with erotic intent as he slowly built the rhythm again, driving them both back towards that same peak. And this time, when she tumbled, she took him with her and he kept his mouth on hers, sharing every cry and every gasp, their bodies locked together in a shimmering heat created by the intensity of their own passion.

CHAPTER SEVEN

'You're insatiable. It's been more than a week—you should be bored with me by now.' Laughing, Evie rolled onto her stomach and leaned on Rio's chest. 'Aren't you ever tired?'

He watched her from beneath lowered lids, his gaze slumberous and unmistakably sexual. 'No. I find sex with you incredibly energizing.'

'So that's how you manage to work such long hours—'

'You should be grateful for that,' he said huskily. 'Otherwise, you wouldn't be getting any sleep at all, *tesoro*.'

'It's only two days until Christmas. You shouldn't be working.' Sometimes, when she woke in the dark, she discovered that he wasn't in bed with her. On one occasion she'd tiptoed sleepily from the bed to find him and discovered him working on the laptop, his gaze fixed intently on the ghostly green glow of the screen.

'I don't need much sleep. I had a few hours.' He slid his hand into her hair, pulled her head down and kissed her. 'Ready for breakfast?'

Evie felt a flutter of nerves in her stomach. Breakfast and mornings meant one thing to her. 'Have the newspapers arrived yet?'

He frowned. 'I have no idea and I don't care.'

'*I* care—I keep thinking about that stupid, horrid photograph.' The mood punctured, she rolled onto her back and stared up at the ceiling.

'Forget it.' Rio shifted over her in a smooth movement, his weight pressing her into the mattress. 'Yesterday they took photographs of you in the front row of the charity fashion show—they'll use one of those. Not one of you naked.'

'But you don't know that for sure—' She felt the sudden tension emanating from his powerful frame.

'I do. You need to trust me.'

Reasoning that he knew a great deal more about the media than she did, Evie forced herself to relax. 'OK. I trust you. But you *do* care, you know you do. That's why we're doing all this. You're worried about your deal going through. Is that still all right? I mean—' Suddenly she felt awkward asking. He didn't talk about stuff, did he? 'I know you don't talk about it but you're always on the phone and I can tell you're stressed about it.'

'I'm not stressed.' Only moments before he'd been relaxed. Now he was frighteningly detached, his handsome face an expressionless mask. 'And everything is fine.'

She shouldn't have asked. 'Good. Whatever it is must be worth a lot for you to care about it so much.'

'Yes. It's worth a lot.' Without warning, he sprang from the bed and prowled towards the bathroom. 'I'm going to take a shower. Order yourself some breakfast.'

His casual dismissal chilled her and Evie pulled the duvet over her naked body, feeling vulnerable and exposed. One minute they were incredibly close—the next, he shut her out.

Listening to the sound of the shower, she wondered what it was about this particular deal that was so important to him. She wished again she'd never raised the subject. Why was he so touchy? Was he worrying about it, or was it just that he didn't like talking about it?

She used the second bathroom to shower and change and was relieved when he joined her for breakfast.

Watching him cautiously, gauging his mood, Evie helped herself to a bowl of fruit. 'I checked the papers. You were right—they printed the photo from the fashion show.'

He poured himself a coffee. 'And what was the headline?'

Evie blushed. 'Something stupid.' She wondered if he minded the media preoccupation with his love life but Rio simply smiled.

'The world appears to be revelling in my rapid and extremely public conversion from never to forever. We're obviously very convincing, *tesoro*.'

Captivated by that smile, Evie felt her breath catch and her heart gave a dangerous lurch. They were so convincing that she was starting to believe it herself. If it weren't for his occasional moments of icy detachment, it would have been frighteningly easy to forget that this wasn't real. *That some day soon he was going to expect her to dump him.*

Reminding herself to live in the moment, she ate a spoonful of fruit. 'We'd better make sure we give them something even more interesting to photograph today then. What are we doing tonight?'

'We have been invited by the Russians to watch a performance of the Bolshoi Ballet at the Royal Opera House at Covent Garden.'

'Wow.' Evie licked her spoon. 'I've never been to the ballet. That's really exciting!'

'Is it? I confess that men in tights don't excite me one little bit.' Rio rose to his feet as his phone rang. 'But, given that you're their new best friend and you speak fluent Russian, I'm sure we can make some use of the evening. Excuse me—I need to take this.'

'Of course.' Basking in the heady knowledge that she was useful to him, Evie felt a rush of pleasure that lasted through the day and the evening. She adored the ballet, was in awe of the elegant grandeur of the world famous Opera House and enjoyed acting as interpreter.

Vladimir was as charming to her as ever, but it was Rio who drew her attention. Cocooned in the private box, under the protection of darkness, she found herself looking at him every other second, her eyes drawn to the perfect symmetry of his arrogant features, fatally fascinated by the breathtaking power and masculinity stamped in every angle of his body.

Once, he caught her looking and raised an eyebrow in silent question. Evie simply smiled, relieved to be able to hide her fascination behind the charade of their 'relationship'. That was what she was supposed to do, wasn't it? She was supposed to look.

Again, the photographers were out in force, stealing photographs at every opportunity, but Evie felt nothing but relief because she knew by now that, providing they managed to get an interesting shot, they were unlikely to use the one she dreaded appearing.

They went from the ballet to another ball and this time Rio needed no persuasion to dance with her. His hand was warm on her bare back as they moved together, the rhythm of their bodies perfectly in tune after so many hours spent locked in intimacy.

'You're not singing tonight?' He murmured the words against her lips and Evie reminded herself that it was essential to breathe or she'd fall over. But, when he held her like this, she felt as though everything inside her was suspended.

No wonder no woman had ever dumped him.

He was so insanely gorgeous, who in their right mind would not want to be with him?

'No singing. They've already had that picture.' Her arms were locked around his neck and she could feel the heat of his body against hers. 'Grandpa liked it, by the way—he said it reminded him of last year when I did the same thing at the village hall.'

'You danced on the table?'

'No—fortunately, they didn't have champagne.' She smiled up at him. 'I'd love to do something really Christmassy. Can we go ice skating? I really envied those people skating when we were at the ball. Or maybe we could go and sing Christmas carols. I noticed an invitation for a celebrity carol concert at St Paul's Cathedral—are we going to that? I know you see Christmas as nothing more than an interruption in your working day, but I love this time of year.'

He didn't answer. At first, she thought he hadn't heard her question and Evie was about to open her mouth and ask again when she saw his eyes. It was like staring into a dark pool, knowing that beneath the still, glassy surface lay nothing but danger.

She shivered.

They'd stopped dancing. Stopped moving. Among the streamers and balloons, the people laughing, dancing and singing, they alone stood still, locked in the small private bubble they'd formed for themselves. Evie felt frozen and she thought absently that there was no reason to be cold when the room was so warm, but then she realised that the chill came from him. His skin was cold to touch, his eyes reflecting not celebration but an acute and bitter pain.

'Rio?' She spoke his name softly. She had no idea what was wrong, but she wanted to help and not just because of what they'd shared. She would have felt the same way about anyone who was suffering as much as he clearly was. 'Are you—' She broke off, frustrated with herself. What was she planning to say? *Are you all right?* Well, obviously, the answer to that was a resounding *no,* but he was hardly likely to tell her that, was he? He was the most fiercely private man she'd ever met.

And yet they must be conspicuous, standing there locked

together but not moving, like some elaborate sculpture of lovers.

Evie placed her hand on his cheek, alarmed by how cold he was. 'Shall we go?'

Finally, he seemed to hear her and he stared down at her blankly, as if he'd forgotten she was there. 'Yes,' he said at last. 'I think that would be a good idea.'

Aware that their behaviour was starting to draw curious glances, Evie stood on tiptoe and kissed him gently on the mouth. *Tomorrow's photograph,* she thought as a camera flashed and a woman sighed with envy.

It was snowing again outside and Evie sat quietly in the limousine as it moved silently through the white streets. Normally snow soothed her, but tonight nothing could ease the tension in the car.

She wanted to know what was going on in his head, but she also knew that he wouldn't want to tell her.

After a moment's hesitation, she reached across and took his hand in hers, oddly pleased when he didn't immediately withdraw his.

Once, during the silent journey, she sneaked a glance at his taut profile but he stared sightlessly into the winter night, apparently oblivious to everything except his own thoughts.

After a silent ride in the elevator, they stepped into the Penthouse and immediately the phone calls started.

So that was it?

Whatever menace lurked beneath the surface had apparently been ruthlessly repressed once more.

Evie stood awkwardly, hovering, while he took one phone call and then another before eventually deciding that she might as well go to bed and wait for him there. She had no expectation that he'd join her this time, but he did—at three in the morning, long after she'd ended her silent vigil.

This time there was no gentle seduction, no talking—just wild, out of control sex that blew her mind.

It was only afterwards, when his side of the bed had long grown cold, that she wondered what he'd been trying to escape. Because he had been trying to escape, of that she was sure. The raw, ruthless passion they'd shared hadn't been energizing sex, it had been oblivion sex.

She had to talk to him.

No one who felt that bad should suffer alone.

Feeling distinctly strange, Evie moved quietly into the living room. How did you approach a man you had wild, crazy sex with but no relationship? What were you supposed to say? Technically, were they friends now?

He had his back to her and he was talking in a low voice, his long fingers toying with a sleek, expensive pen.

She was so busy working out what she was going to say when he finished on the phone that it was a moment or two before she actually paid attention to his conversation.

It was his tone that made her listen. The hardness was tempered by something she hadn't heard in his voice before. There was no hint of the ruthless businessman, or the primitive lover. He was infinitely gentle and it was obvious that the person on the other end of the phone meant a lot to him.

More than a lot.

'Sì tesoro—ti amo.'

Evie froze. *Ti amo.* She didn't speak much Italian but she knew that meant *I love you.* Unable to help herself, she listened to the rest of the conversation and picked up a few more words. This man, who claimed not to believe in happy endings, was telling someone that he loved her. That he hoped to see her soon.

The scent of him still clung to her skin, as did hers to him, no doubt, and yet he was already making plans to see another woman.

Her skin felt icy-cold.

She'd slept with another woman's man.

Was this the secret that simmered beneath the surface? Was this the reason for his pain?

Nausea rose in her stomach and her legs felt as though they'd been turned to water.

She'd had sex with a man who was deeply involved with someone else.

Angry with him but even more angry with herself, Evie was about to move when he turned his head and saw her.

'Evie?' His voice was deep and male, surprisingly normal after the emotional tightrope they'd walked the previous night. 'You're awake early. I didn't see you there.'

'Don't worry about it.' She stood stiff, shivering slightly, feeling slightly detached from her surroundings. 'I'm going to get dressed. Then I'm going.'

He frowned. 'Going where?'

'I don't know.' Her shocked mind was paralysed. It refused to provide her with the words and the thoughts she needed to move forward. 'Anywhere but here.'

His eyes hardened. 'We made a deal. It would be catastrophic if you left now. I need you to stay.'

'Why? What's the point of this charade when you're already involved with someone else?' Emotion thickened her voice and she hated herself for not being the cool, rational person she wanted to be. She wanted to be sophisticated enough to thank him for a perfect no-strings-attached relationship and walk away. Instead, she wanted to claw his flawless features and thump him. She wanted him to hurt the way she was hurting. 'Does she know? Does she know about me?'

A muscle flickered in his cheek and he put his pen down, the movement slow and deliberate. 'You were listening to my phone call.'

'Not intentionally. And if you're expecting me to apologise for eavesdropping on a private conversation then forget it. There are some things that shouldn't be private.'

'*Calma*. Calm down.'

'No, I will not *calma* or calm down! I don't speak much Italian, Rio, but I speak enough to understand the gist of what you just said to her! I'm really astonished you've never been dumped if that's the way you treat women. You're right— you are a complete and utter bastard. This whole week we… you…' She broke off, trying to control herself. 'How could you do that? How could you do those things when you're in love with someone else? I thought you were a free agent— single. You should have *told* me you were involved with someone.'

'I'm not involved.'

Her breathing was shallow. 'When you warned me that you'd break my heart, I didn't expect it to happen quite this quickly.'

'Evie—'

'No! Just don't make pathetic excuses, OK? I don't want to hear them. I heard you! I *heard* you talking to your girlfriend.'

He swore softly in Italian and turned away from her.

For a moment, staring at the rigid tension in those broad shoulders, she thought he wasn't even going to bother defending himself.

And then he turned, a savage look on his face. 'You did *not* hear me talking to my girlfriend. It wasn't a woman.' His voice was raw and Evie stood still, frozen to the spot by the look in his eyes.

'But—'

'You heard me talking to a child. She's four years old. A child, not a woman. My daughter.' He let out a long breath. 'You heard me talking to my daughter.'

'All right. Keep me informed.' Rio terminated the conversation with his lawyer and looked up to see Evie standing there. She'd changed into a pair of jeans and a blue cashmere jumper. Her hair, still damp from the shower, accentuated the extreme pallor of her face.

'Why didn't you tell me you have a child?' Her voice was flat. 'Why didn't you mention it?'

Programmed to keep women at a distance, Rio kept his response cool. 'It isn't any of your business.' Seeing the hurt in her eyes, he wished he hadn't been quite so blunt. 'I don't talk about my private life. To anyone.'

'I'm not some journalist, Rio!' She swept her hand through her hair, her confusion evident in every movement she made. 'We slept together, for God's sake. We shared—'

'Sex,' Rio drawled. 'We shared sex. A physical relationship, however satisfying, doesn't give you access to the rest of my life. Don't make the mistake of thinking that it does.'

Her head jerked as if he'd slapped her and for a moment he thought she was going to do exactly that to him. Instead, she lost still more colour from her cheeks and nodded stiffly. 'Of course it doesn't. My mistake. You have a child. Forgive me for thinking that's something you might have mentioned.' She turned away from him and stalked towards the table that had already been laid for breakfast. 'Are those today's papers?' Her hands shook as she lifted one and flicked through it. 'Have they used the photograph? Or haven't you bothered to check? I'm worried we didn't give them much of interest last night.'

She was rigidly polite and Rio watched her in silence, knowing that he was going to have to tell her the truth and wondering why that felt like a difficult conversation. He'd done what needed to be done. In the same circumstances, he'd make all the same decisions. *So why did he feel so uncomfortable?* 'They haven't used it. They have, however, printed the one they took when you kissed me.' He watched her face as she picked up a tabloid paper and scanned the headline.

Her face was expressionless as she scanned the photograph. *Truly a time for miracles—Rio in love.* Some of the tension left her. 'Well, it seems we're off the hook for another day.'

Rio's jaw tightened. 'Evie—'

'Sorry—it's just that I'm finding this whole thing quite stressful, in case you hadn't noticed. Every morning we go through the same thing. And the worst thing is, there is never going to come a point when it goes away—they have that photo for ever, don't they? They can use it this year or next year—it never ends.'

Wondering exactly when he'd developed a conscience, Rio forced a reluctant confession past his lips. 'Evie, they won't use that photo.'

She looked up from the newspaper. 'It's all very well to say that while you're giving them something more interesting to print, but sooner or later they're going to get bored with our "romance" and then they'll be on the lookout for something more juicy.'

'I can guarantee they're not going to print that photograph.'

'How? Has your security team managed to track the man down?' With a soft gasp, she dropped the newspaper on the table. 'They found him?'

He had to tell her now. 'Yes. We found him.'

Relief crossed her face, to be followed quickly by consternation. 'But that doesn't mean you can stop the photograph. I mean, he's had loads of time to have sent it all over the place. It's probably too late.'

'He hasn't sent it anywhere. My security team confiscated his camera.'

'But how—'

'They confiscated his camera less than fifteen seconds after he took the offending photograph,' Rio confessed in a raw tone, telling himself firmly that he'd do exactly the same thing again in the same circumstances. 'That's how I know for a fact that he didn't send it anywhere. Antonio was outside the door of the Penthouse. He apprehended the guy before he'd taken two steps.'

A heavy silence descended on the room. Evie stared at him, digesting the enormity of his confession and Rio felt the tension inside himself double.

'You're saying—' she swallowed hard '—you're telling me—oh, my God.' She sank down hard on the nearest sofa, her breathing rapid. 'There was never a risk that the photograph would be published. You told me...you let me think...' She lifted her head to look at him and her eyes were huge and shocked. 'How could you do that?'

'Because it was necessary. It was the right thing to do.'

'The right thing?' She lifted her hands to her face and then let them drop again, clearly struggling to find the words to express herself. 'I was almost out of my *mind* with worry! My grandfather is eighty-six years old and I thought...I thought...' Her face was contorted with pain. 'I thought it would crucify him to see that photo. I was *so* worried—'

'Which is why I assured you that they wouldn't use the pictures.'

'But you didn't tell me *why* you were so sure!' She stood up, shock giving way to anger. 'You arranged the photographer! You were in league with creepy Carlos!'

'No—' Rio interrupted her hastily '—that isn't true. It *was* a set-up.' He raked his fingers through his hair, wondering how, of all the difficult negotiations he'd ever made, this one seemed the most challenging. 'But I admit that I turned it to my advantage. I had no choice.'

'You *did* have a choice. There is always a choice. You could have told me the truth.'

'I didn't know if you were involved or not.'

'I *told* you I wasn't.'

He decided not to waste time pointing out that plenty of her sex lied for a living. In the short time he'd known her, he'd started to realise that Evie didn't seem to think the same way as other women. 'By the time I realised that you were telling the truth, we were already deeply involved in the pretence. I was afraid you'd walk out on me.'

'So you used me. Is that what you're trying to tell me?'

Unable to find an alternative take on the situation, Rio felt sweat prickle his brow. 'Yes.'

'But you…' She jabbed her fingers into her hair, an expression of shocked disbelief on her face. 'But we had sex—what was your justification for that? Were there cameras in the room?'

'You initiated the sex.'

She gave a painful laugh. 'Well, that's you off the hook, then.' Her eyes were glazed with tears. 'You warned me you were ruthless and you told me that I'd find it easy to dump you—well, you were right. I'm dumping you. We now have the shortest engagement on record.'

'I accept that I was wrong not to tell you,' Rio breathed, 'but *don't* walk out.'

'Why? Because you haven't closed your precious deal yet? What is *wrong* with you? You don't need more money but you're so desperate to win you're willing to do whatever it takes.' A toss of her head sent her hair flaming down her back and she stalked back into the bedroom without glancing in his direction, flinging words over her shoulder like missiles. 'There are some things in life that are more important than money, Rio. People's feelings are more important. Integrity. Honesty. And if you don't know what any of those words mean then use some of that money of yours to buy a dictionary.'

Rio searched his brain for slick words that would extricate him from this hole, but found none. His instinct was to leave her alone, but his legs had different ideas and, moments later, he found himself standing in the doorway of the bedroom, watching her.

'I understood that you were worried, which is why I

constantly reassured you that the photograph would not be published. You should have trusted me.'

'Trusted you!' She turned on him, her eyes flashing. 'Why would I trust you? You're impossibly arrogant. You think you're right about everything. How was I to know that in this case the reason you knew the photograph wouldn't be published was because you had it in your possession all the time? I don't believe this is happening—' Her breathing was shallow and rapid. 'You were so angry with Carlos. I thought you were going to finish him off—but why would he have arranged that photograph?'

'Because Carlos is the brother of a woman I once had a relationship with,' Rio said savagely. 'It was a difficult relationship. She wanted more—'

'Then she was looking in the wrong place, wasn't she?' Her tone acid, Evie scraped her make-up from the top of the dressing table into her bag. 'Didn't she read the newspapers? Didn't she know that you don't do "more"?'

Telling himself that her anger was only to be expected, Rio ploughed ahead. 'She wanted me to marry her.'

'She wanted to spend the rest of her life with you? Clearly she was deranged.'

Knowing that he deserved that, Rio took it on the chin. 'She stopped taking contraception.'

Evie paused, a tube of lipgloss in her hand. 'She became pregnant? On purpose?' The shock in her voice almost made him smile.

'Yes, on purpose. On purpose, Evie.' He said the word twice, each time with emphasis, knowing that she had absolutely no idea what people could be like. She was such a crazy idealist, wasn't she? 'Are you going to ask me why?'

'I'm not stupid. I presume she thought you'd marry her.' She stuffed the lipgloss into her bag. 'Which, of course, you wouldn't.'

'No, because it never would have worked.' Rio growled

the words angrily. 'I offered her everything but that. I offered to buy her a house near me—I offered her financial support. But all she wanted was marriage and I'd made the mistake of being honest about how much I wanted to see my child. She used that knowledge to carry on blackmailing me. Only this time, instead of "I'm pregnant, marry me", it was "if you want to see your child, marry me".'

Evie stood still. Some of the anger in her face was replaced by uncertainty.

'She used my child as currency,' Rio said thickly. 'An object to be bartered with. I gave her sufficient funds to live in luxury for the rest of her life but she frittered it away on unsuitable friends and people I would not have allowed anywhere near my daughter. Because she had my child, I carried on trying to help. I even gave her useless brother Carlos a job in my hotel, under close supervision. But I was working behind the scenes to get custody of my daughter.'

'Custody?' Her eyes widened in shock and he gave a bitter smile because he'd seen exactly that same look on the faces of others.

'Yes, custody. And, yes, I know I'm a single man. A single man with a self-confessed relationship phobia. I am no one's image of ideal father material. It was easy for her to build a case, making me look unsuitable. I work inhuman hours, I have no history of commitment—' he breathed deeply '—it's possible I would never even have had a chance if it weren't for the fact that Jeanette left Elyssa unattended.'

'She left her child *alone*?'

Rio wanted to tell her not to be so naive, but realised that would be unfair. It wasn't naivety that prevented her from understanding why another woman might leave a child alone; it was her nature. He'd seen the way she cared about her grandfather. She was warm and loving—a nurturer who believed that families stuck together and supported each other through thick and thin.

'Jeanette didn't ever want a child. All she wanted was a tool to manipulate me. She doesn't have a maternal bone in her body.' He watched Evie flinch as he took a hatchet to her illusions. 'I imagine someone like you would find that almost impossible to believe, so let me tell you just how unhappy my daughter's life has been so far and maybe then you'll understand that there are times when "ruthless" is justified.'

'Rio—'

'She was left on her own in the house because there was no way Jeanette was wasting any of the money I gave her caring for a child she never wanted. I sent her staff; she fired them. I interviewed eight nannies personally. None of them lasted a day. Jeanette said she'd care for Elyssa herself, but she didn't. I've been fighting for custody since before my daughter was born but it was only six months ago, after she had a nasty fall in the house while she was on her own, that the tide turned in my favour. The police were called. Elyssa was taken into foster care while they reviewed the case. It's been a long, hard slog but we were almost there.'

'Were?'

'Elyssa is Jeanette's meal ticket,' Rio said, struggling to keep the emotion out of his voice. 'She doesn't want me to have custody. She reinvented herself as a model mother. She's been volunteering at the church, visiting the sick and the elderly, generally behaving like a perfect citizen.'

'And at the same time she's been trying to destroy your reputation? Make you look like an unsuitable carer for a child?'

'Unfortunately, over the years, I've managed to do that for myself. I've made no apology for the fact that I don't want commitment, never realising that the time would come when I'd regret expressing those sentiments in such a public fashion.'

'So that's why Carlos wanted me to spend the night. That's why he arranged the photographer. That's what the deal is.'

Her breathing quickened and her eyes held his. 'This deal isn't about money, is it? It isn't business. It's your daughter. The reason you didn't want those photographs published was because of your daughter. They were trying to make you look bad.'

Rio stood still, watching her. So much was riding on this conversation and yet, for once, his slick way with words had abandoned him. 'I've worked for years to reach this point.'

'But if your security team caught the man immediately— if you knew there was no danger of that photograph being exposed—why go through with that farce?'

'Because I thought you could help my case.' He didn't flinch from the truth. 'My lawyer told me to stay whiter than white or find a wholesome-looking woman. Until Carlos intervened, I'd settled on the first option. Then I saw you lying on the bed.'

'I was naked,' she said dryly. 'Not exactly wholesome.'

'No one looking at you could ever believe you were anything other than a thoroughly decent person,' Rio said roughly. *And he'd used her.* 'I'm a man who has said I'd never settle down—to convince people I'd changed my mind, it would have to be with someone completely different from the usual women I date. You fitted that description.'

She stood for a moment. 'And it didn't occur to you to just tell me the truth? You could have just asked for my help. You could have trusted me.'

'No, I couldn't.'

'Have you ever trusted a woman?'

Rio didn't even hesitate. 'I've never had reason to.'

Pain flickered across her face and he knew she was thinking about everything they'd shared. 'So what happens now?'

He clenched his fists by his sides, wondering why it suddenly felt so hard to remain detached when that was his normal default mode. 'That's your decision,' he said flatly.

'If you want to go home to your grandfather for Christmas, then I can arrange that. And of course you have a job as receptionist. You're overqualified for the position, but if that's what you want then that's fine by me. The one thing I ask is that you dump me, as we agreed, rather than telling the media the truth.'

'How have you kept your daughter's name out of the press?'

'That was part of my deal with Jeanette. And I admit we've been lucky. I suppose because I'm the last man in the world to want a child, they didn't look.'

'So you want me to dump you—' She rubbed her fingers across her forehead. 'But you haven't won your case yet, have you? I could make things difficult for you.'

'Yes.' The thought brought a bitter taste to his mouth. 'But I'll have to take that chance.'

'What makes you think you're the right home for a little girl, Rio? What can you offer a child?'

He didn't hesitate. 'Security. The absolute certainty that I'll always be there for her.' He'd never felt the need to explain or defend his decision to anyone before, but suddenly he had a burning need to defend himself to Evie. 'I'm not planning to nominate myself for super-dad any time soon, but I can offer her a stability that has never been present in her life.'

'That's quite a promise, coming from a man who doesn't believe in commitment.'

'This is one commitment I'm prepared to make.' He didn't expect her to believe him. How could he when he was well aware he'd given her no reason on which to base that belief?

And already his mind was computing the options because he knew she was going to walk out. Why wouldn't she? He'd deceived her. He'd used her. He'd hurt her. *He'd had sex with her—*

And now she was going to make him pay.

He needed to ring the lawyers and warn them, although what they would be able to do, he had no idea.

Reaching into his pocket for his phone, his fingers encountered his wallet. He paused and then pulled it out and retrieved the photograph from behind a stack of dollars. Hesitating for only a fraction of a second, he handed it to her. 'This is Elyssa. It's not a brilliant one—I took it with my phone in the summer. Her hair is darker than it looks in the photograph.' He watched as she stared down at the photograph.

'Please leave me alone,' she said hoarsely. 'I need a minute to myself.'

Rio hesitated, and then turned and walked back into the living room. Conscious of how much he'd hurt her, he retrieved his BlackBerry from his jacket pocket. The only option open to him now was damage limitation.

He was in the process of dialling his lawyer when her voice came from behind him.

'Put the phone down.' She stood in the doorway, stiff and unsmiling, the photograph still in her hand. 'I'll stay and finish this charade if you think it will help you. Not because you shoved a photograph of a vulnerable little girl into my hand and made me feel guilty which, by the way, was yet another example of ruthless manipulation on your part, but because you took that photograph in the first place. It's the first time I've ever known you to use your BlackBerry for anything other than work. If you carry a picture of your daughter around, there must be some good in you somewhere. I have yet to see it, but I live in hope. Unlike you, I'm prepared to take some things on trust. Given that Elyssa seems to have drawn the short straw with her mother, she needs someone who is prepared to stand up and fight for her, *not* that I think that excuses your appalling behaviour.'

Stunned by her words, Rio inhaled deeply. 'Evie—'

'And you need to learn to take some things on trust, too.

You need to show some faith in people.' She walked across the room and placed the photograph carefully in his hand. 'A little girl's future is at stake—you should have known I'd do the right thing. I didn't need a guilt trip to set me on the right path. If you'd told me the truth in the first place—' there were tears in her eyes '—I just wish you had told me the truth, Rio.'

'My daughter's future was all that mattered to me.'

'If you'd told me, I would have helped you.' Her lashes sparkled with moisture. 'You need to stop being such a cynic because the last thing a little girl needs is a father who is a cynic. When you're reading her fairy stories, maybe it's right to adapt the ending—maybe it isn't right to tell children that they all lived happily ever after, I don't know—but neither is it right to bring her up believing that everyone is guilty until proven innocent. That there is no good in anyone. That all people are out to get what they can out of everyone else. If you're going to apply corporate principles to parenting, then it's never going to work.' Taking a deep breath, she squared her shoulders. 'Now, get your coat and phone that driver of yours. We're going shopping.'

Still braced for catastrophe, it took Rio a few moments to assimilate the fact that she wasn't leaving. She was offering to stay. Her generosity floored him. 'Of course I'll take you shopping.' His voice was husky with an emotion he didn't recognise and he lifted his hand and brushed a strand of hair away from her moist cheek. Gratitude, he thought. And admiration. He realised that he'd been wrong about her again. She was far, far stronger than she looked. 'I'll buy you the biggest diamond you've ever seen as long as you tell me I'm forgiven.'

'I didn't say anything about diamonds and I didn't say anything about forgiveness. We're going to a toy shop. If you truly intend to be a father to Elyssa, then you need to start learning what little girls like for Christmas.' Despite everything, there was humour in her gaze. 'I probably ought to warn you that I'm something of an expert. Fasten your seat belt because I have a feeling this is going to be a steep learning curve.'

CHAPTER EIGHT

'Fairy wings?' Rio's tone was incredulous. 'You're sure?'

Evie reached for a pair of pink gossamer wings which hung from a metal hook. She felt devastated. Ripped to shreds by the revelation that he'd lied to her. 'Trust me, fairy wings are always a hit with four-year-olds. Better buy a spare pair, ready for when she breaks these.' It felt strange, having this conversation with this man. She had a sense that what she was saying was as alien to him as the Russian Vladimir spoke.

As if to confirm her suspicions, he looked at her blankly. 'Why will she break them? She's a little girl, not a Sumo wrestler—'

'Yes, but she'll want to sleep in them,' Evie explained patiently, 'because that's what little girls always do and sleeping in them will break them. When that happens you can either explain to her that they're gone for ever or you can spoil her rotten and get her another pair. Normally I'd suggest it's dangerous to spoil her but, given that she's obviously had a completely rubbish time lately, I think an extra pair is probably in order.'

Without hesitation, Rio cleared the shelves of pink fairy wings.

'I meant one spare pair,' Evie said faintly, 'not ten.'

'I'm not risking anything. As you say, she's had enough trauma for one lifetime.' Rio handed them to his stunned bodyguard. 'So we have fairy wings and spare fairy wings and spare spare fairy wings. What next?'

Thrown by the sight of the normally taciturn Antonio struggling to balance a mountain of fairy wings, Evie managed a smile. 'If you're attacked now, this will be interesting. You'll just have to bash them with your magic wand or something—'

Antonio's mouth twitched. 'I'll remember that.'

'Don't worry about Antonio,' Rio drawled. 'He probably trained in the same unarmed combat camp as your grandfather. If the chips were down, he'd find a way to turn fairy wings into an assault weapon.' His gaze met hers. 'It's good of you to do this for me.'

She felt frozen inside. 'I'm doing it for her, not you.' She ignored the tiny part of her that questioned that claim, just as she ignored the commotion in her nerve-endings that told her he was even more lethally attractive when he was vulnerable. 'Let's go. We need dolls.'

'I'm not sure about dolls. Last time I saw her, I took her a doll.' He scanned the rows of toys with something close to despair. 'I think I probably chose the wrong sort. There were millions. The one I picked had a very elaborate costume and she was very frustrated when it wouldn't come off.'

Evie's heart twisted at that image—the arrogant, self assured tycoon taking a serious knock to his self-esteem as he struggled to choose a doll. 'I expect she'd like a doll that can be dressed and undressed. They make one that cries and wets itself.'

His expression was comical. 'There is a market for that?'

'A huge market,' Evie told him, enjoying the look of shock on his face. 'You pour the milk in one end and it comes out the other, just like real life.'

Rio shuddered and he said something in Italian. 'That is *fun*?'

'It's role play. Didn't you ever play mummies and daddies—?' Evie took one look at his face and shook her head. 'Forget I said that. I don't suppose commitment games were ever your thing. Take it from me, most little girls are a sucker for caring for a baby. Put a real baby in a room and the girls are all over it in minutes. Whatever anyone says about feminism, most little girls love pretending dolls are babies.'

'Did you?' Suddenly his gaze became disturbingly acute and Evie felt the slow burn of colour in her cheeks.

'Yes.' She turned away from him and took the stairs two at a time. There were some things it didn't pay to think about. Especially not around this man. She just wanted to get this over with so that she could go into hiding and lick her wounds. 'Here—dolls. I'll grab a shopping trolley. I don't think poor Antonio can carry any more.'

'A whole floor of dolls?' Rio looked horrified. 'How do you know where to start?'

Evie tried to translate it into terms he'd understand. 'Like any product, you have to segment your market. There's a specific market for young children. Then they segment the market again—dolls that cry, dolls that—'

'OK, fine. I get the picture—' he interrupted her hastily '—so which is the market leader?'

'This one.' She pointed and Rio lifted it off the shelf gingerly.

'How many spares do we need?'

'At least one. It's very easy to leave a doll on a plane.' Suddenly realising what she'd said, Evie gave a wry smile. 'On the other hand, you do *own* the plane, so you'd be able to retrieve it without long and fruitless arguments with unhelpful airline staff. You could probably get away without spares.'

Clearly not prepared to take any risks, Rio added five identical dolls to the growing pile of toys in the trolley. 'I have five homes,' he said by way of explanation. 'It's probably best to have a spare in each.'

'Five?' Evie blinked. 'You have *five* homes?'

'You're thinking that it will confuse a small child?' He added a small stack of accessories to the pile. 'I've been thinking the same thing. In fact, I've been restructuring my business so that I can spend as much time as possible at my palazzo in Florence, to give her stability. My team have decorated a room exactly like the one she is in at the moment so that it seems familiar. It's right next to mine and I have already appointed a very experienced English nanny who is ready to move in at a moment's notice.'

Evie felt the hot sting of tears scald her eyes and turned away in horror, blinking rapidly. For crying out loud, what was the matter with her? Why did the thought of him study- ing a child's room and creating an identical version make her want to sob? Struggling for control, she picked up a doll from the shelf and pretended to examine it. Her insides were at war and, when she felt Rio's hand close over her shoulder, the tears formed a lump in her throat. 'This is a good one.' She thrust the doll at him and he studied it in silence.

'Are you sure? I'm no expert, but I don't think so.'

Dragging her gaze from the dark shadow of his jaw to the doll she'd handed him, Evie realised that he was right. The doll she'd selected was completely unsuitable for a young child. Apart from the fact that the clothing was covered in intricate beading, there was a clear warning that it wasn't intended for children under the age of eight. She wasn't con- centrating. Her mind was all over the place.

His hand still on her shoulder, Rio returned the doll to the shelf. 'I've upset you again.' His voice was low and all Evie could do was shake her head, frightened by the intensity of her feelings.

'No.'

'You're trying not to cry. I know enough about women to recognise the signs.'

'I believe you. I'm sure you've made enough women cry in your time.'

'But normally they don't try and hold it back. As usual, you have to be different. If you want to sob, then sob. I know I deserve it. I really have been a bastard to you.' He smoothed her hair away from her face but she moved her head away sharply.

'Don't touch me. And don't use that word in a toy shop.' Evie almost wished she could cry. It would have been easier to hate him. The problem was, she didn't hate him. She didn't hate him at all. He'd used her, he'd lied to her, but she still didn't hate him.

Ignoring her warning not to touch, he closed his hands over her shoulders. 'Evie—'

'Let's just get this done. I'm tired. I haven't had much sleep in the last few days.' She tried to pull away from him but he held her, his physical strength evident in his firm grip.

'We were talking about where Elyssa would enjoy living most. Do you have an opinion on where a little girl would like to live? I assumed a child would rather live in one place as much as possible and Florence is a wonderful city, but if you think—'

'I honestly don't know.' Evie finally managed to pull away from him. 'Why would I know? I'm not a mother. I probably know less than you do.' All she knew was that her mind was a mess. She'd told herself that he was totally the wrong man for her because he wasn't the family sort. He'd emphasised that he wasn't interested in commitment. And now she discovered he had a daughter he clearly adored and every decision he made, even the one to use her so ruthlessly to achieve his own ends, demonstrated the level of his commitment to his child. The fact that he was clearly struggling so hard to do the right thing somehow made the whole thing all the more poignant. He hadn't chosen fatherhood, but he was determined to do it right. He was facing his responsibilities. Despite what everyone said, Rio Zaccarelli didn't have a problem with commitment. His problem was with his own relationships with women. And that was hardly surprising, was it, given the women he'd met in the past?

Thinking about Elyssa's mother, Evie's throat was thick with emotion. Who would do that to a man? Or to a child? A solid lump seemed to have formed behind the wall of her chest. She kept seeing him removing that photograph from his wallet. Kept seeing him piling up fairy wings so that his daughter didn't suffer any more trauma. Her arm brushed against his and an electric current shot through her body and, at that moment, the truth lit up in her brain.

She'd fallen in love with him. At some point during the glittering, glamorous charade, the pretence had turned to reality.

It was a thrilling, sickening feeling. A sudden whoosh of the heart and a sinking of the stomach. Dread and desire intermingled with a knowledge that the whole thing was hopeless.

How could that have happened?

In such a short time and with a man like him?

How could she have been so recklessly foolish?

Parading his faults through her brain, Evie turned sharply and walked towards the end of the store, hiding her panic. 'You need books. Reading together is a great way to bond.' She blocked out an image of Rio sprawled on a bedcover covered in pink dancing fairies, reading to a small, dark haired girl who adored him. This was hard enough without making it worse for herself.

Her hands shook as she selected books from the shelves, conscious of his steady scrutiny.

'What's going on, Evie? When we came into this store you were hell bent on punishing me—you dragged me round pink fairy wings, handed me dolls and stuffed toys bigger than I am—and suddenly you look like the one who is being punished. You look like someone who has had a terrible shock.'

'No,' she answered quickly. Too quickly. 'Not a shock.'

'I wish you'd tell me why you're upset. Or is this still because you're thinking about my daughter?' He sat down on a chair in the reading area. He should have looked ridiculous, stretching his powerful body and long legs amongst the small bean bags and tiny colouring tables, but he didn't look ridiculous. Evie doubted Rio could look ridiculous anywhere. He had that ability to blend with his surroundings that came with confidence and self-assurance.

'Of course I'm thinking of your daughter.' Picking another two books from the shelf, she flicked through them. 'That's what we're doing here, isn't it?' She wished he'd stop looking at her. Suddenly, she was afraid that everything she was feeling might show on her face. The feelings growing inside her were so new she hadn't got used to hiding them yet.

'So we've done fairy wings, dolls, stuffed toys, games—' he listed them one by one, a trace of irony in his voice '—is there anything else you think she would like? What does a little girl really want?'

What does a little girl really want?

Evie stared for a moment, the question opening a deep rift inside her. It was the one thing she was able to answer with complete confidence. 'All a little girl really wants is her daddy,' she said huskily. 'The rest is just icing on the cake.'

'You're sure?' Rio tucked the phone between his ear and his shoulder as he opened the email. 'Yes, I have it here…I'm reading it right now…I'll make all the arrangements.'

When he finally ended the call, he knew his life had altered irrevocably. It was done. The lawyers had finally confirmed it. Elyssa was going to come and live with him. The courts had awarded him custody.

His gaze slid to the small mountain of toys that had been neatly stacked in one corner of the Penthouse, a testament to Evie's dedication to her task. His little girl would want for nothing, not that he was kidding himself for one moment that the future was going to go as smoothly as that one shopping trip. For a start there was his own inexperience to take into account, and then there was the inescapable fact that Elyssa had spent the past few years with a woman so self-absorbed that the needs of her child had largely gone unnoticed. Whichever way you looked at it, there was a rocky road ahead. Staring at the toys, he suddenly wished Evie was there to guide him through more than just his choice of doll.

But that was a crazy thought, wasn't it? A selfish thought, because he had nothing to offer her. Not even a defence against her accusation that he'd used her.

He had.

He'd done what needed to be done, without a flicker of conscience. But he didn't need to use her a moment longer. Their charade could end. Evie could get on with her life—could concentrate on making her grandfather proud.

She could go home for Christmas.

He sat there for a long moment and for once his phones were silent.

Through the wraparound glass of the luxurious Penthouse, he could see that the snow was falling again and immediately he thought how pleased Evie would be.

She loved snow.

Rising to his feet, he decided he needed to tell her, but when he searched the Penthouse there was no sign of her. At some point during his endless phone calls, she'd gone out.

Antonio entered the suite in response to his urgent call. 'Miss Anderson has gone to the park, boss.'

'What do you mean, she's gone to the park? It's seven

degrees below freezing and it's still snowing—' Rio prowled across the thick carpet. The snow was floating past the window, thick flakes that landed on the ground and settled. The streets were virtually empty of people and traffic, everyone trapped indoors because of the weather. For the first time in over a decade the pond in the park had frozen over. A few ducks waddled sorrowfully across the ice. Staring through the window, he peered through the swirling flakes but failed to spot her. 'What the hell is she doing in the park?'

Antonio cleared his throat. 'She's building a snowman, boss.'

'She's—*what?*'

'A snowman.' Antonio was smiling. 'It's surprisingly good, actually. She's managed to—'

'Spare me a description of the snowman.' Rio spoke through his teeth. 'Did she leave a message for me?'

'Yes. She said to tell you that she needed fresh air and that she'd be back when she was finished.'

'Where exactly is she?'

'The far side of the pond, sir. Shall I call your driver?'

Rio strode across the room and snatched his coat from the back of the chair. 'No. I'll walk.'

'In that case, perhaps you would give this to Evie, sir, with my compliments.' Antonio dug his hand in his pocket and withdrew a carrot. 'I went down to the kitchens and found it for her. She might find it useful.'

Rio stared at it. 'Call me stupid,' he said slowly, 'but I can't for a moment imagine what possible use she will have for a single raw carrot.'

'Then you've obviously never made a snowman, boss. It's for his nose. I tried to get a slightly smaller one, but the kitchen—'

'All right—I get the picture.' Feeling out of touch with everyone around him, Rio pushed the carrot into his pocket and strode across the room to the private elevator. As he reached the doors, he paused, his mind exploring an idea. His instinct was to reject it instantly, but for once he fought that instinct.

Why not?

It would please her and he certainly owed her a small bite of happiness after the way he'd treated her.

Having delivered his instructions to a bemused Antonio, Rio left the hotel and crossed the snowy street, wondering what on earth he was doing chasing a girl across a park in the freezing cold.

He found her kneeling in the snow, scooping snow into balls and adding them to a snowman, who was now wearing her hat. Her hair spilled over the shoulders of her quilted jacket and her cheeks were pink from the cold. Her lips were moving and at first he thought she was talking to herself, and then he realised that she was singing.

'Five gold rings, four calling birds, three French hens—'

'—and a girl with double pneumonia,' Rio drawled as he walked over to her. He pulled the carrot out of his pocket and handed it to her. 'Here. Give the guy a nose so that you can come inside and warm up.'

'I'm fine. I'm happy here. Thanks for the carrot.' Without looking at him, she pressed it into the snowman's face and sat back on her heels. 'What do you think?'

Rio decided that this was probably one of those occasions when honesty was not required. 'Spectacular,' he said tactfully. 'A real gladiator of a snowman.' Why wasn't she looking at him? He changed his position so that he could get a better look at her face and saw that her eyes were red.

He'd made her cry.

Forced to confront the damage he'd caused, Rio gave a bitter smile. The fact that she'd still been prepared to help him despite her own personal agony made him feel about as small as the snowflake that landed on his hand.

She pulled off her gloves and blew on her hands to warm them. 'There's no need to go overboard. I know you think I'm crazy.'

He thought she was astonishing. As brave as she was beautiful.

'I'm no judge of snowmen.' He dug his hands in his pockets. 'I've never seen anyone make one before. But you clearly find it an absorbing occupation so I'm willing to be converted.'

'You've never made one yourself?'

'Never.'

'Then you're missing out.' She pushed two pebbles into the snow above the carrot and then sat back to admire her handiwork.

Rio fought the sudden desire to roll her in the snow and warm her up in the most basic way known to man. 'You need to move the pebble on the left up a bit—they're not even. He's squinting.'

Flakes of snow settled on her hair as she shifted the pebble. 'What are you doing out here, Rio? Shouldn't you be on the phone, brokering some deal or sorting out a crisis?'

'I left the phones in the Penthouse.'

She managed a smile. 'All three of them? Won't the business world crumble?'

Rio suddenly discovered that he couldn't care less. 'Come back inside with me.'

The smile vanished. 'I'm happy here.'

'You're soaked through and freezing.'

'I love the snow.' Lifting her face into the falling flakes, she closed her eyes. 'If I keep my eyes shut, I'm a child again.'

Rio felt the tension flash through his body. 'And that's a good thing?'

'Oh, yes.' Clear aquamarine eyes looked into his. 'One of my favourite childhood memories is going to the forest with my grandfather to choose a tree. I used to just stand there, breathing in the smell of pine. Have you ever stood in a forest and just smelt the air? It's the most perfect smell—sharp and pungent—it gets into your nose and then your brain and suddenly you just *feel* Christmas all the way through your body. Smells do that to me. Are you the same?'

He had no idea how to answer that question. 'No,' he said finally. 'I'm not the same.'

The happiness in her eyes dimmed. 'I don't suppose you stand still long enough to notice smells. You're always on the go, pushing another deal through. You don't even take Christmas off.'

Rio looked at her, torn between wanting to know more and wanting to change the subject. 'So what did you do when you and your grandfather had chosen the tree?'

'We took it home and decorated it. That was the best part. We couldn't afford fancy decorations so Grandma and I made stars out of flour and water, baked them in the oven and painted them silver.'

Rio remembered the way she'd stared at the elaborate decorations on the Christmas tree at the ball. He found it all too easy to imagine her sitting at the kitchen table, a huge smile on her face, her hair like a burning bush. 'How long have you lived with your grandparents?'

She reached for a twig and snapped it in half. 'Since I was four years old. My parents had gone away to celebrate their wedding anniversary and I was staying with my grandparents. I remember being really excited about sleeping in their spare bedroom. It's a tiny attic room with a sloping roof and views across the lake and the forest. It felt like the biggest adventure of my life and I couldn't wait to tell my parents every last detail.' She paused and there was a sudden hitch in her breathing. 'And then my grandfather came into my room one morning and told me that they wouldn't be coming to get me. Their car hit black ice. They didn't stand a chance.'

Rio stood still, feeling hopelessly inadequate. He watched in silence as the snow fluttered onto her shoulders. Her vibrant hair was the only warmth and colour in the place. Everything was cold, including him. Her revelation deserved a response, but he had no idea what that response should be. He wasn't used to emotional confessions. People didn't confide in him. They discussed stocks and bonds, mergers and acquisitions—not feelings.

He didn't do feelings.

Wondering what had happened to all the smooth words that were always at his disposal, Rio stumbled awkwardly through foreign territory. 'So you stayed with them?'

'My grandfather had just retired. They were looking forward to enjoying some time together. They'd even booked a world cruise—' her voice was soft '—they cancelled it. They gave me a home.' She breathed deeply. 'They became my parents.'

And the love she felt for her grandfather was a living, palpable thing. He saw it in her eyes and in her smile. In everything she did.

'You're lucky.' The moment he said the words, he braced himself for a sharp comeback. She was going to tell him that he was the lucky one. She was going to remind him that he was a billionaire with five houses and a private jet.

But she didn't say any of those things. Instead, she wiped snow from her cheeks with her gloved hand and nodded. 'I know I'm lucky. That's why I was so upset and worried about that photograph of me naked. After everything they did for me—all the sacrifices they made so that I could have a warm, loving home—I couldn't bear that my grandfather would think I'd let him down like that. All I've ever wanted is to make them proud of me.' She bit her lip. 'I'm still mad with you for not putting me out of my misery sooner, but I'm also just so relieved that Antonio intercepted the guy so quickly. It could have been worse.'

Her pragmatic approach intensified his feelings of guilt and Rio swore softly under his breath. 'I was wrong to do what I did.'

'No, you weren't. You did what you needed to do for your little girl.' She rocked back on her heels and studied her snowman. 'You were prepared to do anything to protect her. I like that. It's good. It's what families should do. They should stick together, no matter what. Family should be the one dependable thing in a person's life.'

'Why is your grandfather so desperate for you to be married?'

'I've told you—he's old-fashioned.' Picking up the other half of the twig, she pushed it into the other side of the snowman. 'He believes that as long as you have family, everything can be all right with the world.'

'All right, *now* I feel seriously guilty,' Rio said gruffly and she smiled up at him, a sparkling smile that warmed the freezing air because it was delivered with such bravery.

'If you're capable of feeling guilt, then there's hope for you, Mr Zaccarelli.'

Was there? He'd lived without that emotion for so long he wasn't even sure he knew how it felt.

'Come back to the hotel. It's absolutely freezing out here.'

'Are you telling me you're cold? Big tough guy like you?' Her voice was teasing and her eyes danced with mockery as she looked up at him. 'You're a wimp. My grandfather will be relieved when I give you the boot. He wants me to find a real man, not some shivering, pathetic creature who can't stand a shift in the weather.'

She squealed with shock and laughter as Rio moved swiftly and tumbled her backwards onto the snow.

'Are you calling me a wimp?' His mouth brushed her soft lips, tasting softness and laughter. He was about to turn the kiss into something less playful when she stuffed a handful of snow down the front of his sweater. Rio swore fluently as the ice froze his skin. 'Is that your test of a real man?'

'That's just one of them. I started with something gentle. I didn't want to be too hard on you.' She was still laughing but, because he had her body trapped under his, he felt the change in her. Looking into her eyes, he saw something that sucked the humour out of the situation—something he'd seen many times before in a woman's eyes.

For a second he couldn't move and he wondered if she even realised what she'd revealed, lying there under him with her hopes and dreams exposed.

And then he sprang to his feet, his withdrawal an instinctive reaction pre-programmed by life experience and a bone-deep cynicism about the durability of relationships. It would be cruel, wouldn't it, to hurt her more than he already had—this child-woman who still believed in happy endings.

'You're shivering.' Keeping his tone matter of fact, he hauled her to her feet and brushed the snow off her jacket. She was looking past him and for a moment he thought she was just avoiding eye contact, and then he saw her expression change. 'What's the matter?'

'Behind you,' she muttered. 'Another photographer. Why are people so interested in your life? Everywhere you go there is a bigger, longer camera lens. We'd better look as though we're in love.' The word tripped off her tongue as if it had no significance and Rio stared down into her sweet, honest face, wondering whether she'd tell him the truth.

But she didn't say anything and he felt something tug inside him.

'We don't have to do that. We can end this charade whenever we like. It's over.' He slid his hands into her hair, suddenly realising he no longer had a legitimate excuse to kiss her.

'What do you mean?' Her eyes widened and then shone as she grasped the implications of his words. 'Are you saying—?

Oh, Rio—you have custody? I'm so pleased! That's fantastic.'
She flung her arms round his neck and hugged him tightly,
whooping with joy and kissing him over and over again. Her
eyes glistened with tears of joy and he brushed them away
with his thumb, fascinated by the way she showed her emotions so freely; touched that her pleasure for his daughter
could transcend her own pain.

'There is still some red tape to play with, but my lawyers
think that Elyssa will come and live with me the week after
Christmas. For what it's worth, they think that seeing me
with you tipped the balance.'

'Well, I'm glad about that. So what does this mean?'

What did it mean? Rio had been searching for the answer
to that question.

When women had fallen in love with him before he'd
always considered it to be a question of 'buyer beware'. They
should have known better.

But Evie lived her life by a different rule book.

'Let's go back to the hotel. I have a surprise for you.'

It was over.

She no longer had a part to play in creating this happy
family.

Evie stood in the elevator, trying to keep the smile on her
face. It was selfish of her, wasn't it, to feel so devastated? The
whole reason this charade could now end was that someone
extremely sensible had decided that a little girl should live
with her daddy. As someone who had known that terrifying
feeling of loneliness and abandonment, she should be thrilled
that another little girl's dreams were going to come true. And
she was. She really was. But was she a wicked person to wish
that she could have had just a couple more days?

Forcing her own feelings aside, she smiled at Rio, determined not to make a fool of herself. *She didn't want his pity.*
The only thing she wanted from him was something quite

different. Something he wasn't able to give. 'You have plans to make. Just let me know what you want me to do.' She kept her voice brisk and practical. 'How you want me to handle things.'

He frowned. 'Handle what?'

'I'm going to dump you, remember? And, boy, am I going to enjoy that part.' Evie rubbed her hands together, wondering whether her voice sounded just a little forced.

'We'll discuss details later.' There was a tension in his shoulders that she attributed to his reaction to the momentous news. Either that or his ego was struggling with the notion of being publicly rejected.

It seemed incredible to her now that only weeks earlier she'd been about to marry another man. What she'd shared with Rio had taught her that what she'd shared with Jeff had been bland and colourless, like existing on a diet of bread and water and then suddenly discovering the variety of colour and texture of real food.

She wondered if she'd ever find anyone else who made her feel the way Rio did.

Blinking rapidly, Evie reinforced her smile as the elevator doors opened. 'Building snowmen is hungry work, so I certainly hope that—' She stopped, the words dissolving in her mouth as she saw the Penthouse.

It had been transformed from an elegant living space into a sparkling winter paradise.

Silver snowflakes were twisted through boughs of holly and an enormous Christmas tree, even bigger than the one she'd decorated, took pride of place next to the fire. It looked like a child's fantasy.

The only thing missing was Santa.

The moment the thought entered her head, Santa appeared from the second bedroom, complete with red robes and full white beard.

Evie blinked. And then she peered closer, through the

clouds of ridiculous white beard, and started to laugh. 'Antonio? Is that you in there?'

'Ho, ho, ho—'

Appalled to find tears in her eyes, Evie kept smiling. 'That doesn't quite work with an Italian accent. First fairy wings, now Santa—your job description seems to have shifted slightly over the past week.'

'I have a gift for you.' Overplaying his role like mad, Antonio reached into his sack with a flourish and pulled out a large square parcel. 'This has your name on it.'

Evie took it, wondering what all this meant. 'Am I supposed to keep it until Christmas?'

'No, you open it,' Rio said immediately as he urged her further into the room, away from Antonio who discreetly let himself out of the Penthouse.

Evie looked around her, unable to believe what she saw. 'But you don't…you hate…' She swallowed. 'You've done this for your little girl. I thought Elyssa couldn't be with you for Christmas.'

'I haven't done this for Elyssa.' His voice was rough and held a touch of uncertainty. 'I've done it for you.'

'For me?'

'Because you love Christmas and, this last week, I've deprived you of Christmas. I'm making up for it. Open the present. I hope you like it.' His eyes were wary and Evie wanted to say that the only present she wanted was him, but she couldn't, could she?

He didn't want that and it took two people to make a relationship work.

Dipping her head, she ripped the paper off the box and opened it. At first she thought there was nothing inside, and then she saw the envelope.

Puzzled, she discarded all the packaging and opened it. Inside was a printed ticket and it took a moment for her to understand what it meant. As the words sank into her brain, she gasped. 'I can spend Christmas Day with my grandfather?'

'Because the snow is so bad and your roads are pathetic, I am going to fly you by helicopter to this place where your grandfather lives—' Looking ridiculously pleased with himself, Rio outlined the plan. 'We will all spend the day together.'

Looking at Rio, with his sleek, expensive clothes and his taste for the best in everything, Evie gave a disbelieving laugh. 'Rio, you eat in hideously expensive restaurants—your chefs are the best in the world—I'm sorry, but I can't see you eating Christmas lunch in the Cedar Court Retirement Home.'

'*Sì*, I have thought the same thing myself,' Rio confessed, 'which is why two of my top chefs are currently preparing to cook lunch in more challenging surroundings than usual.'

'You're kidding.'

'It will be a true test of their talents, don't you agree?'

'But who is cooking lunch in your restaurants?'

'Someone. I don't know.' He spread his hands in a gesture that was pure Italian. 'I don't micro-manage every part of my business.'

'But if they don't do a good job, they're fired.'

'Very possibly. Are you pleased with your gift?'

Evie found it hard to speak. The fact that he'd done this made everything all the more mixed up in her head. Would it have been easier if he hadn't been so thoughtful? *Would it have been easier to walk away cursing him?* 'I'm *so* pleased,' she said huskily, standing on tiptoe and kissing him. 'Thank you. Can I phone him and tell him?'

'He might be rather busy. All the residents are currently with a stylist, choosing new outfits for Christmas Day.'

Overwhelmed by his generosity, Evie swallowed. 'Rio— you didn't have to do this—'

'I wanted to. As a thank you.' He slid his hands into her hair and brought his mouth down to hers and Evie immediately responded, wrapping her arms around his strong neck and pressing her body against his.

As a thank you. Of course. What else?

And she knew it was also a goodbye.

After tomorrow, it would be over. She wouldn't see him again.

He hadn't said what he wanted to do about ending their relationship in public, but presumably he'd chosen to wait until after Christmas Day so that her grandfather wasn't upset.

Rio pressed his mouth to her neck and gave a groan. 'We probably shouldn't be doing this—'

'I want to.' Evie spoke without hesitation, her eyes closing as he slowly unzipped her coat and trailed his mouth lower. 'I want to spend tonight with you.' If this was their last night together, then she wanted something she could remember for ever. She wanted memories to keep her warm.

She couldn't have him for ever, but she could have him for now.

'You're sure?' His voice was deep and husky and she nodded.

'Completely sure.'

It was only later, much later, when she was lying in the darkness, cocooned in his arms and sleepy from his loving, that she asked the question that had been hovering on her lips for days. 'Will you tell me why you hate Christmas? You don't have to if you don't want to, but—'

'It was never a good time of year for me.' He tightened his grip on her. 'Every Christmas was a nightmare. I'm the product of a long-term affair between my mother and a very senior politician who was married with his own family. Christmas Day was the one day he always spent with them. I was eight years old when he finally found the courage to tell her he was never going to leave his wife. I found her body lying under the Christmas tree when I got up in the morning.' He spoke the words in a flat monotone, the same voice he might have used when discussing the share price.

Evie lay immobile, shock seeping through her in icy rivulets, like melting snow. The vision played out in her brain in glorious Technicolor. An excited eight-year-old dashing downstairs to see if Santa had left presents under the tree and discovering death in all its brutal glory.

She wanted to say something—she wanted to find the perfect words that would soothe and heal—but she knew that such words didn't exist. She knew from experience that there weren't always words that could smooth the horrors of life, but she also knew that human comfort could sometimes warm when the temperature of life turned bitter cold. So she tightened her grip on him and pressed her lips against his warm skin, her muffled words intended to comfort, not cure.

'The doctor had given her tablets for depression.' Now that he'd started speaking, he seemed to want to continue. 'She'd swallowed them all, along with a bottle of champagne her lover had given her for Christmas. I called an ambulance but it was too late.'

Evie's eyes filled with tears. 'So what did you do? Where did you go?' She thought of her own loving grandparents and the tears streamed down her face and dampened his skin. 'Did you have family?'

'I gave the hospital the number of my father—' he wiped her tears with his fingers and gave a humourless laugh '—that must have been quite a Christmas lunch, don't you think? I believe it was his wife who answered the phone so he probably had some explaining to do.'

'Did he take you into his family?'

'Yes, on the surface. As a senior politician he had to be

seen to be doing the right thing and I was effectively an orphan. In practice, they sent me to boarding school and tried to pretend I didn't exist. His wife saw me as a reminder of her husband's lengthy infidelity, his daughter saw me as competition and my father saw me as nothing but a bomb ready to explode his career. He told me I'd never make anything of myself.'

'He should have been ashamed of himself—'

'His career disintegrated soon after that, so I don't think life was easy for him.'

Evie pressed her damp cheek against his chest. 'So now I understand why you were prepared to fight so hard for your little girl. Why you wanted to be a father to her.' And she understood why every Christmas tree slashed at the wound he'd buried so deep. And yet he'd put his own feelings aside in order to decorate the Penthouse for her. She wanted to ask why he'd done that—*why he'd put himself through that.* 'I love you, Rio.' Suddenly it seemed terribly important that she tell him, no matter what happened when the sun rose. No matter what he thought of her. 'I love you. I know you don't love me back—I can understand why you're so afraid to love after what you learned about relationships as a child, but that doesn't change the way I feel about you. I want you to know you're loved.'

He gave a low groan and pulled her onto him, wrapping his arms around her. 'I know you love me. I saw it in your eyes when you looked at me in the park.'

'Oh.' Embarrassed, she gave a tiny laugh. 'So much for hiding my feelings. Just don't ever invite me to play poker.'

'Evie—'

'Don't say anything.' She pressed her mouth to his. 'This has happened to you a load of times before. I know it has. It's fine. Don't let's think about tomorrow. Let's just enjoy right now. Right now is all that matters.'

She lay awake in the darkness, holding him, wishing she could hold the moment for ever and stop dawn breaking.

It was the end, she knew that.

For the first time in her life, she didn't want Christmas Day to come.

CHAPTER NINE

Rio was up with the dawn, all dark shadows of the night thrown off as he showered and changed and spoke into two of his three phones while making the arrangements for the day.

Moving more slowly, Evie dressed and collected together the presents she'd bought for her grandfather. A soft cashmere scarf for his walks in the gardens of the home, a reading lamp and some of his favourite chocolates.

As Rio made the final preparations, she wandered back into the sitting room and stared wistfully at the decorations. How much courage had it taken, she thought, to adorn the Penthouse with the flavour of Christmas when the taste must be so bitter to him. A great deal of courage. Obviously, he wasn't a wimp.

He was a real man.

'Are you ready?' He strode up to her and relieved her of the parcels and Evie took a breath.

No, she wasn't ready. But she was never going to be ready for him to walk out of her life.

'I've never been on a helicopter before,' she said brightly. 'Life with you has been one big new experience.'

He smiled and kissed her on the mouth with erotic purpose. 'We're not finished yet.'

No. They had today. One whole day.

Her heart skittered and jumped and she wanted to ask him what his plans were for the announcement, but he was already striding into the elevator, this time going up to the roof, to the helicopter pad.

And then they were flying across the snow-covered English countryside and Evie thought she'd never seen anything more beautiful in her life. Beautiful and poignant because the enforced silence made her mind focus on the fact that everything she did with him today would be for the last time.

By the time they finally landed in the gardens of the Cedar Court Retirement Home, she was barely holding herself together. Even the prospect of seeing her beloved grandfather couldn't lift her sagging spirits. What made the whole thing even harder was that Rio seemed completely energized.

'I am looking forward to finally meeting your grandfather, having spoken to him so many times on the phone.'

So many times? Evie frowned. She knew he'd called her grandfather twice, but she wasn't aware of any other occasions. Before she could question him, the doors opened and she saw all the residents lined up in their finery. She saw Mrs Fitzwilliam with her hair newly styled and then there was her grandfather, dressed in his best suit and smiling proudly at the head of the line.

Within a second she was in his arms and kissing him, her tears mingling with his as they hugged and talked at the same time and he felt solid and safe and such an important part of her life that she wondered why on earth she'd ever thought she could live happily in London. Maybe she'd be all right, Evie thought as she closed her eyes and hugged him. Maybe she'd survive.

They spent precious minutes catching up and it was a few moments before she realised that the entire retirement home had been transformed into a silver and white paradise, just like the Penthouse.

'Your Rio has done us proud, that's for sure. You found

yourself a real man, Evie. I can see how much you love him,'
her grandfather said gruffly and Evie's control almost cracked
as she wondered how on earth she was going to explain to him
when the time came to break it off. She cast a helpless glance
at Rio but he merely smiled and turned to say something in
Italian to Antonio.

Rio's chefs had surpassed themselves but Evie barely
touched her lunch, relieved when her grandfather finally
rose to make a speech and she could give up the pretence of
eating. He thanked the chefs, the styling team and most of
all Rio. And then he looked at Evie, his eyes full of love.

'Sometimes,' he said quietly, 'life doesn't turn out the
way you plan it. When Evie came into our lives, we became
parents all over again and those years were the happiest I've
known. Evie, I want you to know that, no matter what happens, I'll always be proud of you. Not because of what you
do, but because of who you are.'

His words cut the final thread on her control. Evie felt tears
scald her eyes and she had the most awful feeling that her
grandfather knew that her life had tumbled apart in London.
Had he somehow discovered that she'd lost her flat and her
job? Had he guessed that this whole thing with Rio was a
farce? She took a gulp of the champagne Rio had provided,
blinking rapidly to stop the tears from falling. She was so
choked that she was relieved when Rio stood up.

And then she saw the serious look on his handsome face
and relief turned to alarm. Oh, no. Please don't let him decide
that this was a good time to tell the truth. Not on Christmas
Day.

She wanted her grandfather to have the very best day of
his life—

Her anxious gaze met Rio's and she mouthed the word
don't! but he simply smiled as he lifted his glass.

'I agree with every word that has been spoken. Life certainly doesn't turn out the way you plan.' His voice was

smooth and confident and it was clear from the way he spoke and stood that he was comfortable addressing large groups of people. 'When I arrived in London twelve days ago, my plan was to sort out a complicated business issue and then spend the next few days blocking out the fact that it's Christmas, because that's what I do. Every year I try and forget it's Christmas.' A shocked silence greeted his words and Evie felt her mouth dry as she anticipated what he might say next.

'But this year—' he paused and a faint smile touched his hard mouth '—this year I met Evie and all my plans changed. Instead of doing deals, I was dancing. Instead of analyzing shares, I was building snowmen. When I arrived in London I had no plans to fall in love and certainly no plans to get married—' he let the words hang in the air and a stunned silence spread across the room '—but that's because I didn't know that people like Evie existed.'

Nobody moved.

Evie felt as though she was going to pass out. She saw her grandfather beaming at her and several of the elderly women fanning themselves as they watched Rio standing there, tall and impossibly handsome. She felt a burst of hope, followed by a cascade of incredible joy, immediately tempered by caution because she was so terribly afraid she might have misunderstood.

Was this still pretending? Had he decided to take their charade one step further before shattering it for ever?

She glanced around, wondering if the press had somehow gained access to this private event, thinking that only a long lens could have triggered that speech from him. But there were no fancy cameras. There were no journalists or paparazzi scrambling to record the moment.

So why was he saying these things?

'Evie—' He took her hand in his and drew her firmly to

her feet. 'I know how much you love me. What you don't know is how much I love you.'

Her knees felt weak and her body started to tremble. 'Rio—'

'It's real.' Reading her mind, he pressed his mouth to hers, his kiss a lingering promise of a lifetime of love. 'This isn't for the press, or for your grandfather. It's just for us. I want you to marry me.'

'But—'

'I live and work in such a hard, cynical world. I deal with hard, cynical people—and then I met you.' He stroked her hair away from her face, watching her expression as if he were trying to interpret every blink. 'Yesterday, when I finally heard that I had what I wanted, I couldn't work out why I didn't feel more elated. And I realised it was because gaining my daughter meant losing you and I didn't want it to be that way. I'm afraid that my biggest fault is that I want everything.'

Evie was laughing through her tears. 'Greedy.'

'Yes. And selfish, and ruthless—' Smiling, unapologetic, he leaned his forehead against hers. 'You already know that I'll do whatever it takes to get what I want, and I want you, for ever, so you might as well just surrender without a fight.'

For ever?

Happiness flooded through her. 'You don't have to fight.'

'Marry me,' he murmured softly. 'We need to give your grandfather a baby to bounce on his knee and in the meantime he can make a start with Elyssa. She's in desperate need of spare family. She has us, of course, but a wise person once told me that it's useful to have spares of everything so I thought it would be good to collect some more relatives for her.'

Evie buried her face in his neck, half laughing, half crying, thinking that if this was how love felt then from now on every day was going feel like Christmas. 'I—'

'I think the rest of this conversation should be conducted in private,' Rio breathed, sweeping her into his arms so that the toe of her shoe narrowly missed the Christmas pudding. 'Please enjoy the rest of your meal. This afternoon we have dancing. And singing. And Evie will be back to give a private performance of her much acclaimed version of *The Twelve Days of Christmas* but, as that requires dancing on the tables, it has to be after we've finished eating.'

'Rio, you can't just—' Mortified, Evie turned scarlet. 'They're all looking! What do you think you're doing?'

'What am I doing?' There was laughter in his voice. 'I'm behaving like a real man, *tesoro*. If you have any complaints about that, you can take it up with your grandfather.'

Twelve months later

'Can I hold her?'

'Of course you can,' Evie said immediately. 'She's your baby sister.'

Elyssa stepped closer and peered at the baby's face. 'She's very small.'

'Well, she's only three weeks old. You were this small once.'

'But I didn't live with you then.'

'No.' Evie reached out a hand and stroked Elyssa's dark hair. 'But you live with us now. We're a family. Always.'

'I liked being your bridesmaid. I'm pleased you married my Daddy.'

Evie swallowed. 'I'm pleased, too. Now, sit back in the chair and then I'll hand Lara to you. She needs to feel secure.'

The little girl wriggled to the back of the chair and held

out her arms and Evie sat down next to her and carefully gave her the baby, willing the infant not to wake up and cry.

From beyond the windows she heard the sound of a helicopter and moments later Rio appeared in the doorway. His exquisitely tailored suit moulded to his athletic physique and Evie felt her stomach drop. Even after a year together, she still found it hard to breathe when he was in the same room as her.

'I'm sorry I'm late,' he drawled, dropping his briefcase and walking across to them. 'There were a few things I had to arrange. Last minute Christmas shopping. What have I missed?'

'Daddy! Have you bought my present?' Elyssa wriggled with excitement and Rio dropped a kiss on the top of her head and dropped to his haunches.

'I might have done. You're holding Lara.' He shot a questioning look at Evie who smiled reassuringly.

'Isn't she doing brilliantly? She's so good with her sister.' As she spoke, the baby's eyes opened and Evie held her breath. *Don't cry.*

'She's looking at me.' Elyssa looked at her half-sister in fascination. 'Can she see me?'

'Oh, yes.' Watching the two of them together, Evie felt a lump in her throat. 'She loves you, Elyssa.'

'Grandpa and I hung her stocking on the fireplace and I wrote to Santa to tell him she's only a baby so he doesn't leave her unsuitable toys.'

'She's so lucky having you as a big sister.' It had taken months of patience but finally the nightmares had stopped and Elyssa had started to behave like a normal little girl. Far from unsettling her, Lara's birth appeared to have given her greater security—as if the arrival of the baby had somehow cemented their little family.

Elyssa kissed Lara's downy head. 'I can't wait for her to grow big enough to be able to play with me. Can you take her back now? She's really heavy for someone who only drinks milk.'

Rio expertly scooped up his baby daughter, holding her against his shoulder as he sat down on the sofa next to Elyssa. 'Did you decorate the Christmas tree while I was away?'

'Evie wanted to wait for you.'

Knowing how Rio felt about Christmas, Evie cast him an anxious look. It was enough for her that they were together and in England. She was still overwhelmed by his decision to buy the beautiful old Manor House close to the Cedar Court Retirement Home, meaning that she could have her grandfather to stay. He'd declared himself too old to be flying around the world to visit their other homes, so Rio had shifted his business operation to enable him to spend as much time in England as possible.

And her grandfather was delighted that his wish had been fulfilled twice over. He now had two great-grandchildren to hold on his knee.

Rio leaned across Elyssa and delivered a lingering kiss to Evie's lips. 'I missed you. No more work,' he promised, 'for the whole of Christmas. Anyone who phones me is fired.'

'I missed you, too.' She kissed him back, careful not to squash the baby. 'Are you serious? You're not working?'

'I have better things to do with my time. Put your coats on. We're going outside. I have a surprise for you both.'

'Outside?' Excited, Elyssa jumped to her feet. 'Can Lara come, too?'

'Not this time. We're leaving her with Grandpa for a moment.'

Evie's grandfather was obviously in on the surprise because he timed his entrance perfectly. 'Elyssa, there's someone at the front door for you.'

Elyssa shot out of the room and Rio took Evie's hand in his and followed. 'I hope you're not going to be mad with me—'

'That depends on what you've done.' Her eyes teased him and he kissed her again, unable to leave her alone.

'I may have gone a little overboard,' he confessed, 'but, after years of not celebrating Christmas, I'm determined to make up for it big time.'

Overwhelmed with love for him, Evie lifted her hand and stroked his hair. 'I wasn't sure how you'd feel this year—that's why we haven't decorated the tree. I thought you might rather we didn't.' Hesitant, she watched him. 'I know the whole thing has bad memories for you.'

'I'm making new memories—' he captured her hand in his, his voice husky '—with you.'

'Daddy, come on!' Elyssa was waiting impatiently and Rio released Evie and walked to the front door.

'Close your eyes and don't peep until I say so.'

Elyssa squeezed them shut. 'Can I look yet?'

Rio opened the door of the house. '*Now* you can look.'

Evie watched as the little girl opened her eyes. Wonder and happiness lit her whole face. Intrigued as to what had caused such a response, Evie turned her head and gasped as she saw the pretty white pony. He stood quietly, his breath clouding the air, a big red bow in his mane. Behind him was a sleigh piled high with presents.

'Daddy!' Elyssa could hardly speak. 'Oh, Daddy!'

Rio looked smug. 'You like him?'

'He's *mine*? Truly?'

'All yours.' Rio scooped her into his arms and carried her to the pony. 'His name is Snowflake and he's the latest member of our ever-growing family. It's a good job we have a large house.'

Elyssa had her arms around the pony, almost sobbing with excitement. 'He's so beautiful. Oh—oh—Mummy, have you seen him?'

Mummy.

Rio inhaled sharply and so did Evie because she'd waited

for this moment for so long. For almost a year she'd been encouraging the withdrawn, confused little girl to call her Mummy and finally now, on Christmas Eve, she'd said it. To hear her use the word so naturally felt like a miracle.

The best Christmas gift of all.

Warmth spread through her body and Evie walked across to Rio and took Elyssa from him, hugging her tightly, tears on her face.

'I see him, sweetheart, and I think he's completely perfect.'

Her grandfather appeared in the doorway, smiling his approval as he looked at Evie with her family.

Rio looked ridiculously pleased with himself. 'It's cold out here and neither of you are properly dressed. We'll go back inside and get wrapped up and then we can go round to the stables and see Snowflake and his friends.'

Evie glanced up at him. 'Friends?'

A smile transformed his face from handsome to breathtaking. 'I bought a few spares. I have a feeling we're going to be needing them before too long.'

Evie's heart stumbled. He wanted more children. A big family.

Her dream come true.

As she smiled up at him she felt something cold brush against her face and Elyssa gave a squeal of excitement that made the pony throw up his head in alarm.

'It's snowing! Mummy, Daddy, we're going to have snow for Christmas. Can we build a snowman? Do you know how?'

Rio brushed the snow from Evie's cheek. 'Yes, I know how. We need a carrot and some pebbles and a few twigs. And we need your mother because she's brilliant at building snowmen.'

'We also need enough snow,' Evie pointed out practically.

'We need to find something to do while we're waiting for it to settle.'

'I think I can solve that problem.' Rio pulled her back into his arms and held her tightly. 'How would you feel about decorating a Christmas tree?'

BEST MAN UNDER
THE MISTLETOE

JULES BENNETT

To the Harlequin Desire team: Stacy, Charles & Tahra. They say it takes a village to raise a child... The same is true for books.

One

"This investigation has really been a community effort. Thanks to the diligence of so many in Royal, the final piece of the puzzle has been put into place. Maverick has been identified as Royal's own Dale, a.k.a. Dusty, Walsh."

Gabe Walsh muted the TV and tossed the remote onto the leather sofa. He didn't want to hear any more about his late uncle's betrayal. The old bastard had passed away last week from a brain tumor and now the mess he'd caused to so many in the town of Royal, Texas, would have a ripple effect on Gabe's security firm. He would undoubtedly have a hell of a mess to clean up.

He still couldn't believe it. His uncle Dusty was Maverick, the cyber criminal who had terrorized members of the Texas Cattleman's Club for months now, revealing their secrets online and often resorting to blackmail.

Perhaps worst of all, he'd leaked nude photos of Chelsea Hunt, taken without her knowledge in the locker room at her gym.

According to Gabe's law-enforcement sources, all evidence pointed to Dusty working alone, except when it came to the locker room photos. There was now another person of interest in that particular crime. A woman, the police claimed. They were still studying months of surveillance-camera footage from the public areas of the gym to figure out who could have planted the camera.

Who the hell had aided his uncle? And was that the only instance when Dusty had taken on an accomplice? The man had been dying. There was no way Dusty could've done so much on his own. The man had been too feeble, too weak.

Though not so weak that he couldn't plot to destroy lives. Luckily, the citizens of Royal—Chelsea Hunt included—had risen above his attempts to take them down. Investigators had also seen through his elaborate attempt to pin the crimes on someone else.

Gabe raked a hand through his hair and glared at the screen as Sheriff Nate Battle continued his press conference. A picture of Gabe's once robust, smiling uncle filled the top right corner of the TV screen while the sheriff spoke.

How and why Uncle Dusty had pulled off such a grand scheme of blackmail and betrayal were open questions, but one thing was undeniable. He'd managed to put a big dark cloud over the family security firm, the Walsh Group—Gabe's new baby. As if taking over a company wasn't difficult and risky enough, now he was forced to deal with the backlash of questions from clients, both old and new, because of his relationship with Dusty.

How the hell was he supposed to dodge all of this bad press? The business's reputation was on the line. Sure, finances were the least of his concern. He'd busted his ass from the start of his career, saved every dollar, invested wisely and had worked his way up to be the best in the industry. He could close up shop and never work another day in his life, but he valued his reputation and family loyalty. Ironic now, wasn't it?

Gabe once again thought of Chelsea Hunt and it had him seeing red. His uncle had gotten his hands on compromising photos and proceeded to put them out for the town to see. And why? Yes, Chelsea had played an important role in the Maverick investigation, bringing in computer-security experts from out of town to help. But the leak was part of a bigger pattern: Maverick had been especially vicious when targeting women. One theory was that Maverick acted this way because the Texas Cattleman's Club had begun admitting women a few years back. By contrast, Dusty had been passed over for membership, one of the things that incurred his wrath.

Gabe's uncle had certainly been hidebound in his views of women—but going so far as to leak nude photos like that? What had been wrong with the man? Chelsea hadn't deserved the embarrassment and scandal that had been brought upon her by his uncle and some unknown accomplice.

Gabe cursed as he spun away from the television. He had been careful not to look at the photos when they'd been released for all the world to see. He hadn't wanted to be totally disrespectful or to violate her privacy. Plus, where Chelsea was concerned, he had problems of his own to deal with.

Replaying that kiss he and Chelsea had shared last week, it was a wonder he hadn't lost his damn mind.

Gabe and Chelsea had started spending a lot of time together when their best friends, Shane Delgado and

Brandee Lawson, had asked them to be best man and maid of honor in their wedding. Brandee had wanted Gabe and Chelsea to be very hands-on in the process. Gabe had known full well when they'd started working together that they'd be spending quite a bit of time alone.

But the other night, something had shifted. They'd been making name cards for the reception, which had triggered an argument, which had his last ounce of control snapping.

Gabe had grabbed the gold ribbon from Chelsea and tossed it aside, gripping her face and taking what he'd wanted for months.

Raking a hand through his hair, Gabe tried like hell to forget how she'd tasted, how she'd felt against him. But the scene replayed over and over in his head.

He could use a stiff drink and the company of a good woman between the sheets. But right at the moment neither would solve his problems…and the only woman he wanted between his sheets was the very one he needed to forget.

To top it all off on this hellish day, he had to meet Chelsea for some wedding planning nonsense later. How was she handling the news that his late uncle had been Maverick? Would she blame Gabe simply by association?

It was bad enough that he'd been roped into the wedding planning. He may as well have given up his man card for all the flowers and candles he'd been sniffing lately. If Shane and Brandee hadn't specifically asked Gabe and Chelsea to help with the planning, Gabe would've given this project the middle finger. But Shane was as close as family and, even though Gabe didn't believe in happily-ever-after, he was glad to see his best friends so in love.

Gabe just wished Chelsea wasn't the maid of honor because until the Christmas nuptials rolled around, dodging her wasn't an option. Nearly every single day he'd be spending hours looking at seating charts, passing on the bride's playlist to the band, finalizing the caterers and florists…and all of that time would only lead to one more thing. Another kiss.

Why the hell did it have to be this woman who intrigued him? At first he'd wondered if he'd just felt bad for all the negative attention she'd been getting, but he'd quickly squelched that notion. He wasn't one to take pity and turn it into lust.

But there was something about her strength and the fact she wasn't letting this scandal break her when it very well should. He admired anyone who could rise above adversity and still remain in control.

And then there was just plain, old-fashioned, sexual desire.

She was hot, and he was a man with breath in his lungs. He would have been a fool not to be attracted.

That kiss had upped the stakes and now all he could think of was getting another taste. Given everything that had transpired today, was that wrong? Should he even allow himself to crave the woman his uncle had publicly humiliated?

Muttering a curse, Gabe turned the television off and grabbed his keys. He might as well get this little meeting with Chelsea over with and then go back to doing damage control at the Walsh Group. Not only would the clients be pouring in with questions, his employees would, too. The sheriff had told Gabe about his findings before the press conference—and cleared him of any wrongdoing, for that matter—so Gabe had already given a heads-up to his assistants that this was coming and instructed them on how to handle the expected calls.

The people in Royal knew him, knew that he wouldn't

partake in something so heinous. But there were clients who didn't know him and those were the ones he'd be personally calling and meeting face-to-face. He wasn't looking forward to doing damage control, but he'd worked too hard for his impeccable reputation and he'd be damned if he let anyone tarnish it…especially family.

That was business. He knew how to handle all of that, but he had no clue how to approach Chelsea. No doubt she'd heard on the news or directly from Sheriff Battle the identity of her blackmailer and Gabe would be the perfect target for her to take out her frustrations. And then there was the unacknowledged-but-hard-to-ignore attraction between them.

But she was in a vulnerable position and only a complete jerk would take advantage of that. She may put on a strong front, something he commended her for, but no doubt she still hurt. All he could do at this point was to show her he wasn't like his uncle, that he was completely innocent, and he was there for her if she needed him.

The screwdriver hurtled past Gabe's head and Chelsea cursed herself for missing. She was still shaken up by the news, that was all. If she'd been fully on her game, she would've nailed the target. The sexy, arrogant, infuriating target.

She didn't condone violence, but this man had stepped into her bad mood at the wrong time. She'd only just learned of the Maverick's true identity and Gabe Walsh was guilty by association. For all she knew, Gabe had helped cover his uncle's tracks. He was a sneaky PI, after all. Even though the sheriff had assured her there was no evidence Gabe had any involvement whatsoever, she was furious and needed to lash out.

"Is that any way to treat someone who's come to help

you build this archway for the ceremony?" Gabe asked, slowly making his way toward her.

Chelsea grabbed the hammer. "I don't need, nor did I ask for your help."

Gabe cocked his head and kicked up his wicked smile. Gabe had that whole don't-give-a-damn attitude down pat; nothing ever bothered him. He seduced and charmed everyone in his path...but not her. And she wasn't going to think of that kiss, either. She *wasn't*.

"Brandee texted me and asked me to come help you with the arch for the ceremony," he informed her.

Chelsea glanced at the piles of wood, flowers, tulle and wire all spread out in the old barn at Hope Springs, Brandee's ranch. Brandee could've hired a company to take over the decorating and organizing of the big day, but Chelsea had wanted to make things special for her friend. She'd wanted to be hands-on since she knew Brandee better than any stranger would.

But Chelsea would rather have worked her fingers to the bone than ask Gabe for any help. Now that the Maverick had been revealed as his uncle, Chelsea felt utterly betrayed.

"I wasn't sure how Dusty managed to get those images of me and splash them around, but now it's pretty clear he had help." Chelsea continued to stare at the man who was too sexy to be legal. The tattoos, the scruff along his jawline, the arrogant stance. "You were his errand boy."

"What?" Gabe said, jerking back. "I—"

"Anything for the family," she went on, dropping the hammer to the concrete floor at her side instead of hurling it at his head next. "You were trained to take over the family business. Taking orders from your dying uncle just came naturally."

"You have no idea what you're talking about," Gabe

countered, an edge to his voice. "You might want to have evidence before making such claims—evidence you will never find because I had nothing to do with the pictures or the blackmail."

He may have been a former special agent, he may have put the fear of God in many suspects in his time, but Chelsea wasn't afraid. The only thing she worried about was how he managed to infuriate and turn her on at the same time. She hated how her body responded to just the sight of him when her mind told her she knew better. Why did lust have to cloud her judgment?

"I'm not arguing." She turned her attention back to the mess before her. "I have too much to do here. If Brandee doesn't see some progress, she'll worry it won't be done in time, and I won't have my best friend stressed for her special day."

"Then it sounds like you need an extra pair of hands."

Chelsea shuddered. Gabe had used those hands to grip her shoulders and haul her against his hard body as he'd kissed her so fast, so fierce—

"I say we call a truce."

Chelsea swallowed and finally nodded. He was right. They had to work together and she had to believe the sheriff when he'd said Gabe was in the clear. She just wanted someone to blame, someone to take her anger out on.

"A truce," she said. "I think I can handle that."

Gabe flashed that smile again. "So what are we doing here?"

"Brandee wants a large arch for her and Shane to stand beneath to exchange their vows. She wants it to be elegant and Christmassy, not tacky. Everything will be done in whites and golds and clear lights. She told me to order one, but I wanted to make it so she had something special and meaningful."

Chelsea couldn't help but feel a twinge of jealousy at her friend's upcoming nuptials. Chelsea may be hard, she may be independent and run the tech side of Hunt & Co. like a boss, but she was still a woman with dreams. She didn't want a man to take care of her, but she certainly wouldn't mind a man to hold her at night, to appreciate her Italian-lace lingerie collection, to laugh with her and share stories about their days. Was it too much to ask to meet just one man who wasn't a jerk?

"Is there a blueprint for this or are we just winging it?" Gabe asked.

Chelsea came to her feet, dusting her hands against her holey jeans. "No blueprint, but Shane had everything cut and ready to assemble once I told him my ideas. I told Brandee I'd take care of it since it's my idea. I have a picture on my phone of what it should look like. But it's just a mock-up of the picture in my head."

She slid her phone from her pocket and pulled up the image.

Gabe came to stand beside her, having the nerve to brush his shoulder against hers.

She shouldn't be attracted to such a…a…wolfish man. He was a hell of a kisser, but he was also related to the enemy. That was reason enough for her to be leery. Wasn't it? There was only so far a hot bod and toe-curling kiss could take Gabe Walsh. So what if she'd had vivid, detailed dreams of the infamous kiss and all the delicious things her mind conjured up without her permission?

"Subtle," she said as she took a half step to the side. "Don't try using this opportunity to kiss or seduce me or whatever else you're thinking."

Gabe came around and stood directly in front of her. She still held her phone out, her hands frozen in the narrow space between them. His deep eyes held her in place, and Chelsea trembled as if he'd touched her bare skin.

"Darlin', when you were kissing me, you weren't exactly shy about it."

Chelsea opened her mouth to object, but Gabe leaned forward, coming to within a breath of her lips.

"So don't try to deny that you're attracted to me," he murmured. "And I won't deny it, either. But right now, we have more pressing things to do than worry about who is seducing whom."

Keeping his eyes on hers, he eased back and slid the phone from her grip. Damn the man for making her entire body heat up like he'd lit a match from within. The broad shoulders, the scruff along his jawline, the ink peeking from beneath his fitted T-shirt...and the way he'd drawled out "darlin'" had her ready to ignore those red flags and kiss him again. Maybe it hadn't been that good and she'd remembered all wrong. Had her toes actually curled? Had her body tightened with arousal?

Stifling a groan, Chelsea stepped over the supplies and went to the pile of wood. As much as she liked to think she could do everything on her own, she was going to need Gabe's help here.

"This is some setup they're wanting," Gabe said behind her. "I guess we better get started. The wedding is only a couple weeks away and this isn't our only task."

Gabe again came up beside her, this time not touching, and handed over her phone. "Tell me we've decided on the florist. I really don't want to look at one more plant or bloom or branch or anything else that I know nothing about."

"The florist has been nailed down and contacted. Now, we need to finalize the appetizers and beer and wine list for the combined bachelor/bachelorette party," she told him. "I have the final numbers for those who sent in their RSVP."

Gabe blew out a sigh. "I'll handle all the menus if you promise I don't have to pick out tablecloths or do little calligraphy place cards."

Chelsea crossed her arms and turned to fully face him. "Well, Gabriel Walsh, I'm disappointed in your knowledge of contemporary weddings. Calligraphy cards are definitely a thing of the past. I actually already ordered name cards in the same design and font as Brandee's invitations. You really should update your wedding magazine subscriptions if you're ever going to do this yourself."

"If I ever lose my mind and marry, I'll let my bride handle everything." He raked a hand over his stubbled jaw. "Food and alcohol are easy. Especially since we're having the party at the TCC. What else do you want me to do that doesn't involve something frilly or flowery?"

"Someone is grouchy," she muttered. "Is it because I threw the screwdriver at your head or because I'm not throwing myself at you after the kiss?"

Gabe shoved his hands in his pockets and tipped his head sideways to look her in the eyes. "Are we going to be able to get along to get through this together?"

Chelsea shrugged. "Depends. You keep your hands and lips to yourself and we might just. And just so you know, I tend to believe you when you say you didn't know what your uncle was up to. Shane and Brandee wouldn't put their trust in you if you were involved. But you better hope like hell there isn't a connection, because if I find out there is, I won't miss the next time I throw a screwdriver at your head."

Two

"This doesn't look right. Is it leaning a little?"

Gabe stood back and stared at the arch he and Chelsea had been grunting over for the better part of the day. They'd gotten along surprisingly well, as long as they'd kept the topic of conversation on the wedding…or when they weren't talking at all.

When the silence stretched between them, though, his mind started conjuring up all sorts of naughty thoughts and each one starred the woman at his side. The way she wore her holey jeans low on her hips and that fitted tank, she didn't look like an expert hacker and CTO of the most prestigious chain of steakhouses in the South.

She could drive any man out of his mind, even if she was spitting in his face and smarting off with that sweet mouth. It was one of the many reasons he couldn't help but admire her. She didn't take crap from anyone and was her own hero, saving herself from the evils in her own world. Damn if that wasn't sexy as hell.

It didn't go unnoticed how she'd kept glancing his way. The attraction simmering just below that steel barrier she kept around her was going to explode…and he damn well would be the man to experience her passion. He'd had just enough of a taste to crave more, and she could deny all she wanted with her words, her body told a whole different story.

He gave the arch a slight push. "Did that help?"

Chelsea stepped back, angling her head. "That did it."

Gabe's cell vibrated in his pocket. He pulled it out and glanced at the text from one of his assistants. After a quick response, he slid the phone back in.

"Late for a lunch date with your girlfriend?" Chelsea asked as she gathered the tools and put them off to the side.

"If you want to know if I'm seeing anyone, just ask."

She tucked her shoulder-length, honey-blond hair behind one ear and quirked a brow. "I didn't ask."

"I'm not seeing anyone," he informed her, taking long strides to close the distance between them. "A fact you should know before you kiss me again."

Chelsea crossed her arms beneath her chest and it was all he could do to keep his eyes on hers. "You're arrogant enough to think that's going to happen?"

"Arrogant? Perhaps, though I'm positive it's only a matter of time." Whistling, he turned to head from the barn out to his car. Any second he expected a tool to hit the back of his head or go whirling by his ear. But nothing happened. He was proud she showed such restraint. Obviously he was growing on her.

But he'd be lying if he claimed he wasn't irritated by the fact she thought he had something to do with those leaked pictures. What on earth would his motive be? There was no reason for him to go around with his uncle terrorizing the people of this town. Gabe actually liked those who had been affected by his uncle's activities and would never want to see any of them harmed. Shane and Brandee had even been targeted, for pity's sake. Dusty's antics were absolutely inconceivable.

As Gabe slid behind the wheel and started the engine, Chelsea came strutting out of the barn straight toward him. He rolled his window down.

"I knew you'd chase after me."

Rolling her eyes, she propped her hands on her hips. "Brandee just texted me and asked if we'd run to Natalie Valentine's bridal shop so I can get my last fitting."

"As much as I'd love to help you with a fitting, I'm afraid I have work to do. My uncle, as you know, is ruining my name even in his death and I have too many clients to coddle during this sensitive time. Besides, how could you ever bring yourself to trust me at a fitting?"

Chelsea's lips thinned and she gritted her teeth before saying, "Brandee wants us to stop at Priceless to pick up her wedding present to Shane. She bought a table and chairs for their dining room, says it's just like the one his grandmother used to have, and she wants to surprise him. The dress fitting just makes sense because we'll already be there."

Gabe dropped his head back against the headrest and groaned. "You know, I do have a company to run."

"Yes, and here I am with nothing to do. Or maybe you've forgotten I have a demanding position, as well."

"That's not what I meant," he argued. Blowing out a sigh, he glanced back up at her. "Get in. We'll swing by my place and pick up my truck so we can go get this furniture."

"I'll drive myself."

"There's no reason we can't ride together. I have to

take the truck anyway to pick up the table. Unless you're afraid to be alone with me."

Chelsea narrowed her eyes. "I hate your inflated ego."

"Duly noted. Now, get in."

He couldn't help but smile as she rounded the hood of his car. He didn't know why he wanted to provoke her, but he couldn't help himself. In actuality, he wanted to spend more time with her. Seducing her was something he wanted to pursue, sure, but more importantly he wanted her to know that he would never, ever, treat a woman the way she'd been treated by his uncle. Above all else, he needed her to know that. And she wouldn't just take his word for it. She needed to see that he wasn't some jerk that got off on blackmailing people and ruining reputations.

As soon as she got into the car, he put it in gear and set off toward his downtown loft.

He kept his truck in the second bay of his garage, for which he paid a hefty monthly fee to have parking beneath his downtown loft apartment. But a man couldn't live in Texas and not own a truck. It was practically against the law.

"You know—" he began once they'd switched to the truck and were back on the road.

"We don't need to talk."

Well, apparently this was going to be more difficult than he'd thought. Gabe tightened his grip on the wheel.

"Yes, we do," he countered. "As I was saying, you know there are many people in this town who know me and know I would never side with my uncle. I wouldn't have covered up such maliciousness."

"I know you were cleared of any wrongdoing. The sheriff told me he's positive you had nothing to do with the scandal. But at the same time, he was your only family member. How did you not know what he was up to? He was old and feeble. Someone had to know something about what he was doing."

There was bite to her voice, but beneath that gruff exterior there was pain. Gabe hated what she'd gone through, the humiliation and embarrassment. The fact that so many had suffered at the hands of his uncle didn't sit well with him, but he was especially upset about Chelsea. Her betrayal had taken on a darker, more personal feel than the others.

No matter how much anger she projected toward him, he was hell-bent on proving to her that he understood, that he totally agreed with her, that they were on the same page. He knew his uncle was a bastard, but just because Gabe's last name was Walsh didn't mean he knew what had been taking place in the months leading up to his uncle's death.

"I can't imagine how difficult this has been," he started, hoping she let him finish. "I know you're angry, but I swear I didn't know about those photos until they were leaked. I never even looked at them."

Chelsea snorted and shot him a glare. "If you think for a second I believe that lie, you're more of a fool than I thought. You're a guy. You looked."

"We could argue this till we're both blue in the face, you still wouldn't believe me," he growled. "But you'll see. Once the truth is revealed and they catch whoever this accomplice is, you'll realize that I truly knew nothing. You think I'd actually keep information like this to myself? Dusty self-destructed and that has nothing to do with me. I have a reputation, a multibillion-dollar security business to look after. The last thing I want to be involved in is a scandal."

Gabe had to believe she'd eventually come to see that

he wasn't lying. He prided himself on honesty, and liked to think he was a man of integrity. Sure, he could be hard when it came to work, but when it came to his personal life, he could admit he was a bit softer when it was necessary. And this situation called for delicate measures unlike anything he'd ever known.

As he pulled into the Courtyard Shops, Gabe figured that even though he'd rather do anything else than wait on Chelsea to try on her dress, at least this forced time together was giving him the prime opportunity he needed to win her over. Which was important to him, even though he had big problems to deal with at his business right now.

"You can go on into Priceless while I try on the dress."

Gabe hopped out of the truck and shot her a wink. "If it's all the same, I'll just stick with you. You won't be long and then you can help me load the table next door."

Chelsea groaned as she jerked on her door handle. Normally, Gabe would get the door for a woman—he was raised in the South by a well-mannered mother—but he also had a feeling if he tried to get the door for Chelsea, he'd just be taking a step in the wrong direction.

But the moment he stepped inside Natalie's shop, Gabe started to reconsider his ploy to stick close to Chelsea. There were dresses everywhere. Fluffy, lacy, silky dresses, and the place smelled...pink. If a smell could have a color, this place was definitely pink.

The peppy little shop attendant greeted Chelsea and promptly went to get the dress from the back. Gabe spotted a lounge area in that direction and made his way to a white sofa in front of the wall of mirrors. He could catch up on a few emails that needed his attention and check in on his right-hand man doing some security work in Dallas for the next few weeks.

Nothing was as important as his business, especially during this crucial time. He'd already reached out to some of his closest clients and assured them that Dusty's scandal had nothing to do with the Walsh Group. He'd also made sure they knew they could come to him personally with questions or concerns.

The unfortunate, untimely setback wouldn't change the way Gabe handled his business. But it sure did complicate matters. If ole Dusty weren't already dead, Gabe would have no problem driving out to his mansion and beating the ever loving sh—

Every single thought vanished when Chelsea stepped from the dressing room and came to stand in front of the three-way mirror. The fitted gold gown shouldn't have looked so damn sexy, seeing as how it was long, with full sleeves, and a high neck. But the material hugged every single curve and dip on Chelsea's luscious body, mocking him. He'd seen her in jeans, even in little flowy sundresses, but nothing like this, all sultry and glamorous.

She smoothed the dress over her flat stomach and turned from side to side. The innocent gesture shouldn't have gripped his attention, but this woman had him in a total trance.

Emails and damage control forgotten, Gabe set aside his phone. He had nothing else to be doing right this second except for admiring her as she watched her reflection.

Hell. This wasn't the time or the place to be getting uncomfortable in his jeans. Just who the hell was seducing whom here? But from the unsure look on her face—her brows were drawn, her mouth turned down in a frown—it seemed she had doubts about how damn perfect and sexy she looked.

"It's fine," he growled after what seemed like an hour of pure torture. "Can we wrap it up here?"

Hands on her hips, Chelsea glared at him from her reflection in the mirror. "I need to make sure I can breathe and sit without busting a seam, if you don't mind. It seems tight."

Actually he did mind, and it was damn tight…the dress and his pants. He should've gone to the antique store because this was pure hell. Then again, at least he had a heads-up for how she'd look when he had to escort her down the aisle. He'd hate to be all mouth agape and drooling in front of Shane and Brandee's friends and families.

The idea of Chelsea and him walking down the aisle shouldn't have made him feel awkward, yet it did. Weddings in general made him twitchy. That whole happily-ever-after wasn't for everyone; he'd even managed to dodge being in any type of wedding party his entire life. But there was no way he could say no to Shane, his very best friend.

The more Chelsea shifted and turned and smoothed her hands over those luscious curves, the more uncomfortable Gabe became.

Commotion behind him had him tearing his gaze from the mirror and glancing over his shoulder. A slew of teenage girls came in the door, chattering and giggling about homecoming and needing perfect dresses. He could not get out of there fast enough. Between the lace, the satin and the chatter in such high octaves, this place was sucking the testosterone right out of his body.

"This will just have to work because I don't have the time to do more measurements," Chelsea muttered as she stepped off the platform and headed back into her dressing room. "Give me two minutes and we'll be out of here."

Gabe came to his feet, more than ready to get the hell out. As he shoved his hands in his pockets and rocked back on his heels, he heard Chelsea mumbling and cursing from inside the dressing room. Seconds later, the door eased open just a crack.

"Um… I'm stuck."

He eyed the narrow strip of her face showing through the door. "'Scuse me?"

"The zipper," she whispered through gritted teeth. "The damn thing is stuck. Get the salesclerk to come help me."

Gabe glanced over his shoulder at the mayhem of teens and fluffy dresses. The two workers were running in all directions accommodating parents and demanding girls.

He could do this. How hard would it be to get a zipper unstuck? Pulling in a deep breath, Gabe pushed open the dressing room door and offered up his assistance.

Three

"Gabe. What—?"

She backed up and stared as he shut and locked the door behind him. The narrow space seemed to shrink even more with his broad frame filling the area.

"You said you needed help."

Chelsea crossed her arms over her chest. "I said to get the salesclerk."

"Well, darlin', there's about a dozen teenage girls out there and only two staff that I saw. That's not a great ratio, so if you want out of this dress anytime in the next few hours, I'm it."

That gleam in his eye was just about the naughtiest, sexiest thing she'd ever seen. Which was one of the many reasons she shouldn't be closed in with him, and definitely why he shouldn't help unzip her dress. Being half-naked and in close proximity with Gabe would only lead to…

She couldn't even let her mind wander down that path.

"I'll do it myself," she claimed, though she'd already tried that. "Go on to the antique store and I'll be right over."

Gabe took one step and was right against her. "We both have other things to do today, so you might as well let me help you out."

"You seem to be enjoying this a little too much."

His hand skimmed up her side where the zipper was carefully hidden. "I'll be enjoying this even more if you'd let me work this zipper down."

The image that immediately popped into her head had Chelsea thinking for a half second of lifting her arm and letting him have a go. But then she remembered who he was...or rather who his uncle had been.

"This isn't a good idea," she told him. Surely he saw that...didn't he? He knew her feelings and knew full well she didn't trust him.

"What's not a good idea?" he asked, his eyes traveling over her face, landing on her lips. "Us in this confined space alone or the fact that you're attracted to me?"

Chelsea fisted her hands at her sides—to keep from hitting him or grabbing his face and kissing him, she wasn't sure. Her attraction wouldn't be such an issue if Gabe wasn't a Walsh. If his uncle hadn't tried to destroy so many lives, hers included. The guilt by association was enough to have her emotionally pulling back.

But the sizzling attraction didn't let up, no matter how much she tried to shove it aside.

Chelsea's body trembled, betraying her vow to keep him at a distance. When his fingers skimmed over her again, he quirked a half smile as he brought his eyes back up to meet hers.

"Is this the part where you deny your attraction?" he

asked, still using those clever hands. His fingertips circled around to where the dress exposed her back.

Chelsea sucked in a breath and cursed every single goose bump that popped up along her skin. They were both fully clothed, yet his fingertips on her bare back was something too akin to a lover's touch. And it had been too damn long since she'd taken a lover; she was clearly letting this affect her more than it should.

She'd not made the best choices in men. When she'd been younger, she confused attention with attraction. Then as she'd gotten older she'd distanced herself because she didn't trust her judgment. The scandal had her more than hesitant at getting close to any man. Now, here she was attracted to a man who was the next of kin to the bastard who'd humiliated her.

"Turn around," he whispered in her ear.

Without thinking, she turned to face the mirror. Gabe stood directly behind her, his body practically plastered against hers and those fingers still roaming over her heated skin. His eyes met hers in the mirror as he raised his other hand to the top of the zipper. Just the brush of his knuckles on the underside of her arm had her shivering even though the thick material served as a barrier.

Chelsea closed her eyes, hoping that if she didn't have to look at their reflection she could ignore this entire moment.

"Look at me," he demanded.

She gave in way too easily as her gaze met his once again. "Stop," she muttered.

"Stop what exactly?" He gave the zipper the slightest tug. "Stop helping you out of this dress or stop tormenting us both?"

She'd never been one to think of having sex in a public place, but right at this moment, she'd give just about anything to alleviate this ache caused by a man she shouldn't want.

"You had to know when we kissed that there would be more," he whispered. Though he didn't need to keep his voice down. The chaos of teen girls on the other side of that locked door drowned out anything they were saying...or doing.

"There can't be more."

The zipper gave way just as he brushed his lips along the side of her neck. Chelsea's body betrayed her...much as it had ever since Gabe had stepped foot into this tiny room. Closing her eyes, she dropped her head against his shoulder. Maybe she just wanted to take this moment, maybe she wanted to ignore everything and let him pleasure her. He was doing a damn fine job already.

Why did she have to be so torn? Why did he have to be such a mystery?

The hand on her back came around to her throat, tipping her head just enough for him to trail his lips over her exposed skin. He continued to work on her zipper just as expertly as he heated her up. She was about one strategically placed kiss away from moaning.

"Don't lie to me again and tell me you don't want me," he murmured in her ear. "You're shaking in my arms and I haven't even gotten you out of this dress yet."

He cupped her jaw and turned her head toward him. As his mouth crashed onto hers, Chelsea turned in his arms, threading her fingers through his hair and taking what he so freely gave.

Just for a minute. That was all. Then she'd go back to loathing him and believing he was a liar. But right now, common sense and reality had no place here.

Nothing lied about his lips or the hands that roamed

all over her body. He wanted her just as fiercely as she wanted him.

Gabe backed her against the wall and gripped her hips, pulling her toward him. His arousal was obvious.

If he lit her up this quickly, this intensely, what would happen once they were skin to skin? Would he take his time and savor the moment? Would he—?

"Excuse me?" A knock came on the door. "We have several girls who need to try some things on."

Gabe eased back slightly and muttered under his breath. Chelsea wanted the floor to open up and swallow her whole. First, there'd been the naked pictures and now she'd been pretty much caught getting it on in the dressing room of the only bridal shop in town. Could she provide more fodder for the gossip mill? Maybe she should parade down the main street of Royal in the buff.

"My zipper was stuck," she called out, realizing how lame that sounded. "Be right out."

Chelsea pushed Gabe back, but he couldn't go far considering the narrow space. "Either help me with the rest of this zipper or get out."

His dark eyes were heavy with arousal, the bulge in his jeans an added reminder of what they'd nearly done. Heat crept up her neck and flushed her face. She reached to the side of her dress and found that he'd actually gotten the zipper all the way down. When had that happened? Likely somewhere between that first touch and when he'd nearly kissed her to orgasm.

"Your work here is done," she told him, more than ready to get out of this dress and back into her jeans and boots.

Gabe took one step toward her, framed her face in his hands and leaned to within a breath of her mouth. "My work with you hasn't even started."

Releasing her, he stepped from the room and out the door just as casual as you please. Chelsea sank onto the tiny accent chair in the corner and took a deep breath. Right now the least of her worries was the people on the other side of that door when she walked out.

No, her greatest concern was the man who'd just left her aching even more than before. Nobody had ever gotten her so worked up, and here she was still trembling and in desperate need for him to finish the job.

Damn it. How was she going to keep her distance while they worked on this wedding, and not fall into bed with Gabe Walsh?

Four

Gabe shut down his laptop and came to his feet. It had been two days since his close encounter with Chelsea at the bridal shop and he was no closer to finding relief than he was then.

The damn woman had gotten to him. Perhaps it was her sassy mouth, or maybe it was the fact she hadn't initially believed him when he'd said he was in no way involved in leaking those nude photos. Maybe it was the way she wore jeans and tanks like they were made for her. Hell, he didn't know. All Gabe knew was that Chelsea Hunt was an enigma that he simply couldn't solve.

He'd been a damn special agent and still he couldn't figure out how someone as smart-mouthed and difficult as Chelsea had gotten under his skin. He could find any woman to scratch his itch, but he wasn't that guy any-more. In his twenties, he'd been selfish, falling into the bed of any willing woman. He was more particular now, definitely busier with work. And no one had pulled at him like Chelsea Hunt. So, no. No other woman would do.

But right now he had a few other pressing matters. Several of his clients had questioned him about his connection to his uncle. He'd already spoken with quite a few of them and he wasn't done yet. Gabe planned to spend the rest of his day running interference and hopefully smoothing ruffled feathers.

He grabbed his hat and headed out the door of his loft apartment. He loved the prime location in downtown Royal. There were shops, restaurants, and it wasn't too far from the Texas Cattleman's Club. He planned to head over later to get some riding in. Getting on the back of a horse and taking off into the fresh air always calmed him and helped to clear his mind.

The only drawback to living in a loft in town was that he couldn't have his own horses. Growing up outside Dallas on a working farm had been every little boy's dream, and riding had been a staple in his life. At least being a member of the Texas Cattleman's Club offered him anything he could want, including access to the club's stables. So he had the best of both worlds right now.

Gabe's cell vibrated in his pocket as he headed to the garage beneath his loft apartment. Pulling it out, he glanced at the screen and swiped to answer.

"Shane. What's up?"

"Just checking in on you, man. How are you holding up with all the fallout from your uncle?"

Gabe tightened his grip on the phone and resisted the urge to groan. "It's been a bit of a nightmare, but nothing I can't handle."

"Brandee and I are here for you, whatever you need. We know you'd never have a hand in anything this scandalous and cruel."

Gabe slid his sunglasses from the top of his head and settled them in place. "I'm doing damage control with the company. There's not much else anyone can do. I appreciate the offer."

"Of course. I hate how all this is happening on top of the wedding details," Shane added.

"Not a big deal. Like I said, nothing I can't handle."

"Speaking of wedding details, my fiancée is not happy."

Gabe laughed as he settled in behind the wheel of his truck. "Sounds like your problem, not mine."

"Oh, it's every bit your problem," Shane corrected. "Were you in the dressing room at the bridal shop with Chelsea? Wait, I know the answer to that. What the hell were you thinking, man?"

Blowing out a sigh, Gabe started the engine. "Does it matter? Nothing happened. Her zipper was stuck, that's all."

Well, that was all he'd own up to. Whatever was brewing between Chelsea and him was their business. As much as he'd like to claim there was more, things hadn't progressed near to where he wanted them. This was the slowest form of torture and foreplay he'd ever experienced in his life.

"Listen, whatever you do with anyone else is fine."

"Glad I have permission, Dad."

"But," Shane went on, "Chelsea is different. After what she's been through and with her being Brandee's best friend, this is a little more delicate than you just messing around with any other woman."

"I'm well aware of how vulnerable Chelsea is." Anger simmered as Gabe clenched the steering wheel. "And we're not messing around. How the hell did you find out anyway?"

Because he knew for a fact Chelsea wouldn't have run to Brandee and spilled. Even though this was perfect girly gossip, Gabe liked to think he knew Chelsea pretty well and this wasn't the type of chatter she'd take part in.

"You think a shop full of teens and their mothers didn't know you or Chelsea?" Shane asked in disbelief. "This town isn't that big, man. And if I know about it, you don't think Daniel hasn't heard by now?"

Daniel Hunt, Chelsea's brother. Chelsea's older, over-protective brother. He and Chelsea had been through so much with the loss of their parents. Everyone knew their mother had run out on them and their father had passed a year later, some said from a broken heart. Was it any wonder Chelsea was so closed off, so leery and untrusting? Add in the scandal over the photos and she'd had quite a bit thrown at her. More than most people should endure. And other than Daniel and Brandee, who did she have to lean on?

"I'm not worried about Daniel," Gabe said as he put his truck in gear. "As much as I'd love to continue this cheery conversation, I have other things to get done. Even in death, my uncle is ruining my reputation."

Shane blew out a sigh. "Sorry, man. I wasn't thinking."

"No reason to be sorry. You and Brandee were victims, as well."

Hell, there was hardly a member of the TCC who hadn't been affected somehow by his uncle. Gabe still had no clue as to his motives, but he knew Dusty Walsh had been denied membership to the exclusive club three times over the years. And when women had been admitted, it had only made Dusty's grudge worsen.

Perhaps this was his uncle's way of getting back at the club because of the board's decision. Who knew? All Gabe did know was that it would continue to impact his reputation for some time and he'd have to stay on top of things to keep his security business running.

"Just try to calm down with the public displays," Shane warned. "Chelsea is dealing with enough and I'd really like this wedding to go off without drama."

Gabe knew exactly what Chelsea was dealing with and he cursed himself for putting her in such a position. But, damn it, when he was around her, all logical thinking just vanished.

"Your wedding will be drama-free," Gabe assured his best friend. "Go kiss your fiancée and let her know Chels and I have everything under control."

He disconnected the call before Shane could question him further. As much as Gabe wanted to concentrate on Chelsea, on the memory of her sweet body pressed against his and her zipper parting beneath his touch, he had a high-dollar client to see.

Business first. Business always came first. Then he'd check up on his girl.

"I'll make sure they're delivered here if you don't mind being on hand to put everything away in the freezer. They'll come packaged with instructions for how long they need to sit out to thaw and the exact way they should be marinated and cooked."

Chelsea was going over the to-do list for the joint bachelor/bachelorette party with Rose, her contact in the TCC kitchen. Rose smiled and nodded as Chelsea ticked the items in her head off on her fingers.

"I'm sorry," Chelsea said. "I'm sure you know how to cook a steak and this isn't the first party you've done, but this is my company and my best friend we're talking about."

Chelsea may have been the CTO of Hunt & Co., dealing with the computers and the technical end of the business, but she knew how to handle steaks, as well. There were good steaks and then there were Hunt steaks. Chelsea wanted absolutely the best for her friends and that could only come from her family's company.

Rose patted Chelsea's arm. "It's quite all right, dear. I understand."

Chelsea smiled. "Thanks. I promise I'm only neurotic because I want this to be perfect for them."

"And it will be," Rose assured her. "I'll take care of everything."

Chelsea headed from the kitchen area. Since her workday was essentially done, she figured she'd take advantage of her club membership and go riding. She needed the break from reality and being on the back of a horse was always so freeing. It helped to clear her head.

She definitely needed her head cleared because for the past two days she hadn't been able to focus on anything other than Gabe Walsh. The stubborn man wouldn't leave her mind. He took up entirely too much real estate in her thoughts. She'd tried throwing herself further into the wedding planning. She'd tried reading books. She'd even resorted to her old hacking skills and messed with her brother's social media accounts for fun. But nothing had taken away the memory of the dressing room.

The Dressing Room.

It was like the title of an epic romance she couldn't put down. For one, she'd never had a public make-out session. Two, she hadn't allowed any man to wrap her up so tight she feared she'd spring any minute. And for another, damn it…she just wanted to hate the man. Was that too much to ask? He was egotistical, arrogant…and too damn sexy for his own good.

But she couldn't bring herself to hate the way he

kissed, the way he'd touched her. How was it even possible that he had this hold on her? How could one man invoke so many emotions?

Chelsea headed toward the stables. The fresh winter air filled her lungs. She couldn't wait to spend the next few hours just relaxing and enjoying her ride.

When her cell vibrated in her pocket, she ignored it. Nothing was going to get in the way of this much needed alone time. Whoever wanted her could leave a message. If it was Daniel again, she'd get back to him. Any Hunt business could wait since it was after hours. And there was nothing pressing for the wedding at the moment.

In no time, Chelsea had chosen a gorgeous chestnut mare and was on her way. Getting back in the saddle felt so good. It had been too long since she'd taken advantage of the amenities TCC had to offer. Maybe she should schedule a massage and some sauna time after the wedding and holidays were over. She could use a good day of pampering.

Chelsea was just thankful they'd started allowing women to join a few years ago. There was a time when only men were members, but everything had changed when they'd opened the doors and their minds to the ladies.

Chelsea had jumped at the chance to join such an elite club. Who wouldn't want to be part of all of this? The clubhouse sat on gorgeous acreage, the amenities were absolutely perfect and everyone worth anything in this town was a member. Perhaps that's why Dusty was never admitted. Chelsea didn't know him personally, but his actions before his death had proved the guy to be a grade-A bastard.

Settling into an easy rhythm with her horse, Chelsea found a trail and rode off, thankful that with evening falling, there were no other riders. The stables closed at nine, so she had a couple hours to enjoy the open air, the peaceful evening, and to start figuring out her Christmas shopping list because she still had a few people she hadn't bought for. Online shopping was going to be her best friend in these last days leading up to Christmas.

With all the wedding planning, she'd dropped the ball on—

"And here I thought I'd be all alone."

Chelsea cringed at the familiar voice, her grip tightening on the reins. "Then take another path."

Gabe's laughter floated around her as he came up beside her horse. "Now, what fun would that be?"

His thigh brushed hers as he kept a steady gait. Chelsea didn't want any part of his body touching hers. Okay, that was a lie, but if she kept repeating it over and over, maybe the words would penetrate her stubborn heart.

"I came out here to think and be alone," she told him, refusing to look his way. She knew what he looked like— all brooding and sexy—without tormenting herself any further.

"Then by all means, think," he stated. "You won't even know I'm here."

"Are you kidding me?"

She pulled her horse to a stop, not at all surprised when he did the same. Now, she did glance his way. Yup. Just as sexy as two days ago when he'd been wrapped all around her, driving her out of her mind. His black hat shielded his eyes, but not enough that she didn't see that sexy gleam.

"You think I can have a peaceful moment when you're right next to me?"

"Well, darlin', I'll take that as a compliment."

Chelsea narrowed her eyes. "Why won't you go away?"

He rested his forearm on the saddle horn and shrugged. "I haven't seen you for two days. I went by Hope Springs and worked more on the arch, thinking you'd show up and lend a hand, but you never did. I'd say you've had plenty of space."

"Not enough," she muttered.

"You can't hide from me forever, Chelsea. We've got work to do and this tension between us isn't going anywhere."

Why did he have to be so blunt and just lay their attraction right on the table like that? It wasn't often she was speechless, but the man was bound and determined to throw her off her game, and damn it, it was working.

"You seem angry." He offered her a killer smile. "I'd say this fresh air will do you some good. Come on. Ride with me and we'll talk. Not about the dressing room or the fact you want me, and don't deny it. We'll do small talk. We can do that, right? The weather is always a good topic, but so predictable. Maybe we could discuss if you've put your Christmas tree up yet. I haven't."

Was he seriously turning into some chatterbox? She wasn't going to ride along beside him and talk like he was some girlfriend she was comfortable with. Gabe Walsh made her anything but comfortable.

"I don't want to engage in small talk with you." Chelsea pulled the reins and turned her horse back toward the trail. "I can't stop you from riding, but shut up."

Again, his laughter swept over her as he came to an easy trot next to her. Chelsea concentrated on the rocking of the horse, the smell of the fresh air, and not the man a mere foot from her.

"There's something I've been curious about."

She never knew where his thoughts were headed, but it was obvious he was going to keep going no matter what she said, so she just remained quiet.

"Why computers?"

Chelsea turned toward him. "Excuse me?"

"Just wondering why you got into computers."

She should've known he wouldn't honor her wish for silence. But work she could discuss. That was one topic where he wouldn't make her a stuttering, turned-on mess of emotions.

"I've always been interested in how things work," she told him. "When I was little, I tried picking locks. I actually got quite good at it by the time I was seven, but then I grew bored. Dad was always talking business, so I knew we were being raised to take over. When I wasn't learning fast enough, I tried getting into his computer when he was asleep one night. By the time I figured out his password, I'd gotten a little thrill and decided to see what else I could do."

"How old were you then?"

"Ten."

Gabe swore under his breath. "And here I've pissed you off. Are my bank accounts safe?"

Chelsea couldn't stop the smile from spreading across her lips. "For now."

"Did your father know you'd gotten into his system?"

"Of course. I was sloppy, as all beginner hackers are." Chelsea brushed her hair back from her face, wishing she'd thought to put on a headband. "You know, I really don't like that term. It makes me feel… I don't know… illegal."

Gabe tossed her a look with one arched brow. "It pretty much is illegal."

With a shrug, Chelsea forced her attention to the

smooth path in front of her. "Maybe, but I've never done anything terrible with my knowledge. I more do things to see how far I can get and to educate myself."

"So you've never done anything risky or wrong?" he asked.

Chelsea pursed her lips. "I may have changed a couple grades when I was in high school."

"And?" he prompted.

She swallowed. Was she really going to get into this with him?

"I might have hacked into one bank account to add some funds."

"You think hacking into a bank isn't illegal or bad?" he asked, obviously shocked at her admission.

"I admit it was wrong, but hindsight won't change the past."

Silence settled between them and Chelsea figured she shouldn't have told him. It was years ago and nobody had ever figured out what she had done. It had been her first real victory and, illegal or not, she wasn't sorry she'd done it. In fact, she was rather proud of herself.

"Are you going to finish the story or leave me hanging?"

Chelsea came to a stop and glanced toward a nearby cypress grove. Restless energy had her dismounting and tying the reins around a sturdy tree trunk. Gabe did the same and when he propped his hands on his hips and continued to stare at her, she figured she may as well tell him everything.

Five

Sweet, innocent-looking Chelsea had shocked him, but he was more than ready to hear what she had to say. If she claimed her hacking was for good reason, he believed her. He'd built the foundation of his career on reading people and was pretty confident she wasn't vindictive. And he wanted to continue spending time with her. She was opening up. Apparently when they weren't discussing the scandal that had rocked the town, she let her guard slip. He only hoped he could wipe his uncle's actions out of the picture for good.

"There was a husband and wife who worked for Hunt back when I was a teen." Chelsea tucked a stray strand of hair behind her ear and turned to rest against a tree away from the horses. "He had a gambling problem. She was pregnant with their first child, but tried to stick by him despite his addiction. I know my father offered to pay for help if the guy would just go. But, in the end, life became too much and he left her. She couldn't make the mortgage payments on her own and lost her house."

Gabe heard the compassion in Chelsea's tone. This was a whole new side to her he hadn't seen and it only made him want to uncover even more. He'd always figured she was giving, caring, selfless. His instincts hadn't proved him wrong before and they were dead-on now.

"She had her own income, but considering she was pregnant with no home, I couldn't stand it anymore." Chelsea's mouth twisted into a half grin. "I may have hacked into his private account and removed funds. And those funds *may* have found their way into her account."

Gabe honestly didn't know what to say. The woman was constantly a doer. She cared for others and wanted to see everyone around her happy. But he'd never thought once that she'd use her skills for something like this.

"Had you gotten caught—"

Her eyes met his. "At the time, I felt it was worth the risk. Now that I look back, I know it wasn't right to do that, but I got caught up in the moment and acted with my heart instead of my head."

She gave a slight shrug before she continued. "I just thought, what was he going to do? Tell the authorities? Most of his money was obtained illegally, because I uncovered that he was betting on cock fighting. He wouldn't want to open that can of worms and be subjected to proving where his income came from."

Chelsea's eyes misted. "All of that happened around the time when we'd just lost Mom. Actually, she ran off, but she may as well be dead because I haven't seen or heard from her since. I knew what that felt like, what being abandoned does to your soul. I couldn't stand it, Gabe."

Why did she have to have such a vulnerable side that

made resisting her impossible? He'd promised himself when he'd seen her riding up ahead that he'd keep his hands off, but the sorrow lacing her words only had him closing the gap between them.

"You shouldn't touch me. I'm emotional already and if you touch me…"

Her words were barely a whisper and he saw tears swimming in her eyes.

"This is just one friend consoling another," he explained.

Gabe wrapped his arms around her and she instantly returned the gesture. "We're not friends," she argued.

Smiling, he rested his chin on top of her head. "Maybe not, but we're something. I don't think they've created a label for us yet."

When she continued to just be still and let him hold her, Gabe figured she must be gathering her strength. She just needed a minute and he was all too willing to comfort her. As much as he wanted to get her into his bed, he could be patient. Chelsea would be worth the wait.

Hell, his job was based on patience and taking his time, being methodical. And he knew she was much more important than a job. Damn it. When had he let that happen?

Chelsea eased back and glanced up at him. "I'm not sure I can trust you."

Gabe smoothed her hair back and framed her face. "You will."

"Are you always so arrogant?"

Gabe smiled because her tone was light, but her question was genuine. "Confident," he corrected. "I know I did nothing wrong where you're concerned and, in time, you'll realize that, too."

Her eyes darted to his lips and he knew he'd just

knocked another brick off that barrier she kept around herself. She still clung to him and Gabe's last shred of control snapped.

He eased closer, keeping his eyes on hers as he lowered his head. "You plan on stopping me?" he whispered against her mouth.

"Not yet."

The second he covered her mouth, she melted against him. There was no other way to describe the way she simply let go and let him take the lead. But he wasn't naïve. Chelsea held all the power here. As much as he wanted her and was more than ready to seduce her up against this tree, she would ultimately have to give the green light.

Gabe rested one hand on her hip and thrust the other through her hair as he shifted his head and dove back in for more. More was the theme where Chelsea was concerned. He wanted as much as she would give…then he wanted even more.

She arched against him, groaning into his mouth. Gabe trailed his lips across her jaw and down the column of her throat. The neckline of her tank top mocked him, tempted him. So much exposed skin to explore… and still not enough. But he had to tread lightly. Chelsea wasn't just any woman, and their situation was extremely delicate.

"Gabe, please."

Easing back slightly, he took in her flushed cheeks and decided he couldn't leave her hanging. He was a gentleman, after all, and as gently as he needed to treat her, he also planned on giving in to her every desire.

"You don't have to ask twice."

Sliding his hand beneath the hem of her tank, Gabe kept his eyes locked on hers. If she showed the slightest bit of hesitation, he'd stop. But the way she bit on her lower lip and kept her eyes shut, he had to believe he was doing everything right.

He flicked the closure on her jeans, pleased when her hips surged forward. Glancing over his shoulder, he made sure no one was taking a late ride. But they were hidden behind the horses and around the side of a large cypress.

Gabe slid his hand inside the waistband of her panties and kicked her feet apart with the toe of his boot. He rested his forearm alongside her head, against the tree, and dipped his fingers into her heat. The moment she cried out, he covered her mouth with his.

Yes. Finally, this. He had wanted to see her come apart, had wanted to experience every bit of it, and now she was seconds away. He didn't want to just feel it, he wanted to taste it.

Chelsea's fingertips dug into his shoulders as she jerked her body against his. Then she exploded. There was no other way to describe it. She tore away from the kiss and tipped her head back, her mouth open in a perfect O as she clung to him.

Chelsea Hunt was letting every single guard down and giving in to her desires, and it was absolutely the most erotic thing he'd ever seen. He wished he could watch her forever, but he quickly pushed the idea aside. Forever wasn't in his vocabulary.

As she came down and her trembling ceased, Gabe knew for certain that he needed her in his bed. His entire body was wound so damn tight, but he'd have to wait. This was about Chelsea, about her needs and getting her to see that he was serious about this all-consuming need to have her.

But most of all, he wanted her to realize that he wasn't a liar and had never done anything to hurt her or to tarnish her reputation.

The horses shifted behind him and Gabe started to lean forward to kiss her, but she pushed against his shoulders. Her bold green eyes lifted to his and he instantly saw regret.

They'd made too much progress for her to have those walls come back up. Little by little, he was going to make sure she pushed beyond her fears. Why did she have to start letting her doubts and reality sink back in?

He removed his hand and stepped back, giving her a chance to right her clothes.

"I'm not going to apologize."

Her hands froze on the snap of her jeans as she glared up at him. "I didn't ask you to."

"You're angry."

"With myself. Not you."

Well, that was something. But he didn't want her in any way angry about this situation.

"Are you upset because you let yourself feel or because you hate me?"

She finished straightening her clothes and shoved her hair behind her ears. That defiant chin lifted an extra notch as she squared her shoulders and focused solely on him.

"I don't hate you," she retorted. "I just don't make a habit of getting involved with people I'm still on the fence about."

Raking a hand through his hair, he turned away and headed back to his stallion.

"You're not going to say anything?" she called after him.

Gabe tugged at the reins and freed his horse from the tree before glancing back over his shoulder. "You want to fight? You'll have to look elsewhere. A beautiful woman just came apart in my arms. I'm not feeling much like arguing. I want to be here for you, Chelsea. Not because my uncle tried to ruin you and so many others, but because I can't ignore this pull between us or what just happened."

He mounted the horse and turned him toward the stables, but held tight on the reins to keep him in place. "You riding back with me or alone?"

Still flushed and sexy as hell, Chelsea stared up at him. "Unless there's wedding business to attend to, we're better off returning separately."

He had a feeling she'd say something like that. It was expected, but that didn't lessen his frustration any.

Gabe rested his elbow on his knee and leaned down. "You can push me away, but that won't stop what's happening."

A rumble of thunder had him glancing toward the sky then back down to her. "Better get back. Storm's comin'."

He just hoped like hell they could weather it.

Chelsea dropped her keys onto the accent table inside her doorway and wiped her damp hair away from her face. The pop-up storm matched her mood—fierce and full of rage.

The lightning flashed, illuminating her open floor plan as she made her way inside. No sense in turning on the lights. They were set on a timer, anyway, and apparently her electricity had gone out because nothing was on in the entire place.

Perfect. Her phone needed to be charged and she'd wanted to take a hot bath and ignore the world…and the throb between her legs. Because as much as she tried to ignore what had just happened, it was impossible. Gabe was impossible. The stupid man was making her feel things, making her body hum and come alive like never before—all while they were still fully dressed. Her body still sizzled from the orgasm against the tree.

Chelsea made her way to her bedroom using what little battery she had left on her phone to light the way.

First, the man had tried to get it on with her in a dressing room and then he'd pleasured her at the damn club. He was slick, seductive and she'd loved every single minute of both experiences.

Well, she'd loved the way he'd physically made her feel, but the mental side…

Why did he have to keep messing with her head?

Everything circled back to Dusty and how he'd been so meticulous in planting evidence to ruin lives and pointing the finger of blame in so many different directions. The scandal had rocked the entire town and Chelsea wasn't sure she'd ever recover, if she were being honest.

It was humiliating to walk down the street and wonder if passersby had seen the photos of her naked.

Tears filled her eyes once again. She'd shed too many tears caused by a whole gamut of emotions. She'd cried from anger, from frustration, from hurt and resentment… so many things. And she'd had to do it all in private because her very best friend wanted and deserved the wedding of the year and there was no way Chelsea would ruin this monumental moment for her.

Chelsea's cell vibrated in her hand just as she hit her bedroom. When she glanced at the screen, she saw a text from her brother and a missed call from him earlier. With only an eight percent charge left on her battery, she opted to ignore it all. Not that she wouldn't have, anyway.

She definitely wasn't in the mood to talk to Daniel. She loved him and his fiancée, Erin, but right now she just wanted to get into pajamas and lie in bed. With the lightning flashing outside, soaking in her garden tub wasn't the smartest idea. It wasn't late, but late enough, and with the electricity gone, she could at least lie down and read on her electronic reader.

But as she sank to the edge of her bed, all she could think of was how amazing Gabe had made her feel. The man was so, so giving. All the focus had been on her and then, when she'd wanted to battle it out because she'd had no clue what to do with all her emotions, he'd walked away. Some might have said that was cowardly, but she saw it as gentlemanly. He hadn't wanted to make things more difficult than they already were.

Either that, or he'd just wanted to seduce her and that was all.

Unfortunately, she didn't think that was the case. She truly believed he wanted her. That he wanted to get closer to her, and not just for the sex. Yes, Gabe was often seen as a man of mystery, but she was starting to see him for so much more.

All of those reasons were precisely why she was so angry. She'd been furious with him back at the club. No, she'd been furious with herself. It wasn't his fault that when he touched her she went off like a rocket. It wasn't his fault that she'd never had a lover like him before.

Wait. Lover? No. They weren't going to have sex. They *couldn't* have sex. That would go against everything she'd vowed to herself. She wasn't even fully convinced of his innocence in his uncle's controversy, which was all the more reason she needed to keep her distance.

But how could she?

Six

The scream echoed through the barn and made his ears ring. Gabe spun around and spotted Brandee in the doorway, the sunlight illuminating her.

"That is going to be so gorgeous," she squealed as she raced across the open space.

Gabe glanced back at the arch, which he'd just finished. Well, he'd finished the framing and the structure. He'd texted Chelsea to come by later to do the actual decorating because that was not part of his skill set.

"You guys are really going above and beyond," Brandee exclaimed, getting misty-eyed as she came to stand beside him. Her eyes fixed on the arch before her.

Gabe wrapped an arm around her shoulders and pulled her in for a friendly hug. "It's no trouble at all. I'm just glad you've made my best friend so happy."

Disgustingly happy. These two were absolutely perfect for each other. Gabe hadn't believed people could be so in love; he hadn't actually believed in that emotion at all, but if it existed, Brandee and Shane were wrapped up tight with it.

"Where's Chelsea?" Brandee asked, easing back.

It had been three days since he'd seen her and he was getting rather twitchy—not something he wanted to explain to her best friend. He could barely explain his feelings to himself. He wanted Chelsea, but the fierce need that continued to grow inside him was something new. He'd wanted women before, but not like this. The strength she displayed, her loyalty to her friends and her intelligence were all huge turn-ons. There was nothing about her he didn't find mesmerizing.

Originally he'd wondered if it was because he felt sorry for her because of Dusty's actions. But Gabe had quickly discovered that he didn't feel sorry for Chelsea. He admired her. She had a strength he couldn't help but find attractive. She had a take-charge attitude and then, on top of that, with her sexy-as-hell looks, he couldn't help but be drawn.

"I'm sure she's working," he replied. "I told her this would be ready to go today for the flowers or whatever it is you want to decorate it with. I just needed to get the base sturdy enough."

Brandee stepped forward and ran her hand over the oak grain. "This is far more than I'd envisioned and it's not even done. I can't wait for my wedding day."

Gabe hooked his thumbs through his belt loops and rocked back on his heels. "I'm sure Chelsea will be by soon. I texted her earlier."

Brandee tossed him a grin and raised her brows. "You two taking shifts on the wedding preparations? Is that because of the whole dressing room issue?"

On the one hand, he wasn't surprised at all that she'd brought up the incident. On the other hand, he was sure as hell glad she didn't know about their session at the Texas Cattleman's Club. Gabe wanted to keep the stolen moments with Chelsea to himself. They were private and, until he could figure out what the hell they were doing, he wanted to keep things that way.

"I doubt it," he answered with a slight laugh. "She doesn't seem like the type to run over something like that. But I think this attraction has her being extra cautious."

"Attraction?" Brandee said, her brows shooting up and a smile spreading across her face. "Well, she needs something to keep her mind off the bad press caused by those photos. I think it's great you two are working together."

Oh, he did, too. Because when he and Chelsea were together, he couldn't keep his hands to himself and, for the most part, Chelsea wasn't complaining, at least until she started letting her mind take over.

Damn it. He wanted the hell out of her and she still wanted to keep him at a distance. Someone was going to lose this fight…and he'd never lost yet.

"She's still unsure about trusting me," Gabe went on. "She's learning, but given my last name and all, her hesitancy is more than justified."

"You were cleared of any wrongdoing," Brandee said. "Besides, anyone who knows you would never believe for a second you had anything to do with releasing those photos. Shane and I couldn't believe when your name was even mentioned."

"I appreciate that. I would never do something so vile," he declared. "I'm just as disgusted by my uncle's actions as anyone. He's gone and now I'm the one carrying his family name and trying to keep my reputation as far removed from his as possible."

"You're a victim, too," she stated.

Yeah. He was. If only Chelsea could see things from

that angle. But he wasn't one to play the pity card. He didn't want her pity—he wanted her in his bed.

"I'm glad you're here, actually." He was happy to change the subject, he legitimately had something he needed to tell her. "Your wedding present will be arriving tomorrow. It isn't exactly something I could've brought to the reception."

Brandee tipped her head and smiled. "You know you didn't have to get us anything. You and Chels are doing so much already. The load you have lifted from Shane and me is immeasurable."

Gabe shrugged. "Trust me when I say you will want this."

Besides, his uncle had caused so many problems for Brandee and Shane months ago. Their relationship almost hadn't made it at all, let alone to the altar. Gabe was all too happy to give them this extravagant present. They were his friends and Brandee had such a huge heart, giving back so much to the community.

Brandee ran a camp for teens in need. She used her time and her own funding to keep the place on her ranch open for impressionable teens, and it was time she didn't have to carry so much of the load on her own.

"What's that smile for?" she asked.

"Just anxious for a little surprise I have planned," he replied. "Now, if you'll excuse me, I have some business to attend to. Chelsea may be here later."

As he started to head out of the barn, Brandee called out to him, "She's more vulnerable than you think."

Gabe stilled. He knew how fragile Chelsea was, but hearing her best friend confirm it made him wonder what hurt Chelsea kept inside.

He threw a glance over his shoulder. "She's also stronger than you think."

And he wanted her to trust him. Whether she liked it or not, he would protect her. She was done doing everything alone.

Chelsea leaned back in her desk chair in her home office and stared at the bright screen of her laptop. She'd kept tabs on her mother for a year or so now. She'd made sure not to do anything illegal, but some simple investigative work by someone of her skill level...well, it hadn't been too difficult to turn up Shonda Hunt. Or rather, Shonda Patton, since she remarried.

Bitterness burned like acid in Chelsea's gut. She hated that her mother had run out on them. Chelsea had never fully known the reason why and it wasn't a topic she had ever brought up to her father before he'd passed. The poor man had been devastated after his wife left, so much so, he'd died a year later of a heart attack. Chelsea had always figured he'd been so crushed he'd lost his will to go on.

She continued staring at the image she'd uncovered of Shonda and her husband. It was a random photo from a newspaper in Kansas. They were on a park bench attending a town festival or something. There her mother was, enjoying the life she wanted.

Trust didn't come easy to Chelsea and staring back at her was the very reason why. When a foundation was shaken and everything you ever knew turned out to be a lie, it was difficult to see another way, let alone try to rebuild on uneven ground.

The spiral Chelsea spun into after her mother had left had been a cry for help, but her actions, no matter how troubled, had ultimately led her to become the woman she was today. She was damn good at her job and refused to let anyone have control over her life ever again.

That included Gabe Walsh. He'd been smart to keep their interaction to texts these past few days, but part of her really wanted to get into that verbal sparring match she was gearing up for. He had texted earlier that he wanted to talk, but he hadn't said when and he hadn't said why.

How could one man turn her on and infuriate her at the same time?

Closing out her screen, Chelsea came to her feet and secured the knot on her robe. She was done spying on Shonda. Chelsea refused to call her *mother*, because that woman didn't exist. Chelsea knew she needed to let it go and move forward. She had a lucrative career that she loved and she was planning her best friend's wedding. She didn't need anything more.

Right?

Unfortunately, there was that young girl living inside her that wanted answers. That impressionable girl needed to know what she could do to ever fill the void of abandonment.

Chelsea had just stepped into her living room when the doorbell rang. She glanced at the large clock on her mantel and wondered who would be dropping by unannounced at nine at night.

She smoothed her hands down her robe and pulled the lapels a little tighter to her chest. A quick glance out the sidelight caused Chelsea's heart rate to kick up. She pulled in a deep breath and flicked the lock.

When she swung the door wide, she expected Gabe to just walk on in. Instead he gave her a head-to-toe appraisal and propped his arm on the door frame. It caused his bicep to tighten, which only drew her attention to his excellent muscle tone.

"I do like how you greet your guests."

"A heads-up text would've been considerate," she stated, crossing her arms.

The corner of his mouth kicked up. "I texted earlier and said I wanted to talk."

She couldn't help but laugh. "Specifics would've been nice."

"I'll remember that for next time."

He pushed off the frame, but continued to stand in the light of the porch. "But I'm here now and I want you to understand there's no reason to be afraid of what's going on between us. I know you've been dealt a bad hand lately and I also know you're strong. I'd never push you, but I also won't let you run."

Chelsea opened her mouth but Gabe held his hand up to stop her. "I get that you're still reeling from what Dusty did. I even understand that trusting me at first was difficult, but we're past that, aren't we?"

"You confuse me," she whispered. "I can't get into this right now, Gabe. I need to think."

She started to shut the door but he was quicker. His fingers curled around the edge and held it open.

"I want you so much," he replied, stepping in closer until she had to tip her head back to look into those mesmerizing eyes. "Which is why I'm putting the next step on you."

Confused, Chelsea jerked back. "What?"

"There's nothing I want more than to cross this threshold and peel you out of that robe, but I want you to take control. I want you to ache just as much as I do. Because when we finally make it to a bedroom, it will be your decision."

Chelsea swallowed. Her body stirred at his words and his boldness. "Is that why you came here?" she asked, shocked her voice sounded strong at all. "To tell me that we're going to have sex?"

Gabe raked a hand over his face and blew out a breath. "I came here to tell you that I'm not going to coddle you. You're a strong woman and you don't want pity over what happened. I get that you want to be respected, and I respect you. So if anything happens from here on out, it's your call."

Chelsea opened her mouth then closed it.

"Speechless?" he asked with a slight grin. "That wasn't the reaction I expected."

"What did you expect?"

"Well, you didn't slam the door in my face, so I'm already a step above where I thought I'd be."

She bit the inside of her cheek to keep from smiling, but failed.

"And a sexy grin? Hell, I better leave while I'm ahead."

Chelsea tucked her hair behind her ears and took a step back. As much as she wanted to invite him in and take him up on what he was offering, she also had to be smart. She'd never been a woman to just sleep with someone for the sake of getting it out of her system. Then again, no one had ever tempted her the way Gabe Walsh had.

"Do you want me to do anything for the wedding?" he asked, his tone softer as he stared into her eyes. "I have a few hours free tomorrow if you need anything."

"Well, I'm almost done with the arch. I've planned for the steaks to be delivered the day before the bachelor/bachelorette party, so if you want to call and make sure the club has all of the staffing covered for that night, that would help. I just don't want them to be understaffed, because we're expecting quite a few people. The bartenders need to be the best, too. Make sure Tanner and Ellen are on the list to serve."

Gabe nodded. "I can do that. Didn't you message me about some chair covers you wanted picked up?"

Chair covers, yes. She'd forgotten all about those. Maybe it had something to do with the man who stood before her because the past couple of weeks he'd been consuming so much of her time, both in person and in her thoughts. But they needed chair covers for the party. Something elegant, yet something that would fit in at the club with all its dark wood and trophies.

"I can pick them up," she told him. Silence stretched between them and the tension stirred deep within her. "Is that all?"

He flashed her a devilish grin. "Unless you're ready to invite me in now and let me unwrap you."

Oh, she wanted to be unwrapped. Gabe could tempt a saint into stripping and doing naughty deeds.

Chelsea laughed and poked at his chest until he stepped back. "Good night, Gabe."

When he leaned in, Chelsea stilled. His lips feathered across her cheek. "Good night, Chels."

He turned and walked away, bounding down the steps and heading toward his truck. Chelsea closed the door, turning the dead bolt back into place, and rested her forehead against the wood.

What was she going to do about that man? He purposely kept her on her toes and tied up in knots. Part of her loved this catch-and-release game they were playing, but the other part didn't want to play games anymore. She wanted to know for sure that she could trust him. But how? How could she be certain?

Chelsea flicked off the light and headed for bed, knowing full well she wouldn't be getting any sleep tonight.

Seven

"What do you think?"

Chelsea stood back and stared at the archway that was covered in sheer, pale gold material, twinkling clear lights and delicate white flowers.

She then glanced over at her friend, who stood there staring and silent. Okay, maybe it didn't look as great as Chelsea had thought. This wasn't exactly her area of expertise, but she'd like to think it wasn't horrendous.

"It will look better at night for the ceremony when you can see the lights better," Chelsea rushed to say when the silence became too much. "I mean, I can change whatever you want. I'm not really a decorator, but I can look up other ideas—"

"It's perfect."

Chelsea breathed a sigh of relief. She'd honestly had to look at so many wedding planning websites, at images of elegant arches and Christmas-themed weddings just to piece together everything her friend would want.

The expression on Brandee's face made all of that digging worth it.

Because Chelsea had hated every second of searching through blissful pictures of couples deliriously in love. Not that she wasn't happy for Brandee and Shane, but part of her truly didn't believe in the hype of marriage or love. All of that had to be built on trust. But trusting someone with your whole life? No. That just wasn't going to happen. Not for her. And she was okay with living alone.

Chelsea ignored the niggling ache in her heart. Okay, maybe it would be nice to find someone to share her secrets with, to lie with at night and talk about absolutely nothing, to go on trips with and see the world. But all that would require her to fully open up and expose a part of herself she'd shut off far too long ago.

The sound of approaching vehicles had both women turning toward the large entrance to the barn. Brandee headed toward it and Chelsea followed.

As soon as she stepped outside, Chelsea's mouth dropped. There were six, brand-new, shiny white vans and three large pickup trucks sitting in the drive of the Hope Springs Ranch. The driver of the first van got out and crossed the yard toward Brandee.

"I'm looking for Ms. Lawson."

Brandee shielded her eyes from the sun. "That's me."

The middle-aged man held out a clipboard and pen. "I just need you to sign for the shipment of vehicles and let me know where you'd like them all parked. Do you want the keys left in the ignition or brought to you?"

"Excuse me?" she asked. "I didn't… I'm not sure…"

"Oh, I'm sorry," he said with a smile. "These are all paid in full from a Mr. Walsh. He said this was your wedding gift."

What in the world had Gabe done? All of this? He'd paid for every single vehicle here? They were brand-new, not a speck of dirt on any of them, and they were all for Brandee.

Chelsea's heart flipped.

"He said he had something being delivered, but..." Brandee trailed off as she stared at the fleet of new vehicles. "I can't believe he did this."

Chelsea was absolutely stunned. She couldn't take in everything at once. This was a...a *wedding gift*? Weren't you just supposed to get the bride and groom toasters and towels? This went so far above the items on any wedding registry, Chelsea didn't even know what to think.

Gabe had done all of this without fanfare and without mentioning a word to her. He hadn't wanted the recognition or the praise. The man had legitimately wanted to help out with Brandee's work with the teens. How could Chelsea sustain her anger toward him when he kept proving over and over how selfless he was?

Chelsea took in each vehicle as Brandee pointed to where they could be parked. The dollar signs were scrolling through her head. She'd known Gabe was wealthy—from his expensive loft apartment to his luxury cars to his expensive taste in bourbon—but she'd never thought for a second he could do something like this.

"Can you believe this?" Brandee asked when she came back to stand beside Chelsea. "He told me he was having something delivered. I thought maybe it was... I don't know, a horse."

Brandee laughed and raked her hand through her long hair. "I don't even know what to say. A thank-you card isn't even enough. These vehicles will make a huge difference in the camp for my teens. We'll be able to take in more kids."

Brandee's voice broke as she dissolved into tears. "Sorry," she said as she wiped her cheeks. "I'm an emotional mess with the wedding."

Chelsea turned to her friend and pulled her into a hug. "It's understandable. This is a big step in your life. You're entitled to a meltdown. And Gabe's gift was a bit unexpected."

Brandee eased back and smiled. "He's such a great guy, Chels. I spoke with him yesterday and he seemed…"

Chelsea stilled. "What?"

"I don't think it's a stretch to say he's interested in you."

Her friend's misty eyes met Chelsea's. She truly didn't want to have this conversation with anyone, let alone the woman standing there with cupid silhouettes practically bulging out of her eyes.

"He's a guy and I'm single." Chelsea figured shrugging it off would be safest at this point. "But, to answer your veiled question, we're just friends."

Friends who made out like teens in a dressing room. Why didn't she have a friend like him before?

Oh, right. She hadn't trusted him before.

The barrier she'd kept around her soul where Gabe was concerned cracked a little. Okay, more than a little. The very foundation shook. She wanted to give him the benefit of the doubt, and had actually started to.

"You're interested in him, too," Brandee murmured. "Don't bother denying it. This is more than a friendship."

Chelsea jerked her attention back to the moment. "You have too much love and wedding bliss on the mind to think clearly."

But her friend was absolutely correct. Whatever Chelsea and Gabe had going on, it was so much more than friendship. When he'd said there hadn't been a label created for them yet, he'd been accurate. Because they weren't really friends. She didn't trust him. Did she?

Chelsea said farewell to Brandee and headed out to her car. At this point she didn't *not* trust Gabe. The mental sparring match she continued to have with herself was exhausting.

As she drove toward downtown Royal, she realized she was tired of something else, too.

Fighting her needs.

Gabe's doorman had let Chelsea up nearly fifteen minutes ago. He stood at the floor-to-ceiling window, watching as the sun cast a bright orange glow across the horizon as he waited for her. People were starting to really fill the street. Couples were strolling hand-in-hand, heading into restaurants for dinner dates. The little town came alive at night—especially on a Friday.

He watched as people posed in front of the giant Christmas tree in the town square just a block away. The tree stood tall and proud, decorated with what seemed like a million clear lights. There would be an annual candlelight and caroling evening in less than two weeks. He loved this town, loved the traditions it upheld.

Before the doorman had called to announce Chelsea's surprise visit, Gabe had actually been getting ready to head out and grab a drink at the TCC to see who was spending their evening there. Though there likely weren't many people hanging out in the club's bar tonight. These days, nearly everyone was either married, engaged, caring for or expecting a baby.

So much had happened over the past year, both good and bad. Weddings, babies—all of that had brought families together. But the Maverick scandal still left a dark cloud over the club and the town.

Just this afternoon, he'd been in contact with the sheriff to see if there were any updates regarding Dusty's accomplice in planting the camera in the locker room. There had to have been someone and Gabe wanted to know who it was. Until that person was brought to justice, this nightmare wouldn't fully be over.

At least he had been cleared of any involvement early on in the investigation. And even more importantly, Chelsea had started trusting him more and more.

Something had changed Chelsea's mind about him, otherwise she wouldn't have come of her own accord to his loft.

Which made him wonder why she hadn't knocked on his door yet. Gabe had given the doorman a small list of guests who didn't need an okay from him before they were automatically rung up. Chelsea had been at the top of the list for over a month now. But the doorman had called Gabe fifteen minutes ago to tell him she was on her way up.

Yet his unexpected guest hadn't made her presence known to him. She was most likely hesitating out in the hallway, wondering why she'd come. He knew exactly why she'd come.

Gabe shoved his hands in his pockets and smiled. He'd put the proverbial ball in her court and it had been excruciating waiting on her to come to the conclusion that they needed to get this out of their system. Those two make-out sessions hadn't even come close to alleviating his ache.

Turning from the window, Gabe crossed his loft and went to the door. If she'd come this far, the least he could do was give her a hand and help her the rest of the way.

Gabe opened the door wide and spotted Chelsea leaning against the wall directly across from him. Clearly startled, she jerked and clutched her purse in front of her…as if trying to use something to shield her from the big bad wolf. Didn't she know? There was nothing he couldn't knock down to get what he wanted.

"How long were you going to wait before you knocked?" he asked.

Squaring her shoulders and tipping her chin, she cleared her throat. "I wasn't sure I was going to knock. I was thinking of leaving."

"No, you weren't."

Chelsea blinked, opened her mouth then closed it and continued to stare.

"Are we going to do this in the hallway or are you coming in?"

"Do what?" she asked.

"Whatever brought you here." He stepped back and gestured her in. "Don't look so worried, Chels. I only bite when I'm asked to."

Her eyes widened for a fraction of a second before she blinked and stepped forward, turning sideways to pass without actually touching him. Gabe bit back a grin as he closed the door, securing it with a click of the lock. He had the entire top floor to himself, and knew they wouldn't be bothered, but he still wanted that extra layer of privacy between the outside world and his Chelsea.

No. She wasn't his. Gabe needed to stop thinking along those lines. He wanted her. That was all. Once, not so long ago, he'd let emotions over a woman cloud his judgment and it had resulted in his partner being killed. He'd let his need override his job, thinking he could handle an attraction to a woman and still think clearly out in the field. He'd been wrong and his partner had paid the ultimate price.

He couldn't forget the promise he'd made to himself

after that to stay focused on work. Any extracurricular activities had to remain strictly physical, which was more than fine with him. Especially where a certain computer hacker and CTO was concerned.

After the hell that she'd been through, she deserved respect. She may keep that steely front in place, but he knew there was an underlying vulnerability after the leak of those photos.

Gabe appreciated Chelsea enough to place the control in her hands. And now she'd risen above her vulnerability and had come to him.

Damn, she smelled amazing. That familiar jasmine scent he'd come to associate with her surrounded him. Gabe crossed his arms and watched as she did a slow circle, taking in his space.

He'd imagined her in his bed many times, but never had he imagined her in his living room for a casual visit. That would have been too personal.

"You're sneaky," she muttered. "I mean vans and trucks, Gabe."

She turned to face him and raised her brows as if waiting for him to answer, but he'd missed the actual question.

"I take it the fleet arrived at Hope Springs."

Her eyes narrowed. "Your wedding gift was incredible. A fleet of expensive vans and trucks. I was buying them the china set they registered for and you go and spend...well, more than the cost of the entire wedding, reception, and honeymoon combined."

Clearly he was on shaky ground here, so he dropped his arms to his sides and crossed to her. "I can't tell if you're angry or shocked. Regardless, I wanted to help Brandee with the camp. It seemed like the logical thing to do."

"Logical." She lifted her head to hold his gaze and those green eyes definitely pinned him in place. "You're not a logical man. You're reckless, unpredictable, maddening, but never logical."

"Well, darlin', I think you just gave me a compliment."

Chelsea rolled her eyes and threw her hands out as she turned to head toward the wall of windows. Gabe remained where he was, waiting on her to say something.

"Only you would find those words to be flattering." With her back still to him, she tucked her hair behind her ears and blew out a sigh. "I want to hate you. I want to keep not trusting you, but then you go and do this. It's so unselfish and giving and…damn it."

One step after another, Gabe closed the distance between them and came to stand directly behind her. As the sun started to set and the evening grew dim, their reflections were easy to make out in the window. He saw the uncertainty on her face, the passion in her eyes. She had come to his door for one reason and one reason only.

"You're frustrated," he murmured against her ear, still holding on to his amazing restraint by not touching her. "Tell me the real reason you're here. It's not to pat me on the back for giving the best wedding gift."

"Part of it is." She met his gaze in their reflection. "I was standing there watching as one truck after another pulled onto the ranch. And I realized, maybe you're not a jerk."

Gabe smiled and smoothed her hair away from her neck. "What else did you realize?"

She trembled beneath his lips and he gave up all restraint. Trailing his fingertips up her arms and back down, he took a half step to bring his chest against her back.

"That I want you. I want this."

Finally.

"I'm done fighting," she went on as he continued gliding his fingers over her silky skin. "I never take what I want."

"And you want me."

"Yes," she whispered.

He hadn't asked, but hearing her repeat her affirmation had arousal consuming him. He'd put her at the helm and she was going after what she wanted. Him.

"If I'd known it was going to get you to my door, I would've bought the fleet a month ago," he joked, figuring she needed the tense moment to ease her nerves.

She smiled, which was exactly his intent. Her body relaxed against his and he reached around, flattening one palm against her stomach. His fingers splayed across the fabric of her tank top, pulling her back against him. Chelsea continued to watch in the window.

Gabe curled his pinky finger beneath the hem of her tank and slid it just inside the waistband of her jeans. Her swift intake of breath had him nipping at her ear. He wanted her as off balance as possible, because he'd been that way for weeks now. He wanted her so achy and needy that she begged him, that she came apart in his arms and cried out his name.

Gabe began to pull her shirt up over her head but Chelsea gasped and attempted to cover herself.

"The windows—"

"Are mirrored on the other side," he stated. "Nobody can see you and I want you right here, right now."

"But—"

"You came to me," he reminded her, turning her so she could face him. "We're playing by my rules now."

Chelsea relaxed a little as he finished taking off her shirt and tossed it over his shoulder. Then he crushed his mouth to hers and was instantly rewarded with a groan.

This time, nothing would stop them. They weren't in public anymore and he was damn well going to take his time. Later. This first round was going to be quick and fierce because he'd waited long enough.

Gabe pressed her back against the glass and started working on the button on her jeans. In no time she was wiggling those hips and helping him remove the unwanted garment. Now that she was only clad in lacy panties and a matching bra that would bring any man to his knees, Gabe lifted her by her waist and nipped at her swollen lips.

"You knew exactly why you were coming here."

Chelsea bit down on her lip and met his gaze.

"Say it," he commanded. "Tell me exactly why you're here."

He wanted her begging, pleading.

Gabe ground his hips against hers as she locked her ankles behind his back.

"Tell me, Chels."

Eight

"You," she ground out. "I want to be with you in every way. Now, Gabe."

He knew full well just how to get her begging and, for once, she was all too anxious to give up control. She needed him, needed this. Trust issues, worrying who was exactly behind what would come later. She couldn't think of one time in her life she'd done something rash, for purely selfish reasons, without analyzing it to death.

Gabe Walsh was the perfect reason to be selfish. He was also the perfect man to prove that she was still in control after the scandal. She wanted to be here. She wanted him. And she was going to have him.

"Damn right you do."

He released her, easing her legs back to the floor, but only long enough to perform the quickest strip she'd ever seen. By the time he was completely bare and he'd procured protection from his wallet and covered himself,

Chelsea's body was aching in ways she'd never known. She continued to stare into his gray eyes as he rid her of the last pieces of lace. Then he was on her.

Once again, he lifted her and she wrapped her legs around his waist. He slid into her like they were made for each other. Chelsea tipped her head back against the glass as a groan escaped her.

"Look at me," he murmured.

The fact they were doing this against the window had a shiver of excitement coursing through her. Still, she was thankful for the mirrored glass on the other side.

Chelsea locked her eyes on Gabe and smiled. "You're bossy," she panted.

He smacked her backside as he jerked his hips faster. "You wouldn't have it any other way. You're enjoying this just as much as I am."

She was. Oh, mercy, she was. This experience with this man made her feel so much more in control of her body, of how a man looked at her. How did Gabe make her feel so treasured and so erotic at the same time? She didn't know she would be this comfortable with intimacy so soon after the Maverick scandal, but Gabe made her feel alive and sexy.

When she opened her mouth to speak, he reached between them and touched her in just the right spot to have her eyes rolling back and a groan escaping her. Her entire body tightened as she clutched his shoulders and let him do whatever he wanted...because he clearly knew her body better than she did.

"Chels," he strained to say as his own body trembled. His grip on her hips tightened.

She remained wrapped all around him, taking in every bit of his release. Feeling all of that taut skin beneath her hands, having such a powerful man at her mercy right now was absolutely incredible. Gabe Walsh was doing things to her mind and body that she wasn't ready for, but she'd started this roller coaster and it was too late to jump off now.

He was perfect, and had come along at the perfect time—when she didn't even realize she needed someone. But she did. She needed him to show her she was a passionate woman and not defined by those photos.

Their bodies ceased trembling, but she wasn't ready to let go. Not quite yet.

"Stay here tonight," he whispered in her ear.

The warm breath tickling her skin had her fisting her hands on his shoulders. There was nothing more she wanted than to stay and do this all over again, maybe in a bed this time, but she couldn't let her post-coital feelings dominate her common sense. She still had questions and she still had concerns.

"You're thinking too hard." He turned from the window, still holding on to her, and headed toward the hallway leading deeper into the loft. "Apparently, I didn't do my job if you're still able to have coherent thoughts."

"My thoughts are jumbled, if that counts."

He tightened his hold on her and Chelsea had to suppress a moan of pleasure. Being skin-to-skin after sex was even more intimate than the act itself. This moment was… Chelsea suddenly realized she couldn't do this. Not with a man she was still so unsure about.

Gabe turned into a bedroom—his bedroom. The dark navy and rich wood tones screamed masculine dominance. She'd just voluntarily come to the lion's den.

"Gabe, I can't—"

"You can."

Her arms and legs were still draped around him. He held their bodies together so tight, she just knew when he let go she would feel cold, alone. But this was fun while it lasted, right? She hadn't come here for a sleepover or to do anything other than what had just happened.

"No," she told him, pressing against his shoulders. "I can't."

He studied her face for just a moment before easing her down to stand on her own. But he kept his hands on her hips.

"I don't want a relationship, Gabe."

"Is that right?" he asked, gliding his hands up the dip in her waist and back down.

The way he continued to stare at her made her feel foolish for making assumptions, but he had to see her side. "I came here for sex. That's all. Staying overnight implies more."

She'd wanted him, plain and simple. She'd also wanted this man to help her get over the feeling that she'd been tarnished somehow. The things he did to her, with her, had helped Chelsea realize she was still in control despite the scandal that followed her.

The corners of Gabe's mouth twitched as he continued that maddening feathering of his fingertips over her heated skin. Her heartbeat had yet to slow down from the moment she'd walked through his door. She was seriously out of her element here and, judging from the relaxed manner of the frustrating man in front of her, he'd clearly been in this position of power before.

"So now what?" he asked. "You're going to get dressed and leave?"

Honestly, she hadn't thought all of this through. The man was wearing her down and she couldn't even think straight.

"This isn't something I do," she admitted. "So, yeah. I guess I'll, um, I should just get dressed and go."

Gabe towered over her, leaning forward until she sank back onto the bed. His hands dipped into the mattress on either side of her hips as he came within a breath of her mouth.

"Don't be ashamed that you're here, that you took what you wanted." His eyes seemed a darker gray now, desire filling them. "This doesn't have to be awkward or complicated."

"I'm not ashamed," she stated, trying to seem strong and in control when her bare butt was on his duvet and he was a breath away from getting her flat on her back and having his way again. "I just don't know what to do from here."

That naughty grin kicked up a second before he nipped at her lips. "I'll show you exactly what we're going to do from here and then you can decide if you want to stay the night or leave."

Chelsea wanted to protest, she really should stick to her guns, but the only thing she could think as Gabe's weight settled over hers and she lay back was, *Finally.* They'd finally made it to the bed.

"Missed again, Walsh."

Gabe muttered a curse. "I didn't miss."

"But you didn't hit the bull's-eye," Shane countered. "What's up, man?"

Playing darts and drinking a beer with his buddies at TCC usually calmed Gabe. Not today.

He headed back to the bar and grabbed his beer, taking a hearty swig. What the hell was wrong with him? He'd thought once he got Chelsea in his bed, he'd be over this need. If anything, though, he was achier than ever and, damn, if he wasn't pissed about it.

"Nothing," Gabe replied, setting his bottle back on

the glossy bar top. "Getting ready for the big day? Did you get your vows all written?"

Shane's smile widened, as it always did when his fiancée was mentioned. The two were so obviously in love and Gabe couldn't be happier for them. After all Dusty had done to try to ruin Brandee, she deserved a happy ending.

Gabe just hated that there were so many amazing people, *innocent* people, who were still recovering from being the Maverick's victim. Since discovering Dusty had been at the helm of the scandal that shook Royal, Gabe had personally reached out to each of the victims. Apologies were just words, but he hoped they understood his sincerity.

With the exception of Chelsea—and even she seemed to have come around to believe his innocence—nobody had blamed him or accused him of guilt by association. He'd been a victim, as well, considering the impact on his reputation and on the business that carried Dusty's last name. But Gabe could take care of himself—he was taking care of himself. He'd been more concerned with making things right for the Maverick's true victims.

The majority had moved on with their lives. And the strange thing was, for some of them, their experiences with Maverick had led to positive outcomes. They'd married, had children, settled deeper roots in Royal. Gabe was just thankful the repercussions Dusty's dark, twisted games hadn't been worse.

"My vows are done," Shane replied, pulling Gabe's attention back to the conversation. "Brandee is a little stressed."

Shane sank onto a bar stool and ordered another bourbon. "I told her so long as the minister shows up, nothing else matters. That was the wrong thing to say."

Gabe laughed as he leaned his elbow on the bar. "Chelsea and I have everything covered. You two just show up and worry about remembering those vows you're preparing."

Shane's brows shot up. "How is Chelsea? Brandee said she wasn't too talkative over the past couple days. Her texts are to the point and only about wedding details. Would you have any idea what's up?"

"Not a clue."

Shane took the tumbler from the bartender and swirled the amber liquid around. "You're a terrible liar."

"Actually, I'm an exceptional liar and my bank account proves it."

Being in the security field occasionally had him going undercover in disguise. He was a remarkable actor, if he did say so himself. But there were just some aspects of his life he wasn't ready to share and Chelsea was one of them.

Shane tipped back the bourbon and finished it in one long gulp before setting his glass down and motioning for another. "Fine. But you can't lie to me, and I know something is up with the two of you. She's beautiful and you're, well, you. Might as well tell me what's going on."

"What the hell is that supposed to mean? I'm me? Are you calling me a player?"

"Calm down. I just meant you two have been spending quite a bit of time together over the past several weeks."

Before Gabe could defend himself, Daniel Hunt walked in the door. Seeing Chelsea's brother, Gabe felt a momentary pang of guilt. But he shouldn't feel bad about whom he wanted...and whom he'd had. Chelsea was a big girl and she had come to him—then left in the middle of the night.

He wasn't sure if he was more upset about her silent

departure or relieved that she'd held up their agreement to keep things simple. Although he had to admit, just to himself, he wished she'd stuck around because there was nothing he would've liked better than to roll over and feel her by his side in the morning.

Which was precisely why it was good she had left. A woman like Chelsea could make a man forget all about reality. Gabe was growing his business, doing damage control where needed, and the last thing he had time for was a relationship.

"Hey, man," Shane called to Daniel. "Didn't know you were in Royal."

Daniel came up to the bar on the other side of Shane and nodded for the bartender. "Erin wanted to do some shopping for Christmas and insists on the local shops here rather than Seattle. She said she wants to stay through Christmas because she loves this small-town feel and wants to experience her first Christmas here. Plus, she didn't want to miss the wedding or the annual candlelight and caroling ceremony on Christmas Eve."

Gabe raked his thumb over the condensation on his glass of beer and wished he'd ordered something stronger and stayed home.

"How's the wedding coming?" Daniel asked then leaned around to glance at Gabe. "You and my sister have everything covered? Knowing her, she's taken control."

An image of Chelsea straddling him last night when they'd finally made it to his bed flooded his mind. She'd taken control, all right, and he'd been more than okay with relinquishing the reins.

"It's more like divide and conquer," Gabe replied, refusing to say much more.

Shane threw him a glance, but Gabe merely picked

up his beer and drained the glass. "I need to head out," he said, pushing away from the bar.

"Stay," Daniel said. "Next round is on me."

Tempting as another drink was, he didn't want to sit around with his best friend who knew too much and the overprotective brother of the woman he was sleeping with. He could think of a hundred other things that sounded more appealing.

"I still have some work to tend to this evening." Not a total lie. He was always checking on his clients and staff. "And tomorrow is an early day for me."

Actually he had nothing planned, but it sounded like a good excuse. Besides, there was always something to be done and he was always up early and hitting work hard.

"I wanted to ask you about the Maverick case."

Gabe stilled. "Sheriff Battle said there are no new leads as to who helped Dusty. I've had my team working on this, as well. The security cameras outside the gym locker room had been tampered with."

Daniel rubbed the back of his neck and shook his head. "This is absurd. I don't know what I'll do when I get hold of the person who made my sister's life a living hell."

Gabe was right there with him, but best not to say that or to express too much interest in Chelsea. Daniel was definitely the overprotective big brother. What Daniel didn't know was that Gabe had also appointed himself to that role.

"I'll be sure to keep you informed," Gabe assured Daniel. "I'm hoping this is wrapped up soon and we can all move on for good."

"I appreciate that, Walsh."

Gabe tossed some bills onto the bar and grabbed his black hat off the stool. "Shane, I'll talk to you later. Daniel, hope to see you at the bachelor/bachelorette party."

"Wouldn't miss it," he answered. "Oh, Gabe, if you see my sister soon, tell her to stop dodging my calls and texts. I have a feeling you're with her more than anyone lately."

Gabe didn't miss the narrowed gaze or the knowing tone. He smiled and couldn't resist replying, "I'll tell her tonight."

"I don't need to tell you to be careful with my sister."

Blowing out a sigh, Gabe tapped his hat against the side of his leg. "You don't need to tell me. I'm well aware of how raw her emotions are right now, but you also need to understand she's stronger than people give her credit for."

Turning away, Gabe whistled and headed for the exit. As he plopped his hat on his head, he heard Shane say something to Daniel, but couldn't quite make it out. Gabe didn't care. He wasn't trying to be purposefully rude, but he also wasn't going to have anyone, especially Chelsea's brother, try to wedge his way into whatever it was they had going on.

Daniel had every right to worry about Chelsea because of the photos and the scandal. But Gabe also wanted the man to be aware that Chelsea was a strong woman and getting stronger every day.

The chatter about the scandalous photos had died down. Now, the town had shifted its focus to the breaking news about Dusty and figuring out what had motivated him to lash out at so many.

The questions swirled around the small town and were discussed everywhere from beauty salons to bar stools. Nobody really knew why Dusty Walsh had opted to make such poor life choices that had affected so many. Perhaps he was upset because he hadn't been admitted into the TCC, or maybe he was jealous of so many new members. Maybe he was just a bitter, terminally ill man who wanted others to be miserable, as well. Nobody truly knew what had motivated him to be so evil and conniving.

Even Gabe didn't have a clue. But now that Dusty was gone, the healing had begun and the town of Royal was getting back to normal. There was no greater way to celebrate than with Shane and Brandee's Christmas wedding.

Gabe headed toward his loft downtown, but before his turnoff, he decided to take a slight detour. He had a message to deliver, after all.

Nine

Chelsea glanced over her spreadsheet again. Hope filled
her as she realized that this spring her dream would become a reality. She'd wanted to do something to give back
and help struggling teens for so long, but had never really known how or what to do.

Smiling, she closed out her computer program. She
couldn't wait to get her counseling center for teens suffering from depression and suicidal tendencies up and
running. And once the idea started to become more of
a reality, she'd discuss partnering with Brandee and her
camp for teens. Between the two of them, they could
really do some good for a whole new generation. Nobody should ever have to feel isolated or hopeless the
way she'd felt.

Chelsea had known that crippling fear and loneliness
all too well. She'd experienced it twice in her life. The
first time, after her father passed, Chelsea had had Dan-

iel. But a brother wasn't the same as a father and he'd been dealing with his own grief.

She'd experienced it again just months ago when so many in this town had seen photos of her in various states of nakedness in the TCC locker room.

When the compromising photos emerged, she'd gotten angry. She'd felt like she'd been stranded on a deserted island, that no one understood her.

Then she'd realized that there were people out there who had been hurt like her and that's when she'd circled back to the idea of giving back and helping others. So, in a warped sort of way, the Maverick scandal had helped her come to the conclusion that it was time to step forward and reach out to others.

Chelsea wanted to open a place that would help young people realize that they weren't alone, that there was always hope. She'd already started vetting counselors and had just purchased an old office building outside of town. Soon she would start renovations and then the true work would begin. Souls and lives would be changed.

This was her baby, something she was keeping close to her chest until she was ready to reveal everything. She wanted all the plans in place before she made a big announcement. Besides, she hadn't wanted to detract attention from the wedding of the year.

The name of her new organization still eluded her. She'd racked her brain and still nothing came to mind. It needed to be meaningful, simple, something that would call out and make troubled people feel safe, comfortable. Everything hinged on the name: the reputation, the feel of the business, the marketing. There was so much to think about other than just helping those in need.

Chelsea came to her feet and stretched. She'd yet to

change from her running gear after her evening jog. Several more ideas for the counseling center had come to her while she'd been out pounding the pavement and she'd rushed home to enter them in the computer. Now, it was time for a shower and to get ready for bed.

Chelsea loved her lacey bras and panties to be delicate and sexy and utterly feminine, and much of her sleepwear was the same. But tonight she just wanted her old cut-off shorts and her well-worn tank.

If she put on anything silky or lacy, she'd instantly think of Gabe and she needed to not go there.

She'd snuck out of his bed at promptly eighteen minutes after one the other morning, and hadn't spoken to him since. He was long overdue to come charging back into her life. Someone like Gabe probably didn't like the fact that she'd walked away without a word. She'd say that sex was his area of expertise and she couldn't help but wonder if anyone had ever left him like that before.

Chelsea was surprised he hadn't stopped by unannounced with some lame wedding question since then. But knowing Gabe, it was only a matter of time.

She quickly showered and pulled her hair back into a messy bun at the nape of her neck. This in-between length was driving her crazy. She either needed to cut it short or to let it grow. But right now she had so many other pressing matters, she couldn't even make the time for an appointment.

With work at Hunt & Co., the wedding planning, her secret project, which wouldn't be a secret much longer, and Gabriel Walsh consuming her mind every waking minute, was it any wonder she was exhausted?

It was Friday night and she was home alone. That right there should have told her something about her nonexistent social life. She was literally all work and no play.

Well, she'd played, but she didn't figure playing with Gabe counted. He was more like work, when it came to how impossible he was. At least with Hunt & Co. and the upcoming counseling center she was in control, whereas with Gabe, she never had a clue what would happen next. They both wanted to take charge, which meant that control volleyed back and forth between them.

As she finished putting on her nightclothes, the chime of her doorbell echoed through her house. Chelsea stilled then smiled. Well, it had taken him longer to come to her than she'd first thought. Though the fact he was standing outside her door right now had her stomach doing all sorts of girl-crush flips, which was absurd considering they weren't a couple or dating or anything.

Padding barefoot toward the front door, Chelsea instantly made out his silhouette through the etched glass of the door. Some might have said Gabe was predictable, but he was far from it. More like determined. He knew what he wanted and apparently wasn't stopping until he had it. She knew he wanted her, but that was just physical. Besides, he'd gotten what he wanted, so shouldn't he be done?

Chelsea flicked the lock on her door and pulled it open. Without waiting for an invite, Gabe removed his hat and stepped in, placing a kiss on her forehead as if to smooth over his abruptness.

"Won't you come in?" she muttered with a wave of her hand.

He didn't stop in the foyer. No, he went on into the living room as if he had every right to barge into her personal space.

Chelsea closed the door and followed, not at all surprised that he thought he could just take charge like he owned the place. He took a seat on her sofa, casual as you please, but she remained in the wide doorway. Practicing restraint around Gabe Walsh was difficult on a good day. This being the first time seeing him since they'd slept together, she figured she deserved some type of award for her control.

"Are you staying long?" she asked as she crossed her arms and leaned against the doorjamb.

"Not long," he replied. "I ran into your brother at TCC. He said you're not answering his texts."

Chelsea snorted. "So you're his messenger boy now? Since when did you two become so chatty?"

Gabe stretched his arm along the back of the couch and shifted his focus to her. "He offered to buy me a drink and asked about the Maverick case."

Chelsea wasn't quite sure how she felt about her brother and the man she'd just slept with discussing her without her present. She could only imagine the two alphas going head to head, both trying to protect her.

She licked her lips and kept her focus on Gabe. She didn't want him to know just how much he affected her simply by being in her space, large and masculine, taking up a good portion of her couch. She hadn't had a man in here in so long, and definitely not a man as sexy as Gabe.

"So why did you stop by?" she asked, hoping her voice didn't come across as breathy as it sounded to her. "You could've texted or called."

"Maybe I wanted to see you." That Southern voice warmed her just the same as if he'd touched her.

His words were often just as potent as his touch. She shivered at the passion, the desire shining back at her from his gray eyes.

"You should probably go," she whispered. If he stayed, they'd tumble into bed—and then what? She didn't think Gabe was looking for more, and she certainly wasn't, either. But the more time they spent together, the more she trusted him and wanted to explore. Surely that would be a mistake. Right?

Gabe didn't move. He barely blinked. Yet somehow from across the room he captured her attention.

"You don't really want me to go," he stated. "Besides, I want to know why you snuck out of my bed without a goodbye."

Clearly, this was going to take some time and he wasn't going anywhere without answers. Pulling in a deep breath, Chelsea went to the front window where she'd created a perfect window seat with plush, colorful pillows. She got comfortable and leaned back.

"I didn't want to wake you and I told you I wasn't staying."

"You didn't want a confrontation," he corrected. "What are you afraid of, Chels? I won't hurt you, I won't exploit you and everything we do is private. I'm aware of your sensitivity and I'd never make you uncomfortable. Unless you're afraid that you might want more than one night?"

That was exactly what scared her. There was no *might* about it. She did want more, but wanting more would lead to emotions and that was one area she couldn't afford to go to with someone like Gabriel Walsh.

"I can hear your mind working from over here," he stated. "Don't make this any more complicated than it needs to be."

"Says the man who doesn't have a past that haunts him."

Something dark came over his face in an instant. "You have no idea what's in my past, so don't assume."

"I'm sorry." Chelsea clutched the floral pillow tighter to her chest. "I never thought—"

"I had a life before I came to Royal, Chels. I had a demanding job and was too naïve. I thought I could have it all, but it was just another lie I told myself."

Chelsea waited for him to go on, listening as his voice took on a lonely, sad tone. He glanced around her living room then came to his feet. Raking a hand through his hair, he pulled in a deep breath. She didn't want him to feel like he owed her anything. He paced like a caged animal and she got the feeling he actually wanted to let her in on this portion of his life.

"I don't know how much you know about my time in Dallas, but I was an agent for the FBI."

"I was aware of that," she told him. "Listen, you don't have to tell me anything—"

"I do." He tipped his head to the side, raking his hand over his scruffy jawline. "I consider you a friend, even though I'm not sure how much you trust me at this point. You need to know the reasons for my actions, for why I'm so adamant about putting strict limits on relationships."

Again she remained silent and waited on him to continue.

He paced through the room in a random pattern before coming to stand by the fireplace. Resting his elbow on the mantel, he examined the photos she had on display.

There were older ones of her and Daniel and their parents, a couple of her and Brandee, and one Chelsea had taken of the most amazing sunset from the time she went on vacation in the Bahamas. She liked to keep the happy memories on display to showcase just how blessed she was in her life and how far she'd come since her darker days.

"I found myself attracted to a woman," he finally went on. "That attraction grew into something more, something I'd never experienced before. But there was a case—I can't get into specifics—and my loyalties were torn."

A sliver of jealousy spiraled through Chelsea at the thought of another woman getting so close to Gabe. But why? It wasn't like she was in love with him or anything. The night they'd shared meant nothing. Right?

Actually, no. That night meant something, more than it should have, and that was precisely the reason she'd had to scurry out and save herself the walk of shame the next morning. She'd left in the dark of night, praying he didn't wake and question her. All he'd had to do was roll over and ask her to stay and she had a feeling she would've done just that.

Gabe was getting to her. Beneath that mysterious aura, the tattoos, the smoldering eyes, he was a man she couldn't ignore. She hadn't trusted him at first, had been convinced he'd had something to do with the leaked photos. She knew better now. Gabe had just been the obvious target for her rage. She'd needed someone to take her anger, her humiliation, out on. Considering they'd been working together and he was a Walsh, he'd been too convenient.

"My partner was killed over a woman who interfered with our investigation. I let it happen because, where she was concerned, I was naïve. And the result was fatal. I'd let my feelings for her cloud my judgment and she'd been playing me the entire time. She was working for the guys we were trying to take down."

Gabe's stunning declaration jerked her back to the moment. "Oh, Gabe. How awful."

He turned from her mantel and crossed to her, taking a seat at the other end of the long cushion. Even though he was only a few feet away, the manner in which he stared off into the distance indicated he was back in the past and not here with her at all. Whatever scene played through his mind gave his face a pinched, tormented expression, as if the pain was still fresh.

"I vowed never to get tangled up with a woman again," he said, glancing down at his hands resting on his knees. "I can control work. I can control how good I am at my job. But not when I get blindsided by someone I'm supposed to trust."

The final brick in the wall of her defenses crumbled. This man hadn't betrayed her with those photos. He was a man of worth and integrity and loyalty. Someone who had experienced such a tragic loss at the hands of someone he'd trusted couldn't have done such horrific things to her—or anyone else in this town, for that matter. Gabe was definitely a man to be trusted. He had a big heart and was loyal to a fault.

Gabe sought justice. He was a man who valued his career and making sure the truth was revealed. No doubt this whole scenario involving Maverick disturbed him on a level she hadn't even thought of.

"Is that really why you came here?" she asked. "Did you need me to know about that time so I'd see a different side of you?"

Gabe stared at her for a minute before shaking his head and glancing away. "No. Maybe. Hell, I don't know. You deserve to know the real me."

"The guy not many people see," she muttered mostly to herself.

"I'm the same guy everyone sees," he whispered, still not looking her way. "Maybe I just want you to view me differently."

Why did he have to be so noble? It had almost been easier when she'd believed him to be the accomplice of her betrayer. Then she could keep him at a distance, protecting her heart in the process. But now that wasn't an option. Not anymore.

Chelsea came to her feet. She took a couple steps and sank to her knees in front of him. Taking his hands in hers, she stared into those unique gray eyes that never failed to captivate her. Now, though, she had a glimpse into his soul and all the insecurities he kept so well hidden. Maybe they were alike in more ways than she'd ever considered.

"I do see you differently."

His eyes widened, with surprise, with arousal. The muscle in his jaw clenched, as did his grip on her hands.

"You changed your mind about me over what I just told you?" he asked. "That fast?"

Chelsea offered a smile. "Let's say my defenses have been crumbling before now."

Gabe leaned forward, briefly touching his lips to hers. When she started to ease back, he released her hands and framed her face, taking the kiss even deeper.

In an instant, he had them both on their feet and had swept her up into his arms. Looping her arms around his neck, she threaded her fingers through his hair and opened to him. Feeling him touch her, knowing exactly what was to come, had anticipation pulsing through her.

"I'm staying the night," he muttered against her lips.

She didn't reply, because he hadn't asked. Gabe was finally going to claim her and nothing was going to stand in their way.

Ten

Sunlight slashed through the windows, waking Gabe. He stirred, but stilled when he realized he was alone... and not in his bed.

He sat up, rubbing his hands over his face. Coarse hairs bristled against his palms. He was in desperate need of a razor, though Chelsea hadn't complained a bit last night when he'd raked his scruff along her bare skin. In fact, the way he recalled, she'd moaned and jerked her hips against him as if silently begging for more.

Gabe glanced toward the empty side of the bed, at the indention in the crisp, white pillowcase. The sweet jasmine scent still permeated the air as if she were still there. That was twice now she'd left him to wake up alone. He'd always thought himself to be a light sleeper, but apparently not with this woman.

And now that he sat there surrounded by everything that was Chelsea, he realized he didn't like being alone.

For now, he wanted to be with her—whatever the hell that meant. He'd gotten a taste of her and needed more, and that scared the hell out of him.

Part of him was glad he'd told her about his past. At least now she saw him in a different light; he wasn't the monster she'd taken him for. On the other hand, he hated being exposed and vulnerable. He'd hated opening that wound from his past and letting her see into his soul.

He'd kept the details vague. Even if he had been at liberty to discuss a federal case, he wouldn't have. The emotion over being betrayed by a woman he'd cared for, the pain of losing his partner and friend, was still too raw. So much had changed in his life in that instant when he'd realized he'd been played and he'd put the life of a man who trusted him on the line.

Gabe had been on the brink of a major breakdown when he'd come to the realization he needed to move on and leave Dallas for good. He'd forced himself to put the nightmare of that botched assignment behind him. The move hadn't been easy, but for the sake of his sanity, he'd had to remove himself from the life that was sucking away his soul. Coming to Royal and taking over his family's security company had only made sense.

Of course after coming here he'd had to face the entire Maverick scandal. Out of the frying pan and into the proverbial fire was not his idea of a good time, but he wasn't leaving. He was seeing this through and standing his ground because he had nothing to be ashamed of. He'd done nothing wrong.

Stifling a yawn, Gabe looked around for a clock but didn't see one. From the way the sun was shining through the curtains, he guessed it wasn't too early. He should be making calls, checking emails, making sure he wasn't on the brink of losing any clients. Because not only did he want to hold on to the ones he had, he also wanted to expand and possibly go global. Nothing screamed confidence like expansion, so now was the time for him to go all-in, proving to his clients that he was the most reputable name in the business.

Besides, he truly didn't want to have to start over again. Granted, he could retire and never work another day in his life, but he would go positively insane if he had nothing to do other than travel and live the high life. He'd made wise investments over the years, he'd cashed in at the right times and reinvested. He may have been a kickass agent, but he'd also been a brilliant businessman.

While Gabe did enjoy getting away to one of his homes either in Miami or in the mountains in Montana, he had to work. After what had happened in Dallas and the Maverick situation here in Royal, the pursuit of justice would remain his lifelong calling.

Tossing the covers aside, Gabe searched the floor for his boxer briefs and jeans and put them on. Shirtless, he padded down the hallway and heard the clanging of a pan in the kitchen. Well, at least she hadn't completely left him.

Gabe stood in the doorway and watched as Chelsea mumbled to herself and scrolled through her phone. She muttered something about casserole and eggs then scrolled again. A grin tugged at the corners of his mouth. She had quite the creative way to curse about breakfast foods.

Her hair was messy on one side and flat on the other, she still had a sheet mark on the side of her cheek, and her oversize T-shirt had slipped down to reveal one slender shoulder. Arousal pumped through him and it wasn't breakfast he was hungry for anymore.

"I've never had a woman make me breakfast."

Chelsea started, flattening her hands on the island in front of her and glancing up at him. "You scared me to death."

"Were you expecting another man to greet you this morning?"

"I never remember which one I've left in my bed."

Gabe growled as he closed the gap between them and wrapped his arms around her waist. "There's no other man in your bed but me for now."

With a quirk of a perfectly arched brow, Chelsea patted his cheek. "Then I guess you're the one I'm making breakfast for."

"You don't have to make me breakfast." He nipped at her ear. "I'll make breakfast while you sit here and keep me company."

Without asking, he circled her waist with his hands and lifted her to sit on the counter. She squealed and laughed, smacking him on the shoulder.

She paused and then her fingertips started tracing the pattern of his tattoos from his biceps up over his shoulder and down onto his chest. Just that light touch had him ready to throw her over his shoulder and take her right back to those rumpled sheets he'd just left.

"I never thought tattoos were attractive before," she murmured almost to herself. "Now, I'm not sure I'll ever want a man without them."

The egotistical side of Gabe was thrilled he was ruining her for other men, but the other side, the one he didn't want to think too much about, couldn't stand the idea of her with someone else. For now, she was his and he damn well planned to take advantage of the situation.

Gabe kissed her chin then worked his way down the column of her throat. "Sit here while I cook."

Her body arched against his touch. "I'm not sitting here."

Gabe's hands covered the tops of her bare thighs, giving a gentle squeeze as he lifted his gaze to meet hers. "You are," he commanded. "Right here, wearing my shirt, while I make our food. You're going to need your strength."

Her eyes widened with shock, arousal. "Don't you have work to do today?"

He did. He'd gotten an email late last night about a client that was threatening to pull out and go elsewhere because they'd heard of the scandal surrounding the Walsh name. Gabe had already put his best man on the job and planned to follow up himself later today. That client wasn't going anywhere and neither was Chelsea.

"Right now I have a sexy woman wearing my clothes and I plan on stripping her and showing her how very thankful I am that she believes in me." He covered her lips with his for a quick kiss, a kiss that promised more. "But first, we're eating."

"I won't argue with you about that." She raked her hand through the top of his hair. "My cooking skills aren't what they should be."

Gabe jerked back. "The heiress of a steak empire can't cook?"

She lifted one slender shoulder, causing his shirt to slide down farther, exposing creamy skin he couldn't resist touching. Gabe curled his fingers around her shoulder and stroked his thumb over her collarbone.

"I mean, I can cook steak," she amended. "But most other things terrify me. Mixing ingredients, that's the hard part. Steak is simple."

"Your restaurants have the best steaks, so don't say

it's easy," he retorted. "Nobody even compares to what you guys do to a hunk of beef."

Her smiled widened. "That's the nicest thing you've ever said to me."

"I call you sexy and gorgeous, but I compliment your family's meat and you get all soft."

Chelsea tipped her head to the side. "I'm a simple girl."

Gabe laughed and shook his head as he turned away to look in her fridge. Chelsea Hunt was not simple, not by any stretch. She was as complex as his jumbled feelings for her.

There was no room for feelings, not unless they stayed superficial. Chelsea was fun, she was sexy and she wasn't looking for anything long-term, either. In short, they were perfect together, at least for now.

"So how long is this going to last?"

Her question threw him off, but he remembered Chelsea was nothing if not logical. He thought about his response as he cracked the eggs over the edge of a bowl and then whisked them to a nice froth.

"Done with me already?" he asked, purposely dodging the question.

"I'll at least let you feed me before I kick you out. But I may keep this comfy shirt."

Gabe threw her a glance and a wink. "You're all heart."

And he didn't even want the shirt back because it looked a hell of a lot better on her than him.

"I don't think our hearts are getting involved here."

Good answer. Because their hearts *couldn't* get involved here.

"I'd say last night was…fun," she continued.

"Fun?" he repeated, whisking the hell out of the eggs.

"It was spectacular and you know it. And your screaming and the scratches on my back prove you had more than fun."

"Fine," she amended. "It was fabulous and I wouldn't mind doing it again. So long as we're still on the same page about this not getting too serious."

Her words grated on his last nerve and annoyed the hell out of him. Gabe wanted to do the whole this-isn't-a-serious-relationship talk and she'd totally beat him to it. At least they were on the same page, though. Wasn't that what mattered? Shouldn't he be thanking every last star that she wasn't clingy and wanting more?

"There's no reason we can't go on seeing each other in this capacity," she added.

"Capacity? You mean having sex?"

"Yes. Just until the wedding."

His hand stilled on the whisk and the bowl as he turned to face her. "You're putting a deadline on sex?"

With a simple shrug, she met his gaze. "I think that's best considering neither of us want more. Besides, once the wedding passes, we won't have a reason to see each other. Right?"

Gabe swallowed, not liking the way his heart kicked up. But he wasn't allowing his heart to be involved. He'd just scolded himself about that very rule.

"Right," he agreed, turning back to breakfast. "We'll enjoy each other's company, keep this private and, after the wedding, go our separate ways."

"Perfect."

Gabe worked on getting some filets going and then the eggs. "Steak and eggs are a great source of protein and good for energy. Which you will need. If we've only got two weeks left, then I'm taking full advantage."

He turned and wiggled his brows at her. Chelsea took

her time uncrossing and recrossing her legs, giving him a glimpse of exactly the goal he had for the morning.

"If you keep that up, these steaks will go to waste."

She groaned and leaned back on her hands on the counter, arching her back. Even though his shirt was large on her, her breasts strained against the fabric and the hem inched up even higher on her bare thighs.

Keeping his gaze locked on hers, Gabe reached behind him and flicked off the burners. In two short steps he was on her, gripping her hips and pulling her toward the edge of the counter.

"What about breakfast?" she asked, quirking one brow and offering him that sultry smile that went straight to his gut.

"Oh, I'm still having breakfast."

And with that, he jerked the shirt up and over her head before taking exactly what she'd taunted him with.

"What about this one?" Brandee held up a lacy number with a matching thong. "Red or black?"

"Both," Chelsea replied, searching for her size in a short, sheer gown she knew would have Gabe's eyes rolling back in his head. She so enjoyed being the one who made him lose control.

"You didn't even look," Brandee complained.

Chelsea glanced up. "Again, both. It's lingerie. Men can never get enough and they rip it off you, anyway, so color doesn't matter."

"True. But what's Gabe's favorite color?"

Brandee's teasing tone and mocking grin had Chelsea biting the inside of her cheek. "You think you're so smart."

"Oh, I'm brilliant," Brandee stated, full-on smiling now. Her diamond ring glistened as she waved a hand toward Chelsea. "You two have spent quite a bit of time together and the kind of bickering and heated looks I've witnessed between you always leads to the bedroom."

And the kitchen. Mercy sakes, Chelsea would never look at her center kitchen island the same again. The things that man had done to her right there on her marble countertop should be illegal.

Chelsea hadn't intended to shop for lingerie, but since she was here with her friend, why not? Just because she and Gabe were only physical didn't mean she couldn't put a little flair into their time together.

"I actually haven't seen Gabe in two days," she returned defensively.

Granted, she'd only missed seeing him because he had some important business to attend to in Dallas with a new client and she had her own workload to take care of. She actually did have to work, as much as she'd rather spend her time between the sheets—or on the island—with her new lover.

Even though he was gone, Gabe had most definitely left her with a glorious goodbye and the promise of an even better return.

Actually, he'd advised her to rest up because he fully planned on making up for those two days, especially since their time together was limited anyway.

Which was why she was all too eager to find something in this little lingerie boutique that would drive him out of his mind. Her body heated up just thinking of all the things they'd get into when he returned.

But if they didn't slow down somewhat, Chelsea knew full well she'd fall head-over-boots and be a lost cause. Her heart had already taken a tumble after his soulful admission about his past and if things between them dragged on, the end would only be more difficult. At least this way she could prepare herself for the end…and enjoy the ride all the way to their final day.

"I thought you only came with me to help me choose honeymoon wear and get some Christmas shopping done."

Chelsea ignored her best friend's questioning stare and returned to searching for her size. "I am Christmas shopping—my purchases just happen to be for selfish reasons."

Well, maybe they weren't totally selfish because Gabe would absolutely love unwrapping her. Oh, maybe she should just get a silky piece of fabric and tie herself up in a big bow. Just the thought of him jerking the knot and having the fabric wisp across her body as it floated down to puddle at her feet…

"This must be serious if you're dodging my questions."

Chelsea's hand stilled on the satin hanger. "Honestly, I don't know what's going on between us. We're keeping things private, but I do know that my feelings are stronger than I want to admit."

"Yet you just did."

Brandee came and stood on the other side of the rack, offering a sympathetic smile. "I know how you feel. I was there with Shane, remember? I went through a scandal of my own with Maverick and Shane pulled me through. We finally found our happily-ever-after."

Chelsea recalled all too well the emotional ride her friends had gone through before finally finding their destiny. Chelsea wasn't looking for a ring on her finger or the promise of a lifetime, but she couldn't stop the desire for Gabe that had settled deep in her soul. And this wasn't sexual desire, though there was an abundance of that. No, this was the desire to know more, to learn more, to have more with Gabe.

So where did that leave her? She still wasn't convinced she was looking long-term, but she wanted more than a romp while they were planning the wedding.

Damn it. She never should've put an expiration date on their interlude, but she sure as hell hadn't wanted to be on the receiving end of his conditions, either. This way, she'd set the terms and held all the power. At least she was well aware of how and when things would end. That was the only way she could cope because heartache was not something she wanted to experience again.

Chelsea knew she'd knocked Gabe off his game when she'd brought up an end date. But he'd gone along with her plan like he thought it was brilliant. It just proved he wasn't looking for anything more than a few nights together.

"The sex is amazing, but I'm to the point I want a real date."

Brandee's mouth dropped. "You've already had sex and you're just now telling me?"

Chelsea hated keeping secrets from her best friend, but everything had happened so fast. And then things had kept happening, so Chelsea had been a bit busy. Plus, they were supposed to be keeping it a secret. *Oops.*

"He'd been pursuing me for a while," Chelsea admitted.

Giving up on finding her size, she crossed the store and went to the back where a wall of drawers held other sultry treasures. Brandee, of course, followed. They were the only ones shopping and the clerks were always great in giving customers privacy and only assisting if asked.

"First he drove me out of my mind in the dressing room when my dress was stuck."

"Wait, what?"

"Then there was horseback riding." Chelsea went

on, ignoring her friend's shocked look because she just wanted to get all this out there. "Then he had to go and give you that extravagant wedding present and I totally melted at his selflessness."

"Back up for a second." Brandee held her hands up. "We'll get to all the details of the dressing room and the riding in a minute. I thought you were skeptical of him, that you believed he was in cahoots with his uncle."

"I did. But the more time I've spent with him, I've seen a side I never thought existed."

"Gabe wouldn't purposely hurt anyone, especially in such a callous way."

Chelsea nodded. "I know that now. I see the man he is."

"Oh, Chels. Are you in love with him?"

"What? No." She wasn't. She *wasn't*. "It's complicated."

"That's the exact way love is described."

Love. What a preposterous word for a relationship that wasn't even a *real* relationship.

Chelsea's father had thought himself in love, but in the end, that myth had shattered him. Chelsea wasn't going to follow the same path.

"Trust me. This isn't love." Great sex and a healthy dose of desire, absolutely. "And don't say anything to anyone. We really want to keep this private. Once we're done seeing each other, we don't want to answer a bunch of questions from people who thought we were a couple. You can see that would get confusing, not to mention annoying."

She thought no-strings sex was supposed to be uncomplicated. Yet there were suddenly so many rules with Gabe, including this whole term-limit thing and the secrecy.

She'd never actually had no-strings sex before be-

cause she'd been in solid relationships with all her partners. Those encounters actually hadn't had rules, so how
was this any easier?

Brandee's skeptical gaze held hers, mirroring the exact
doubts Chelsea had in her own mind. Brandee pursed her
lips and crossed her arms over her chest. Chelsea didn't
like the scrutiny, so she tugged open one of the wide
drawers and started checking the merchandise inside.

There were peacock-colored bra and panty sets, peach
teddies, so many choices all delicately displayed. Each
one she could imagine wearing for Gabe, but then, would
he wonder what her intentions were…other than the obvious? Would he wonder if she wanted more?

On a groan, Chelsea slid the drawer shut. "What am
I going to do?"

Brandee wrapped her arm around Chelsea's shoulder.
"We're going to pick out some killer lingerie that will
have our men begging. Then we're going to go get some
ice cream drenched in hot fudge and whipped cream.
After that, who knows what we'll get into. Maybe wine.
We definitely need some wine."

Chelsea laughed. "At some point I need to actually
Christmas shop. I have nothing for you yet."

Her friend gave her a slight squeeze before letting go.
"You're planning my bachelorette party and my wedding.
I'd say that's more than present enough."

"Speaking of the party, what are you wearing tomorrow?" Chelsea asked.

Brandee blew out a sigh. "I have no clue. I was thinking a cute dress and my boots, but then I think maybe I
should be dressier since I'm the bride. What about you?"

"I bought a white, off-the-shoulder dress and I'm pair-
ing it with my new cowgirl boots. I need some jewelry
to go with it."

Brandee's face lit up. "Then let's finish up here. I'll buy your jewelry for your Christmas present and you can buy me a dress for mine."

Chelsea drew her friend into a hug. "You've got a deal."

Now, all that was left before the promised ice cream and wine was to select the killer lingerie. Chelsea had no clue what turned Gabe on in the way of lace or silk so she opted to buy herself a few different options. Maybe after the bachelorette party, he'd get a little surprise.

Eleven

Gabe saw a flash of white turn the corner and he looked around to make sure nobody saw him follow. That damn dress had driven him crazy for the past three hours and he was done letting this temptress seduce him from afar. He wanted his hands on her. Now.

The coed bachelor/bachelorette party was in full swing at the club and everyone was having a great time. Brandee and Shane wanted all their friends to celebrate and have one last bash before the big day. Everyone loved gathering at TCC, especially since women were such a big part of the club now. Having a joint party here just made sense.

They'd gone with classic mason jars with candles for the center of the tables. Rope was used as cording around the edge of the tablecloths. On the food table was a large S and B wrapped in raffia and propped up with small, twinkling lights surrounding them.

Chelsea had seriously outdone herself on working with the in-house decorator. Brandee and Shane had been so thrilled with the results when they'd arrived.

But right now Gabe was twitching to see Chelsea. Alone.

When he'd arrived before the party officially started and seen Chelsea, he'd nearly swallowed his tongue. She was wearing a short, tight dress and those new cowboy boots, leaving a portion of her legs exposed. He wanted to feel those legs wrapped around his waist and he wanted to hike the skirt of her dress up to see what she wore beneath.

The last few days had been hell in terms of all the ass-kissing he'd had to do to appease his clients. One had threatened to pull all of his business, which would have been a significant loss. But Gabe had assured him that no other scandals would tarnish the company. Gabe knew he was riding a fine line and one more issue would be the end of this working relationship.

Gabe didn't intend to let anything happen again. He was in complete control now. But some of the clients handled by his staff weren't yet convinced. Gabe planned to keep a close eye on the situation and to reassure everyone that they were in the safest hands with the Walsh Group.

Now that he'd handled the damage control, Gabe was more than ready to get back to Chelsea.

When Gabe got to the hall she'd disappeared into, there was no sign of her. There were a couple offices and restrooms along the corridor but he had no idea where she'd gone.

A faint sound of sniffling had Gabe going still. He turned his attention toward one of the offices and crossed the hallway. He knocked on the door, but no answer.

That's when he heard colorful cursing from behind the closed door.

Gabe let himself in and found Chelsea. Her back was to him, her shoulders hunched as she pulled in a shaky breath. She pounded her fist on the desk with each curse word as if the inanimate object had offended her.

"Chels?"

She flinched and turned, her hand over her chest. "Sorry, I just needed a minute."

"To cry?"

"I'm not crying."

Maybe not, but she was on the verge of angry tears if that quivering chin was any indicator.

Gabe moved into the room, closing the door at his back and flicking on the light since he'd shut out the glow from the hall. Something at the party had bothered her because just moments ago he'd seen her laughing with guests and playing darts with some other ladies.

"What is it?"

Shaking her head, she attempted a smile. Did she truly think he'd just let her lie to his face and suffer alone? He wanted to know who the hell had hurt her so much that her cheeks were tinged pink and her eyes were practically shooting fire.

"It's nothing. I just needed to get away from the chaos out there for a second." Chelsea slid her palms over his chest and cocked her head. "I've missed you."

Gripping her wrists before she could distract him, he leaned forward. "Don't change the subject. Tell me what happened."

"Just some jerk thinking he can make crude comments about the photos." She slid her hands up around his neck and ran her fingers through his hair. "I didn't want to make a scene so I just walked out."

Rage pumped through him. "Tell me who."

Chelsea shook her head. "He's not ruining this night. That's why I didn't say anything. Daniel would go all big brother on me if he knew and Shane and Brandee would feel guilty for inviting someone here who was so ill-mannered."

To hell with Daniel or what anyone else would do. Gabe wanted his hands around the bastard's throat right this second. Nobody would ever make Chelsea feel inferior or knock her self-esteem down...not as long as he was around. Hell, even after they were through, he'd still consider her a friend and he'd never stand for anyone being cruel to her.

Gabe gritted his teeth and attempted to rein in his anger. He would find the bastard and make sure he understood never to mention Chelsea's name again or even to glance her way. If Shane knew about this, he'd haul the guy out of the party, but Gabe wouldn't let this dark cloud hang over the night and he sure as hell wasn't going to let it hang over Chelsea.

Daniel and Shane didn't need to know anything had happened. Gabe knew and he would damn well take care of things.

Forcing himself to remain calm, he nipped at her lips. "You look so damn sexy," he murmured against her mouth. "Did you wear this to drive me crazy? Because I'm ready to make our excuses and find someplace where we can be alone so I can see what you're wearing under this."

With that bright smile that never failed to pack a punch of lust, Chelsea tickled the nape of his neck with her fingertips. "Maybe I had someone in mind when I put this on."

"Is that right?" he growled.

She nodded and met his gaze beneath her heavy lids. "I may have also had that same person in mind when I made a special purchase yesterday. Maybe something lacy."

His entire body tightened as he plunged his hands into her hair and covered her mouth with his. Damn this party. He wanted her right now. It had been too long—days—since he'd had her and each second that ticked by brought them closer to the end. The need had grown stronger and stronger and, right at this moment, he was hanging on by a thread.

Chelsea pulled away. "We can't do this here."

"We can," he argued, reaching down to haul her hips flush with his. "I can clear off that desk and have you bent over in a second."

Her moan vibrated through her chest. "If we got caught here, Shane and Brandee would kill us. Besides, just think of all this as foreplay."

He'd been in foreplay mode all night. Seeing her hips in motion beneath that flimsy material had been like watching a slow-motion strip tease and he was damn tired of waiting for his prize.

"I want to know what's under this dress."

She gripped his jaw, wiping her thumb over his bottom lip. "I assure you, it will be worth the wait once we get back to my place."

"My place is closer. We'll go there."

Before Chelsea, he'd never taken a woman back to his place, but he'd never had a need like this. Chelsea was different in every respect. She'd already been to his loft and, he had to admit, having her there hadn't freaked him out. He'd actually enjoyed it.

He'd also exposed a part of himself, of his past, that he never would've divulged had Chelsea not gotten to him deeper on some level. Those were thoughts he wasn't ready to dive into right now.

The second this party was over, he wanted that dress off and he suddenly had the all-consuming desire to see her spread across his sheets. Any meaningful thoughts or questioning why he'd opened up to her had no place here.

"So impatient," she mocked. Dropping a quick kiss on his lips, she pulled away from his arms and adjusted her dress. "We better get back out there or people will wonder where we went."

Nobody knew about their current situation and Gabe wanted to keep things that way. Whatever was going on between Chelsea and him didn't concern anyone else. She was his and he wasn't too keen on sharing. And he was determined to track down the jerk who'd upset her. The party was large, but Gabe knew most everyone in attendance. It wouldn't be too difficult to figure it out.

"You go," he told her. "I'll be out in a minute."

She slipped out the door and Gabe needed more than a minute to gather his thoughts. Between the desire pumping through him and the fury over some guy who didn't have any manners, Gabe needed to rein it in before he went out there in a fit of rage.

Gabe let a good five-minute gap pass before he headed back out. The party was still in full swing. The drinks were flowing, laughter and conversation filled the open area, and couples were dancing to a slow country song by the hired band.

Standing back, Gabe surveyed the room, trying to pinpoint guests he didn't know. There was no way a friend of theirs would make snide remarks to Chelsea, so this guy had to be someone outside of their inner circle. Maybe a business associate of Shane's or Brandee's.

Within minutes Gabe had narrowed the options to

three guys. Gabe shoved his hands in his jeans and watched each of them for a few minutes. He needed to have absolutely no doubt which one he needed to rip apart.

Chelsea and Brandee were throwing darts in the corner. Erin stood near them, sipping on a glass of water and chatting with her friends. Shane and Daniel were at the other dartboard. Gabe figured he should mingle so he didn't look like he wanted to commit murder, but if any of those three guys said something to Chelsea again, Gabe wouldn't be responsible for his actions.

"Looks like you owe me a bourbon," Daniel stated, slapping Shane on the back as Gabe joined them near the dartboards.

"Considering it's an open bar, I'm paying for it anyway," Shane replied.

"Actually, Chelsea and I paid for it," Gabe interjected. "But feel free to drink all you want. We also have drivers to make sure everyone gets home safely."

"You guys really thought of everything," Shane said. "Thanks, man."

Gabe didn't want the accolades. Shane was his best buddy and there wasn't anything he wouldn't do for him. Besides, working with Chelsea was worth all the money and time he'd spent. She trusted him now. She believed in him. And he couldn't wait to get back to his place and make good on his promise to rip that dress off her body.

"I'll go get drinks," Shane offered. "What do you guys want?"

Daniel and Gabe gave their orders and Shane headed toward the bar. Risking a glance at the women, Gabe smiled when Chelsea threw the last dart in her hand and it hit the bull's-eye. She threw her arms in the air and spun toward her friends with a huge smile on her face. That punch of lust to his gut always caught him off guard—though it was something he really should have been used to by now.

"I'll go get us some drinks," she told them.

Gabe forced himself to look away, but when he turned back, Daniel was eyeing him.

"Something you want to tell me?" Chelsea's brother asked.

"No."

"You dodged that question before, Walsh."

Gabe shrugged. He'd continue dodging it until Chelsea wanted her brother in on what was going on...if she ever did.

Even if he and Chelsea hadn't agreed to keep things private, he wouldn't be chatting with her brother about this. Chelsea was Gabe's business. Simple as that.

"This is none of your concern."

Daniel lifted his brows. "Is that right? Because you were looking at my sister like... I can't even finish that without getting graphic. What the hell is going on with you guys?"

Gabe crossed to the board and plucked out the darts. "We're planning a wedding. You want to know anything else, you'd have to ask her."

"I'm asking you."

Gabe handed Daniel the red-tipped darts. "Winner gets the final say-so in this argument."

Taking the darts from Gabe, Daniel nodded. "I'll want the truth when I win."

Like Gabe would ever lose.

The crash of breaking glass had Gabe and Daniel spinning around. Chelsea stood in the midst of the mess, and some guy Gabe didn't know was clutching her elbow.

Oh, hell no. Gabe was across the room before he could

even think twice. Rage bubbled within him and all he saw
was Chelsea's shocked face, her mouth open, her eyes
wide. And fear. He saw fear and he damn well didn't like
it one bit because his Chelsea never cowered from anything. She was a fighter.

"C'mon, baby. Everyone has already seen everything
you have. Why don't you give me a private show?"

The guy slurred his words as the reek of alcohol
wafted off him. Before Gabe could make a move, Chelsea rammed her elbow into the man's stomach, causing
him to grunt and double over.

"You don't have to be a b—"

Gabe reached down, grabbing the guy by the throat
and pulling up so he could look him in the eye. He wanted
this jerk to know exactly who was threatening him.

"Get the hell out of here and don't come back. If I see
you near Chelsea—if I even think you've spoken her
name—you will find out just how difficult your life can
be. Are we clear?"

Daniel came up beside Chelsea, wrapping an arm
around her. Gabe knew she was fine, but he wanted the
trash taken out.

Yanking the guy by the back of the neck, Gabe escorted him to the door and made sure he headed toward
the parking lot. No way in hell was he going to allow
Chelsea to continue living with this black mark over her.
Everything that had happened to her wasn't her fault, but
the fault of his uncle.

Gabe wished the old bastard wasn't gone because he'd
go kick his ass and knock some sense into him. How did
one even get revenge on a dead man? Rage was a difficult
emotion to control, but Gabe forced himself to breath in
and out and get back to Chelsea without ripping someone's head off.

Chels was a strong woman, but there were only so many times someone could be knocked down, and in public, no less. Damn it all. Even though none of this was his fault, it was his family member who had set this ball in motion, ruining lives.

That was all in the past now and Gabe was hell-bent on making sure the whole nightmare stayed that way. The town was moving on. These people were moving on. Until that jerk made a scene, this party was proof that every one of his friends had found their own happiness despite Dusty's antics.

Gabe stepped back into the main room and made a beeline for Chelsea, who sat on a bar stool beneath a large bundle of mistletoe. It was almost as if he was being given the green light.

Several friends surrounded her: Erin, Brandee, Shane and her brother Daniel. Gabe didn't care how rude he was or what others thought. The whole secrecy thing be damned. He wanted her to know she wasn't alone and he wasn't just consoling her as a pal. No, he planned on consoling her like her lover.

Pushing past Shane, Gabe reached for Chelsea. Her eyes went wide when she spotted him and he wondered exactly what she saw written all over his face. Most likely, she saw every blasted thought racing through his head. Every instinct in him wanted to haul her out of there, but throwing her over his shoulder would only piss her off more.

Gabe said nothing as he framed her face and captured her mouth. He swallowed her shocked gasp and eased her to her feet. Cheers and music surrounded them, but he blocked everything out except Chelsea's sweet taste.

When he feathered the kiss and released her lips, her

lids took an extra moment to open. Desire and surprise stared back at him.

"Well, that was unexpected," she muttered. "Guess we're not keeping this private anymore."

Gabe grabbed her hand. "We're leaving."

"Don't be absurd, Gabe. We—"

He shot her a look that shut her up immediately.

"Go," Brandee stated from behind him. "The party is almost over, anyway."

"And we paid for people to clean up," he reminded her, never taking his eyes from Chelsea.

Her lips thinned as she nodded and gripped his hand.

Gabe turned to find Daniel with his arms crossed, his eyes narrowed.

"That dart game is going to have to wait," Gabe stated as he pushed by.

Daniel's eyes went to his sister. "Chels."

"I'll call you later," she told him.

Later? Maybe tomorrow. Right now they were going to be alone, away from people, phones. The world. Gabe wasn't in a sharing mood.

Something about having another man put his hands on his woman and terrorize her made Gabe even more protective, even more territorial, than ever.

Hadn't he wanted to keep this purely physical? Hadn't he wanted to keep things private?

Well, apparently manhandling the jerk who'd approached her and then kissing Chelsea beneath the mistletoe had blown that plan all to hell. But he'd answer everyone's questions another time.

Chelsea was his for another week and he damn well planned to take every opportunity to show her just how a woman should be treated. She deserved everything and, for now, he was going to be her everything. Once the wedding was over, well, he'd worry about that when the time came.

The valet brought Gabe's truck around and Gabe gave him a hefty tip before helping Chelsea get in. There were so many emotions pumping through him right now, he needed a minute. If she touched him, if she said anything, he was afraid his control would snap. He was that desperate to be with her and to prove that she was not defined by the scandal that continued to plague her. Gabe had never felt the need to prove something to someone and he'd never had this desperation before.

But this wasn't about him. Everything about this moment, about these emotions, was about Chelsea.

Being with this woman was like walking a tightrope. One wrong step and he could plummet into a territory he wasn't ready for. Gabe was already teetering as it was and he had a sinking feeling he wasn't going to be able to hang on much longer.

The second he settled in behind the wheel and put the truck into Drive, Chelsea turned in her seat. "Gabe—"

"Not now," he growled, gripping the wheel tightly.

Once they got to his place, they would talk. Or not. He'd much rather work his tension and stress out another way. He had a sinking feeling if he started opening up about his emotions now, he'd say things he'd vowed never to say to another woman and the last thing he wanted was for Chelsea to get hurt again.

Twelve

Anger rolled off Gabe in waves. She'd never seen him like this, had never thought someone so reserved could dole out such rage. But the man was practically shaking.

He'd been pissed back at the party. The way he'd handled that drunk guy, Chelsea wasn't so sure what would've happened had the room not been full of family and friends. Would Gabe have been so controlled or would he have pounded on the man? She'd been scared, not that Gabe would hurt her in his anger, but of what he'd do to the other guy and how she couldn't prevent it.

If she thought Daniel had been protective growing up, that was nothing compared to Gabe right now. How would Gabe react if he knew her past? Would he look at her differently? Would he see her as weak?

It didn't matter, though. Their time was drawing to a close and no matter how much her heart kept trying to get involved, Chelsea had to hold back at least some part of herself. If she gave him everything…well, she'd suffer even more heartache in the end.

Gabe ushered her into his penthouse loft apartment. She'd briefly been there before and hadn't paid much attention, but now that she was back, she could easily see this was his domain. The industrial yet country vibe surrounded her. The exposed brick walls were masculine, the chrome finishes and high-tech electronics taking up one entire end of the loft screamed money and power. There were closed-circuit TVs showing the outside of the apartment building, the parking garage beneath, the street in both directions.

Being so paranoid must be an occupational hazard for a former FBI agent turned security analyst.

"You sure do have quite a bit of surveillance," she casually commented.

"I own the building."

Chelsea didn't even bother hiding her surprise. "Seriously? How did I not know that?"

Gabe gave a shrug. "It's not something I talk about. I actually own several properties in Royal, but most are held under my company names."

Yet again, the man of mystery had more up his sleeve. He tended to keep her guessing on who the real Gabriel Walsh was. Just when she thought she'd uncovered the final layer, he revealed another.

Chelsea continued to peruse the open living area. There was a black metal outline of the state of Texas hanging on the wall at the other end of the room. The simple wall art was tasteful yet very Gabe. There was a pair of old cowboy boots over in the corner and several hats that hung on pegs near the front door. While the loft was neat and tidy, Gabe's presence was everywhere.

The gleaming kitchen with a long, concrete island

lined by eight bar stools just begged for a party. But she didn't think Gabe was too much of a partier, let alone a host. Still, she saw herself getting steaks ready, him serving up sides and handing out bourbon.

Wait, no. This wasn't some fantasy that would come to life. He'd brought her here for sex. Isn't that what they'd discussed in the office back at the club? But then he'd gone and gotten angry and now she wasn't so sure why she was there because there was still fury pouring from him.

This final week was going to be full of Gabe and the wedding. Gabe in private was going to be vastly different than Gabe as a cohost of the nuptials and a best man. The idea of walking down the aisle with him on her arm gave her heart a little extra beat. She absolutely couldn't get caught up in that image or that fantasy.

Gabe stalked to the living area and stared out the floor-to-ceiling windows. With jerky movements, he unbuttoned the cuffs on his sleeves and rolled them up his forearms. He'd hung his black hat by the others near the door and hadn't spoken a word.

"If you're just going to be angry, I'm not sure why I'm here."

She remained near the entryway, crossing her arms over her chest and waiting for him to respond. But he kept looking out onto the city, his hands shoved into the pockets of his perfectly fitted jeans.

"I'll just call someone to pick me up."

"Stay."

That one word settled between them and Chelsea softened just a bit. What the hell was he so angry about? It wasn't like this was his life that kept getting thrown back in his face. She had a feeling there would be jerks for some time to come who were all too eager to bring up those nude photos, thinking she was easy and willing to give them a private showing. It was humiliating, but right now all she could do was keep her head high and move on.

"You didn't see your face," Gabe said, still keeping his back to her. "When you dropped those glasses and I turned to see what happened... Chels, your face was pure terror. You'd gone white and I saw that guy's hand on you and I wanted to kill him right there."

The hurt in his tone had her moving toward him. She'd been so worried about what type of scene she'd caused and if she'd ruined the party to even think about how all of that had affected Gabe. Obviously he'd been angry with the guy. Someone like Gabe, so powerful and prominent, would see it as a setback, an embarrassment. They were just a fling, anyway, so why should he have to put up with her scandal?

"I completely understand if you want to call this quits between us." She stood only a few feet away now. Even though she wanted to reach out and touch him, she clasped her hands in front of her dress. "I know the scandal surrounding me is embarrassing. I wouldn't want someone else to have to bear the burden of the crass jokes or the mocking."

Gabe whirled around. "You think I'm trying to tell you...what? That I'm leaving you alone to deal with this mess? That I don't want to be associated with you because of it? Do you honestly think I'm that big of a jerk?"

Chelsea swallowed the burn in her throat. Why did love have to be complicated?

Wait. Love?

Well now was not the time for her to realize she'd completely fallen head-over-boots with this man. Not only was she completely unsure about where he stood, she knew he didn't do relationships. Fantastic. There was nothing like this feeling of despair when she was already battered and bruised.

"I don't think you're a jerk," she whispered, ignoring the extra thump of her heart. "I just wouldn't blame you for wanting to bring this to an end now instead of after the wedding."

She wouldn't blame him; she would be devastated. But the end was inevitable. Next week or now, did it really matter? Both ways she'd be alone, which she was used to. But being with Gabe had changed her into someone who didn't want to be alone, not when she knew how amazing he could be.

Damn it. When had she fallen in love? Somewhere between not trusting him and seeing him come to her defense tonight. She'd known for a few days that she was sinking deeper into territory she knew nothing about. She'd fought every step, but she couldn't lie to herself anymore.

Gabe reached out and hooked an arm around her waist. "I'm not ending a day sooner than we planned," he growled. "I'm angry you had to deal with that guy. I'm angry because you should never be afraid of what my family did and there's not a damn thing I can do to go back and change what happened to you."

Wait. Gabe was blaming himself for Dusty's actions?

Chelsea reached up, smoothing his unruly blond hair back from his forehead. Framing his face, she leaned in and briefly touched his lips.

"You aren't to blame," she assured him. "And you can't control what others say."

"Maybe not, but I can try to shield you from the hurt."

Her heart tumbled in her chest, but she knew he didn't want any part of her heart or her love. Which was such a shame, because she would give them both so freely to her knight in shining armor.

"I've never been so angry in my life," he murmured. "When my partner was killed, I was hurt and broken, yes. Angry? Yes. But I was able to stop the killer and bring him to justice. But all of this? I have no idea how to stop it completely and it rips me apart."

Chelsea eased back from his arms. "Well, for now I know something you can control. I believe you said something about wanting to see what I have on beneath my dress."

The darkness in his eyes mixed with arousal. Chelsea reached for the hem and eased it up and over her head. She tossed the dress onto the back of the sofa only a few feet away. When she turned her focus back to Gabe, the arousal in his eyes had turned to hunger and she knew she'd made the right decision in terms of lingerie tonight.

The white, lacy, strapless bustier and matching thong indeed had Gabe speechless. Most women trying to seduce a man would pair the outfit with heels, but she was all about her cowgirl boots.

"You bought this for me?" he asked, slowly making his way toward her.

"You know I did."

Because there was no one else.

Gabe muttered a curse beneath his breath. "I've never wanted someone more than you right now. You're breathtaking and sexy and…damn, Chels. You're killing me."

She couldn't help but smile because she'd finally managed to make him a stuttering mess. Feeling a tad saucy, she propped her hands on her hips and tipped her head.

"Maybe if you're good, I'll show you some other items I purchased."

His eyes snapped to hers. "You bought others?"

"Something in green to match my eyes and then there was this racy black number that I simply couldn't pass up."

With a growl, Gabe was on her. His arms circled her waist, his mouth crashed down onto hers, and he backed her against the window. The cool glass did nothing to calm the heat racing through her.

Gabe nipped at her lips before roaming over her jaw, down her neck, to the swell of her breasts. Her entire body felt as if she was lit up from within. As his hands seemed to touch her everywhere, his mouth was doing wonders driving her mad.

"I want you in my bed," he murmured against her skin. "I've envisioned you there all spread out, reaching for me."

The image in her mind had her arching against him. She'd take him anywhere he wanted.

"But the bed is too far away," he stated. "And my need for you is too great."

She thrust her fingers through his hair and held him as he yanked the top of her bustier down and covered her flesh with his mouth. She cried out, but then he started ridding her of the rest of her clothes and Chelsea could only hang on.

Once she was bare—except for her boots—Gabe took a half step back and raked his heavy-lidded gaze over her.

"Take off your clothes," she demanded.

His grin kicked up, wrinkling the corners of his eyes and making him seem all the more menacing. "You take them off."

In her next breath, she was making frantic work of his buttons and when she was down to the last two, she just jerked the shirt open. Gabe's laugh had his abs clenching, as if he was showing off just how spectacular his build truly was.

Chelsea's hands shook as she removed his pants. He toed off his boots and finally stood before her wearing nothing but desire.

He reached into his pants' pocket, pulled out protection and slipped it on. Chelsea's blood pumped faster, her nerves dancing with anticipation, and when he finally turned those gray eyes back to her, she didn't hesitate to reach for him.

Gabe lifted her off the floor. She toed off her boots and let them clunk to the floor before locking her ankles behind his back.

Gabe closed his mouth over hers at the same time he plunged into her. Then he stood still, right there in the middle of the room. Their bodies were joined, but he didn't move, and the erotic sensation was driving her absolutely out of her mind.

"I have no control with you," he murmured against the side of her neck. "I need you, Chels."

He spun around, sending them tumbling to the sofa. He cradled her face as his weight settled her deeper against the cushions.

Chelsea opened to him as he covered her mouth with his. He trailed one of his hands down her side and held tight to her hip, his fingertips gripping her skin.

This wasn't enough. She wanted more, needed more. Beyond the sex—though it was the best she'd ever had—she needed Gabe for everything.

He muttered something in her ear she didn't understand at the same time he tipped his hips just right to send her over the edge. She tightened around him, arched her back and dug her heels into his backside.

When Gabe's body shuddered against hers, he whispered something else, something she still didn't quite catch. She clung to him, though, taking his release as hers ebbed. He held his weight just off her, but she wanted all of him.

Chelsea circled his shoulders with her arms and pulled him closer as his body ceased trembling. His head rested in the crook of her neck. Darkness had fallen across the apartment. Only the glow of a small desk lamp across the room gave any light. She wanted this moment to carry on; she didn't want words or movement to break the spell of their time together.

Closing her eyes, Chelsea willed time to stop. If she held on tighter maybe he'd stay.

Fortunately, though, she wasn't a clinging woman. She'd never begged for a man and she wasn't going to start now. If there was ever a time or a man, though, Gabe was definitely worthy of her begging.

When he started to move, she trailed her fingertips up through his hair.

"What did you whisper in my ear earlier?"

Gabe froze, cringed actually. "I don't recall."

He was lying. It had been mere moments ago and he'd said it twice.

"Don't move," she murmured. "Let's just lie like this for another minute."

His hand softened on her hip as his hips shifted. "If I stay here too long, I'm going to want you again and the rest of my protection is in the bedroom."

Chelsea smiled up at him. "Then maybe we should make our way there."

Thirteen

The wedding was only four days away now. Chelsea couldn't believe the time had almost come for her best friend to say "I do." She'd be lying if she didn't admit, just to herself, that she was jealous. Chelsea hadn't thought she wanted romance and forever, but getting swept away in this real-life, fairy-tale ending had her wishes shifting.

Suddenly Hunt & Co. wasn't her only focus. If Gabe knew how much real estate he took up in her mind, her *heart*, he'd likely run fast and far. She had to keep this to herself. She knew deep in her soul that there was no future for them, not together, anyway. He'd made it abundantly clear from the start that he couldn't trust his heart that way again.

Trust. Hadn't that been the entire theme of their relationship? No matter if they were enemies, then friends, then lovers, everything surrounding them always circled back to trust.

He'd pursued her and she'd backed away, but now that she was fully on board, he was backing away. The dance they continued to perform was confusing, frustrating, and she wished like hell they were doing the same steps.

Chelsea pulled up her spreadsheet and attempted to get the new system up and running for the accounting department. That was her goal today, not to focus on the fact she'd enjoyed two days at Gabe's loft. The weekend had flown by in a blur of sex and time spent doing nothing but enjoying each other.

Monday was even harsher to handle after such an amazing few days with the man she loved.

She seriously needed to stop using that word. Love wasn't a good idea. Admitting her feelings this close to the end game...damn it. None of this was a game. Every single moment she'd spent with him had been real, had been amazing, and something she wanted forever.

A gentle tap on her door had Chelsea glancing across her office. Before she could mutter a reply, the door eased open and Daniel stepped in. She figured he'd be making his presence known. She'd known he was spending the holidays in Royal as opposed to Dallas, especially with the wedding coming up. Erin wanted to be at Crescent Moon, the Hunt family ranch, for Christmas. Chelsea made a mental note to swing by to see her soon-to-be sister-in-law and take her Christmas present. Well, she'd take the present just as soon as it was delivered, because she'd purchased nearly everything online.

Chelsea offered her brother a smile. Surprisingly he hadn't contacted her since she and Gabe had left the party abruptly the other night. Well, he'd texted her, but she'd been preoccupied.

"Your assistant said you don't have a meeting for another hour." Daniel closed the distance between them and took a seat opposite her desk. He crossed one ankle over his knee and settled in. "Hope this isn't a bad time."

"You wouldn't care if it was," she replied, turning her chair to fully face him. "You're here to question me about Gabe, so let's have it."

Daniel blew out a breath as he removed his cowboy hat and placed it over the arm of the chair. "What are you thinking, Chels? The guy is a loner and you're going to get your heart broken."

She'd expected nothing less from her big brother. "Did you rehearse that or just decide to wing it?"

"I'm winging it, so have pity on me when I'm trying to play the concerned older brother."

"You're not playing anything. You *are* the concerned older brother." Chelsea offered him a smile as she folded her arms across her desktop and carefully thought of what to say next. "Listen, I know you care about me and I get that you don't want me hurt. I'm not a fan of heartache myself, but Gabe and I know what we're doing. We have no preconceived notion that this is long-term."

No notions, but wishes...definitely.

"That's not like you."

She couldn't help but laugh. "And you know about my sex life? Is that really where you want to go?"

Daniel cringed. "Definitely not, but you're going to get hurt."

Most likely, but she couldn't live her life worrying about the future. If things were going to end with Gabe— no, *when* they ended—she at least wanted to enjoy the here and now. And she'd enjoyed the hell out of their weekend together.

"Daniel, I realize over this past year Royal has been overrun with happily-ever-afters and you and Erin want everyone to be as blissful as you guys, but right now I'm not looking for love."

Yet it had found her, anyway. She'd have to worry about that later. She vowed that she'd enjoy Gabe until the very last minute, and then she'd stock her fridge with her favorite ice cream and allow herself the pity party she would no doubt deserve. What a way to ring in the New Year.

"I swear, Gabe and I are fine, and at the end of the day, we're just friends."

Who give each other toe-curling orgasms and spend weekends together.

"Friends, huh?" Daniel asked with a grunt. "The man looked like he wanted to strangle that guy the other night and then he kissed you like he was staking his claim."

"Maybe he was," she replied simply. This was not a conversation she wanted to have with Daniel. And the truth was, he wouldn't want her honest opinion or feelings on the matter. It was best to keep him as far away from this as possible. "Was there something else you wanted to discuss?"

Daniel pursed his lips as if he were contemplating his next move.

Chelsea arched her brow, silently daring him to circle back to the topic she'd just closed.

"Erin and I wanted to have you over for dinner."

"That sounds great. When were you thinking?"

Daniel came to his feet and tapped his fingers on the edge of her desk. "Tonight, actually. We have something we want to discuss with you."

Chelsea stood, as well. "That sounds serious. Is everything okay?"

"We're fine," he assured her with his smile, one that matched their father's. "Does seven work for you?"

"I'll be there."

When he blew out a breath and looked into her eyes, she knew they weren't done with their heart-to-heart.

"You know I love you and just want what's best, right?"

Chelsea circled her desk and wrapped her arms around her great protector. She'd always looked up to him, always admired his opinion, and loved how he continually put her first.

"I feel the same about you," she told him then eased back. "Now, get out of here so I can finish this program for the accounting department or we're going to have a whole host of angry employees when their checks are messed up."

Daniel kissed her on the cheek and left her office, closing the door behind him. That talk had gone better than she'd thought. She wasn't quite sure how he'd react to Gabe's very public display of affection. Hadn't Gabe been the one to want to keep things under wraps? Yet when she was threatened, he hadn't cared one bit. He had to have some feelings for her…didn't he?

Regardless of what Daniel thought, or anyone else for that matter, Chelsea was going to enjoy this time with Gabe. Once the wedding was over and they were done working together, they wouldn't see each other as often. Maybe she'd get lucky and the desire would fizzle out.

The likelihood of that happening was about as great as her getting Gabe to fall in love with her—and that was never going to be a reality. He didn't do love, didn't do long-term, and even though she didn't know the full details of the case involving his partner's death, she had to respect his desires.

That didn't mean she had to like them.

Blowing out a breath, Chelsea went back to her computer. There was no sense in worrying about this now.

She had so much work to get done, surely she could block Gabe and focus.

The second she pulled up the program she'd been working on, her cell vibrated on her desktop. She glanced at the screen only to find a simple message from Gabe: Tonight you're mine.

So much for focusing on work.

Chelsea let herself into the main house at Crescent Moon. She'd grown up here, and returning as an adult always felt like coming home. She loved her house in Pine Valley, but Crescent Moon held such a special place in her heart.

She made her way through the open foyer. Erin's laughter filtered through the first floor and Chelsea could tell her brother and his fiancée were in the back of the house. When she got to the enclosed four-seasons room with three walls of windows overlooking the stables, she smiled. She'd always loved this room. She'd spent hour upon hour reading her favorite books in the corner chaise, which had since been replaced with another in a pretty pale yellow.

Erin slid her legs over the side of the chair and offered a bright smile. "Hey, glad you could make it." Coming to her feet, Erin closed the gap between them and wrapped her arms around Chelsea.

"A dinner that I didn't have to prepare?" Chelsea said, easing back. "I'm always up for that."

Daniel crossed to the minibar in the opposite corner. "Can I get you a drink? Dinner should be ready in about fifteen minutes."

"I'd love a glass of wine. White, please." While Daniel busied himself getting her wine, Chelsea glanced at Erin. "I'm sorry I've been so scarce lately. This wedding planning, plus work, has taken up a good bit of my time."

"And Gabe Walsh?" Erin asked, her brows rising as her smile widened.

Why deny it? The man had kissed her in front of nearly the entire town at that party. Her brother had already speculated about their connection and Brandee knew the truth. There wasn't much of a thread of secrecy to hold on to at this point.

"He has occupied a good portion of my time." Mainly the nights, but there was no need to get into that. "So what did you guys need to see me about?"

Daniel handed her the glass and clutched his own tumbler, most likely filled with bourbon. "We're pregnant."

Chelsea gripped the stem of her glass. "'Scuse me?"

"Way to go, Daniel." Erin shook her head and rested a hand over her stomach. "We are expecting, but I'd hoped to deliver the news in a little more of an exciting manner."

Chelsea sat her glass on the table and pulled Erin into another hug. "I'm so thrilled for you guys! I'm going to be an aunt."

She eased back and glanced down at Erin's flat belly. "How far along? Are you feeling okay? What can I do to help?"

Erin laughed and patted Chelsea's shoulder. "I'm fine. I went to the doctor today and I am six weeks."

Chelsea squealed and turned to her brother. "You guys are going to be such awesome parents. I can't wait to see Baby Hunt."

Daniel wrapped an arm around her. "We were hoping you'd agree to be the godmother. I know not many people do that anymore, but we want you to be a big part of our kids' lives."

"Of course," she answered then froze. "'Kids'?"

Erin beamed. "Twins."

Chelsea jerked her attention back to her brother. "Two babies? I'm going to need something stronger than wine."

Erin laughed and nodded. "I know, it's a shock. Believe me. We were stunned, but we knew we wanted a large family and I guess we're just getting a jump start. I'd been having some pain and they just did an ultrasound to make sure things looked okay. Apparently the pain is my uterus stretching faster than normal."

Two babies? Chelsea couldn't even imagine being a mother to one, let alone two. But Erin and Daniel were beaming and Chelsea couldn't be happier for them.

Tears pricked her eyes. "I don't even know what to say."

"Well, damn. Don't cry." Daniel picked up her wineglass. "I can't handle tears."

"I'm happy," Chelsea insisted. "Really. I'm just overwhelmed and excited and I can't even imagine how you guys feel."

"All of that and more," Erin assured her. "I've gotten used to the ups and downs of my emotions lately, but I know you're still taking it all in. Dinner should be ready. What do you say we go eat and discuss baby registries and nursery décor?"

"Maybe I should eat in the kitchen," Daniel groaned.

Chelsea smacked his chest. "You're eating with us, and we're going to have a nice family dinner. And we need to figure out which room to put the nursery in, and colors, and names. We need names."

Daniel groaned as he turned and headed toward the kitchen where his chef had no doubt prepared something fabulous. "We have a long time still to go," he growled as he walked away. "Why do I have a feeling my credit card is going to take a hard hit?"

Chelsea smiled as she looped her arm through Erin's. "Because it is."

* * *

He'd told her to be at his place at seven, yet it was now nearing eight and there was no sign of Chelsea. No call, no text. Absolutely nothing.

Gabe didn't like to be kept waiting, especially by the woman warming his bed.

The doorman buzzed him, letting him know Chelsea was on her way up. Had something happened that had prevented her from getting in touch to tell him she'd be late? Had she been delayed by some jerk harassing her again when she was out?

Everything in him stirred, churning toward anger. He wanted to shield her from all the flack she was taking. Even beyond that, he wanted to be her…what? They only had a few more days left together before their agreed-upon date to end things. And she'd never given any indication she wanted more.

Why the hell was he now choosing to think of something beyond sex? He'd done that once. His partner had been killed because Gabe had trusted the wrong woman. He'd let her into his personal life, thinking she loved him, only to find out she had actually been playing him all along to feed information to the drug cartel Gabe had been working to bring down.

He'd been such a damn fool.

But Chelsea was different. She'd dodged him and he'd continued to chase her. Gabe always got what he wanted, but now he wasn't so sure what that was. He knew for certain he didn't want things to end, yet at the same time he wasn't looking for a relationship.

Maybe all these wedding plans and seating charts and dress fittings were getting to him. He was just surrounded by the prospect of "forever" and "I do" and clearly getting caught up in the moment.

And most troubling was how he'd whispered his need to her the other night. He'd slipped and whispered how much he needed her, how much he cared for her. Not once but twice. Those words bordered on a confession he certainly wasn't ready to make now...if ever.

Here a quiet knock on his door, Gabe turned from the view of downtown and glanced toward the entryway. Chelsea let herself in, but the moment he spotted her, Gabe was crossing the room in long strides.

"What happened?" he asked, gripping her arms and studying her tear-streaked face. "Are you hurt?"

She smiled and shook her head, her eyes bright with unshed tears. "These are happy tears."

Happy tears? That always sounded like an oxymoron to him, just one more thing he would never understand.

"You're an hour late and you come in crying," he persisted. "What's going on?"

"Daniel and Erin are having twins."

Her declaration was made on another burst of tears. Gabe wasn't quite sure what to do, so he pulled her into his arms. "And you're sure these are happy tears?" he asked again.

She nodded against his shoulder. "I'm so excited for them. My best friend is getting married. My brother is having babies. I mean, it's all so life-changing and makes me think about my own life goals and—"

She jerked back, eyes wide. "I'm not saying that to scare you," she quickly amended. "I don't mean us. I'm just happy and excited, and I want that in my life. I want to have a family and a husband, and I never thought I did, but..."

Yeah, all this talk was making his gut tighten. Seeing Chelsea having an epiphany like this had him wondering about his own future. Hell, he'd just admitted to himself he may want more with her, but marriage and kids?

Let's not get too out of control here.

He framed her face in his hands, using the pads of his thumbs to wipe her tears. "Have you eaten dinner? I can call and have something brought to us."

"I ate at Daniel's." Her gaze held his; moisture glistened on her lashes. "Sorry I'm late. Erin and I got carried away with looking at baby things online. I may have already bought nursery furniture for them."

Gabe could see her getting so involved and wanting to play the doting aunt. How would she be with her own children? Would she want a large family?

The idea of her starting a life with some nameless, faceless, man had jealousy curling low in his gut. But who was Gabe to put a stop to this new goal she'd created? He was merely passing through her life.

"Want to help put up my Christmas tree?"

Chelsea jerked back and her eyes widened. "Tonight?"

"Might as well."

"It's only a few days until Christmas," she reminded him as if he didn't know the date. "Why do anything at this point?"

Because, surprisingly, he wanted to spend time with her, and not just in the bed. As crazy and absurd as that sounded, he found it to be true. He wanted to do something with Chelsea that was normal, something that would create memories.

Damn it. He was getting in deep here. Deeper than he'd anticipated. And he knew full well that in a few days, after the wedding was over, he wasn't going to want to let her go.

Hell, maybe he couldn't let her go.

Fourteen

"I can't believe those are the only ornaments you have."

Gabe glanced over at her, his brows drawn. "What's wrong with them?"

Chelsea didn't even attempt to hide her laughter. "You used one of your hats as the tree topper and the rest of your ornaments are shot glasses from around the world and plastic horseshoes. Don't you have any beads or ribbon or even a star for the top?"

Crossing his arms over his broad chest, Gabe glanced from the tree back to her. "I suppose your tree has all of that and is weighed down with glittery ornaments?"

Chelsea shrugged. So he'd described her tree perfectly. Well, the tree she'd always put up. This year she'd been so preoccupied with so many other things and she'd rarely been home.

"I may like a little glitter in my Christmas decorations," she admitted. "It's festive and happy. Besides, most of my stuff belonged to my father. They're ornaments we hung when I was little."

She remembered her dad letting her pick out most of the decorations. Even though she'd been young, she'd chosen all the sparkles and, still as an adult, she loved the shiny stuff.

"Do the holidays upset you?" he asked, glancing over his shoulder to meet her eyes. "I imagine it's difficult without your parents at times like this."

Chelsea wasn't quite sure what to say. Yes, it was hard, but she couldn't quite focus on her response. Was Gabe trying to get to know her more? Did he want to take this relationship somewhere they hadn't discussed? Because placing her past front and center in the conversation was most definitely putting them on another level.

"Losing my father was the worst," she admitted, staring at the tree because it was easier than looking into those caring gray eyes. "I know he died of a broken heart. He gave up his will when the only woman he loved walked out and was never heard from since."

Chelsea bit her lower lip, willing the burn in her throat and the threat of more tears to cease. "I actually know where my mother is. I have for years."

"Chels." Gabe crossed to her, sliding his hands up her arms, curling his fingers over her shoulders. "Have you contacted her?"

"No. Why would I?" Now, she did meet that mesmerizing gaze. "She made her choice. At first I just wanted to see if I could use my skills to find her, and I did. She doesn't live that far from here. She has a new life, and is clearly not concerned with what she left behind."

"Baby, I'm sorry."

Baby. He'd not called her such an endearing term before. Well, he'd drawn out darlin' once or twice, but always in that devil-may-care attitude. The way he spoke to her now, the way he *looked* at her, was completely different.

She found she wanted to open up more now that she'd started. Never before had she felt like this, like she could trust a man with more than her body. Gabe was worth the risk.

"When she left and then Dad passed, I didn't handle things very well. I was on the verge of a breakdown and I broke."

Shame filled her. She'd never actually said the words out loud. When everything had happened, Daniel and Brandee were well aware of the situation and had gotten her the help she needed. She'd never had to fully tell the story. Even when she spoke with counselors, Chelsea had glossed over details or kept her feelings veiled.

"Hey." Gabe slid his finger beneath her chin and tipped her face up. "Whatever it is, you don't have to tell me. I want to help, but don't torture yourself."

She pulled in a breath and reached up to grip his wrist, as if drawing strength from him. "I tried to end my life."

Gabe's gasp had her cringing. "Chelsea." Her name came out somewhere between pain and fear as Gabe pulled her into his arms. He encircled her in a vise-like grip. "I don't even know what to say."

He held her another moment, the silence settling heavily around them. She knew by the way he held her that he was stunned, struggling with how to react.

"I felt so alone," she went on, clinging to him. "I know I had Daniel and Brandee, but my foundation was gone. My trust had been shattered when my mom left. I didn't know how to approach my dad to talk because he was so distraught. Then once he was gone..."

Gabe eased her back and framed her face, forcing her

to hold his attention. "I hate that you had to go through all of that. I hate that you felt alone and that there was no choice but to... Damn it, I can't even think it, let alone say it."

There was so much affection in his tone, so much, dare she hope love? Had his feelings changed toward her? It certainly hadn't been her intent to influence him when she'd decided to open up about her past. She'd grown to love and trust him, and decided that if she was going to go after what she truly wanted, then he needed to know the full story.

"Needless to say, that's why Daniel has always been so protective." Chelsea pulled in a breath, thankful the story was out and off her chest. "I guess I wanted you to know."

"You trust me."

There was almost a relief in his voice. Chelsea smiled through her tears and nodded. "I do trust you, Gabe."

She went up onto her toes and kissed him. She wanted to feel him, to taste him. She wanted to ignore the pain from her past and concentrate on what she hoped was her future.

Gabe flattened his hands on her back, urging her closer. From mouths to hips, they were joined. Chelsea knew she could never get enough. She only hoped he was starting to feel the same way.

When Gabe eased back, she had to stifle a groan. She wanted him to take her to the bedroom—or here on the floor would be fine—and finish what that kiss promised. She wanted to feel alive after the anguish of her admission.

"Want to go put your Christmas stuff up?" he asked, his brows drawn in.

Seriously? He was worried about her tree?

But the closer she looked at him, the more she realized he was out of his element here. He was unsure of how to approach her now, of how to handle her. There was so much affection in his eyes. She was used to the desire, the passion and fire. But seeing this side of Gabe warmed every single part of her and only added to the growing hope she had for them.

"It's late and we're so close to Christmas." Chelsea waved a hand in a silent gesture to just forget it. "Besides, is that really how you want to spend our time together? I mean, I could probably procure some mistletoe and we could toy with that. You can even decorate me if you want."

Longing instantly filled his eyes. "I can think of several ways for us to spend the rest of the night and you won't need to go get mistletoe. I'll have you unwrapped and begging in no time." He nipped once again at her lips. "You're staying, by the way."

Little did he know she'd never had any intention of leaving.

As he lay in the dark with Chelsea sleeping in the crook of his arm, Gabe couldn't stop replaying their conversation. The idea that this strong, independent woman had thought there was no way out of her stressful life, well, it absolutely crushed him. A world without Chelsea would be dull and lifeless.

Gabe realized now that he didn't want a world without her. She'd become part of him, part of everything he did and every thought he had. Somehow she'd managed to consume more space in his mind than work and that had never happened. Ever.

Chelsea made his days brighter. As silly and adolescent as that sounded, it was true. When he knew they were going to see each other, he found himself counting down the hours. Yes, the sex was amazing, better than he'd ever had, actually, but there was more. So much more.

He trailed his fingers up her arm and over the curve of her shoulder. They were supposed to end things in a couple of days but he wasn't planning on letting her go. She'd exposed too much of herself, of her troubled past, and he knew his Chelsea wouldn't have done that if she weren't having strong feelings for him.

Between the wedding and Christmas, Gabe figured this was about as magical as the timing could get. He wanted Chelsea to know that she was it for him. He wanted her to know that she would never feel alone again, not as long as he was in her life.

But he wanted her to know he meant it. He wanted her to see that he wasn't just in this for their time between the sheets. He wasn't sure when he'd started falling for her, but he'd done it just the same.

Their quick, whirlwind affair had forced him to realize that she was so much more than just a sexy woman who challenged him. She'd overcome so much in her past, yet she'd come out on top in her career and her life.

Still, the guilt hadn't subsided. She'd suffered even more than he ever suspected and hadn't said a word to anyone except her brother, her best friend, and now him.

That in and of itself told him all he needed to know about her feelings.

Gabe smiled into the darkness and rolled over to face her. Even though she continued to sleep, he couldn't let himself relax. He wanted to formulate the perfect plan to show Chelsea just how much he wanted her in his life, just how much he cared for her and, yes, just how much he loved her.

This would be the greatest Christmas yet.

146

BEST MAN UNDER THE MISTLETOE

* * *

Chelsea ended up going into Hunt & Co., after she'd gone home, showered and changed her clothes. After their emotional night, she'd woken with a smile on her face and Gabe had promptly given her something else to smile about.

Gabe couldn't wait until this evening. They planned on taking more decorations to the church for the wedding, which was closing in on them. That meant the deadline to achieve his goal of keeping Chelsea in his life was also closing in on him.

They hadn't spoken about it since before her heartfelt admission last night. He hoped she'd forget all about it, that she'd ignore the end date they'd set.

As much as he wanted to be with her, he was glad to have this time alone because he needed to plan. As soon as the wedding was over, he intended to bring her back to his place and tell her everything. That he didn't want to be without her, that he was so proud of her for learning to trust, and that he trusted her, too…with his heart.

Gabe headed down to the first floor to check his mail. He planned on swinging by the TCC to make sure everything was in place for the outdoor reception. He'd promised Chelsea he would and she'd even sent him a text of her notes so he didn't forget anything. Which was fine, considering he didn't have the first clue about wedding receptions.

Fortunately, he'd discovered quite a bit on this journey, though, and if Chelsea wanted a large wedding, he'd damn well give her one. Anything she wanted, so long as he was in her life.

Once upon a time the thought of a wedding with him as the groom would've scared the hell out of him, but not anymore. Having Chelsea all to himself forever had quickly become a dream he wanted to make a reality.

Gabe exited the elevator on the first floor and nodded to the daytime doorman standing at his post. Sunshine flooded the floor of the old building, highlighting the gleaming black-and-white-checkered flooring.

When Gabe checked his mailbox, he was surprised to only have one piece of mail. He hadn't checked it for nearly a week. But considering that most everything he did was online, and with the holidays fast approaching, it probably made sense there wasn't much mail.

He flipped the envelope over and noticed a note taped to the front.

This letter was placed in my box by mistake. I was out of town so I wasn't able to get it back to you until now.
Your Neighbor in 2C.

So the elderly lady who lived below him had received his mail. That rarely happened. She'd been out of town for the past several weeks visiting her kids across the state.

Gabe tore off the note and stilled. The letter was postmarked four weeks ago, but that wasn't the part that chilled him.

The return address was Dusty's. Seeing his uncle's handwriting, receiving this from him after his death, was a bit eerie.

Gabe had no clue what Dusty could've sent out only one day before his death, so he sure as hell didn't want to open this without privacy. He couldn't get back to his loft fast enough. Gabe had a sinking feeling whatever Maverick had started almost a year ago was about to come back to life in this piece of mail.

Once Gabe finally made it to his apartment, he barely got his door closed before he was tearing into the oversize envelope. He pulled out the contents, cursing under his breath when black-and-white glossies spilled out onto the floor at his feet. Glossies of the woman he loved.

Gabe crouched down and sifted through the images, one after another after another. His heart sank, his stomach turned.

He searched through each photo, but they all had the same theme. She was naked or partially dressed, in the locker room of her gym. From the angle, Gabe could tell someone had planted the camera in a vent or a light fixture. Each photo brought a new wave of rage. She'd had no clue these were taken. Were these just copies of the others that were out there? Because he'd deliberately never looked at those.

Or were these completely new?

Dread coiled in his gut as he gathered the photos and stalked to his kitchen. He tossed the images on the counter and started reading the letter.

Gabriel,
I don't know how much longer I have, so I'm reaching out to my only living relative.

By now, you may have figured everything out. Yes, I'm Maverick. I have my reasons for doing what I did, which I'll lay out below. But I also have some unfinished business and need your help.

As you know I was shunned at the Texas Cattleman's Club. My attempts to gain membership were constantly turned down. They let women in a man's club and kept me out? Well, I had to take matters into my own hands and, once I explain

why, you'll understand. I hope you carry on where
I had to leave off.

Years ago I had an affair with Colleen Hum-
phreys. Her husband was a longtime president of
the TCC and on the board until his death just a
year ago. When he found out about the affair, he
threatened to ruin me. But blacklisting me only
backfired on his precious club. I mean, who had
the last laugh? The revenge I took on the members
was so sweet. I do feel a tad guilty for the lives I
ruined, but they were merely pawns caught in the
game. I had no choice.

Gabe gritted his teeth at his uncle's words. So Dusty
had done all of this, terrorizing Royal for months on end,
to get back at a man who'd been his victim to begin with?
What kind of sick person had his uncle been?

Disgust filled Gabe as he focused on the rest of the
letter.

Here are some final photos of Chelsea Hunt. I never
shared these and I know you'll help me out by finishing this. You always were so loyal. I'm counting on you, Gabriel. Do what you see fit to ruin
the TCC and all those who were allowed in when
I was not. Women like Chelsea and so many others think they're too good, walking around all high
and mighty. It's not right, but we'll make sure they
suffer.

Gabe gripped the paper so tightly that it crinkled in
his hand. Then he tossed it onto the counter, unable to
even touch it another second. He had no clue what to do.
He had to think. He'd believed this situation was behind

them but it had just reared its ugly head once again. Now, he was in control…whether he wanted to be or not.

At least Dusty had mailed the photos and letter to him. Gabe hated to think what would've happened had they gotten into the wrong hands.

Disgusted, Gabe turned away from the heap of photos on the counter. He didn't want to see them anymore, didn't want *anyone* to see them. Gabe would have to turn them over to Sheriff Nathan Battle to be processed with the rest of the items. They were still trying to figure out who could've helped Dusty because obviously the man couldn't have planted a camera in a women's locker room by himself. Not with his poor health.

Gabe would get to the bottom of this. He'd find out who was helping his uncle, he'd make sure this was all in the past, and then he and Chelsea could move forward with their future.

Fifteen

"Can you believe tomorrow is the day?" Chelsea resisted a girlish squeal, but she hugged her best friend tight. "Everything is going to be perfect."

The rehearsal dinner was going exactly as planned. The food was perfect, the décor similar to what would be used in the actual wedding. Chelsea couldn't be more excited for her best friend.

"Everything is going to be perfect," Chelsea exclaimed.

Brandee eased back and nodded. "You and Gabe have gone above and beyond. I can't thank you guys enough."

"We were happy to help."

Brandee's brows rose as her smile widened. "Maybe we'll be planning your wedding next?"

As much as the idea gave Chelsea the warm fuzzies, she wasn't sure Gabe was ready for that. She wasn't even sure he was ready to hear her say how she truly felt. But, after the wedding tomorrow, she was going to tell him.

This was their last night together and she had every intention of making it unforgettable. She would love to open herself up to him tonight and tell him every emotion she'd kept bottled up, but if he turned her down, she didn't want the awkward tension at the wedding, especially since they were walking down the aisle together.

"We're just…" Chelsea wasn't quite sure how to describe the current situation. "Taking this one day at a time."

"You love him."

The chatter around them, the music from the DJ, the soft breeze, everything faded away at those three words. There was no use denying them, not to Brandee. The girl knew Chelsea better than she knew herself.

"I just hope he feels the same."

Brandee tipped her head. "If the way he's staring at you right now is any indicator, I'd say he feels more than lust."

A thrill shot through Chelsea. She so wanted Gabe to be on the same emotional page as she was. They'd had a breakthrough moment when she'd fully opened herself to him. He'd taken her to his bed and made love to her like she was the most fragile, most precious thing in his life. She only prayed that was true.

"Just be honest," Brandee urged. "I almost lost Shane, but we both fought for what we wanted. You're going to have to do the same."

Chelsea opened her mouth to reply, but Brandee squeezed her hands and shot a look over Chelsea's shoulder.

"I better go talk to the other guests," Brandee stated. "I'll see you in the morning at the church."

Chelsea watched as her friend went to talk to a couple of the other bridesmaids. The outdoor rehearsal dinner at

Hope Springs Ranch was perfect. With the temperatures hovering around fifty, they were able to have the event outside in comfort thanks to the heated tents.

This laid-back atmosphere was perfect before the rush and drama of tomorrow. The caterers had done a phenomenal job; of course, they'd used some beef tips from Hunt & Co. for the main course.

Strong hands curled around Chelsea's shoulders and she didn't even hesitate when Gabe eased her back against his chest.

"These little dresses of yours drive me out of my mind," he growled into her ear. "I think you enjoy teasing me."

Chelsea smiled and reached up to cup her hands over his. "I love wearing dresses with boots when the occasion calls for it. Driving you out of your mind is just a bonus."

"What are you wearing under this? Something else new?"

"Perhaps."

She'd put on the slinky teddy with him in mind, and had been counting down the time until they could leave so he could take it off.

"We practiced coming down the aisle and going back up, plus we've eaten." He nipped at her earlobe. "Are we done here yet?"

Chelsea turned in his arms. "You know, if we keep leaving parties early, people are going to know what we're up to."

His hands settled easily on her waist. Those gray eyes she'd come to love sought her from beneath the rim of his black hat.

"I don't care what people think," he told her. "I care about you and that's it."

He cared about her. Not quite a declaration of love,

but it was more than what they'd originally started with. Hope blossomed.

"We should at least say goodbye to our friends," she told him.

"Fine. Say your goodbyes. Be quick." He smacked a kiss on her mouth and stepped back. "Be at my place in fifteen minutes."

Chelsea laughed. "It takes me fifteen minutes to get there from here."

"Then you better just wave goodbye instead of saying it."

He turned and headed toward Shane. Chelsea watched as they did the one-armed man hug and then Gabe headed off toward the field where they'd all parked their cars.

"I imagine you'll be leaving, too."

Chelsea turned to see her brother eyeing her with concern. "I am," she confirmed.

"You're going to get hurt, Chels. I know guys like Walsh. Hell, I know Gabe. I can see the hearts in your eyes."

She attempted to tamp down her anger as she crossed her arms over her chest. "You've tried to warn me before. Do I look like I'm hurt? Don't interfere, Daniel. I've got this under control."

When she started to turn away, he grabbed her elbow and forced her to focus on him. "I hope your eyes are wide-open here. And I hope that he feels the same way as you do because you're in deep."

She hoped Gabe was on the same page with her feelings, too.

With a simple nod, Chelsea pulled her arm from Daniel's grasp. She knew he was just looking out for her, but this was ridiculous. No one was going to come between her and what she wanted—and she wanted Gabe Walsh in her life.

By the time she made it to his loft, her entire body was humming. Chelsea smiled at the doorman as she entered the building. The elevator ride seemed to take forever, then finally she was at Gabe's door. She didn't bother knocking as she turned the knob beneath her palm and eased the door open.

The only light in the loft was the sparkle from the Christmas tree and the city lights streaming through the wall of windows.

She'd barely gotten the door closed when Gabe's arms banded around her. Chelsea melted against him, more than ready to spend the night here.

"You're three minutes late."

Chelsea pushed away from him and crossed the apartment. She wasn't quite done driving him out of his mind.

"I had to talk to my brother," she explained. "And say goodbye to Brandee and Shane. Then I thanked the caterers."

"Take off your dress."

Chelsea turned back to face him. The large loft seemed to close in on her as Gabe took one slow step after another toward her. His eyes never left hers, giving her all the thrills. How could a look make her feel like he was touching her all over? How did he have so much control over not just her body but her mind?

"Come take it off me," she countered.

A low growl emanated from him as he closed the distance between them. In a flash move, he gripped the hem of her dress and jerked it up and over her head. The second he tossed it aside, his swift intake of breath had her confidence soaring. She propped her hands on her hips, thrusting her chest out and cocking her head to the side.

"Was it worth the wait, cowboy?"

"Damn," he whispered. "Had I known you were wearing that, we never would've made it to the dinner."

Chelsea couldn't help but laugh. "I'm pretty sure there's a rule against that."

"Maybe, but nobody would blame me."

She reached out, jerking on his silver buckle. "Why don't you just take me here? This is technically the last night in our agreement, right?"

As soon as the words were out of her mouth, she wanted to take them back. But seeing the flicker of annoyance in his eyes told her he wasn't ready to see this end.

Maybe she should tell him now. Maybe she should just throw it all out there and take the risk now.

But, no. Because if she'd read him wrong, she would never forgive herself for the resulting awkwardness at Brandee and Shane's wedding.

Gabe lifted her into his arms. With one arm behind her back, one arm behind her knees, he nipped at her lips as he walked through the loft. Romance had entered their relationship. This had all started with frenzied, passionate sex. Somewhere along the way love had settled in deep.

Chelsea wrapped her arms around his neck and nestled her head against his shoulder. "I expected you to take me against the window again," she murmured into his ear.

"Maybe tonight is different."

Maybe it was. As Gabe kicked the door shut to his bedroom, Chelsea finally felt like things were going her way. She'd found her happily-ever-after.

Early the following morning, Chelsea slid from bed. The sun still hadn't come up, but she couldn't sleep. Between the wedding, the fantastic night in Gabe's arms, and the talk she wanted to have with him later today about their future, there was just too much going on and her mind simply wouldn't shut down.

Chelsea glanced back to the bed where Gabe lay sprawled on his stomach, his light hair in disarray after she'd run her fingers through it. Her body still hummed as she snagged his T-shirt and put it on. She eased the door closed behind her as she made her way to the kitchen. Gabe was every bit the bachelor, but hopefully he had something she could make for their breakfast. She didn't have to be at the church for a few hours, so maybe breakfast in bed was a great way to start the day.

Humming as she started searching through his cabinets, Chelsea figured if all else failed, she could do coffee, eggs and toast. He at least had those on hand.

She pulled out a pan and the eggs. Once she had them cracked into a bowl, she tugged on a drawer for a whisk. Of course his utensils weren't in a drawer she would put them in. She tried another, only to find a junk drawer. She started to shut it when something caught her eye.

It was a black-and-white photograph. Chelsea focused on it, her heart hammering in her throat. No. That couldn't be. Gabe wasn't the accomplice. Was he? The sheriff had said they were searching for a female.

With a shaky hand she pulled the picture from the drawer, only to find more underneath it. She pulled them all out, then she saw a letter with Gabe's name on it.

Nausea settled in the pit of her stomach as she shuffled through each picture. These weren't the same ones that had circulated months back. These were actually newer, maybe a couple of months old. She knew that because she remembered the exact day at the gym. She recognized the outfit; she'd tried racquetball for the first time. Pretty soon after that, the first nude photos had been leaked and she hadn't been back to that gym since.

Pulling in a deep breath, she set the pictures on the counter, facing down. Her attention went to the letter; she quickly saw it was from Dusty. Did she really want to read this? Did she want to know what he and Gabe had discussed?

Her eyes scanned the scratchy penmanship first before she went back to the top and absorbed every single word.

She couldn't be reading this right. She just...she couldn't. This was important evidence that had been sent to Gabe weeks ago. Why was he hiding these photos in a drawer? Shouldn't he have turned these over to the sheriff by now? Was Gabe covering something up?

Dropping the letter on top of the pictures, Chelsea took a step back and stared at the pile. Such damning evidence of Gabe's involvement with his uncle mocked her and the future she'd been foolish enough to believe in.

Trust hadn't come easy and now she knew why. She should've trusted her instincts to begin with where Gabe was concerned.

The tears came before she even realized it. All the hurt, all the anger, and so much resentment flooded her. She should've listened to her initial suspicions. Hell, she should've listened to Daniel. Hadn't he been trying to warn her she'd get hurt?

She wasn't just hurt, she was utterly, completely, destroyed.

The glow from the Christmas tree in the living room mocked her, trying to pull her back to that night when they'd put it up. He'd completely played her for a naïve fool.

At least she hadn't told Gabe how she felt. He'd probably get a great kick out of knowing he'd duped her.

Chelsea blinked the tears away and went to the living room where her clothes were. She quickly changed, trying to figure out exactly what her next move should be. Did she really want to confront him? Did she want to hear more lies?

And that's what all of this had been. A relationship built on lies.

Once she was dressed, Chelsea tucked her hair behind her ears and glanced at the closed bedroom door. As much as she didn't want to even look at him and hear his excuses, she deserved answers. She deserved to know the real man…not just the one she'd fallen in love with. That man didn't exist.

Sixteen

The sound of the bedroom door creaking woke him. But it was the lights flashing on and the papers that were tossed onto the bed that had Gabe sitting straight up.

No. Not papers. Pictures.

His gut tightened as he glanced up at Chelsea. The brokenness and pain staring back at him told him all he needed to know. She believed he had deceived and betrayed her.

He now regretted that he hadn't done a better job securing the papers. He had intended to turn them over to the sheriff as soon as the wedding was over; he just hadn't wanted to risk more press attention to ruin Brandee and Shane's—not to mention Chelsea's—special day. She had worked so hard on this wedding and he didn't want it ruined for her. He'd had every intention of doing things the right way—or what he thought was right—but now he just looked like he'd been deceiving her all along.

"I don't even want you to defend yourself," she said, crossing her arms over her dress.

Damn it. She'd put her clothes back on, which meant he had about two seconds to get her to listen to the truth. Mentally, she'd already left.

"I just want to know what your motivation is," she went on. "What could you get from having these pictures just lying around your house? Were you planning on humiliating me further? Is this just family loyalty?"

Gabe came to his feet, jerking on a pair of shorts lying by the bed. "I have never set out to hurt you, Chels. I had nothing to do with these pictures being taken."

"Maybe not," she agreed then let out a harsh laugh. "But you know what? Dusty's letter spells things out pretty clearly. You were to take over since he was too sick. You could've destroyed these or turned them over to the sheriff, or hell, given them to me. Yet here you are with them tucked away in your apartment."

He started to take a step forward, but she held up a hand. "No. All this time you were with me, you made me believe you cared, but under the same roof you were hiding these pictures. I was a fool to trust you."

"You can trust me," he insisted. Gabe crossed the room, ignoring her when she shook her head and held her hands out to keep him back. "Look at me. Damn it, I was going to take them to Nathan, but not until after the wedding. I put them away so nobody would see them."

Chelsea kept her head turned away, refusing to look at him. "Convenient," she muttered.

Nothing he said now would make her believe. She'd seen the pictures and the letter, and had decided he'd been lying all along. He hated her thinking he would ever be involved in something like this, but most of all, he hated that she was hurting and he couldn't comfort her.

"What can I say to make you believe me?" he asked.

He wanted to reach out and hold her, but she would never allow that. Her red-rimmed eyes tore him apart. How long had she been in the other room tormenting herself with this?

The automatic bedroom shades rolled up right on time, the soft hum breaking the tension in the room. The sun was starting to rise, but the day that should've been one of the happiest for them had turned into anything but.

"There's nothing you can say," she whispered, her voice thick with tears. "I trusted you with a piece of me I've never given to another man. I thought…"

Her words died off as she bit her lower lip to compose herself. Gabe did reach for her now. He didn't give a damn what she wanted because he knew he hadn't done a thing wrong and he just wanted to hold her, to comfort her. She was absolutely breaking his heart and he'd promised her she'd never feel alone again.

Damn it. He *promised*.

Now, she stared up at him, unshed tears swimming in her eyes. "I thought after the wedding I'd tell you that I didn't want to end things. Stupid, right? I mean, all this time you've chosen to side with your uncle."

"No." He gently took her by the shoulders. "I never sided with him. I got all of that in the mail after he died. Just two days ago."

Chelsea broke free of his grip. "I'm not convinced that you had nothing to do with the first set of pictures, but let's pretend I do believe you. These pictures should never have been here. You should've turned them over. If you care for me at all, if you truly wanted me to believe you were innocent, you wouldn't have kept them."

"I was going to give them to Nathan," he insisted.

Stepping back, Chelsea wiped at her damp cheeks.

"Then you should've told me the second you got them. You have no excuse for that."

She was right. He didn't, other than the fact he didn't want to cause her any more pain.

When she turned away, Gabe's heart clenched. "Don't go. Don't leave this upset. Stay. We can talk this out and then I'll take you to the church."

Chelsea's shoulders straightened, but she didn't face him again. "I'm leaving and I'll get myself to the church. Brandee and Shane deserve this day to be perfect and I'll not let you ruin it for them. After the wedding and our duties are done, I never want to see or speak to you again."

It was difficult, but Gabe let her go.

Right now she needed space, and he needed to figure out how the hell he could fix this. Because he would fix it and he would make her realize that he was never that guy. He could never purposely cause her so much pain.

Though he had to admit beneath his denial and defensiveness, hurt started spreading through him. She actually thought he'd been capable of doing such heinous things. Maybe she'd never fully trusted him. Maybe in the back of her mind she'd always kept those suspicions in reserve.

He would have to put on a front for the wedding because Chelsea was right. This day belonged to Brandee and Shane. But if she thought for a second that he was just going to let her go and never hear from him again... well, she would be in for a surprise.

Gabe gathered the pictures and the letter and went out into the living room. Once he had them secured in an envelope, he laid them on the sofa table. Tomorrow he'd take them to the sheriff and be done with the likes of his uncle. Even dead, the man was ruining lives. Then he'd find out who the hell had assisted Dusty in obtaining the photos to begin with.

Padding barefoot to the kitchen, Gabe noticed the eggs on the counter, the pan on the stove, the bowl. His heart flipped and he gripped the edge of the countertop. She'd been prepared to make him breakfast. She'd found the pictures shoved in the drawer.

Damn it. He was a fool. He should've told her but, in his defense, he just hadn't wanted her to have to deal with that mess any longer. He'd been trying to protect her, but all he'd managed to do was to crush her hopes further and to destroy the trust they'd built.

He had to find a way to get her back. Gabe had never given up before and he sure as hell didn't intend to start now—not when this was the most important moment of his life.

Chelsea smoothed a hand down her gold dress and tried to forget the last time she'd had this on. She flashed back on the dressing room, on Gabe, his clever hands and magical touch.

Pain squeezed like a vise around her chest and she pushed the memory aside. She'd doubled up on concealer and powder, hoping to hide her puffy red eyes. Her waterproof mascara was definitely going to be put to the test.

When Chelsea had first arrived at the church, Brandee had questioned her, but Chelsea had just played it off as wedding tears.

Chelsea spun away from the mirror, not wanting to see herself in this dress. She could practically feel Gabe's hands at the side zipper.

Would his memory fade over time or would she be forced to battle him in her mind forever?

Chelsea crossed to the adjoining room where Brandee

was getting ready. It was time to get into full maid-of-honor mode. Pulling in a deep breath, Chelsea let herself into the room and gasped.

Brandee stood in front of the floor-length mirror, her gaze meeting Chelsea's in the reflection. Chelsea had seen the dress, but now it seemed different. With Brandee's long hair falling in simple waves down her back and the subtle makeup, she looked angelic.

"Can you help me with my veil?" Brandee asked, a wide smile on her face. "My hands are shaking."

Chelsea offered her best friend a smile and crossed to where the veil hung on the back of a closet door. Carefully, she removed it from the plastic wrap and hanger.

"Squat down just a tad," Chelsea told Brandee as she came to stand behind her. "Tip your head back a bit."

After adjusting the pins to be hidden in the soft curls, Chelsea stepped back. "There. How does that look?"

Seeing her best friend smile in the mirror—no, she wasn't just smiling, she was glowing—helped heal a portion of Chelsea's wounded heart. Love did exist, she was absolutely certain of that. She'd just misplaced hers.

"Everything okay?"

Chelsea focused her attention on Brandee's reflection and nodded. "Couldn't be better. You're the most beautiful bride I've ever seen. And this Christmas wedding is going to be magical."

Brandee turned and reached for Chelsea's hands. "I'm more focused on my happily-ever-after. Too many people focus on the wedding details and making a big show of things. I just want to spend my life with Shane."

"He's a lucky man."

"I'm the lucky one." Brandee tipped her head down and narrowed her eyes. "What's up, Chels? Something is off with you today."

There was no sense in lying again. Brandee wasn't buying it. "Just a mishap with Gabe. Nothing for you to worry about on your special day."

Brandee's brows drew in as she squeezed Chelsea's hands. "Oh, honey, what happened?"

The threat of tears burned the back of her throat. "He's not the man I thought he was."

"Did he hurt you?"

Chelsea dabbed beneath her eyes, already knowing she was going to have to have a makeup redo. "I found more pictures at his place. Pictures of me from the gym locker room."

Brandee jerked back. "What did he say?"

"He denied any involvement with his uncle. Dusty sent the photos with a letter—I read it. He wanted Gabe to carry on with what he'd started."

Brandee pursed her lips. "But Gabe didn't do anything with them, right?"

"Not yet. But he didn't tell me he had them," Chelsea replied. "He kept them hidden when he could've destroyed them or just explained what happened and why he had them in the first place."

Brandee reached up and wiped a tear from Chelsea's cheek before squeezing her hands once again. "Gabe wouldn't hurt you. Did you ever think that's the reason he didn't tell you? Maybe he's protecting you."

Or maybe he was still being loyal to his uncle.

There were just so many questions, and she was an emotional wreck. Now wasn't the time to try to solve all of her problems. She had a wedding to partake in…and a man waiting to walk down the aisle with her.

"Forget it," Chelsea said, squaring her shoulders and sniffling back the tears. "This is your day and what-

ever Gabe and I have going on, I swear it won't interfere with this."

"Of course it won't." Brandee smiled and dropped
her hands to smooth down her gown. "I know how Gabe
feels, though. Remember the way he manhandled that
jerk who was mistreating you? And the way Gabe looks at
you when you don't know is enough to set panties on fire.
He cares for you and, if I'm not mistaken, he loves you."

Chelsea closed her eyes, willing those words to be
true, but his actions said different...didn't they? Had she
jumped to conclusions?

"We've all been through so much." Chelsea reached
out to adjust her friend's veil around her face. "Let's
just focus on the happiness of today. It's two days before
Christmas and everything is finally settling back down
after a year of scandal. This is going to be the best day
and a new beginning."

Brandee nodded. "Let's fix your makeup and get ready
for the pictures. But I want you to keep in mind, Gabe is
exactly the man he claims to be. I'd stake my life on it."

Chelsea wasn't so sure she could say the same, but
she'd laid her heart on the line, which was pretty much
the same. She needed some space to think. Unfortunately,
she'd be walking arm in arm with the only man she'd ever
loved in a very short time.

Right now she needed to put on her happy face and
coat of armor. This day was about to test every bit of
her strength.

Seventeen

"You look stunning."

Gabe whispered the compliment as Chelsea slid her arm over his elbow. She clutched her gold ribbon that secured a ball of mistletoe. In lieu of bouquets, Chelsea and Brandee had gone with mistletoe…and now he was being mocked by the classic flower.

The late afternoon wedding at the TCC was perfect. As he glanced around, Gabe saw every detail that he and Chelsea had a hand in. He had to focus on things like that because the woman at his side was driving him out of his mind with want and need.

The way Chelsea's body shifted beneath the material of her dress, the way she delicately brushed against his body, had his mind pumping into overdrive.

The last time he'd seen her in that dress…

Gabe focused on making it down the aisle, his hand securing hers over his arm. He needed to touch her, needed to feel her. Regardless of whether this was just for the sake of appearances, he'd take what he could get at this point.

The way she'd left so hurt and angry only hours ago—yeah, he had to have some sort of contact. He'd sat in his apartment and slowly driven himself insane with what he should have done differently and how he could have avoided hurting her.

But he honestly didn't know that he would have done things differently. Yes, he could have informed her that he'd received the mail from his uncle, but he'd planned on doing that when he turned them over to the authorities.

She was understandably upset, but just as she had at the start of their relationship, she would come to see that she was wrong. His actions would speak for themselves. He just had to figure out how the hell to get her to understand that he had been protecting her.

Chelsea remained silent as they reached the end of the aisle and parted ways. His arm and hand instantly chilled. Holding this winter wedding outdoors had nothing to do with it, either. The tent where Brandee and Shane were about to exchange their vows was heated.

No, his chill came from the fact that the one woman he'd allowed himself to truly love, the one woman who'd entered his life like a whirlwind and settled deep into his heart, had pushed him away.

In her defense, she had good reasons for being wary. But where he was concerned, her fears and suspicions were misplaced.

Canon in D chimed through the very well hidden speakers and everyone in attendance came to their feet. Gabe glanced to the end of the aisle as Brandee came around the corner. Shane tipped his head down and rubbed his eyes. Gabe reached up and squeezed his shoulder in silent encouragement.

He couldn't imagine what was going through his best friend's mind. What would it be like to find the one you wanted to spend your life with? What would it be like to have her coming toward you, ready to take a risk together like nothing else in the entire world mattered?

Gabe turned his attention to Chelsea. Her eyes were locked on the bride, but her shoulders were stiff and she held tight to the ribbon of mistletoe. There was a hint of a smile on her face, but Gabe saw the hurt in her eyes and knew she was anything but relaxed.

Gabe paid little attention to the vows and ring exchange. He didn't take his eyes off Chelsea and when she met his gaze, he didn't look away. Neither did she.

He had no idea what was going through her mind, or what was even going on around them. He didn't care. All that mattered was Chelsea. Damn it. His heart flipped in his chest. She'd gone and worked her way right into the deepest part of him—and he realized that's exactly where he wanted her.

This wasn't just him wanting to prove his innocence to her and make sure she wasn't hurting. Yes, he did want both of those things, but the obvious reason was literally staring right back at him. He wanted Chelsea in his life, now, tomorrow, forever.

He wanted what Brandee and Shane had; he wanted what so many of their friends had found. There had never been another to grab his heart the way Chelsea had and he wasn't about to just let her walk out of his life.

As soon as the ceremony was over, Gabe waited for the newly married couple to turn to the guests and make their way back down the aisle. The music started up in celebration of the milestone moment.

Gabe stepped up, extending his elbow for Chelsea to take. She didn't meet his eyes as she did so.

"We need to talk," he murmured out the side of his mouth as they made their way off the elevated platform.

"Not yet."

Well, at least she'd replied and hadn't completely shot him down. That was a step in the right direction.

As they joined the party lining up in the back to greet guests, Chelsea quickly let go of him and went to stand next to Brandee.

The evening seemed to drag on for him, but he was positive the newly married couple was having the time of their lives. Chelsea always seemed busy or missing when he went to find her. Most likely she was avoiding him, and that was okay, but it was only so long before he caught up with her. He had no idea what he planned to say, no idea how to make this all go away, but he would.

Gabe caught a flash of gold in the distance, but by the time he crossed the patio area just off the TCC ballroom, he realized it wasn't Chelsea but another guest.

Cursing, Gabe turned and nearly tripped a waiter carrying a tray of drinks.

"'Scuse me," he said, holding his arms out to make sure the tray stayed level.

"Care for a bourbon?" the waiter asked.

Gabe grabbed one of the tumblers and muttered his thanks before moving on. He wasn't in the mood to mingle or dance; he only wanted to talk to Chelsea. As he rounded the back of the building near the walking trails and stables, he found Daniel and Chelsea in an embrace.

Clearly he'd stumbled upon something private. As he started to turn away, Chelsea's words stopped him.

"You warned me," she said, her voice slightly trembling. "You told me I'd get hurt and I didn't want to hear it."

Gabe slid behind some landscaping near the corner of the building so as not to be seen. He'd just listen for a minute, then he'd give them their privacy. He knew he should walk away now, but damn it, this was the woman he loved and he wanted to know what he was up against in this fight.

"I never wanted to be right about this," Daniel said. "I want you to find happiness, Chels. I just didn't think Gabe was the guy for you."

What the hell? Her brother had warned her off? Anger bubbled within Gabe and he started to step away from his hiding place, but Chelsea's cry stopped him in his tracks.

"But I love him."

Hope quickly replaced the anger. She loved him? So all the hurt he'd seen in her eyes was about thinking the man she loved had betrayed her trust. As much as he wanted to be angry over this whole situation—with his uncle and with himself for hurting Chelsea—all he could focus on was the fact that she loved him.

It was almost like a weight had been lifted from his chest. Those words were all he needed to know he'd get her back. Between his determination and her declaration, that was all the ammunition he needed to secure Chelsea in his life. Forever.

Chelsea pulled back from Daniel's embrace and dabbed beneath her eyes. "I didn't want to have a meltdown, but I wanted to let you know what was going on."

"You weren't acting like yourself," he replied, pulling a handkerchief from his pocket.

Chelsea smiled as she took it. "You always were a gentleman."

"So what are you going to do?" he asked. "You don't trust him, but you love him."

That about summed up this complex situation. Seeing Gabe in his tux, having him hold on to her for the briefest of moments before the wedding vows, had been almost too much to take. She'd tried to focus on the ceremony but keeping her eyes away from Gabe had been near impossible. He'd caught her looking at him once and she'd been unable to turn away. When those gray eyes had locked onto hers, Chelsea swore he was looking into her soul.

"I want to believe him." She looked up at her brother, knowing she'd find concern in his expression. "My heart and my head are saying two different things. I just need to talk to him, but I need time first."

"What can I do?"

Chelsea smoothed a hand down her gown and shook her head. "Nothing at all. Take care of Erin and those babies. I'll handle my love life."

Daniel's lips thinned as he shoved his hands into his suit pockets. "I know you're smart, but I just don't want you to be taken advantage of or to be wrapped up in another scandal."

"I won't be," she assured him. "We're all moving on now that Maverick has been pinpointed. I won't let anyone hurt me like that again. Whoever the accomplice is, they're likely lying low right now."

The words were for her brother's peace of mind, but they were a vow to herself. She refused to ever be the victim again.

"I should get back to the reception." Chelsea wrapped her arms around her brother once more. "Thanks for always listening."

"I wouldn't be anywhere else when you need me."

Chelsea turned away and made her way back to the reception. Thankfully it was wrapping up and Brandee and Shane would head off on their honeymoon soon. They were escaping to someplace tropical and private, so private they hadn't disclosed their destination to friends and family.

Now that the excitement and the hustle and bustle were over, Chelsea planned to take the next two days and do nothing but enjoy the Christmas season. She'd drink hot chocolate topped with whipped cream and peppermint flakes, she'd watch classic movies that were sure to take her mind off her current issues, and she'd not have any contact with Gabriel Walsh until she knew exactly what she wanted to say to him.

And until she could get her emotions under control because damn if she still didn't want the man.

Eighteen

It was Christmas Eve morning and he still hadn't heard a word from Chelsea. She'd slipped from the reception shortly after the bride and groom. In the few minutes Gabe had stayed beyond that, he'd been greeted with a glare from Daniel. Just when Chelsea's brother had started to make his way over to Gabe, Erin had intervened and they had left.

As much as Gabe wanted to stand his ground and talk to Daniel, the most important person he needed to see wasn't returning his texts. He got that she needed space, but her timeframe was about to expire.

Gabe had already taken steps to secure their future. He'd already made sure that nothing else incriminating or embarrassing would crop up out of nowhere down the road. Above all else, he had made sure she was protected. Even if she didn't accept his love, his commitment to her, Gabe still wanted to put a shield of protection around her.

Tonight would be the perfect time to approach her. The annual candlelight and caroling event around the twenty-foot tree in Royal's town square couldn't provide a better setting. He knew Chelsea would be there. Everyone went to the event to light candles, join family and friends, and sing carols. Then they'd all fellowship together afterward as the area businesses provided hot chocolate and baked goods and the shops that lined the square stayed open late. Everyone, no matter their background, their financial status or their age came to celebrate the season.

Chelsea would feel comfortable there. They'd be surrounded by people, so there would be no pressure, but there would also be nowhere for her to run.

Considering he had several more hours to worry about her response, Gabe decided to fill the time making calls and checking on his clients. The swift damage control he'd run in the last couple weeks had paid off. The reputation of his company was strong as ever and more potential clients were pouring in. His career couldn't be better and his global prospects seemed to be a great possibility.

He'd turned the photos over to Nathan, but Gabe wasn't relinquishing control of everything. The hunt for Dusty's accomplice would be over and done with soon and Chelsea could truly move on...hopefully with him. But Gabe was keeping his men on this search. He wanted to find the person who had helped his uncle.

Once Chelsea was back in his life, in his home, he would truly have it all. And Gabe always got what he wanted.

Chelsea went with her favorite emerald-green sweater, dark jeans, and her cowgirl boots. She did her hair in loose curls and applied a thin layer of gloss. There was no way she'd avoid Gabe tonight and she wanted to look good but not overly made up.

He'd texted over the past two days, but every time she'd started to reply, she simply hadn't found the right words. How did she get into such a dramatic conversation via text? What she needed to say to him had to be said in person.

Royal's candlelight and caroling was one of her favorite events of the entire year. When everyone gathered together, it almost seemed as if the outside world didn't exist, as if there were no problems, and peace on earth was indeed the reality. She wanted peace, not just for herself, but the town. The past year had been trying for so many, but this seemed to be a new hope and a new day to start over and move forward.

Dare she hope the same was true for her own life? She wasn't so much worried about the gossip regarding her photos anymore. Those who loved and cared for her had already forgotten and those who made rude remarks... well, she wasn't going to concern herself with them.

Her heart warmed as she thought back to how protective Gabe had been that night he'd handled one such jerk. Even though they'd agreed to keep their relationship private, he hadn't cared one bit about his secrecy because he'd been set on defending her. Shouldn't that tell her all she needed to know about the man she'd fallen for?

Sometimes what seemed to be the truth was just a haze covering up the reality. Those pictures in his loft were damning, yes, but what motive would he have had to put them out there? Just because Dusty asked him to? Chelsea didn't see Gabe doing such a thing. He had been angry about the scandal that had ensnared so many members of the TCC. And Gabe had been furious and mortified when Maverick's identity had been revealed.

Chelsea parked several blocks away from the town square and used the walk to clear her head. This was the first year she hadn't come with Brandee, but she knew her friend was having a much better time on her honeymoon.

The shops were all set up with their tables of last-minute Christmas items, baked goods, and hot chocolate and hot cider at the ready. Chelsea couldn't resist getting a cup of cider on her way to the tree. Each table also had candles, so she grabbed one of those, as well.

When she glanced at the white taper in her hand, she couldn't help but inwardly roll her eyes. There was a sprig of mistletoe tied around the base, just below the clear disc to catch any wax drippings.

Mistletoe seemed to be mocking her lately. She was having a difficult time dodging it—and dodging the man who stood only a few feet in front of her holding his own candle.

Chelsea's heart kicked up as she made her way toward Gabe. He'd spotted her already and his eyes held hers as she drew closer.

"I've been watching for you."

She'd missed his voice, missed looking into his face and seeing…everything. The desire, the concern, the love.

Could their relationship be so simple? Could she believe everything he told her and let down her guard again?

"I don't know what to say," she admitted, toying with the tie holding her mistletoe to the taper. "I want so much, Gabe. But I'm afraid."

Kids squealed and ran by; a mother chased them demanding that they stop. Gabe took hold of Chelsea's elbow and steered her toward the side of a building, away from the chaos.

"You think I'm not afraid?" he asked. With her back against the brick building, he shifted so his body blocked out the festivities behind them. "Having you walk out, thinking even for a second that I could hurt you in such a way, put more fear in me than I'd ever known."

Chelsea stared up into his eyes, her heart beating so fast. Gabe wasn't lying; he wasn't just saying pretty words. Everything he told her was from his heart.

"I didn't know what to think." She still didn't, but she couldn't ignore the pull of emotions steering her toward him. "I didn't want to believe the worst, but I panicked when I saw the letter. I know Dusty was all the family you had, so I got scared that your loyalty would override anything you felt for me."

Gabe dropped his candlestick to the ground and instantly framed her face, forcing her to hold his gaze. "Override love? Nothing and no one can replace what I feel for you."

Chelsea's breath caught in her throat. "Love?"

"Damn it, you know I love you." He closed his lips over hers briefly before easing back and resting his forehead against hers. "I can't live without you, Chels. I don't want to even try."

"I—"

"Wait." He shifted back to look at her once again, but he didn't let go. "You need to know that I've turned everything over to Nathan. I've also launched my own investigation into who could've helped Dusty because I agree he didn't act alone."

Tears pricked her eyes. She tried to blink them away, but they spilled over. Gabe gathered her against his chest, rubbing his hand up and down her back. He took the candle from her hand as she clutched his shirt and attempted to pull herself together. How could she, though, when everything she wanted was right here? The risk she was about to take would change her entire life.

"You really love me," she murmured.

She felt the soft rumble of laughter reverberate through his chest. "I really do. There's nothing I wouldn't do for you."

Chelsea slid her arms up and wrapped them around his neck. Pressing her lips to his, she held him tight, never wanting to let this moment go. The moment when he confessed his love, the moment when she decided to let it all go and trust in what they'd built.

"Tell me again," she muttered against his mouth. "Tell me you love me."

Gabe slid the pads of his thumbs over her damp cheeks. "No one will ever love you more. I ached when you left. That's how I knew what we had was real. The pain was too strong to be just casual. I want to build a life with you, Chelsea. No matter what we're doing or where we live, I want it with you."

"I want my life with you, too." Chelsea smiled. "But you should probably know I'm going to be opening a counseling center for young adults."

Gabe's eyes widened then he smiled. "That's a great idea."

"No. It's not just an idea. I bought the building, I'm searching for counselors now, and I want this up and running by spring. The focus will be on teens suffering from depression, anxiety, and suicidal tendencies."

Gabe kissed her hard, fast. "You're so damn remarkable, darlin'. Of course, you're already on the ball with this. Tell me what to do to help and I'm there."

Chelsea threaded her fingers through his hair. "Love me. That's all I need to get through."

The singing started up behind them. The cheerful chorus quickly spread through the street. The magical evening had begun and she stood in her lover's arms. Right now, nothing could destroy her happiness.

"I'll always love you, Chelsea. Always."

She went up onto her toes and kissed him. "I love you more."

Epilogue

"What are you thinking?"

Chelsea lay beside him, her head on the pillow. Soft moonlight filtered in through the blinds he'd left open because he'd wanted to make love to her by the pale light.

After a month of bouncing from her house in Pine Valley to his loft, he'd finally asked her to move in with him. But he knew they'd eventually get their own place and start fresh. Actually he didn't want to wait much longer.

"Gabe?"

He smiled at her, reaching up to stroke her hair away from her face. Touching her, watching her while she slept, just the mundane things they did together, made him anxious, and he was done waiting to ask.

Gabe leaned back and reached into his nightstand, pulling out the small velvet box. He tapped the remote on the nightstand one time, to add the softest light in the room. He wanted to see her face, but he didn't want harsh light to ruin the moment.

Chelsea gasped when he rolled back over and she saw what he was holding.

"I had something elaborate and romantic planned for next week, but—"

"Yes," she squealed.

Gabe laughed. "Will you let me at least ask?"

Chelsea shot up in bed, the sheets pooling around her waist as she took it from him. "No. I want to marry you, now. This minute."

Shaking his head, he took the box back. "We'll get to that, but let me be somewhat of a gentleman here."

He lifted the lid, keeping his eyes on hers. "Since you already answered, I guess I should tell you that your brother already approved this."

Her eyes darted from the ring to him. "You talked to Daniel?"

"Considering he had his doubts about us a month ago, yes. Besides, I always thought a man should ask permission from the father of the woman he wants to marry. For you, I knew I should go through Daniel."

Chelsea's eyes misted as she looked back at the ring. "It's a pearl. It's lovely, Gabe."

He felt a little silly now since he hadn't gone the traditional route with a diamond.

"I saw the pearl and immediately thought of how they're made. How they're the toughest, yet come from something so soft. It just reminded me of you."

She took the ring, but he tossed the box onto the covers and plucked the ring from her hand. "I'm at least putting this on you."

When he slid it onto her finger, she held it up and admired the way it looked on her hand.

In the last month so much had happened in their lives. Gabe had worked closely with Nathan and discovered that Dusty's once lover, whose husband had been on the TCC board, had indeed been the one to help plant the cameras. She apparently had divorced her husband some time back and was still secretly involved with Dusty, claiming her love until his death.

Her home had since been searched and all hard drives and any computers taken. Charges were pending and Gabe was confident Nathan would handle matters from here on out.

Maverick's reign of terror was indeed over. The town had moved on. Chelsea was gearing up to open her counseling center by late March and Brandee was completely on board with joining forces in the project, as well.

"I don't want a big wedding," Chelsea told him, reaching over to join their hands. "Something simple at the Crescent Moon is perfect for me. For us."

Gabe leaned forward and kissed her, sending them tumbling back to the pillows. "We can discuss wedding plans later. I want to celebrate."

Chelsea laughed as he jerked the covers up and proceeded to show her just how happy he was that she'd said yes.

* * * * *

A WHITE WEDDING CHRISTMAS

ANDREA LAURENCE

Prologue

A lot had changed in the past fourteen years.

Fourteen years ago, Natalie and her best friend, Lily, were inseparable, and Lily's older brother Colin was the tasty treat Natalie had craved since she was fifteen. Now, Lily was about to get married and their engagement party was being held at the large, sprawling estate of her brother.

He'd come a long way since she saw him last. She'd watched, smitten, as he'd evolved into the cool college guy, and when Lily and Colin's parents died suddenly, Natalie had watched him turn into the responsible guardian of his younger sister and the head of his father's company. He'd been more untouchable then than ever before.

Lily and Natalie hadn't seen much of each other over the past few years. Natalie had gone to college at the

University of Tennessee and Lily had drifted aimlessly. They exchanged the occasional emails and Facebook likes, but they hadn't really talked in a long time. She'd been surprised when Lily called her at From This Moment, the wedding company Natalie co-owned, with a request.

A quickie wedding. Before Christmas, if possible. It had been early November at the time, and From This Moment usually had at least fourteen months of weddings scheduled in advance. But they closed at Christmas and for a friend, she and the other three ladies that owned and operated the wedding chapel agreed to squeeze one more wedding in before the holiday.

Natalie's invitation for the engagement party arrived the next day and now, here she was, in a cocktail dress, milling around Colin's huge house filled with people she didn't know.

That wasn't entirely true. She knew the bride. And when her gaze met the golden hazel eyes she'd fantasized about as a teenager, she remembered she knew a second person at the party, too.

"Natalie?" Colin said, crossing a room full of people to see her.

It took her a moment to even find the words to respond. This wasn't the boy she remembered from her youth. He'd grown into a man with broad shoulders that filled out his expensive suit coat, a tanned complexion with eyes that crinkled as he smiled and a five-o'clock shadow that any teenager would've been proud to grow.

"It is you," he said with a grin before he moved in for a hug.

Natalie steadied herself for the familiar embrace. Not everything had changed. Colin had always been a hugger. As a smitten teen, she'd both loved and hated those hugs. There was a thrill that ran down her spine from being so close; a tingle danced across her skin as it brushed his. Now, just as she did then, she closed her eyes and breathed in the scent of him. He smelled better than he did back when he wore cheap drugstore cologne, but even then, she'd loved it.

"How are you, Colin?" she asked as they parted. Natalie hoped her cheeks weren't flushing red. They felt hot, but that could just be the wine she'd been drinking steadily since she got to the party.

"I'm great. Busy with the landscaping business, as always."

"Right." Natalie nodded. "You're still running your dad's company, aren't you?"

He nodded, a hint of suppressed sadness lighting in his eyes for just a moment. *Good going, Natalie, remind him of his dead parents straight off.*

"I'm so glad you were able to fit Lily's wedding in at your facility. She was adamant that the wedding happen there."

"It's the best," Natalie said and it was true. There was no other place like their chapel in Nashville, Tennessee, or anywhere else she knew of. They were one of a kind, providing everything a couple needed for a wedding at one location.

"Good. I want the best for Lily's big day. You look amazing, by the way. Natalie is all grown up," Colin noted.

Natalie detected a hint of appreciation in his eyes as his gaze raked over the formfitting blue dress her business partner Amelia had forced her into wearing tonight. Now she was happy her fashion-conscious friend had dressed her up for the night. She glanced at Colin's left hand—no ring. At one point, she'd heard he was married, but it must not have worked out. Shocker. That left the possibilities open for a more interesting evening than she'd first anticipated tonight.

"I'm nearly thirty now, you know. I'm not a teenager."

Colin let out a ragged breath and forced his gaze back up to her face. "Thank goodness. I'd feel like a dirty old man right now if you were."

Natalie's eyebrow went up curiously. He *was* into her. The unobtainable fantasy might actually be within her grasp. Perhaps now was the time to make the leap she'd always been too chicken to make before. "You know, I have a confession to make." She leaned into him, resting a hand on his shoulder. "I was totally infatuated with you when we were kids."

Colin grinned wide. "Were you, now?"

"Oh yes." And she wouldn't mind letting those old fantasies run wild for a night. "You know, the party is starting to wind down. Would you be interested in getting out of here and finding someplace quiet where we could talk and catch up?"

Natalie said the words casually, but her body language read anything but. She watched as Colin swallowed hard, the muscles in his throat working up and down as he considered her offer. It was bold, and she knew it, but she might not have another chance to get a taste of Colin Russell.

"I'd love to catch up, Natalie, but unfortunately I can't."

Natalie took a big sip of her wine, finishing her glass, and nodded, trying to cover the painful flinch at his rejection. Suddenly she was sixteen again and felt just as unworthy of Colin's attentions as ever. Whatever.

"Well, that's a shame. I'll see you around then," she said, shrugging it off as though it was nothing but a casual offer. Turning on her heel with a sly smile, she made her way through the crowd and fled the party before she had to face any more embarrassment.

One

Putting together a decent wedding in a month was nearly impossible, even with someone as capable as Natalie handling things. Certain things took time, like printing invitations, ordering wedding dresses, coordinating with vendors... Fortunately at From This Moment wedding chapel, she and her co-owners and friends handled most of the work.

"Thank you for squeezing this last wedding in," Natalie said as they sat around the conference room table at their Monday morning staff meeting. "I know you all would much rather be starting your holiday celebrations."

"It's fine," Bree Harper, the photographer, insisted. "Ian and I aren't leaving for Aspen until the following week."

"It gives me something to do until Julian can fly back

from Hollywood," Gretchen McAlister added. "We're driving up to Louisville to spend the holidays with his family, and working another wedding will keep me from worrying about the trip."

"You've already met his family, Gretchen. Why are you nervous?"

"Because this time I'm his fiancée," Gretchen said, looking down in amazement at the ring he'd just given to her last week.

Natalie tried not to notice that all of her formerly single friends were now paired off. Gretchen and Bree were engaged. Amelia was married and pregnant. At one time, they had all been able to commiserate about their singleness, but now, it was just Natalie who went home alone each night. And she was okay with that. She anticipated a lifetime of going home alone. It's just that the status quo had changed so quickly for them all. The past year had been a whirlwind of romance for the ladies at From This Moment.

Despite the fact that she was a wedding planner, Natalie didn't actually believe in any of that stuff. She got into the industry with her friends because they'd asked her to, for one thing. For the other, it was an amazingly lucrative business. Despite the dismal marriage statistics, people seemed happy to take the leap, shelling out thousands of dollars, only to shell out more to their divorce attorneys at some point down the road.

As far as Natalie was concerned, every couple who walked through the door was doomed. The least she could do was give them a wedding to remember. She'd do her best to orchestrate a perfect day they could look back on. It was all downhill from there, anyway.

"I'll have the digital invitations ready by tomorrow.

Do you have the list of email addresses for me to send them out?" Gretchen asked.

Natalie snapped out of her thoughts and looked down at her tablet. "Yes, I have the list here." Normally, e-invites were out of the question for a formal wedding, but there just wasn't time to get paper ones designed, printed, addressed, mailed and gather RSVPs in a month's time.

"We're doing a winter wonderland theme, you said?" Amelia asked.

"That's what Lily mentioned. She was pretty vague about the whole thing. I've got an appointment with them on the calendar for this afternoon, so we'll start firming everything up then. Bree, you're doing engagement photos on Friday morning, right?"

"Yep," Bree said. "They wanted to take their shots at the groom's motorcycle shop downtown."

Natalie had known Lily a long time, but her choice in a future husband was a surprise even to her. Frankie owned a custom motorcycle shop. He was a flannel-wearing, bushy-bearded, tattooed hipster who looked more like a biker raised by lumberjacks than a successful businessman. Definitely not who Natalie would have picked for her best friend, and she was pretty sure he was not who Colin would've picked for Lily, either.

He seemed like a nice guy, though, and even Natalie could see that under the tattoos and hair, the guy was completely hormone pair-bonded to Lily. She wouldn't say they were in love because she didn't believe in love. But they were definitely pair-bonded. Biology was a powerful thing in its drive to continue the species. They could hardly keep their hands off each other at the engagement party.

"Okay. If that's all for this morning," Bree said, "I'm going to head to the lab and finish processing Saturday's wedding photos."

Natalie looked over her checklist. "Yep, that's it."

Bree and Amelia got up, filing out of the conference room, but Gretchen loitered by the table. She watched Natalie for a moment with a curious expression on her face. "What's going on with you? You seem distracted. Grumpier than usual."

That was sweet of her to point out. She knew she wasn't that pleasant this time of year, but she didn't need her friends reminding her of it. "Nothing is going on with me."

Gretchen crossed her arms over her chest and gave Natalie a look that told her she was going to stand there until she spilled.

"Christmas is coming." That pretty much said it all.

"What is this, *Game of Thrones*? Of course Christmas is coming. It's almost December, honey, and it's one of the more predictable holidays."

Natalie set down her tablet and frowned. Each year, the holidays were a challenge for her. Normally, she would try going on a trip to avoid all of it, but with the late wedding, she didn't have time. Staying home meant she'd have to resort to being a shut-in. She certainly wasn't interested in spending it with one of her parents and their latest spouses. The last time she did that, she'd called her mother's third husband by her second husband's name and that made for an awkward evening.

Natalie leaned back in the conference room chair and sighed. "It's bothering me more than usual this year." And it was. She didn't know why, but it was. Maybe it was the combination of all her friends being blissfully in love colliding with the holidays that was making it doubly painful.

"Are you taking a trip or staying home?" Gretchen asked.

"I'm staying home. I was considering a trip to Buenos Aires, but I don't have time. We squeezed Lily's last-minute wedding in on the Saturday before Christmas, so I'll be involved in that and not able to do the normal end-of-year paperwork until it's over."

"You're not planning to work over the shutdown, are you?" Gretchen planted her hands on her hips. "You don't have to celebrate, but by damn, you've got to take the time off, Natalie. You work seven days a week sometimes."

Natalie dismissed her concerns. Working didn't bother her as much as being idle. She didn't have a family to go home to each night or piles of laundry or housework that a man or child generated faster than she could clean. She liked her job. "I don't work the late hours you and Amelia do. I'm never here until midnight."

"It doesn't matter. You're still putting in too much time. You need to get away from all of this. Maybe go to a tropical island and have a fling with a sexy stranger."

At that, Natalie snorted. "I'm sorry, but a man is not the answer to my problems. That actually makes it worse."

"I'm not saying fall in love and marry the guy. I'm just saying to keep him locked in your hotel suite until the last New Year's firework explodes. What can a night or two of hot sex hurt?"

Natalie looked up at Gretchen and realized what was really bothering her. Colin's rejection from the night of the engagement party still stung. She hadn't told anyone about it, but if she didn't give Gretchen a good reason now, she'd ride her about it until the New Year. "It can hurt plenty when the guy you throw yourself at is your best friend's brother and he turns you down flat."

Gretchen's mouth dropped open and she sunk back down into her seat. "What? When did this happen?"

Natalie took a big sip of her soy chai latte before she answered. "I had too much chardonnay at Lily's engagement party and thought I'd take a chance on the big brother I'd lusted over since I'd hit puberty. To put it nicely, he declined. End of story. So no, I'm not really in the mood for a fling, either."

"Well that sucks," Gretchen noted.

"That's one way of putting it."

"On the plus side, you won't really have to see him again until the wedding day, right? Then you'll be too busy to care."

"Yep. I'll make sure I look extra good that day so he'll see what he missed."

"That's my girl. I'm going to go get these email invitations out."

Natalie nodded and watched Gretchen leave the room. She picked up her tablet and her drink, following her out the door to her office. Settling in at her desk, she pulled out a new file folder and wrote *Russell-Watson Wedding* on the tab. She needed to get everything prepared for their preliminary meeting this afternoon.

Staying busy would keep Christmas, and Colin, off her mind.

Colin pulled into the parking lot at From This Moment, his gaze instantly scanning over the lackluster shrubs out front. He knew it was winter, but they could certainly use a little more pizzazz for curb appeal.

He parked and went inside the facility. Stepping through the front doors, he knew instantly why Lily had insisted on marrying here. Their box holly hedges might have left something to be desired, but their focus was clearly on the interior. The inside was stunning with high ceilings, crystal chandeliers, tall fresh flower arrangements on the entryway table and arched entryways leading to various wings of the building. Mom would've loved it.

He looked down at his watch. It was a minute to one, so he was right on time for the appointment. Colin felt a little silly coming here today. Weddings weren't exactly his forte, but he was stepping up in his parents' place. When he'd married a year and a half ago, it had been a quick courthouse affair. If they'd opted for something more glamorous, he would've let Pam take the lead. Pam wasn't interested in that, though, and apparently, neither was his sister, Lily.

If she'd had her way, she and Frankie would've gone down to the courthouse, too. There was no reason to rush the nuptials, like Colin and Pam, but Lily just wanted to be done. She loved Frankie and she wanted to be Mrs. Watson as soon as possible. Colin had had to twist her arm into having an actual wedding, reminding her that their mother would be rolling over in her grave if she knew what Lily was planning.

She'd finally agreed under two circumstances: one, that the wedding be at Natalie's facility. Two, that he handle all the details. He insisted on the wedding, he'd offered to pay for it; he could make all the decisions.

Lily intended to show up in a white dress on the big day and that was about it.

Colin wasn't certain how he'd managed to be around so many women who weren't interested in big weddings. Pam hadn't wanted to marry at all. Hell, if it hadn't been for the baby and his insistence, she wouldn't have accepted the proposal. In retrospect, he realized why she was so hesitant, but with Lily, it just seemed to be a general disinterest in tradition.

He didn't understand it. Their parents had been very traditional people. Old-fashioned, you might even say. When they died in a car accident, Colin had tried to keep the traditions alive for Lily's sake. He'd never imagined he would end up raising his younger sister when he was only nineteen, but he was determined to do a good job and not disappoint his parents' memory.

Lily was just not that concerned. To her, the past was the past and she wasn't going to get hung up on things like that. Formal weddings fell into the bucket of silly traditions that didn't matter much to her. But it mattered to him, so she'd relented.

Colin heard a door open down one of the hallways and a moment later he found himself once again face-to-face with Natalie Sharpe. She stopped short in the archway of the foyer, clutching a tablet to her gray silk blouse. Even as a teenager, she'd had a classic beauty about her. Her creamy skin and high cheekbones had drawn his attention even when she was sporting braces. He'd suppressed any attraction he might have had for his little sister's friend, but he'd always thought she would grow up into a beautiful woman. At the party, his suspicions had been confirmed. And better yet, she'd looked at him with a seductive smile and an openness he hadn't expected. They weren't kids anymore, but there were other complications that had made it impossible to take her up on her offer, as much as he regretted it.

Today, the look on her face was a far cry from that night. Her pink lips were parted in concern, a frown lining her brow. Then she took a breath and shook it off. She tried to hide her emotions under a mask of professionalism, but he could tell she wasn't pleased to see him.

"Colin? I wasn't expecting to see you today. Is something going on with Lily?"

"Lots of things are going on with Lily," he replied, "but not what you're implying. She's fine. She's just not interested in the details."

Natalie swung her dark ponytail over her shoulder, her nose wrinkling. "What do you mean?"

"I mean, she told me this is my show and I'm to plan it however I see fit. So here I am," he added, holding out his arms.

He watched Natalie try to process the news. Apparently Lily hadn't given her a heads-up, but why would she? He doubted Lily knew about their encounter at the engagement party. She wasn't the kind of girl to give much thought to how her choices would affect other people.

"I know this is an unusual arrangement, but Lily is an unusual woman, as you know."

That seemed to snap Natalie out of her fog. She nodded curtly and extended her arm. "Of course. Come this way to my office and we can discuss the details."

Colin followed behind her, appreciating the snug fit of her pants over the curve of her hips and rear. She was wearing a pair of low heels that gave just enough lift to flatter her figure. It was a shame she walked in such a stiff, robotic way. He wouldn't mind seeing those hips sway a little bit, but he knew Natalie was too uptight for that. She'd always been a sharp contrast to his free-spirited sister—no-nonsense, practical, serious. She walked like she was marching into battle, even if it was a simple trip down the hallway.

After their encounter at the engagement party, he'd started to wonder if there was a more relaxed, sensual side to her that he hadn't had the pleasure of knowing about. He could only imagine what she could be like if she took down that tight ponytail, had a glass of wine and relaxed for once.

He got the feeling he would know all about that if he'd accepted her offer at the party. Unfortunately, his rocky on-again, off-again relationship with Rachel had been *on* that night. As much as he might have wanted to spend private time with Natalie, he couldn't. Colin was not the kind of man who cheated, even on a rocky relationship. Especially after what had happened with Pam.

After realizing how much more he was attracted to Natalie than the woman he was dating, he'd broken it off with Rachel for good. He was hopeful that now that he was a free man, he might get a second chance with Natalie. So far the reception was cold, but he hoped she'd thaw to his charms in time.

He followed her into her office and took a seat in the guest chair. Her office was pleasantly decorated, but extremely tidy and organized. He could tell every knickknack had its place, every file had a home.

"Can I get you something to drink? We have bottled water, some sparkling juices and ginger ale."

That was an unexpected option. "Why do you have ginger ale?"

"Sometimes the bride's father gets a little queasy when he sees the estimate."

Colin laughed. "Water would be great. I'm not that worried about the bill."

Natalie got up, pulling two bottles of water out of the small stainless steel refrigerator tucked into her built-in bookshelves. "On that topic, what number makes you comfortable in terms of budget for the wedding?" she asked as she handed him a bottle.

Colin's fingers brushed over hers as he took the bottle from her hand. There was a spark as they touched, making his skin prickle with pins and needles as he pulled away. He clutched the icy cold water in his hand to dull the sensation and tried to focus on the conversation, instead of his reaction to a simple touch. "Like I said, I'm not that worried about it. My landscaping company has become extremely successful, and I want this to be an event that my parents would've thrown for Lily if they were alive. I don't think we need ridiculous extras like ice bars with martini luges, but in terms of food and decor, I'm all in. A pretty room, pretty flowers, good food, cake, music. The basics."

Natalie had hovered near her chair after handing him the water, making him wonder if she'd been affected by their touch, too. After listening to him, she nodded curtly and sat down. She reached for her tablet and started making careful notes. "How many guests are you anticipating? Lily provided me a list of emails, but we weren't sure of the final total."

"Probably about a hundred and fifty people. We've

got a lot of family and friends of my parents that would attend, but Frankie doesn't have many people nearby."

He watched her tap rapidly at her screen. "When I spoke with Lily, I suggested a winter wonderland theme and she seemed to like that. Is that agreeable?"

"Whatever she wants." Colin had no clue what a winter wonderland wedding would even entail. White, he supposed. Maybe some fake snow like the kind that surrounded Santa at the mall?

"Okay. Any other requests? Would you prefer a DJ or a band for the reception?"

That was one thing he had an answer for. "I'd like a string quartet, actually. Our mother played the violin and I think that would be a nice nod to her. At least for the ceremony. For the reception, we probably need something more upbeat so that Lily and her friends can dance and have a good time."

"How about a swing band? There's a great one locally that we've used a couple times."

"That would work. I think she mentioned going swing dancing at some club a few weeks back."

Natalie nodded and finally set down her tablet. "I'm going to have Amelia put together a suggested menu and some cake designs. Gretchen will do a display of the tablescape for your approval. I'll speak with our floral vendor to see what she recommends for the winter wonderland theme. We'll come up with a whole wedding motif with some options and we'll bring you back to review and approve all the final choices. We should probably have something together by tomorrow afternoon."

She certainly knew what she was doing and had this whole thing down to a science. That was good because Colin wasn't entirely sure what a tablescape even was.

He was frankly expecting this process to be a lot more painful, but perhaps that was the benefit of an all-in-one facility. "That all sounds great. Why don't you firm up those details with the other ladies and maybe we can meet for dinner tomorrow night to discuss it?"

Natalie's dark gaze snapped up from her tablet to meet his. "Dinner won't be necessary. We can set up another appointment if your schedule allows."

Colin tried not to look disappointed at her quick dismissal of dinner. He supposed he deserved that after he'd done the same to her last week. Perhaps she was just angry with him over it. If he could convince her to meet with him, maybe she could relax and he could explain to her what had happened that night. He got the distinct impression she wouldn't discuss it here at work.

"If not dinner, how about I just stop by here tomorrow evening? Do you mind staying past your usual time?"

Natalie snorted delicately and eased up out of her chair. "There's no usual time in this business. We work pretty much around the clock. What time should I expect you?"

"About six."

"Great," she said, offering her hand to him over the desk.

Colin was anxious to touch her again and see if he had the same reaction to her this time. He took her hand, enveloping it in his own and trying not to think about how soft her skin felt against his. There was another sizzle of awareness and this time, it traveled up his arm as he held her hand, making him all the more sorry she'd turned down his dinner invitation. He'd never had that instant of a reaction just by touching someone. He had this urge to lean into her and draw the scent of her perfume into his lungs even as the coil of desire in his gut tightened with every second they touched. What would it be like to actually kiss her?

He had been right before when he thought Natalie was caught off guard by their connection. He was certain he wasn't the only one to feel it. Colin watched as Natalie avoided his gaze, swallowed hard and gently extracted her hand from his. "Six it is."

Two

Discuss it over dinner? *Dinner!* Natalie was still steaming about her meeting with Colin the next afternoon. As she pulled together the portfolio for his review, she couldn't help replaying the conversation in her mind.

That look in his eye. The way he'd held her hand. Dinner! He was hitting on her. What was that about? Natalie was sorry, but that ship had sailed. Who was he to reject her, then come back a week later and change his mind? He had his shot and he blew it.

As she added the suggested menu to the file, she felt her bravado deflate a little. Natalie would be lying if she said she didn't want to take him up on the offer. She really, really did. But a girl had to draw the line somewhere. Her pride was at stake and if she came running just because he'd changed his mind, she'd look needy. She was anything but needy.

He had passed up on a one-night stand and what was done, was done. Now that she knew they were working together on the wedding plans, it was just as well. She didn't like to mix business with pleasure.

Natalie looked at the clock on her computer. It was almost six. The rest of the facility was dark and quiet. It was Tuesday, so the others were all off today. Natalie was supposed to be off, too, but she usually came into the office anyway. When it was quiet, she could catch up on paperwork and filing, talk with their vendors and answer the phone in case a client called. Or stopped by, as the case was tonight.

She slid open the desk drawer where she kept all her toiletries. Pulling out a small hand mirror, she checked her teeth for lipstick, smoothed her hand over her hair and admired her overall look. She found her compact to apply powder to the shinier areas and reapplied her lipstick. She may have put a little extra effort into her appearance today. Not to impress Colin. Not really. She did it more to torture him. Her pride stung from his rebuffing and she wanted him to suffer just a little bit, too.

Satisfied, she slipped her things back into the drawer. A soft door chime sounded a moment later and she knew that he'd arrived. She stood, taking a deep breath and willing herself to ignore her attraction to him. This was about work. Work. And anytime she thought differently, she needed to remind herself how she'd felt when he rejected her.

Natalie walked quickly down the hallway to the lobby. She found Colin waiting for her there. At the party and at their meeting yesterday, he'd been wearing a suit, but tonight, he was wearing a tight T-shirt and khakis. She watched the muscles of his broad shoulders move beneath the fabric as he slipped out of his winter coat, hanging it on the rack by the door.

When he turned to face her, she was blindsided by his bright smile and defined forearms. When he wore his suit, it was easy to forget he wasn't just a CEO, he was also a landscaper. She'd wager he rarely got dirt under his nails these days, but he still had the muscular arms and chest of a man who could move the earth with brute strength.

Colin looked down, seemingly following her gaze. "Do you like the shirt? We just had them made up for all the staff to wear when they're out on job sites."

Honestly, she hadn't paid much attention to the shirt, but talking about that was certainly better than admitting she was lusting over his hard pecs. "It's very nice," she said with a polite smile. "I like the dark green color." And she did. It had the Russell Landscaping logo in white on the front. It looked nice on him. Especially the fact that it looked painted on.

"Me, too. You didn't call to say there was an issue, so I assume you have the wedding plans ready?"

"I do. Come on back to my office and I'll show you what we've pulled together."

They turned and walked down the hallway, side by side. She couldn't help but notice that Colin had gently rested a guiding hand at the small of her back as she slipped into the office ahead of him. It was a faint touch, and yet she could still feel the heat of it through her clothes. Goose bumps raised up across her forearms when he pulled away, leaving her cold. It was an unexpected touch and yet she had to admit she was a little disappointed it was so quick. Despite their years apart, her reaction to Colin had only grown along with his biceps. Unfortunately, those little thrills were all she'd allow herself to have. She was first and foremost a professional.

They settled into her office and Natalie pulled out the trifold portfolio she used for these meetings. She unfolded it, showing all the images and options for their wedding. Focusing on work was her best strategy for dealing with her attraction to Colin.

"Let's start with the menu," she began. "Amelia, our caterer, would normally do up to three entrees for a wedding this size, but with such short notice, we really don't have time for attendees to select their meals. Instead, she put together a surf and turf option that should make everyone happy. Option one pairs her very popular beef tenderloin with a crab cake. You also have the choice of doing a bourbon-glazed salmon, or a chicken option instead if you think fish might be a problem for your guests."

She watched Colin look over the options thoughtfully. She liked the way his brow drew together as he thought. Staring down at the portfolio, she could see how long and thick his eyelashes were. Most women would kill for lashes like those.

"What would you choose?" he asked, unaware of her intense study of his face.

"The crab cake," Natalie said without hesitation. "They're almost all crab, with a crisp outside and a spicy remoulade. They're amazing."

"Okay, that sounds great. Let's go with that."

Natalie checked off his selection. "For the cake, she put together three concept designs." She went into detail on each, explaining the decorations and how it fit with the theme.

When she was finally done, he asked again, "Which one of these cakes would you choose?"

Natalie wasn't used to this. Most brides knew exactly what they wanted. Looking down at the three concept sketches for the cake, she pointed out the second option. "I'd choose this one. It will be all white with an iridescent shimmer to the fondant. Amelia will make silver gum paste snowflakes and when they wrap around the cake it will be really enchanting."

"Let's go with that one. What about cake flavors?"

"You won't make that decision today. If you can come Thursday, Amelia will set up a tasting session. She's doing a couple other appointments that day, so that would work best. Do you think Lily would be interested in coming to that?"

"I can work that out. I doubt Lily will join me, but I'll ask. I'm sure cake is cake in her eyes."

Natalie just didn't understand her friend at all. Natalie had no interest in marriage, therefore no interest in a wedding. But Lily should at least have the party she wanted and enjoy it. It didn't make sense to hand that over to someone else. Her inner control freak couldn't imagine someone else planning her wedding. If by some twist of fate, she was lobotomized and agreed to marry someone, she would control every last detail.

"Okay." Natalie noted the appointment in her tablet so Amelia could follow up with him on a time for Thursday. From there, they looked at some floral concepts and bouquet options. With each of them, he asked Natalie's opinion and went with that. Sitting across from her was a sexy, intelligent, wealthy, thoughtful and agreeable man. If she *was* the kind to marry, she'd crawl into his lap right now. Whoever did land Colin would be very lucky. At least for a while.

Everything flowed easily from there. Without much debate, they'd settled on assorted tall and low arrangements with a mix of white flowers including rose, ranunculus, stephanotis and hydrangea. It was everything she would've chosen and probably as close as she'd get to having a wedding without having to get married.

"Now that we've handled all that, the last thing I want to do is to take you to the table setup Gretchen put together."

They left her office and walked down to the storage room. She kept waiting for him to touch her again, but she was disappointed this time. Opening the doors, she let him inside ahead of her and followed him in. In their storage room, amongst the shelves of glassware, plates, silver vases and cake stands, they had one round dinner table set up. There, Gretchen put together mock-ups of the reception tables for brides to better visualize them and make changes.

"Gretchen has selected a soft white tablecloth with a delicate silver overlay of tiny beaded snowflakes. We'd carry the white and silver into the dishes with the silver chargers, silver-rimmed white china, and then use silver-and-glass centerpieces in a variety of heights. We'll bring in tasteful touches of sparkle with some crystals on white manzanita branches and lots of candles."

Colin ran the tip of his finger over a silver snowflake and nodded. "It all looks great to me. Very pretty. Gretchen has done a very nice job with it."

Natalie made a note in her tablet and shook her head with amazement. "You're the easiest client I've ever had. I refuse to believe it's really that easy. What are you hiding from me?"

Colin looked at her with a confused expression. "I'm not hiding anything. I know it isn't what you're used to, but really, I'm putting this wedding in your capable hands."

He placed his hand on her shoulder as he spoke. She could feel the heat radiating through the thin fabric of her cashmere sweater, making her want to pull at the collar as her internal temperature started to climb.

"You knew my parents. You know Lily. You've got the experience and the eye for this kind of thing. Aside from the discussion about flowers, I've had no clue what you were talking about most of the time. I just trust you to do a great job and I'll write the check."

Natalie tried not to frown. Her heated blood wasn't enough for her to ignore his words. He was counting on her. That was a lot of pressure. She knew she could pull it off beautifully, but he had an awful lot of confidence in her for a girl he hadn't seen since she wore a retainer to bed. "So would you rather just skip the cake tasting?"

"Oh no," he said with a smile that made her knees soften beneath her. "I have a massive sweet tooth, so I'm doing that for sure."

Natalie wasn't sure how much her body could take of being in close proximity to Colin as friends. She wanted to run her hand up his tanned, muscular forearm and rub against him like a cat. While she enjoyed indulging her sexuality from time to time, she didn't have a reaction like this to just any guy. It was unnerving and *so* inappropriate. This wedding couldn't come fast enough.

* * *

"Thank you for all your help with this," Colin said as Natalie closed up and they walked toward the door.

"That's what I do," she said with the same polite smile that was starting to make him crazy. He missed her real one. He remembered her carefree smile from her younger days and her seductive smile from the engagement party. This polite, blank smile meant nothing to him.

"No, really. You and your business partners are going out of your way to make this wedding happen. I don't know how to thank you."

Natalie pressed the alarm code and they stepped outside where she locked the door. "You and Lily are like family to me. Of course we'd do everything we could. Anyway, it's not like we're doing it for free. You're paying us for our time, so no worries."

Their cars were the only two in the parking lot, so he walked her over to the cherry-red two-seat Miata convertible. Had there been another car in the lot, he never would've guessed this belonged to Natalie. It had a hint of wild abandon that didn't seem to align with the precise and businesslike Natalie he knew. It convinced him more than ever that there was another side to her that he desperately wanted to see.

"Let me take you to dinner tonight," he said, nearly surprising himself with the suddenness of it.

Natalie's dark brown eyes widened. "I really can't, Colin, but I appreciate the offer."

Two up at bats, two strikeouts. "Even just as friends?"

Her gaze flicked over his face and she shook her head. "You and I both know it wouldn't be as friends."

Turning away, Natalie unlocked her car and opened the door to toss her bag inside.

"I think that's unfair."

"Not really. Listen, Colin, I'm sorry about the other night at the party. I'd been hit by a big dose of nostalgia and too much wine and thought that indulging those old teenage fantasies was a good idea. But by the light of day, I know it was silly of me. So thank you for having some sense and keeping me from doing something that would've made this whole planning process that much more awkward."

"Don't thank me," Colin argued. "I've regretted that decision every night since it happened."

Natalie's mouth fell agape, her dark eyes searching his face for something. "Don't," she said at last. "It was the right choice."

"It was at the time, but only because it had to be. Natalie, I—"

"Don't," Natalie insisted. "There's no reason to explain yourself. You made the decision you needed to make and it was the right one. No big deal. I'd like to just put that whole exchange behind us. The truth is that I'm really not the right kind of woman for you."

Colin wasn't sure if she truly meant what she said or if she was just angry with him, but he was curious what she meant by that. He was bad enough at choosing women. Maybe she knew something he didn't. "What kind of woman is that?"

"The kind that's going to have any sort of future with you. At the party, I was just after a night of fun, nothing serious. You're a serious kind of guy. Since you were a teenager, you were on the express train to marriage and kids. I'm on a completely different track."

They hadn't really been around each other long enough for Colin to think much past the ache of desire she seemed to constantly rouse in him. But if what she said was true, she was right. He wanted all those things. If she didn't, there wasn't much point in pursuing her. His groin felt otherwise, but it would get on board eventually.

"Well, I appreciate you laying that out for me. Not all women are as forthcoming." Pam had been, but for some reason he'd refused to listen. This time he knew better than to try to twist a woman's will. It didn't work. "Just friends, then," he said.

Natalie smiled with more warmth than before, and she seemed to relax for the first time since he'd arrived. "Friends is great."

"All right," he said. "Good night." Colin leaned in to give Natalie a quick hug goodbye. At least that was the idea.

Once he had his arms wrapped around her and her cheek pressed to his, it was harder to let go than he expected. Finally, he forced himself back, dropping his hands at his sides and breaking the connection he'd quickly come to crave. And yet, he couldn't get himself to say good-night and go back to his truck. "Listen, before you go can I ask you about something?"

"Sure," she said, although there was a hesitation in her voice that made him think she'd much rather flee than continue talking to him in the cold. She must not think he'd taken the hint.

"I'm thinking about giving Lily and Frankie the old house as a wedding present."

"The house you and Lily grew up in?" she asked with raised brows.

"Yes. It's been sitting mostly empty the last few years. Lily has been living with Frankie in the little apartment over his motorcycle shop. They seem to think that's great, but they're going to need more space if they want to start a family."

"That's a pretty amazing wedding present. Not many people register for a house."

Colin shrugged. "I don't need it. I have my place. It's paid for, so all they'd have to worry about are taxes and insurance. The only problem is that it needs to be cleaned out. I never had the heart to go through all of Mom's and Dad's things. I want to clear all that out and get it ready for the newlyweds to make a fresh start there."

Natalie nodded as he explained. "That sounds like a good plan. What does it have to do with me?"

"Well," Colin said with an uncharacteristically sheepish smile, "I was wondering if you would be interested in helping me."

She flinched at first, covering her reaction by shuffling her feet in the cold. "I don't know that I'll be much help to you, Colin. For one thing, I'm a wedding planner, not an interior decorator. And for another thing, I work most of the weekends with weddings. I don't have a lot of free time."

"I know," he said, "and I'm not expecting any heavy lifting on your part. I was thinking more of your organizational skills and keen aesthetic eye. It seems to me like you could spot a quality piece of furniture or artwork that's worth keeping amongst the piles of eighties-style recliners."

There was a light of amusement in her eyes as she

listened to him speak. "You're completely in over your head with this one, aren't you?"

"You have no idea. My business is landscaping, and that's the one thing at the house that doesn't need any work. I overhauled it a few years ago and I've had it maintained, so the outside is fine. It's just the inside. I also thought it would be nice to decorate the house for Christmas since they get back from their honeymoon on Christmas Eve. That way it will be ready to go for the holidays."

The twinkle in her eye faded. "I'm no good with Christmas, Colin. I might be able to help you with some of the furniture and keepsakes, but you're on your own when it comes to the holidays."

That made Colin frown. Most people enjoyed decorating for Christmas. Why was she so opposed to it? In his eyes it wasn't much different from decorating for a wedding. He wasn't about to push that point, however. "Fair enough. I'm sure I can handle that part on my own. Do you have plans tonight?"

Natalie sighed and shook her head. "I'm *not* going out with you, Colin."

He held up his hands in surrender. "I didn't ask you out. I asked if you were busy. I thought if you weren't busy, I'd take you by the old house tonight. I know you don't have a lot of free time, so if you could just take a walk through with me this evening and give me some ideas, I could get started on it."

"Oh," she said, looking sheepish.

"I mean, I could just pay a crew to come and clean out the house and put everything in storage, but I hate to do that. Some things are more important than others, and I'll want to keep some of it. Putting everything in storage just delays the inevitable. I could use your help, even if for just tonight."

Natalie sighed and eventually nodded. "Sure. I have some time tonight."

"Great. We'll take my car and I'll bring you back when we're done," Colin said.

He got the distinct impression that if he let Natalie get in her car, she'd end up driving somewhere other than their old neighborhood, or make some excuse for a quick getaway. He supposed that most men agreed to just being friends, but secretly hoped for more. Colin meant what he'd said and since she'd agreed, there was no need to slink away with his tail between his legs.

Holding out his arm, he ushered her reluctantly over to his Russell Landscaping truck. The Platinum series F-250 wasn't a work truck, it was more for advertising, although he did get it dirty from time to time. It was dark green, like their shirts, with the company logo and information emblazoned on the side.

He held the passenger door open for her, a step automatically unfolding along the side of the truck. Colin held her hand as she climbed inside, then slammed the door shut.

"Do you mind if we listen to some music on the way?" she asked.

Colin figured that she wanted music to avoid idle conversation, but he didn't mind. "Sure." He turned on the radio, which started playing music from the holiday station he'd had on last.

"Can I change it to the country channel?"

"I don't care, although you don't strike me as a country girl," he noted.

"I was born and raised in Nashville, you know. When

I was a kid, my dad would take me to see performances at the Grand Ole Opry. It's always stuck with me." She changed the station and the new Blake Wright song came on. "Ooh. I love this song. He's going to be doing a show at the Opry in two weeks. It's sold out, though."

Colin noted that information and put it in his back pocket. From there, it wasn't a long drive to the old neighborhood, just a few miles on the highway. Blake had just finished singing when they arrived.

They had grown up in a nice area—big homes on big lots designed for middle-class families. His parents honestly couldn't really afford their house when they had first bought it, but his father had insisted that they get the home they wanted to have forever. His parents had wanted a place to both raise their children and entertain potential clients, and appearances counted. If that meant a few lean years while the landscaping business built up, so be it.

The neighborhood was still nice and the homes had retained an excellent property value. It wasn't as flashy or trendy with the Nashville wealthy like Colin's current neighborhood, but it was a home most people would be happy to have.

As they pulled into the driveway, Natalie leaned forward and eyed the house through the windshield with a soft smile. "I've always loved this house," she admitted. "I can't believe how big the magnolia trees have gotten."

Colin's father had planted crepe myrtles lining the front walkway and magnolia trees flanking the yard. When he was a kid they were barely big enough to provide enough shade to play beneath them. Now the magnolias were as tall as the two-story roofline. "I've maintained the yard over the years," he said proudly. "I knew how important that was for Dad."

It was too dark to really get a good look at the outside, even with the lights on, so he opened the garage door and opted to take her in through there. His father's tool bench and chest still sat along the rear wall. A shed in the back housed all the gardening supplies and equipment. He hadn't had the heart to move any of that stuff before, but like the rest of it, he knew it was time.

They entered into the kitchen from the garage. Natalie instantly moved over to the breakfast bar, settling onto one of the barstools where she and Lily used to sit and do their homework together.

He could almost envision her with the braces and the braids again, but he much preferred Natalie as she was now. She smiled as she looked around the house, obviously as fond of his childhood home as he was. He wanted to walk up behind her to look at it the same way she was. Maybe rub the tension from her tight shoulders.

But he wouldn't. It had taken convincing to get her here. He wasn't about to run her off so quickly by pushing the boundaries of their newly established friendship. Eventually, it would be easier to ignore the swell of her breasts as they pressed against her sweater or the luminous curve of her cheek. Until then, he smoothed his hands over the granite countertop and let the cold stone cool his ardor.

"How long has it been since you've lived here, Colin? It seems pretty tidy."

"It's been about three years since I lived here full-time. Lily used it as a home base on and off for a while, but no one has really lived here for a year at least. I have a service come clean and I stop in periodically to check on the place."

"So many memories." She slipped off the stool and went into the living room. He followed her there, watching her look around at the vaulted ceilings. Natalie pointed at the loft that overlooked the living room. "I used to love hanging out up there, listening to CDs and playing on the computer."

That made him smile. The girls had always been sprawled out on the rug or lying across the futon up there, messing around on the weekends. Natalie had spent a lot of time at the house when they were younger. Her own house was only the next block over, but things had been pretty volatile leading up to her parents' divorce. While he hated that her parents split up, it had been nice to have her around, especially after his own parents died. Colin had been too busy trying to take care of everything and suddenly be a grown-up. Natalie had been there for Lily in a way he hadn't.

"Lily is very lucky to have a brother like you," she said, conflicting with his own thoughts. "I'm sure she'll love the house. It's perfect for starting a family. Just one thing, though."

"What's that?"

Natalie looked at him and smiled. "The house is exactly the same as it was the last time I was here ten years ago, and things were dated then. You've got some work ahead of you, mister."

Three

After a few hours at the house, Colin insisted on ordering pizza and Natalie finally acquiesced. That wasn't a dinner date, technically, and she was starving. She wasn't sure that he had put the idea of them being more than friends to bed—honestly neither had she—but they'd get there. As with all attractions, the chemical reactions would fade, the hormones would quiet and things would be fine. With a wedding and the house to focus on, she was certain it would happen sooner rather than later.

While he dealt with ordering their food, she slipped out onto the back deck and sat down in one of the old patio chairs. The air was cold and still, but it felt good to breathe it in.

She was exhausted. They'd gone through every room, talking over pieces to keep, things to donate and what renovations were needed. It wasn't just that, though. It was the memories and emotions tied to the place that were getting to her. Nearly every room in the house held some kind of significance to her. Even though Lily and Colin's parents had been dead for nearly thirteen years now, Natalie understood why Colin had been so reluctant to change things. It was like messing with the past somehow.

Her parents' marriage had dissolved when she was fourteen. The year or so leading up to it had been even more rough on her than what followed. Lily's house had been her sanctuary from the yelling. After school, on the weekends, sleepovers…she was almost always here. Some of her happiest memories were in this place. Colin and Lily's parents didn't mind having her around. She suspected that they knew what was going on at her house and were happy to shelter her from the brunt of it.

Unfortunately, they couldn't protect her from everything. There was nothing they could do to keep Natalie's father from walking out on Christmas day. They weren't there to hold Natalie's hand as her parents fought it out in court for two years, then each remarried again and again, looking for something in another person they couldn't seem to find.

Her friends joked that Natalie was jaded about relationships, but she had a right to be. She rarely saw them succeed. Why would she put herself through that just because there was this societal pressure to do it? She could see the icy water and jagged rocks below; why would she jump off the bridge with everyone else?

She heard the doorbell and a moment later, Colin called her from the kitchen. "Soup's on!"

Reluctantly, Natalie got back up and went inside the

house to face Colin and the memories there. She found a piping hot pizza sitting on the kitchen island beside a bottle of white wine. "Did they deliver the wine, too?" she asked drily. The addition of wine to the pizza made this meal feel more suspiciously like the date she'd declined earlier. "If they do, I need their number. Wine delivery is an underserved market."

"No, it was in the wine chiller," he said as though it was just the most convenient beverage available. "I lived here for a few weeks after I broke up with Pam. It was left over."

Natalie had learned from Lily that Colin got a divorce earlier this year, but she didn't know much about the details. Their wedding had been a quiet affair and their divorce had been even quieter. All she did hear was that they had a son together. "I'm sorry to hear about your divorce. Do you still get to see your son pretty often?"

The pleasant smile slipped from his face. He jerked the cork out of the wine bottle and sighed heavily. "I don't have a son."

Natalie knew immediately that she had treaded into some unpleasant territory. She wasn't quite sure how to back out of it. "Oh. I guess I misheard."

"No. You heard right. Shane was born about six months after we got married." He poured them each a glass of chardonnay. "We divorced because I found out that Shane wasn't my son."

Sometimes Natalie hated being right about relationships. Bad things happened to really good people when the fantasy of love got in the way. She took a large sip of the wine to muffle her discomfort. "I'm sorry to hear that, Colin."

A smile quickly returned to his face, although it seemed a little more forced than before. "Don't be. I did it to myself. Pam had been adamant when we started dating that she didn't want to get married. When she told me she was pregnant, I thought she would change her mind, but she didn't. I think she finally gave in only because I wouldn't let it go. I should've known then that I'd made a mistake by forcing her into it."

Natalie stiffened with a piece of pizza dangling from her hand. She finally released it to the plate and cleared her throat. "Not everyone is meant for marriage," she said. "Too many people do it just because they think that's what they're supposed to do."

"If someone doesn't want to get married, they shouldn't. It's not fair to their partner."

She slid another slice of pizza onto his plate. Instead of opting for the perfectly good dining room table, Natalie returned to her perch at the breakfast bar. That's where she'd always eaten at Lily's house. "That's why I've made it a policy to be honest up front."

Colin followed suit, handing her a napkin and sliding onto the stool beside her. "And I appreciate that, especially after what happened with Pam. You're right though. I'm the kind of guy that is meant for marriage. I've just got to learn to make better choices in women," he said. Pam had been his most serious relationship, but he had a string of others that failed for different reasons. "My instincts always seem to be wrong."

Natalie took a bite of her pizza and chewed thoughtfully. She had dodged a bullet when Colin turned her down at the engagement party. She'd only been looking for a night of nostalgic indulgence, but he was the kind of guy who wanted more. More wasn't something she could give him. She was a bad choice, too. Not lie-about-the-paternity-of-your-child bad, but definitely not the traditional, marrying kind he needed.

"Your sister doesn't seem to want to get married," Natalie noted, sending the conversation in a different direction. She'd never seen a more reluctant bride. That kind of woman wouldn't normally bother with a place like From This Moment.

"Actually, she's very eager to marry. It's the wedding and the hoopla she can do without."

"That's an interesting reversal. A lot of women are more obsessed with the wedding day than the actual marriage."

"I think she'll appreciate it later, despite how much she squirms now. Eloping at the courthouse was very underwhelming. We said the same words, ended up just as legally joined in marriage, but it was missing a certain something. I want better for my little sister's big day."

"She'll get it," Natalie said with confidence. "We're the best."

They ate quietly for a few moments before Colin finished his slice and spoke up. "See," he said as he reached for another piece and grinned. "I told you that you'd have dinner with me eventually."

Natalie snorted softly, relieved to see the happier Colin return. "Oh, no," she argued with a smile. "This does not count, even if you add wine. Having dinner together implies a date. This is not a date."

Colin leaned his elbows on the counter and narrowed his eyes at her. "Since we're sharing tonight, do you mind telling me why you were so unhappy to see me yesterday at the chapel?"

"I wouldn't say unhappy. I would say surprised. I expected Lily. And considering what happened the last time I saw you, I was feeling a little embarrassed."

"Why?"

"Because I hit on you and failed miserably. It was stupid of me. It was a momentary weakness fueled by wine and abstinence. And since you passed up the chance, this is definitely not a date. We're on a nondate eating pizza at your childhood home."

A knowing grin spread across Colin's face, making Natalie curious, nervous and making her flush at the same time. "So that's what it's really about," he said with a finger pointed in her direction. "You were upset because I turned you down that night at the party."

Natalie's cheeks flamed at the accusation. "Not at all. I'm relieved, really." She took a large sip of her wine and hoped that sounded convincing enough.

"You can say that, but I know it isn't true. You couldn't get out of the house fast enough that night."

"I had an early day the next morning."

Colin raised his brow in question. He didn't believe a word she said. Neither did she.

"Okay, fine. So what?" she challenged. "So what if I'm holding it against you? I'm allowed to have feelings about your rejection."

"Of course you're allowed to have feelings. But I didn't reject you, Natalie."

"Oh really? What would you call it?"

Colin turned in his seat to face her, his palms resting on each knee. "I would call it being the good guy even when I didn't want to be. You may not have noticed, but I had a date at the party. She was in a corner sulking most of the night. It wasn't really serious and we broke it off the next day, but I couldn't very well ditch her and disappear with you."

Natalie's irritation started to deflate. She slumped in her seat, fingering absentmindedly at her pizza crust. "Oh."

"Oh," he repeated with a chuckle. "Now if you were the kind of woman that *would* date me, you'd be feeling pretty silly right now."

Natalie shook her head. "Even if I were that woman, this is still not a date. You can't just decide to be on a date halfway through an evening together. There's planning and preparation. You'd have to take me someplace nicer than this old kitchen, and I would wear a pretty dress instead of my clothes from work. A date is a whole experience."

"Fair enough," Colin agreed, taking another bite of his pizza. "This isn't a date."

Natalie turned to her food, ignoring the nervous butterflies that were fluttering in her stomach. It wasn't a date, but it certainly felt like one.

They cleaned up the kitchen together and opted to climb in the attic to take a look at what was up there before they called it a night. Colin's father had had the attic finished when they moved in, so the space was a little dusty, but it wasn't the treacherous, cobweb-filled space most attics were.

"Wow," Natalie said as she reached the top of the stairs. "There's a lot of stuff up here."

She was right. Colin looked around, feeling a little intimidated by the project he'd put on himself. He'd put all this off for too long, though. Giving the house to Lily and Frankie was the right thing to do and the motivation he needed to actually get it done.

He reached for a plastic tote and peeked inside. It was filled with old Christmas decorations. After further investigation, he realized that was what the majority of the items were. "My parents always went all out at Christmas," he said. "I think we've found their stash."

There were boxes of garland, lights, ornaments and lawn fixtures. A five-foot, light-up Santa stood in the corner beside a few white wooden reindeer that lit up and moved.

"This is what you were looking for, right?" Natalie asked. "You said you wanted to decorate the house for the holidays."

He nodded and picked up a copy of *A Visit From St. Nicholas* from one of the boxes. His father had read that to them every year on Christmas Eve, even when he and his sister were far too old for that sort of thing. In the years since they'd passed, Colin would've given anything to sit and listen to his father read that to him again.

"This is perfect," he said. "I have to go through all this to see what still works, but it's a great start. I'll just have to get a tree for the living room. What do you think?"

Natalie shrugged. "I told you before, I'm not much of an expert on Christmas."

He'd forgotten. "So, what's that about, Grinch?"

"Ha-ha," she mocked, heading toward the stairs.

Colin snatched an old Santa's hat out of a box and followed her down. He slipped it on. "Ho-ho-ho!" he shouted in his jolliest voice. "Little girl, tell Santa why you don't like Christmas. Did I forget the pony you asked for?"

Natalie stopped on the landing and turned around to look at him. She tried to hide her smirk with her hand, but the light in her eyes gave away her amusement. "You look like an idiot."

"Come on," he insisted. "We've already talked about my matrimonial betrayal. It can't be a bigger downer than that."

"Pretty close," Natalie said, crossing her arms defensively over her chest. "My dad left on Christmas day."

The smile faded from his face. He pulled off the Santa hat. "I didn't know about that."

"Why would you? I'm sure you were spared the messy details."

"What happened?"

"I'm not entirely sure. They'd been fighting a bunch leading up to Christmas, but I think they were trying to hold it together through the holidays. That morning, we opened presents and had breakfast, the same as usual. Then, as I sat in the living room playing with my new Nintendo, I heard some shouting and doors slamming. The next thing I know, my dad is standing in the living room with his suitcases. He just moved out right then. I haven't celebrated Christmas since that day."

"You haven't celebrated at all? In fifteen years?"

"Nope. I silently protested for a few holidays, passed between parents, but once I went to college, it was done. No decorations, no presents, no Christmas carols."

He was almost sorry he'd asked. So many of Colin's favorite memories had revolved around the holidays with his parents. Even after they died, Christmas couldn't be ruined. He just worked that much harder to make it special for Lily. He'd always dreamed of the day he'd celebrate the holidays with his own family. He'd gotten a taste of it when they celebrated Shane's first Christmas, but not long after that, he learned the truth about his son's real father.

"That's the saddest thing I've ever heard." And coming from a guy whose life had fallen apart in the past year, that was saying a lot.

"Divorce happens," Natalie said. A distant, almost ambivalent look settled on her face. She continued down the stairs to the ground floor. "It happens to hundreds of couples every day. It happened to you. Heck, it's happened to my mother three times. She's on her fourth husband. My sad story isn't that uncommon."

"I actually wasn't talking about the divorce." Colin stepped down onto the first-floor landing and reached out to grip the railing. "I mean, I'm sure it was awful for you to live through your parents' split. I just hate that it ruined Christmas for you. Christmas is such a special time. It's about family and friends, magic and togetherness. It's a good thing we've decided to just be friends because I could never be with someone who didn't like Christmas."

"Really? It's that important?"

"Yep. I look forward to it all year. I couldn't imagine not celebrating."

"It's easier than you think. I stay busy with work or I try to travel."

Colin could only shake his head. She wasn't interested in long-term relationships or holidays, both things most people seemed to want or enjoy. Her parents' divorce must've hit at a crucial age for her. He couldn't help reaching out to put a soothing arm around her shoulder. "You shouldn't let your parents' crap ruin your chances for having a happy holiday for the rest of your life."

"I don't miss it," she said, shying away from his touch, although she didn't meet his eyes when she said it.

He didn't fully believe her. Just like he didn't believe her when she said she wasn't interested in going on a date with him. She did want to, she was just stubborn and afraid of intimacy. As much as he might be drawn to Natalie, he wasn't going to put himself in that boat again. He was tired of butting his head against relationship brick walls. But even if they were just friends, he couldn't let the Christmas thing slide. It was a challenge unlike any he'd had in a while.

"I think I could make you like Christmas again."

Natalie turned on her heel to look at him. Her eyebrow was arched curiously. "No, you can't."

"You don't have much faith in me. I can do anything I put my mind to."

"Be serious, Colin."

"I am serious," he argued.

"You can't make me like Christmas. That would take a lobotomy. Or a bout of amnesia. It won't happen otherwise."

He took a step closer, moving into her space. "If you're so confident, why don't we wager on it?"

Her dark eyes widened at him and she stepped back. "What? No. That's silly."

"Hmm…" Colin said, leaning in. "Sounds to me like you're too chicken to let me try. You know you'll lose the bet."

Natalie took another step backward until her back

was pressed against the front door. "I'm not scared. I'm just not interested in playing your little game."

"Come on. If you're so confident, it won't hurt to take me up on it. Name your victor's prize. We're going to be spending a lot of time together the next two weeks. This will make it more...interesting."

Natalie crossed her arms over her chest. "Okay, fine. You're going to lose, so it really doesn't matter. You have until the wedding reception to turn me into a Christmas fan again. If I win the bet, you have to pay for me to spend Christmas next year in Buenos Aires."

"Wow. Steep stakes," Colin said.

Natalie just shrugged it off. "Are you confident or not?"

Nice. Now she'd turned it so he was the chicken. "Of course I'm confident. You've got it. I'll even fly you there first class."

"And what do you want if you win?"

A million different options could've popped into his mind in that moment, but there was only one idea that really stuck with him. "In return, if I win the bet, you owe me...a kiss."

Natalie's eyebrow went up. "That's it? A kiss? I asked for a trip to South America."

Colin smiled. "Yep, that's all I want." It would be a nice little bonus to satisfy his curiosity, but in the end, he was more interested in bringing the magic back to Christmas for her. Everyone needed that in their life. He held out his hand. "Shall we shake on it and make this official?"

Natalie took a cleansing breath and nodded before taking his hand. He enveloped it with his own, noting how cold she was to the touch. She gasped as he held her, her eyes widening. "You're so warm," she said.

"I was about to mention how cold you are. What's the matter? Afraid you're going to lose the bet?"

She gave a soft smile and pulled her hand from his. "Not at all. I'm always cold."

"It *is* Christmastime," Colin noted. "That just means you'll need to bundle up when we go out in search of some Christmas spirit."

She frowned, a crease forming between her brows. "We're both really busy, Colin. What if I just kiss you now? Will you let the whole thing drop?"

Colin propped his palm on the wall over her shoulder and leaned in until they were separated by mere inches. He brought his hand up to cup her cheek, running the pad of this thumb across her full bottom lip. Her lips parted softly, her breath quickening as he got closer. He had been right. She was attracted to him, but that just wasn't enough for her to want more.

"You can kiss me now if you want to," he said. "But there's no way I'm dropping this bet."

His hand fell to his side as a smirk of irritation replaced the expression on her face. This was going to be more fun than he'd expected.

"It's getting late. I'd better get you home."

He pulled away, noting the slight downturn of Natalie's lips as he did. Was she disappointed that he didn't kiss her? He'd never met a woman who sent such conflicting signals before. He got the feeling she didn't know what she wanted.

She didn't need to worry. They might just be friends, but he would kiss her, and soon. Colin had no intention of losing this bet.

Four

Natalie was on pins and needles all day Thursday knowing that Colin would be coming for the cake tasting that afternoon. She was filled with this confusing mix of emotions. First, there was the apprehension over their bet. Colin was determined to get her in the Christmas spirit. Wednesday morning when she'd stepped outside, she found a fresh pine wreath on her front door with a big red velvet bow.

She was tempted to take it down, but she wouldn't. She could withstand his attempts, but she knew the more she resisted, the more she would see of Colin. That filled her with an almost teenage giddiness—the way she used to feel whenever Colin would smile at her when they were kids. It made her feel ridiculous considering nothing was going to happen between the two of them, and frankly, it was distracting her from her work. Thank goodness this weekend's wedding was a smaller affair.

She was about to call the florist to follow up on the bride's last-minute request for a few additional boutonnieres when she noticed a figure lurking in her doorway. It was Gretchen.

Natalie pulled off her earpiece. "Yes?"

"So Tuesday night, I was meeting a friend for dinner on this side of town and I happened to pass by the chapel around nine that night. I noticed your car was still in the parking lot."

Natalie tried not to frown at her coworker. "You know I work late sometimes."

"Yeah, that's what I thought at first, too, but none of the lights were on. Then I noticed on your Outlook calendar that you had a late appointment to discuss the Russell-Watson wedding." A smug grin crossed Gretchen's face.

Natalie rolled her eyes. "It was nothing, so don't turn it into something. We finalized the plans for the wedding, that's all. Then he asked me for help with his wedding present for Lily. He's giving her a house."

"A house? Lord," Gretchen declared with wide eyes. "I mean, I know I'm engaged to a movie star and all, but I have a hard time wrapping my head around how rich people think."

"It's actually the home they grew up in. He asked me to help him fix it up for them."

Gretchen nodded thoughtfully. "Did you help him rearrange some of the bedroom furniture?"

"Ugh, no." Natalie searched around her desk for something to throw, but all she had was a crystal paperweight shaped like a heart. She didn't want to knock

Gretchen unconscious, despite how gratifying it might feel in the moment. "We just walked around and talked about what I'd keep or donate. Nothing scandalous. I'm sorry to disappoint you."

"Well, boo. I was hopeful that this guy would make it up to you for his cruel rebuffing at the engagement party."

"He didn't make it up to me, but he did explain why he'd turned me down. Apparently he had a date that night."

"And now?"

"And now they've broken up. But that doesn't change anything. We're just going to be friends. It's better this way. Things would've just been more…complicated if something had happened."

Gretchen narrowed her gaze at her. "And you helping him with the house now that he's single won't be complicated?"

Natalie swung her ponytail over her shoulder and avoided her coworker's gaze by glancing at her computer screen. There were no critical emails to distract her from the conversation.

"Natalie?"

"No, it won't," she said at last. "It's going to be fine. We've been family friends for years and that isn't going to change. I'm going to handle the wedding and help him with the house and everything will be fine. Great, really. I think it's just the distraction I need to get through the holidays this year."

Gretchen nodded as she talked, but Natalie could tell she wasn't convinced. Frankly, neither was Natalie. Even as she said the words, she was speaking to herself as much as to her friend. She certainly wasn't going to tell her that she was fighting her attraction to Colin like a fireman with a five-alarm inferno. Or that she'd gotten herself roped into a bet that could cost her not only a kiss, but a solid dose of the holidays she had just said she was avoiding.

"Okay, well, whatever helps you get through the holidays, hon."

"Thank you."

"Uh-oh. Speak of the devil," Gretchen said, peeking out Natalie's window.

"He's here?" Natalie said, perking up in her seat, eyes wide with panic. "He's early." She was automatically opening her desk drawer and reaching for her compact when she heard Gretchen's low, evil laugh.

"No, he's not. I lied. I just wanted to see how you'd react. I was right. You're so full of it, your eyeballs should be floating."

Natalie sat back in her chair, the panic quickly replaced by irritation. Her gaze fell on the drawer to the soft foam rose stress ball that the florist had given them. She picked it up and hurled it at Gretchen, who ducked just in time.

"Get out of my office!" she shouted, but Gretchen was already gone. Natalie could hear her cackling down the hallway. Thank goodness there weren't any customers in the facility this morning.

There would be several clients here after lunchtime, though. Amelia had three cake tastings on the schedule today, including with Colin.

Hopefully that would go better than just now. Gretchen had already called her on the ridiculous infatuation that had reignited. Amelia would likely be more tactful. She hoped. Natalie didn't think she'd been that obvious. In the end, nothing *had* happened. They'd finalized plans, she'd helped him with the house and they'd had pizza. They hadn't kissed. She had certainly wanted to.

It was hard to disguise the overwhelming sense of disappointment she felt when they had their near miss. Natalie had been certain he was about to kiss her. She thought maybe dangling that carrot would serve her on two levels: first that they could call off the silly bet, and second, that she'd finally fulfill her youthful fantasy of kissing the dashing and handsome Colin Russell.

Then…nothing. He knew what he was doing. He'd turned up the dial, gotten her primed, then left her hanging. He was not letting her out of the bet. It might be a painful two weeks until the wedding while he tried, but in the end, she'd get a nice trip to Argentina out of it.

Colin was well-intentioned, but he wasn't going to turn her into a jolly ol' elf anytime soon. It wasn't as though she wanted to be a Humbug. She'd tried on several occasions to get into the spirit, but it never worked. The moment the carols started playing in the stores, she felt her soul begin to shrivel inside her. Honey-glazed ham tasted like ash in her mouth.

With her parents' marriages in shambles and no desire to ever start a family of her own, there wasn't anything left to the season but cold weather and commercialism.

That said, she didn't expect Colin to lose this bet quietly. He would try his damnedest, and if last night was any indication, he was willing to play dirty. If that was the case, she needed to as well. It wouldn't be hard to deploy her own distracting countermeasures. The chemistry between them was powerful and could easily derail his focus. She wouldn't have to go too far—a seductive smile and a gentle touch would easily plant something other than visions of sugarplums in his head.

Natalie reached back into the drawer for the mirror she'd sought out earlier. She looked over her hair and re-applied her burgundy lipstick. She repowdered her nose, then slipped everything back into her desk. Glancing down at her outfit, she opted to slip out of her blazer, leaving just the sleeveless burgundy and hunter-green satin shell beneath it. It had a deep V-neck cut, and the necklace she was wearing today would no doubt draw the eye down to the depths of her cleavage.

Finally, she dabbed a bit of perfume behind her ears, on her wrists and just between her collarbones. It was her favorite scent, exotic and complex, bringing to mind perfumed silk tents in the deserts of Arabia. A guy she'd once dated had told her that perfume was like a hook, luring him closer with the promise of sex.

She took a deep breath of the fragrance and smiled. It was playing dirty, but she had a bet to win.

"I brought you a gift."

Colin watched Natalie look up at him from her desk with a startled expression. From the looks of it, she'd been deep into her work and lost track of time. She recovered quickly, sitting back in her chair and pulling off her headset. "Did you? What is it now? A light-up snowman? A three-foot candy cane?"

"Close." He whipped out a box from behind his back and placed it on her desk. "It's peppermint bark from a candy shop downtown."

Natalie smirked at the box, opening it to admire the

contents. "Are you planning to buy your way through this whole bet?"

"Maybe. Either way, it's cheaper than a first-class ticket to Buenos Aires."

"You added the first class part yourself, you know, when you were feeling cocky." She leaned her elbows on the desk and watched him pointedly.

His gaze was drawn to a gold-and-emerald pendant that dangled just at the dip of her neckline. The shadows hinted at the breasts just beyond the necklace. He caught a whiff of her perfume and felt the muscles in his body start to tense. What were they talking about? Cocky. Yes. That was certainly on point. "Do you like the wreath?" he asked, diverting the subject.

"It's lovely," she said, sitting back with a satisfied smile that made him think she was teasing him on purpose.

That was definitely a change from that night at the house. She'd been adamant about being the wrong kind of woman for him and that they should be friends. Now she was almost dangling herself in front of him. He couldn't complain about the view, but he had to question the motivation.

"It makes my entryway smell like a pine forest."

At least she hadn't said Pine-Sol. "You're supposed to say it smells like Christmas."

"I don't know what Christmas is supposed to smell like. When I was a kid, Christmas smelled like burned biscuits and the nasty floral air freshener my mom would spray to keep my grandmother from finding out she was smoking again."

Colin winced at her miserable holiday memories. It sounded as though her Christmas experiences sucked long before her dad left. His next purchase was going to be a mulling spice candle. "That is not what Christmas smells like. It smells like pine and peppermint, spiced cider and baking sugar cookies."

"Maybe in Hallmark stores," she said, pushing up from her chair and glancing at her watch. "But now we need to focus on cake, not sugar cookies."

Colin followed her into a sitting room near the kitchen. It had several comfortable wingback chairs and a loveseat surrounding a coffee table.

"Have a seat." Natalie gestured into the room.

"Are you joining me?" he asked as he passed near to her.

"Oh yes," she said with a coy smile. "I've just got to let Amelia know we're ready."

He stepped inside and Natalie disappeared down the hallway. He was happy to have a moment alone. The smell of her skin mingling with her perfume and that naughty smile was a combination he couldn't take much more of. At least not and keep his hands off her.

Something had definitely changed since Tuesday. Tuesday night, she'd been more open and friendly once he told her why he'd turned her down, but nothing like this. Not even when she'd leaned into him, thinking he was about to kiss her.

Perhaps she was trying to distract him. Did she think that keeping his mind occupied with thoughts of her would shift the focus away from bringing Christmas joy back into her life? This had all happened after the bet, so that had to be it. *Tricky little minx.* That was playing dirty after her big speech about how she wasn't the right kind of woman for him. Well, two could play at that game. If he was right, now that he knew her ploy he'd let her see how far she was willing to push it to win.

No matter what, he wouldn't let himself be ensnared by her feminine charms. They were oil and water that wouldn't mix. But that didn't mean he wouldn't enjoy letting her try. And it didn't mean he'd let himself lose sight of the bet in the process.

He heard a click of heels on wood and a moment later Natalie came back into the room. She settled onto the loveseat beside him. Before he could say anything, the caterer, Amelia, blew in behind her.

"Okay," Amelia said as she carried a silver platter into the room and placed it on the coffee table. "Time for some cake tasting. This is the best part of planning a wedding, I think. Here are five of our most popular cake flavors." She pointed her manicured finger at the different cubes of cake that were stacked into elegant pyramids. "There's a white almond sour cream cake, triple chocolate fudge, red velvet, pistachio and lemon pound cake. In the bowls, we've got an assortment of different fillings along with samples of both my buttercream and my marshmallow fondant. The cake design you selected will work with either finish, so it's really just a matter of what taste you prefer."

"It all looks wonderful, Amelia. Thanks for putting this together."

"Sure thing. On this card, it has all the flavors listed along with some popular combinations you might like to try. For a wedding of your size, I usually recommend two choices. I can do alternating tiers, so if a guest doesn't one like flavor, they can always try the other. The variety is nice. Plus, it makes it easier to choose if you have more than one you love."

"Great," Colin said, taking the card from her and setting it on the table. He watched as the caterer shot a pointed look at Natalie on the couch beside him.

"And if you don't mind, since Natalie is here with you, I'm going to go clean up in the kitchen. I've got another cake to finish piping tonight."

Colin nodded. He was fine being alone with Natalie. That left the door open for her little games anyway. "That's fine. I'm sure you've got plenty to do. Thanks for fitting me in on such short notice."

"Thanks, Amelia," Natalie said. "If we have any questions about the cake, I'll come get you."

Amelia nodded and slipped out of the room. Colin watched her go, then turned back to the platter in front of them. "Where should we start?"

Natalie picked up the card from the table. "I'd go with Amelia's suggestions. She knows her cake."

"Great. What's first?"

"White almond sour cream cake with lemon curd."

They both selected small squares of cake from the plate, smearing them with a touch of the filling using a small silver butter knife. Colin wasn't a big fan of lemon, but even he had to admit this was one of the best bites of cake he'd ever had.

And it was just the beginning. They tried them all, mixing chocolate cake with chocolate chip mousse, lemon pound cake with raspberry buttercream and red velvet with whipped cream cheese. There were a million different combinations to choose from. He was glad he'd eaten a light lunch because by the time they finished, all the cake was gone and his suit pants were a bit tighter than they'd been when he sat down.

"I don't know how we're going to choose," he said

at last. "It was all great. I don't think there was a single thing I didn't like."

"I told you she did great work."

Colin turned to look at Natalie, noticing she had a bit of buttercream icing in the corner of her mouth. "Uh-oh."

"What?" Natalie asked with concern lining her brow.

"You've got a little…" his voice trailed off as he reached out and wiped the icing away with the pad of his thumb. "…frosting. I got it," he said with a smile.

Natalie looked at the icing on the tip of his thumb. She surprised him by grasping his wrist to keep him from pulling away. With her eyes pinned on his, she leaned in and gently placed his thumb in her mouth. She sucked off the icing, gliding her tongue over his skin. Colin's groin tightened and blood started pumping hard through his veins.

She finally let go, a sweet smile on her face that didn't quite match her bold actions. "I didn't want any to go to waste."

For once in his life, Colin acted without thinking. He lunged for her, capturing her lips with his and clutching at her shoulders. He waited for Natalie to stiffen or struggle away from him, but she didn't. Instead, she brought up her hands to hold his face close to her, as though she was afraid he might pull away too soon.

Her lips were soft and tasted like sweet vanilla buttercream. He'd had plenty of cake today, but he couldn't get enough of her mouth. There was no hesitation in her touch, her tongue gliding along his just as she'd tortured him with his thumb a moment ago.

Finally, he pulled away. It took all his willpower to do it, but he knew he needed to. This was a wedding chapel, not a hotel room. He didn't move far, though. His hand was still resting on Natalie's upper arm, his face mere inches from hers. She was breathing hard, her cheeks flushed as her hands fell into her lap.

He could tell that he'd caught her off guard at first with that kiss, but he didn't care. She'd brought that on herself with her distracting games. If her body was any indicator, she hadn't minded. She'd clung to him, met him measure for measure. For someone who thought they were unsuitable for each other, she'd certainly participated in that kiss.

He just wished he knew that she wanted to, and she wasn't just doing it as a distraction to help her win the bet. There was one way to find out. She wasn't good at hiding her initial emotional responses, so he decided to push a few buttons. "So, what do you think?" he asked.

Natalie looked at him with glassy, wide eyes. "About what?"

"About the cake. I'm thinking definitely the white cake with the lemon, but I'm on the fence about the second choice."

Natalie stiffened, the hazy bliss vanishing in an instant. He could tell that cake was not what she'd had on her mind in that moment. She'd let her little game go too far. He was glad he wasn't the only one affected by it.

"Red velvet," she said. She sniffed delicately and sat back, pulling away from him. Instantly, she'd transformed back into the uptight, efficient wedding planner. "It's a universal flavor. I'm told it's a Christmas classic, so it suits the theme. It's also one of my favorites, so admittedly I'm partial."

"Okay. The choices are made. Thanks for being so... helpful."

Natalie looked at him with a narrowed gaze that softened as the coy smile from earlier returned. "My pleasure."

Five

Monday afternoon, Colin made a stop by Frankie's motorcycle store on his way home from his latest work site.

When he'd first found out that his sister was dating a guy who looked more like a biker than a businessman, he'd been hesitant. Meeting Frankie and visiting his custom bike shop downtown had changed things. Yes, he had more tattoos than Colin could count and several piercings, but he was a talented artisan of his craft. The motorcycles he designed and built were metal masterpieces that earned a high price. Over the past year, Frankie's business had really started to take off. It looked like he and Lily would have a promising future together.

Slipping into the shop, Colin walked past displays of parts, gear and accessories to the counter at the back. Lily was sitting at the counter. Frankie had hired her to run the register, making the business a family affair. Living upstairs from the shop had made it convenient, but he couldn't imagine they had enough space to raise a family there or even stretch their legs.

"Hey, brother of mine," Lily called from the counter. "Can I interest you in a chopper?"

"Very funny." Colin laughed.

Lily came out from behind the counter to give him a hug. "If not for a bike, to what do I owe this visit?"

"Well, I thought you might want to know about some of the wedding plans Natalie and I have put together." Colin had a copy of the design portfolio to show her. He hoped that by showing her the designs, she would start getting more excited about the wedding.

Lily shrugged and drifted back to her post behind the counter. "I'm sure whatever you've chosen will be great."

"At least look at it," Colin said, opening the folder on the counter. "Natalie and her partners have worked really hard on putting together a beautiful wedding for you. We went with the winter wonderland theme you and Natalie discussed. For the cake, we chose alternating tiers of white almond sour cream cake with lemon curd filling and red velvet with cream cheese. Natalie said those were two of their most popular flavors, and they were both really tasty."

"Sounds great," Lily said, sitting back onto her stool. "I have no doubt that it will come together beautifully. As long as I have someone to marry us, it's fine by me. The rest of this is just a bonus."

"Have you ordered a dress yet?"

His sister shook her head. "No."

Colin frowned. "Lily, you don't have a dress?"

"I was just going to pull something from my closet. I have that white dress from my sorority induction ceremony."

"Are you serious? You've got to go get a wedding dress, Lily."

His sister shrugged again, sending Colin's blood pressure higher. He couldn't fathom how she didn't care about any of this. Pam hadn't been very interested in planning their wedding either. Since they were in a hurry, they'd ended up with a courthouse visit without frills. It was a little anticlimactic. He didn't want that for Lily, but she seemed indifferent about the whole thing.

"I've got a job, Colin. Frankie and I work at the shop six days a week. I can't go running around trying on fluffy Cinderella dresses. If you are so concerned with what I'm wearing, you can pick it out. I wear a size six. Natalie and I used to be able to share clothes when we were teenagers. At the engagement party she looked like she might still wear the same size as I do. I'm sure you two can work it out without me."

Colin fought the urge to drop his face into his hands in dismay. "Will you at least go to a dress fitting?"

"Yeah, sure."

"Okay. So we'll get a dress." He pulled out his phone to call Natalie and let her know the bad news. He knew she had been busy over the weekend with a wedding, so he hadn't bothered her with wedding or holiday details. He couldn't wait any longer, though. He was certain this was an important detail and could be the very thing that pushed his cool, calm and collected wedding planner over the edge.

She didn't answer, so he left a quick message on her

phone. When he slipped his phone back into his pocket, he noticed Lily watching him. "What?"

"Your voice changed when you left her a message."

"I was trying to soften the blow," he insisted.

Lily shook her head. "I don't know. That voice sounded like the same voice I remember from when you would tie up the house phone talking to girls in high school. What's going on between you two?"

"Going on?" Colin tried to find the best way to word it. "I don't know. We've spent a lot of time together planning the wedding. Things have been…interesting."

"Are you dating?"

"No," Colin said more confidently. He was determined not to wade into that territory with Natalie. She was beautiful and smart and alluring, but she also had it in her to crush him. "Natalie and I have very different ideas on what constitutes a relationship."

Lily nodded. "Natalie has never been the princess waiting for her prince to save her. She always kept it casual with guys. I take it you're not interested in a booty call. You should consider it. Going from serious relationship to serious relationship isn't working for you either."

Colin did not want to have this conversation with his little sister. Instead, he ignored the kernel of truth in her words. "I am not going to discuss booty calls with you. I can't believe I even said that phrase out loud."

"Have you kissed her?"

He didn't answer right away.

"Colin?"

"Yes, I kissed her."

Lily made a thoughtful clicking sound with her tongue. "Interesting," she said slowly, her hands planted on her hips. "What exactly do you—?"

Colin's phone started to ring at his hip, interrupting her query. He'd never been so relieved to get a call. "I've got to take this," he said, answering the phone and moving to the front of the shop. "Hello?"

"There's no dress?" It was Natalie, her displeasure evident by the flat tone of her query.

"That is correct," he said with a heavy sigh. "And like everything else, she says to just pick something. Lily says she's a size six and that you used to share clothes, so fake it."

"Fake it?" Natalie shrieked into his ear.

"Yep." He didn't know what else to say.

Natalie sat silent on the other end of the line for a moment. "I need to make a few calls. Can you meet me at a bridal salon tonight?"

Colin looked down at his watch. It was already after five. Did they have enough time? "Sure."

"Okay. I'll call you back and let you know where to meet me."

Colin hung up, turning to see a smug look on his sister's face.

"I told you she could handle it."

"That well may be, but she wasn't happy about it." At this point, they'd probably be lucky if Lily didn't go down the aisle in a white trash bag. They had about two weeks to pick the dress, order it, have it come in and do any alterations. He wasn't much of a wedding expert, but he got the feeling it would be a rough road. "What about Frankie? Do I need to dress him, too?"

Lily shook her head and Colin felt a wave of relief wash over him. "He's good. He's got a white suit and picked out a silver bowtie and suspenders to go with the theme."

He should've known a bit of hipster style would make its way into this wedding. Whatever. It was one less person he had to dress.

Returning to the counter, he closed the wedding portfolio. He was anxious to get out of here before Lily started up the conversation about Natalie again. "Okay, well, I'm off to meet Natalie at some bridal salon. Any other surprises you're waiting to tell me until an inopportune time?"

The slight twist of Lily's lips was proof that there was. "Well…" she hesitated. "I kind of forgot about this before, but it should be fine."

Somehow, he doubted that. "What, Lily?"

"Next week, Frankie and I are flying to Las Vegas for a motorcycle convention."

"Next week? Lily, the wedding is next week."

"The wedding isn't until Saturday. We're flying back Friday. No problem."

Colin dropped his forehead into his hand and squeezed at his temples. "What time on Friday? You've got the rehearsal that afternoon and the rehearsal dinner after that."

"Hmm…" she said thoughtfully, reaching for her phone. She flipped through the screens to pull up her calendar. "Our flight is scheduled to arrive in Nashville at one. That should be plenty of time, right?"

"Right." He didn't bother to point out that it was winter and weather delays were a very real concern this time of year. With his luck, she was connecting in Chicago or Detroit. "When do you leave?"

"Monday."

Colin nodded. Well, at the very least, he knew he

could work on the house without worrying about her stopping by and ruining the surprise.

A chime on his phone announced a text. Natalie had sent him the name and address of the bridal shop where they were meeting.

"Anything else I need to know, Lil?"

She smiled innocently, reminding him of the sweet girl with pigtails he remembered growing up. "Nope. That's it."

"Okay," he said, slipping his phone back into his pocket. "I'm off to buy you a wedding dress."

"Good luck," she called to him as he slipped out of the store.

He'd need it.

Natalie swallowed her apprehension as she went into the bridal shop. Not because she had to get Lily a dress at the last minute—that didn't surprise her at all. They were close enough to sample size to buy something out of the shop and alter it.

Really, she was more concerned about trying on wedding dresses. It wasn't for her, she understood that, but it still felt odd. She'd never tried on a wedding dress before, not even for fun. Her mother had sold her wedding dress when her parents divorced.

She knew it was just a dress, but there was something transformative about it. She didn't want to feel that feeling. That was worse than Christmas spirit.

She'd avoided the bulk of Colin's holiday bet by staying busy with a wedding all weekend. But now it was the start of a new week and she had no doubt he would find some way to slip a little Christmas into each day.

In addition to the wreath and the peppermint bark,

she'd also received a Christmas card that played carols when she opened it. A local bakery had delivered a fruitcake to the office on Friday, and a florist had brought a poinsettia on Saturday morning.

What he didn't know was that she'd received plenty of well-meaning holiday gifts throughout the years. That wasn't going to crack her. It just gave her a plant to water every other day.

As she entered the waiting room of the salon, she found Colin and the storekeeper, Ruby, searching through the tall racks of gowns. Ruby looked up as she heard Natalie approach.

"Miss Sharpe! There you are. Mr. Russell and I were looking through a few gowns while we waited."

"Not a problem. Thanks for scheduling us with such late notice."

"This is the bridal business," Ruby said with a dismissive chuckle. "You never know what you'll get. For every girl that orders her gown a year in advance, I get one pregnant and in-a-hurry bride that needs a gown right away. After being in this industry for twenty years, I've learned to keep a good stock of dresses on hand for times like this."

Ruby was good at what she did. Natalie referred a lot of brides to her salon because of it. "Did Colin fill you in on what we need?"

"Yes. He said you need something in a street size six that will fit a winter wonderland theme. He also said the bride won't be here to try them on."

"That's correct. We wear the same size, so I'll try on the dresses in her place."

"Okay. I'd recommend something with a corset back. You don't have a lot of time for alterations and with a corset bodice, you can tighten or loosen it to account for any adjustments in your sizes."

Brilliant. She'd have to remember this in the future for quick-turnaround brides. "Perfect."

"Great. If you'd like to take a seat, Mr. Russell, I'll take Miss Sharpe to the dressing room to try on a few gowns to see what you like."

"Have fun," Colin said, waving casually at her as she was ushered into the back.

She was officially on the other side now. She'd passed the curtain where only brides went. It made her stomach ache.

"I've pulled these three dresses to start with. I think you're pretty close to the sample size, so this should be a decent fit. Which would you like to try first?"

Natalie looked over the gowns with apprehension. She needed to think like Lily. Everything else about the wedding had turned out to be Natalie's choice, but when it came to dresses, it seemed wrong to pick something she liked. "It doesn't matter," she said. "I'm going to let her brother choose."

"Then let's start with the ruched satin gown."

Natalie slipped out of her blouse and pencil skirt and let Ruby slip the gown over her head. She was fully aware how heavy bridal gowns could be, but for some reason, it seemed so much heavier on than she had expected it to.

She held the gown in place as Ruby tightened the corset laces in the back. Looking in the mirror, she admired the fit of the gown. The corset gave her a curvy, seductive shape she hadn't expected. She never felt much like a sex kitten. Her shape had always been a little lanky and boyish in her opinion, but the gown changed that.

The decorative crystals that lined the sweetheart neckline drew the eyes to her enhanced cleavage.

"Do you like the snowflake?"

Natalie narrowed her gaze at her reflection and noticed the crystal design at her hip that looked very much like a snowflake. Perfect for the theme. "It's nice. It's got a good shape and the crystals give it a little shine without being overpowering."

"Let's go show him."

There was more apprehension as Natalie left the dressing room. This wasn't about her, but she wanted to look the best she could when she stepped onto the riser to show him the gown. She focused on her posture and grace as she glided out into the salon.

Her gaze met his the minute she cleared the curtain. His golden hazel eyes raked up and down the length of the gown with the same heat of appreciation she'd seen that night at the engagement party. Natalie felt a flush of heat rise to her cheeks as she stepped onto the pedestal for his inspection.

"It's beautiful," he said. "It's very elegant and you look amazing in it. But I have to say that it's not right for Lily at all."

Natalie sighed and looked down. He was right. "Ruby, do we have one that's a little more whimsical and fun?"

Ruby nodded and helped her down. "I have a few that might work. How fun are we talking?" she asked as they stepped back into the dressing room. "Crazy tulle skirt? Blush- or pink-colored gowns?"

"If she was here, probably all that and more. But she should've shown up herself if she had that strong of an opinion. Let's go for something a little more whimsical, but still classically bridal."

The minute Ruby held up the gown, Natalie knew this dress was the one. It was like something out of a winter fantasy—the gown of the snow queen. It was a fitted, mermaid style with a sweetheart neckline and sheer, full-length sleeves. All across the gown and along the sleeves were delicate white-and-silver-stitched floral designs that looked almost like glittering snowflakes dancing across her skin.

She held her breath as she slipped into the gown and got laced up. Ruby fastened a few buttons at her shoulders and then it was done. It was the most beautiful dress she'd ever seen, and she'd seen hundreds of brides come through the chapel over the years.

"This gown has a matching veil with the same lace trim along the edges. Do you want to go out there with it on?"

"Yes," she said immediately. Natalie wanted to see the dress with the veil. She knew it would make all the difference.

Ruby swiftly pinned her hair up and set the veil's comb in. The veil flowed all the way to floor, longer than even the gown's chapel-length train.

It was perfect. Everything she'd ever wanted.

Natalie swallowed hard. Everything she'd ever wanted *for Lily*, she corrected herself. Planning a wedding in the bride's place was messing with her head.

She headed back out to the salon. This time, she avoided Colin's gaze, focusing on lifting the hem of the skirt to step up on the pedestal. She glanced at herself for only a moment in the three-sided mirror, but even that was enough for the prickle of tears to form in her eyes.

Quickly, she jerked away, turning to face Colin. She covered her tears by fidgeting with her gown and veil.

"What do you think of this one?" Ruby asked.

The long silence forced Natalie to finally meet Colin's gaze. Did he hate it?

Immediately, she knew that was not the case. He was just stunned speechless.

"Colin?"

"Wow," he finally managed. He stood up from the velour settee and walked closer.

Natalie felt her chest grow tighter with every step. He wasn't looking at the gown. Not really. He was looking at her. The intensity of his gaze made her insides turn molten. Her knees started trembling and she was thankful for the full skirt that covered them.

Just when she thought she couldn't bear his gaze any longer, his eyes dropped down to look over the details of the dress. "This is the one. No question."

Natalie took a breath and looked down to examine the dress. "Do you think Lily will like it?"

Colin hesitated a moment, swallowing hard before he spoke. "I do. It will look beautiful on her. I don't think we could find a dress better suited to the theme you've put together." He took a step back and nodded again from a distance. "Let's get this one."

"Wonderful!" Ruby exclaimed. "This one really is lovely."

The older woman went to the counter to write up the slip, completely oblivious to the energy in the room that hummed between Natalie and Colin. Natalie wasn't quite sure how she didn't notice it. It made it hard for

Natalie to breathe. It made the dress feel hot and itchy against her skin even though it was the softest, most delicate fabric ever made.

Colin slipped back down onto the couch with a deep sigh. When he looked up at her again, Natalie knew she wasn't mistaken about any of this. He wanted her. And she wanted him. It was a bad idea, they both knew it, but they couldn't fight it much longer.

She also wanted out of this dress. Right now. Playing bride was a confusing and scary experience. Before Colin or Ruby could say another word, she pulled the veil from her head, leaped down from the pedestal and disappeared behind the curtains into the dressing room as fast as she could.

Six

"I'd like to take you to dinner," Colin said as they walked out of the shop with the gown bagged over his arm. "I'm serious this time. You really bailed me out on this whole dress thing."

It was a lame excuse. It sounded lame to his own ears, but he couldn't do anything about it. There was no way he could look at Natalie, to see her in that dress looking like the most beautiful creature he'd ever set his eyes on, and then let her just get in her car and go home. It no longer mattered if they were incompatible or had no future. The taste of her already lingered on his lips, the heat of her hummed through his veins. He wanted her. End of story.

Natalie stopped and swung her purse strap up onto her shoulder. "Dinner? Not a date?"

This again. You'd think after their kiss, and after the intense moment they'd just shared in the salon, that she wouldn't be so picky about the details. "No, it's not a date, it's a thank-you. I believe that I have yet to meet your stringent qualifications for a date."

Natalie's lips curled into a smile of amusement. He expected her to make an excuse and go home, but instead she nodded. "Dinner sounds great."

Colin opened the door of his truck and hung the gown bag up inside. "How about the Italian place on the corner?"

"That's perfect."

He closed up the truck and they walked down the sidewalk together to the restaurant. Colin had eaten at Moretti's a couple of times and it had always been good. It was rustic Italian cuisine, with a Tuscan feel inside. The walls were a rusty brown with exposed brick, worn wood shelves and tables, warm gold lighting and an entire wall on the far end that was covered in hundreds of wine bottles. It wasn't the fanciest place, but it was a good restaurant for a casual dinner date, or a thank-you dinner as the case was here.

It was a pretty popular place to eat in this area. Typically, Moretti's was super busy, but coming later on a Monday night the restaurant was pretty quiet. There were about a dozen tables with customers when they arrived and no waiting list.

The hostess immediately escorted them to a booth for two near the roaring fireplace. Nashville didn't get very cold in the winter, but with the icy December wind, it was cold enough that the fire would feel amazing after their walk down the street. Colin helped Natalie out of her coat, hanging it on one of the brass hooks mounted to the side of the booth.

The waiter arrived just as they'd settled into their

seats, bringing water and warm bread with olive oil. He offered them the daily menus and left them alone to make their choices. After a bit of deliberation, Natalie chose the angel-hair primavera and Colin, the chicken parmesan. They selected a bottle of cabernet to share and the waiter returned with that immediately.

The first sip immediately warmed Colin's belly and cheeks, reminding him to go slow until he ate some bread. He'd had a quick sandwich around eleven, but he was starving now and wine on an empty stomach might make him say or do something he'd regret, like kissing Natalie again. Or maybe he'd do something he wouldn't regret, but shouldn't do. At the moment, Lily's suggestion that he indulge himself in something casual with Natalie was sounding pretty good. He took a bite of bread as a precaution.

"Well, this is certainly not how I envisioned this evening going," Natalie noted as she tore her own chunk of bread from the loaf.

"It's not bad, is it?"

"No," she admitted. "But when I woke up this morning, I didn't figure I'd be trying on wedding dresses and having dinner with you."

It hadn't been on his radar either, but he was happy with the turn of events. There was something about spending an evening with Natalie that relaxed him after a stressful day. "Did you have plans for tonight that I ruined?"

"Not real plans. I'd anticipated a frozen dinner and a couple chapters of a new book I downloaded."

"I was going to grab takeout and catch up on my DVR. We're an exciting pair. Are you off tomorrow?"

Natalie shrugged, confusing him with her response

to a simple question. "Technically," she clarified. "The chapel is closed on Tuesday and Wednesday, but I usually go in."

"That means you don't get any days off."

"I don't usually work a full day. And I only work half of Sunday to clean up."

Colin shook his head. "You sound as bad as I used to be when I took over Dad's business. I worked eighteen-hour days, seven days a week trying to keep afloat. Is that why you put in so many hours? How's the wedding business?"

If the bill he'd received for the upcoming wedding was any indication, they were doing very well. He'd told her money was no object and she'd believed him. It was well worth it for Lily, but he'd been surprised to see so many digits on the invoice.

"Business is great. That's why it's so hard not to come in. There's always something to do."

"Can't you hire someone to watch the place and answer the phones while you all take time off? Like a receptionist?"

Natalie bit her lip and took a large sip of wine as though she were delaying her response. "I guess we could. Anyways, I'm the only one without a backup, but I'm the only one of us without a life. It's kind of hard to swap out the wedding planner, though. I'm the one with the whole vision of the day and know all the pieces that have to fall into place just perfectly."

"Getting a receptionist isn't the same as getting a backup planner. It just frees you up so you're not answering the phones and filing paperwork all the time. You should look into it. Of course, that would require you not to be such a control freak."

Natalie perked up in her seat. "I am not a control freak."

At that, Colin laughed. "Oh, come on now. Your office is immaculate. You're always stomping around with that headset on, handling every emergency. I'm beginning to think you run a one-stop wedding company because you won't let anyone else do any of it."

She opened her mouth to argue, then stopped. "Maybe I should look into a receptionist," she admitted.

"If you had one, you could spend the next two days with me instead of sitting alone in that lonely office of yours."

Natalie's eyebrow raised in question. "Spend the next two days with you doing what?"

"Working on the house. Helping me decorate. What we discussed last week. I've turned over the reins of the company to my second-in-command to manage our remaining projects through the end of the year so I can focus on what I need to do before the holidays."

"Oh."

That wasn't the enthusiastic response he was hoping for. "Oh, huh? I guess I should sweeten the deal, then. Spending time with me to help your childhood best friend isn't enough incentive."

"Quit it," Natalie chided. "I told you I'd help you with the house. Since I work on weekends, it makes sense to come over tomorrow, you're right. And I will. I was just expecting something else."

"Like what?"

"I don't know…a trip to the Opryland Hotel to look at the Christmas decorations and visit Santa, maybe?"

Opryland! Colin silently cursed and sipped his wine to cover his aggravation. The hotel in central Nashville was practically its own city. They went all out every holiday with massive decorations. They usually built a giant ice village with slides kids could play on. They even hosted the Rockettes' Christmas show. That would've been perfect, but of course he couldn't do it now that she'd brought it up. He refused to be predictable.

There wasn't really time for that, either. When he'd made that impulsive bet, he hadn't given a lot of thought to how much they both worked and how incompatible their schedules were. Between their jobs, working on the house and the wedding, there wasn't much time left to reintroduce Natalie to the holiday magic. He'd find a way, though. He was certain of it.

"I figured it was something related to the bet, although I don't know why you'd bother after that kiss we shared at the cake tasting. I'm not sure the one you'll win will be better than that."

Colin smiled wide. "Are you serious?" he asked.

She looked at him blankly. "Well, yes. It was a pretty good kiss, as kisses go."

"It was an amazing kiss," Colin conceded. "But it won't hold a candle to the kiss I'll get when I win."

Natalie sucked in a ragged breath, her pale skin growing a more peachy-pink tone in the golden candlelight. "I guess as a teenager I never realized how arrogant you were."

"It's not arrogance when it's fact. I intend to make your pulse spike and cheeks flush. I want you to run your fingers through my hair and hold me like you never want to let me go. When I win this bet, I'll kiss you until you're breathless and can't imagine ever kissing anyone else."

He watched Natalie swallow hard and reach a shaky hand out for more wine. He hid away his smile and focused on her so she knew he meant every word.

"Y-you've still g-got to win the bet," she stammered. "I'm pretty sure you've run out of Christmas stuff to mail to the office."

"Don't underestimate me," Colin said. "Those holiday gifts were just to get you in the right mindset." There were a lot of sensory elements to Christmas— the smell of pine and mulling spice, the taste of peppermint and chocolate, the sight of bright lights and colorful poinsettias. "I wanted to…prime the pump, so to speak. When you're ready, that's when I'll move in for the kill."

The waiter arrived with their salads, but Colin had suddenly lost his appetite. He knew what he wanted to taste and it wasn't on the Moretti's menu. A part of him knew it was a mistake to let himself go any further with Natalie, but the other part already knew it was too late. He needed to have her. Knowing nothing would come of it going in, he would be able to compartmentalize it. Just because he rarely had sex for sex's sake didn't mean he couldn't. What they had was a raw, physical attraction, nothing more. Natalie was certainly an enticing incentive to try to start now.

Perhaps if he did, he could focus on something else for a change. He had plenty going on right now, but somehow, Natalie's full bottom lip seemed to occupy all his thoughts.

As they ate, Natalie shifted the conversation to the wedding and his sister, even asking about his business, but he knew neither of them was really interested in talking about that tonight. They just had to get through dinner.

It wasn't until they were halfway through their pasta that she returned to the previous discussion. "I've been thinking," she began. "I think you and I started off on the wrong foot at the engagement party. I'd like us to start over."

"Start over?" He wasn't entirely sure what that meant.

"Yes. When we get done eating, I'm going to once again ask if you'd like to go someplace quiet to talk and catch up. This time, since you're not dating anyone, I hope you'll give a better response."

Was she offering what he thought she was offering? He sincerely hoped so. He finished his wine and busied himself by paying the bill. When the final credit card slip was brought to him, he looked up at Natalie. She was watching him with the sly smile on her face that she'd greeted him with the first time.

"So, Colin," she said softly. "Would you be interested in getting out of here and finding someplace quiet where we could talk and catch up?"

Colin had replayed that moment in his mind several times since the engagement party and now he knew exactly what he wanted to say.

"Your place or mine?"

It turned out to be his place, which was closer. Natalie's heart was pounding as she followed Colin down the hallway and into his kitchen. She'd only been here once before, the night of the engagement party. The house looked quite different tonight. There were no huge catering platters, no skirted tables, no jazz trio. It was just the wide open, modern space he called home.

It actually looked a little plain without everything else. Spartan. Like a model home.

She couldn't help but notice the sharp contrast between it and the warm, welcoming feel of his parents' house. It was about as far as you could get between them. Natalie had no doubt that this was a million-dollar house, but it was far too contemporary in style to suit her.

"May I offer you more wine?" he asked.

"No, thank you," she said, putting her purse down on the white quartz countertop. "I had plenty at dinner." And she had. She was stuffed. Natalie had focused on her food to avoid Colin's heated appraisal and now she regretted it. If she'd fully realized that her fantasies would actually play out after dinner, she would've held back a touch. She didn't exactly feel sexy, full to the gills with pasta, bread and wine.

"May I offer you a tour, then? I'm not sure how much you got to see of the place the other night."

"Not much," Natalie admitted. Since she'd only known the bride and her brother, she hadn't done much socializing. She'd hovered near the bar, people watching most of the evening.

Colin led her out of the sleek kitchen and through the dining room to the two-story open living room with a dramatic marble fireplace that went up to the ceiling. She followed him up the stairs to his loft office, then his bedroom. "This is the best part," he said.

"I bet," Natalie replied with a grin.

"That's not what I meant." He walked past the large bed to a set of French doors. He opened them and stepped out onto a deck.

Natalie went out behind him and stopped short as

she caught a glimpse of the view. They'd driven up a fairly steep hill to get here, she remembered that, but she hadn't realized his house virtually clung to the side of the mountain. While precarious, it offered an amazing view of the city. The lights stretched out as far as the eye could see, competing with the stars that twinkled overhead.

She had a really nice townhouse she liked, but it couldn't hold a candle to this. She could sit out here all night just looking up at the stars and sipping her coffee. Natalie bet it was amazing at sunrise, too.

"So, what do you think?"

Natalie hesitated, trying to find the right words. She turned to Colin, who was leaning against the railing with his arms crossed over his chest. "The deck is amazing."

"What about the rest of the house?"

"It's very nice."

"Nice, huh? You don't like it at all."

Natalie avoided the question by stepping back into the bedroom with him on her heels. "It's a beautiful home, really. The view alone is worth the price you paid for it. The aesthetic is just a little modern for my taste."

Colin nodded. "Me, too. To be honest, Pam picked this place. If I hadn't been so mad about Shane, I probably would've let her keep it."

Natalie stiffened at the mention of his ex-wife and the son who'd turned out not to be his. She still wasn't sure exactly what had happened, but prying seemed rude. Since he brought it up… "Does she ever let you see Shane?"

Colin shook his head once, kind of curt. "No. I think it's better that way though since he's still a baby. If he'd been any older, it would've been harder to help him understand where his daddy was. He's probably forgotten who I am by now."

"I don't know about that," Natalie said, stepping toward him until they were nearly touching. "I know I've never been able to forget about you."

"Is that right?" Colin asked, wrapping his arms around her waist. The pain had faded from his face, replaced only with the light of attraction. "So, did you fantasize about what it would be like to kiss me?"

Natalie smiled. How many nights had she hugged her pillow to her chest and pretended it was Lily's handsome older brother? "An embarrassing number of times," she admitted.

"Did our first kiss live up to those expectations?"

"It did, and then some. Of course, when I was fifteen, I didn't know what was really possible like I do now."

"Oh really?"

"Yes. And now I want more."

Colin didn't hesitate to meet her demand. His mouth met hers, offering her everything she wanted. She ran her fingers through his hair, tugging him closer. Natalie wasn't letting him get away this time. He was all hers tonight. She arched her back, pressing her body against the hard wall of his chest.

He growled against her lips, his hand straying from her waist to glide along her back and hips. He cupped one cheek of her rear through the thin fabric of her skirt, pushing her hips against his until she could feel the firm heat of his desire.

Natalie gasped, pulling from his mouth. "Yeah," she said in a breathy voice. "There's no way I would've imagined a kiss like that."

Pulling back, she reached for the collar of his jacket. She pushed his blazer off his shoulders, letting it fall to the floor. Her palms moved greedily over his broad shoulders and down the front of his chest, touching every inch of the muscles she'd seen in that tight T-shirt. Starting at his collar, she unbuttoned his shirt, exposing the muscles and dark chest chair scattered across them.

Colin stood stiffly as she worked, his hands tightly curled into fists at his sides. When Natalie reached his belt, he sprang into action, grasping her wrists. "That's not really fair, is it?"

"Well," she reasoned, "I've been fantasizing about seeing you naked for years. I think it's only right I shouldn't have to wait any longer."

Colin gathered the hem of her blouse and lifted it slowly over her head. Natalie raised her arms to help him take it off. He cast her shirt onto a nearby chair. "I don't think a few more minutes will kill you."

He focused on her breasts, taking in the sight before covering the satin-clad globes with the palms of his hands. Natalie gasped when he touched her, her nipples hardening and pressing into the restraining fabric. He kneaded her flesh, dipping his head down to taste what spilled over the top of the cups. Colin nipped at her skin, soothing it with the glide of his tongue. Tugging down at her bra, he uncovered her nipples, drawing one, then the next into his mouth.

Natalie groaned, pulling his head closer. The warmth of his mouth on her sensitive flesh built a liquid heat in her core. She wasn't sure how much longer she could take this kind of torture.

"I need you," she gasped. "Please."

In response, Colin sought out the back of her skirt

with his fingers. He unzipped it, letting it slide down over her hips. She stepped out of the skirt and her heels, then let Colin guide her backward through the room until the backs of her legs met with the mattress. She reached behind her, crawling onto the bed.

While Colin watched, she unclasped her bra and tossed it aside, leaving nothing on but her panties. His eyes stayed glued to her as he unfastened his pants and slipped them off with his briefs. He pulled away long enough to retrieve a condom from the bedside stand before he climbed onto the bed.

The heat of his body skimmed over hers. He hovered there, kissing her as one hand roamed across her stomach. It brushed the edge of her panties, slipping beneath to dip his fingers between her thighs. Natalie arched off the bed, gasping before meeting his lips once more. He stroked her again and again, building a tension inside her that she was desperate to release.

Colin waited until she was on the very edge, then he retreated, leaving her panting and dissatisfied. "Just a few more minutes," he reassured her with a teasing grin.

He moved down her body, pulling the panties over her hips and along the length of her legs as he moved. Tossing them aside, he sheathed himself and pressed her thighs apart. He nestled between them and positioned himself perfectly to stroke her core as his hips moved forward and back. He rebuilt the fire in her belly, then, looking her in the eye, shifted his hips and thrust into her.

Natalie cried out, clawing at the blankets beneath her. He started slow, clenching his jaw with restraint, then began moving faster. She drew her legs up, wrapping them around his hips as they flexed, eliciting a low groan deep in Colin's throat.

"Yes," Natalie coaxed as he moved harder and faster inside her.

The release he'd teased at before quickly built up inside her again and this time, she knew she would get what she wanted. She gripped his back, feeling the knot tighten in her belly. "Please," she said.

"As you wish." He thrust hard, grinding his pelvis against her sensitive parts until she screamed out.

"Colin!" she shouted as the tiny fire bursts exploded inside her. Her release pulsated through her whole body, her muscles tightening around him as she shuddered and gasped.

Thrusting again, Colin buried his face in her neck and poured himself into her. "Oh, Natalie," he groaned into her ear.

The sound of her name on his lips sent a shiver down her spine. She wrapped her arms around him as he collapsed against her. She gave him a few minutes to rest and recover before she pushed at his shoulders. "Come on," she said.

"Come where?" He frowned.

"To the shower. You and I are just getting started. I've got fourteen years to make up for."

Seven

Colin was making coffee downstairs the next morning when he heard the heavy footsteps of a sleepy Natalie coming down the stairs. He peeked around the corner in time to see her stumble onto the landing. She'd pulled her messy hair into a ponytail and was wearing her professional office attire, but it was rumpled and definitely looked like a day-two ensemble for her.

He watched as she hesitated at the bottom of the stairs. She looked around nervously, almost like she was searching for an exit route. Was she really trying to sneak out without him seeing her? Yes, there wasn't anything serious between them, but she didn't need to flee the scene of the crime. She started slinking toward the front door, but he wasn't about to let her off so easily.

"Good morning, Natalie," he shouted.

She stiffened at the sound of his voice, and then reluctantly turned and followed the noise toward the kitchen. "Good morning," she said as she rounded the corner.

He loved seeing this unpolished version of her. With her wrinkled clothes, her mussed-up hair and day-old makeup, it was a far cry from the superprofessional and sleek wedding planner at the chapel. It reminded him of just how she'd gotten so messy and made him want to take her back upstairs to see what more damage he could do to her perfect appearance in the bedroom.

From the skittish expression on her face, he doubted he'd get the chance. Last night was likely a one-time event, so he'd have to be content with that. Instead, Colin returned to pouring the coffee he'd made into a mug for each of them. "How do you take your coffee? I have raw sugar, fake sugar, whole milk and hazelnut creamer. Oh, and getting it in a go-cup isn't an option, by the way."

She smiled sheepishly, clearly knowing she'd been caught trying to make a quick getaway. "I promise not to drink on the run. A splash of milk and a spoonful of raw sugar, please."

He nodded and worked on making her the perfect cup. "Would you like to have coffee downstairs or on the deck?"

She looked up at the staircase to the bedroom, which they'd have to pass through to get to the deck. "The kitchen nook is fine," she said, obviously unwilling to risk the pleasurable detour. "I'm sure we missed the best of the sunrise a long time ago."

Colin handed over her mug and followed her to the

table with a plate of toasted English muffins with strawberry jam and butter. He sat down and picked up one muffin, taking a bite with a loud crunch. He finished chewing and let Natalie sip her coffee before he pressed her about her great escape.

"You seem to be in a hurry this morning. What's the rush?"

Natalie swallowed her sip of coffee and set the mug on the kitchen table. "I was hoping you wouldn't notice. It's just that I'm, uh, not used to staying over. I'm sort of a master of the four a.m. vanishing act. I prefer to avoid the awkward morning-after thing."

"You mean coffee and conversation?"

"I suppose," she said with a smile.

"What kept you from leaving last night?" Colin wasn't quite sure what he would've done if he'd woken up and she was gone. He wasn't used to this kind of scenario with a woman. He was a relationship guy, and that usually meant enjoying a nice breakfast after a night together, not cold empty sheets beside him in bed.

"I think it was all the wine we had at dinner on top of the…exercise I got later. When I fell asleep, I slept hard. I didn't so much as move a muscle until I smelled the coffee brewing downstairs."

Colin considered her answer. He tried not to let it hurt his pride that she hadn't stayed because she felt compelled, or even wanted to. "You know, despite what happened last night, we're still friends. I don't want this to change that, so there's no need to run before you turn back into a pumpkin. Do you mind me asking why you feel the need to leave?"

Natalie bit at her lip before nodding. "Like I told you

before, I'm not much on the relationship thing. I like to keep things simple and sweet. Uncomplicated."

What was more complicated than this? Colin couldn't think of anything else. A normal relationship seemed a lot more straightforward. "What does that even mean, Natalie?"

"It means that what we shared last night is all I'm really wanting."

"I get that. And I'm on board with that or I wouldn't have let it go that far last night. I'm just curious as to why you feel this way about guys and relationships in general."

"There's nothing really in it for me after that first night or two because I don't believe in love. I think it's a chemical reaction that's been built up into more. I also don't believe in marriage. I enjoy the occasional companionship, but it's never going to come to any more than that with any man."

Colin listened to her talk, realizing this was worse than he'd thought. It could've just as easily been his ex-wife, Pam, sitting across the table talking to him. Yes, Natalie had said she wasn't the marrying kind, but this was more than just that. She didn't believe in the entire concept. He raised his hand to his head to shake off the déjà vu and the dull throb that had formed at his temple. It was a good thing he knew about her resistance going into this or it could've been a much bigger blow. "A wedding planner that doesn't believe in love or marriage?"

She shrugged. "Just because I don't believe in it doesn't mean that other people can't. I'm organized and I'm detail-oriented. I was made for this kind of work, so why not?"

The whole thing seemed a little preposterous. "So even though you spend all your days helping people get married, you never intend to marry or have a family of your own?"

"No," Natalie said, shaking her head. "You know what I grew up with, Colin. My mother is on the verge of dumping her fourth husband. I've seen too many relationships fall apart to set myself up for that. The heartache, the expense, the legal hassles... I mean, after everything that happened, don't you sometimes wish that you'd never married Pam?"

That wasn't a simple question to answer. He'd spent many nights asking himself the same thing and hadn't quite decided on what he'd choose if he had the power to bend time and do things differently. "Yes and no. Yes, never marrying or even never dating would've been easier on my heart. But more than not getting married, I just wish Shane had been mine. I don't know how long Pam and I would've been able to hold our marriage together, but even if we'd divorced in that case, I'd still have my son. I'd have a piece of the family I want. Now I have nothing but the lost dream of what I could've had. As they say, 'a taste of honey is worse than none at all,' but I wouldn't trade away my time with Shane. The day he was born was the happiest day of my life. And the day I found out he wasn't my son was the worst. I lost my son and I wasn't even allowed to grieve the loss because I never truly had him to begin with."

Natalie frowned into her coffee cup. "That's exactly the kind of heartache I want to stay away from. I can't understand how someone could go through that and be willing to dust themselves off and try again."

"It's called hope. And I can't understand how someone could go through their life alone. Having a family, having children and seeing them grow up is what life is all about."

"Exactly. It's survival of the species, our own biology tricking us into emotional attachments to ensure stability for raising the next generation. Then it fades away and we're left feeling unfulfilled because society has sold us on a romantic ideal that only really exists in movies and books."

Colin could only shake his head. "That's the worst attitude about love I've ever heard."

"I don't force anyone else to subscribe to my ideas. I didn't come up with this overnight, I assure you. I learned the hard way that love is just a biological impulse that people confuse with Hallmark card sentiment. Have you ever noticed that all the fairy tales end when the Prince and Princess get married? That's because the story wouldn't be that exciting if it showed their lives after that. The Prince works too much. The Princess resents that she's constantly picking up his dirty socks and wiping the snotty noses of his children, so she nags at the Prince when he comes home. The Prince has an affair with his secretary. The Princess throws the Prince out of the palace and takes him to court for child support. Not exactly happily ever after."

"Don't ever write children's books," Colin said drily.

"Someone needs to write that book. That way little girls won't grow up believing in something that isn't going to happen. It would save them all a lot of disappointment."

Colin had tasted every inch of Natalie last night and there hadn't been the slightest bitterness, but now, it seemed to seep from every pore. He was frankly stunned by her attitude about love. It was even more deep-seated and angry than Pam's negative ideas. Pam just didn't want the strings of marriage and monogamy. Natalie didn't believe in the entire construct.

"Hopefully you weren't disappointed with last night."

"Of course not. Last night was great, Colin. It was everything that I'd hoped it would be, and more. And by stopping right now, we get to preserve it as the amazing night that it was."

He knew she was right. He could feel it in his bones. But he also couldn't just let this be the end of it. He wouldn't be able to finish dealing with the wedding plans and the house, being so close to her, without being able to touch her again. "What if I wanted another night or two like last night?"

Natalie watched him with a suspicious narrowing of her eyes. "Are you suggesting we have a little holiday fling?"

He shrugged. Colin had never proposed such a thing, so he wasn't entirely sure. "I did bet you that I could put a little jingle in your step. I think the time we spend together would be a lot more fun for us both if we let this attraction between us be what it is. No promise of a future or anything else, and you don't have to dash from the bed like a thief in the night. What do you think?"

"It sounds tempting," she admitted. "I wouldn't mind getting a little more of those toe-curling kisses you promised me. But you have to agree that after the wedding, we part as we started—as old friends. No hard feelings when it's over."

"Okay, it's a deal. I promise not to fall in love with you, Natalie."

"Excellent," she said with a smile before leaning in to plant a soft kiss on his lips. "I don't plan on falling in love with you either."

"So, what do you think?"

Natalie hovered in the doorway of Colin's family home, her mouth agape in shock. It had only been a week since she was in the house, but it had been completely transformed. "Is this the same place?"

Colin smiled. "A lot has happened since you were here. While I have been busy planning Lily's wedding and seducing you, I couldn't just sit around doing nothing all weekend while you were working, you know."

He'd worked magic in Natalie's opinion. A lot of the old furniture and things they didn't want to keep were gone. In their place were new pieces that looked a million times better. There was new paint on the walls, updated light fixtures and window coverings...the place looked better than she ever remembered. "You've worked a miracle."

"I didn't do it alone, I assure you. The Catholic charity came and picked up all the old things we didn't want to keep. I've had contractors in and out all week. We didn't do any major renovations, so it's mostly cosmetic, but I think it turned out nicely."

"Well, what's left for me to do?"

Colin took her hand and led her into the formal dining room. There, in front of the bay window, was a giant Christmas tree. Apparently her plan to distract him with sexual escapades hadn't worked the way she'd thought.

"Colin," she complained, but he raised a hand to silence her.

"Nope. You agreed to go along with the bet. It's not fair if you stonewall my plans. If you're confident enough to win, you're confident enough to decorate a Christmas tree without being affected by the cloying sentimentality of it all."

Natalie sighed. "Okay, fine. We'll trim the tree."

Colin grinned wide. "Great! I got all the decorations down from the attic."

They approached the pile of boxes and plastic totes that were neatly stacked by the wall. He dug around until he found the one with Christmas lights.

"When did you have the time to get a live tree?"

"I went by a tree lot while you went back to your place to shower and change. It took some creative maneuvering to get it into the house, but I was successful. Would you like a drink before we get started?" he asked as he walked into the kitchen.

"Sure. Water would be fine."

"How about some cider?" he called.

Cider? Natalie followed him into the kitchen, where she was assaulted by the scent of warm apple, cinnamon, orange zest and cloves. It was almost exactly like the scented candle she still had sitting on her desk from one of his holiday deliveries. She could hardly believe it, but Colin actually had a small pot of mulled cider simmering on the stove. Sneaky.

She wasn't going to acknowledge it, though. "Some cider would be great," she said. "It's a cold day."

"All right. I'll be right out and we can get started on that tree."

Natalie wandered back into the dining room and stared down the Christmas tree. She hadn't actually been this close to one in a long time. The scent of pine was strong, like the wreath on her door. She'd never had a real tree before. Her mother had always insisted on an artificial tree for convenience and aesthetics. While perfectly shaped and easy to maintain, it was lacking something when compared to a real tree.

The soft melody of music started in another room, growing louder until she could hear Bing Crosby crooning. Before she could say anything, Colin came up to her with a mug of cider and a plate of iced sugar cookies.

"You're kidding, right? Did you seriously bake Christmas cookies?"

"Uh, no," he laughed. "I bought them at a bakery near the tree lot. I didn't have time to do everything."

"You did plenty," she said, trying to ignore Bing's pleas for a white Christmas. "Too much." She sipped gingerly at the hot cider. The taste was amazing, warming her from the inside out. She'd actually never had cider before. It seemed she'd missed out on a lot of the traditional aspects of the holiday by abstaining for so long.

While it was nice, it wasn't going to change how she felt about Christmas in general. Natalie reluctantly set her mug aside and opened the box of Christmas lights. The sooner they got the tree decorated, the sooner she could get out of here.

They fought to untangle multiple strands, wrapping the tree in several sets of multicolored twinkle lights. From there, Colin unpacked boxes of ornaments and handed them one at a time to Natalie to put them on the tree. They were all old and delicate: an assortment of glass balls and Hallmark figurines to mark various family milestones.

"Baby's First Christmas," Natalie read aloud. It was a silver rattle with the year engraved and a festive bow tied around it. "Is this yours?"

Colin nodded. "Yep. My mom always bought a few ornaments each year. This one," he said, holding up Santa in a boat with a fishing pole, "was from the year we went camping and I caught my first fish."

Natalie examined the ornament before adding it to the tree with the others. "That's a sweet tradition."

"There are a lot of memories in these boxes," Colin said. "Good and bad." He unwrapped another ornament with a picture of his parents set between a pair of pewter angel wings.

When he handed it to Natalie, she realized it was a memorial ornament and the picture was one taken right before their accident. It seemed an odd thing to put on the Christmas tree. Why would he decorate with bad memories?

"Put it near the front," Colin instructed. "I always want our parents to be a part of our Christmas celebration."

Natalie gave the ornament a place of honor, feeling herself get a little teary as she looked at the two of them smiling, with no idea what was ahead for them and their children. "I miss them," she said.

Colin nodded. "Me, too." He took a bite of one of the iced snowman cookies. "Mom's were better," he said.

That was true. Mrs. Russell had made excellent cookies. But as much as Natalie didn't like the holidays, she didn't want to bring down the evening Colin planned with sad thoughts. "Do we have many more ornaments?"

The sad look on Colin's face disappeared as he focused on the task of digging through the box. "Just one more." He handed over a crystal dove. "Now we just need some sparkle."

Together, they rolled out the red satin tree skirt with the gold-embroidered poinsettias on it, then they finished off the last decorating touches. Colin climbed onto a ladder to put the gold star on the top of the tree while Natalie wrapped some garland around the branches.

"Okay, I think that's it," Colin said as he climbed down from the ladder and stepped back to admire their handiwork. "Let's turn out the lights and see how it looks."

Natalie watched him walk to the wall and turn out the overhead chandelier for the room. She gasped at the sight of the tree as it glowed in front of the window. The red, green, blue and yellow lights shimmered against the walls and reflected off the glass and tinsel of the tree.

Colin came up behind her and wrapped his arms around her waist. She snuggled into him, feeling herself get sucked into the moment. The tree, the music, the scents of the holidays and Colin's strong embrace... it all came together to create a mood that stirred long-suppressed emotions inside her.

"I think we did a good job," Colin whispered near her ear.

"We did a great job," she countered, earning a kiss on the sensitive skin below her earlobe. It sent a shiver through her body with goose bumps rising up across her flesh.

"Are you cold?" he asked. "I can turn on the gas fireplace and we can drink our cider there. Soak in the ambience."

"Sure," Natalie said. She picked up her cider and the plate of cookies and followed Colin into the living room. Natalie noticed that above the fireplace were a pair of stockings with both Lily's and Frankie's names embroidered on them. There was pine garland with lights draped across the mantel with tall red pillar candles and silk poinsettias. It was perfect.

With the flip of a switch, the fireplace roared to life. Colin settled down on the love seat and Natalie snuggled up beside him. She kicked off her shoes and pulled her knees up to curl against him. It was soothing to lie there with his arm around her, his heartbeat and the Christmas carols combining to create a soundtrack for the evening.

It had been a long time since Natalie had a moment like this. She didn't limit herself to one-night stands, but her relationships had focused more on the physical even if they lasted a few weeks. She hadn't realized how much she missed the comfort of being held. How peaceful it felt to sit with someone and just be together, even without conversation.

Sitting still was a luxury for Natalie. Once they had opened the chapel there was always something to be done, and she liked it that way. Now she was starting to wonder if she liked it that way because it filled the holes and distracted her from what she was missing in her life. Companionship. Partnership. Colin hadn't convinced her to love Christmas again, but he had opened her eyes to what she'd been missing. She could use more time like this to just live life.

Unfortunately, time like this with a man like Colin came with strings. It had only been a few short hours since they'd agreed to a casual fling, but in her heart, Natalie still worried.

While the decisive and successful owner of Russell Landscaping was driven and in control of his large company, the Colin she'd always known was also sentimental and thoughtful on the inside. The business success and the money that came with it were nice, but she could tell that he'd done all that to honor his father's memory. And more than anything, he wanted his own family, and had since he lost his parents. No little fling would change that.

She liked Colin a lot, but even her teenage infatuation couldn't turn it into more than that. More than that didn't exist in her mind. She could feel her hormones raging and her thoughts kept circling back to Colin whether she was with him or not, but that wasn't love. That was biology ensuring they would continue to mate until she conceived. He might be attracted to her now, but she would never be the wife and mother he envisioned sitting around the Christmas tree with their children. She just wasn't built for that.

Natalie knew she had to enjoy her time with Colin, then make sure it came to a swift end before either of them got attached to the idea of the two of them. She was certain that their individual visions of "together" would be radically different.

"That wasn't so bad, was it?" Colin asked.

The question jerked Natalie from her thoughts and brought her back to the here and now, wrapped in Colin's arms. "It wasn't," she admitted. "I have to say that was the most pleasant tree decorating experience I've had in ten years."

"Natalie, have you even decorated a Christmas tree in ten years?"

Of course he'd ask that. "Nope. I appreciate all your efforts, but even if it had been a miserable night, it still would've been the best. So sorry, but you haven't won the bet yet."

Eight

in her you?"

Eight

Tomorrow night, Natalie's cell phone screen had read
on Wednesday.

Colin followed it up with another text. You and I are
going on a date. Per your requirements, you will wear
a pretty dress and I will take you someplace nice. I will
pick you up at seven.

She ignored the warning bells in her head that insisted a real date fell outside their casual agreement.
While going on a date with Colin had the potential to
move them forward in a relationship with nowhere to
go, it also might do nothing other than provide them
both with a nice evening together. She tried not to read
too much into it.

Natalie made a point of not staying at work too late
on Thursday so she could get home and get ready for
their date. She ignored the pointed and curious glare

of Gretchen when she announced that she was leaving early. She would deal with that later.

Back at her townhouse, she pored through her closet looking for just the right dress. She settled on a gray-and-silver lace cocktail dress. It was fitted with a low-plunging scalloped V-neckline that enhanced what small bit of cleavage she had. It also had shimmering silver bands that wrapped around the waist, making her boyish figure appear more seductively hourglass-shaped.

Once that was decided, she spent almost a half hour flatironing her hair. She wore it in a ponytail most every day. At work, she liked it off her face, but tonight, she wanted it down and perfect.

The doorbell rang exactly at seven and Natalie tried not to rush toward the door. She took her time, picking up her silver clutch on the way.

"Hello there," Natalie said as she opened the door.

Colin didn't respond immediately. His gaze raked over her body as he struggled to take it all in. Finally, he looked at her and smiled. "I like going on dates with you, pretty dress and all."

She preened a little, taking a spin to show off how good her butt looked in the dress before pulling her black wool dress coat from the closet. "I made a big deal of tonight's requirements so I wanted to hold up my end of the bargain."

Colin held out her jacket to help her into it. "You certainly have. You look amazing tonight."

"Thank you."

"Your chariot awaits," Colin said, gesturing toward a silver Lexus Coupe in the driveway.

"Where's the truck?" she asked.

"I didn't think you'd feel like climbing up into it when you're dressed up. Besides, this car matches your dress. It's fate."

He helped her into the car and they drove through town, bypassing some of the usual date spots and heading toward one of the high-end outdoor shopping plazas in Nashville. "Where are we going?" she asked as they pulled into the crowded parking lot. She made a point of avoiding any major shopping areas in December. She was guaranteed to run into Christmas music, decorations and grumpy people fighting their way through their chore lists.

"You'll see," Colin replied, ignoring her squirming in the seat beside him.

"Is this part of the Christmas bet? Telling me you're taking me on a date, letting me get all dressed up and then taking me to see Santa at the mall is cruel. I can assure you it won't fill me with Christmas spirit. More than likely, it will fill me with impatience and a hint of rage. These heels are pretty and expensive, but I'm not above throwing them at someone."

Colin just laughed at her and pulled up to the valet stand at the curb. "Keep your shoes on. I doubt you'll have need to use them as a weapon. I didn't bring you here for the holiday chaos. I brought you here for the best steak and seafood in Nashville."

"Oh," she said quietly. There *were* some nice restaurants here; it was just hard to think about going to them in mid-December. Natalie waited until Colin opened her door and helped her out of the car. "What's that under your arm?" she asked as they made their way through the maze of shops.

Colin looked down at the neatly wrapped package

beneath his arm and shrugged. "It's just a little something."

Natalie wrinkled her nose in a touch of irritation. She
hated surprises, hated not knowing every detail of what
was going on in any given situation. Being a wedding
planner allowed her to legitimately be a control freak.
She wanted to press the issue with him but let the subject go since they were approaching the heavy oak doors
of the restaurant. A man opened one for them, welcoming them inside the dark and romantic steakhouse. They
checked in and were taken back to a private booth away
from the main foot traffic of the restaurant.

They ordered their food and a bottle of wine, settling
in for a long, leisurely dining experience. "So, now will
you tell me what's in the box?"

Colin picked up the shiny silver package. "You mean
this box?" he taunted.

"Yes. That's the one."

"Not right now. I have something else to discuss."

Natalie's eyebrow went up. "You do, do you?"

"Yes. I was wondering what you're doing Sunday
evening."

Natalie wished she had her tablet with her. "Sunday
morning, we clean and break down from Saturday's
wedding. I don't think I have plans that night, aside
from kicking off my shoes and relaxing for the first
time in three days."

"That doesn't sound like it's any fun. I think you
should consider coming with me to a Christmas party."

"Oh no," Natalie said, shaking her hand dismissively.
"That's okay. I'm not really comfortable at that kind
of thing."

"What's there to be uncomfortable about? We'll eat,

drink and mingle. Aside from the reason for the party, you might even forget it's a holiday gathering."

"Yes, but I won't know anyone there. I'm awful at small talk."

"Actually, you'll know everyone. It's Amelia Dixon's party."

"Amelia?" Natalie frowned. "My friend Amelia invited *you* to a Christmas party?"

Colin took a sip of his wine and nodded. "She did. Why are you so surprised? Did she not invite you?"

Honestly, Natalie wasn't sure. She didn't really pay much attention to her mail this time of year if it didn't look like an important bill of some kind. A few folks, Amelia included, always seemed to send her a Christmas card despite her disinterest. If she'd gotten an invite, it was probably in her trash can.

"I typically don't attend Amelia's Christmas party. I'm more curious as to how you got invited. You don't even know her."

"I know her well enough for a little Christmas gathering when I'm dating her close friend."

"Are we dating?" Natalie asked.

"And more importantly," he continued, ignoring her question, "I think she understands you better than you'd like to think. I get the feeling she invited me to make sure you showed up this time."

"I wouldn't be surprised." Amelia had proved in the past that she was a scheming traitor when it came to men. She'd lured Bree to a bar to see Ian after they broke up. Natalie had no doubt she would stoop to similar levels to push her and Colin together *and* get her to come to her annual Christmas soirée. "Despite how much she pesters me, she knows I won't come."

"Well this year, I think you should make an exception and go. With me."

She could feel her defenses weakening. It all sounded nice, and she couldn't wait to see what kind of party Amelia could throw in their big new house with all that entertaining space. But she wished it didn't have to be a Christmas party. The last Christmas party she went to was for kids. Santa was there handing out little presents to all the children, they ate cupcakes and then they made reindeer out of clothespins. She was pretty certain that wasn't what they'd be doing at Amelia and Tyler's. What did adults even do at Christmas parties? "I don't know, Colin."

"It's settled, you're coming." Colin picked up his phone and RSVP'd to Amelia while they were sitting there. Natalie opened her mouth to argue, but it was too late. There was no getting out of it now. Amelia would insist and there would be no squirming.

"Why do you hate me?" Natalie asked as he put his phone away.

"I don't hate you. I like you. A lot. That's why I'm so determined to make the most of our short time together. It also doesn't hurt that it might help me win that kiss." His hazel eyes focused on her across the table, making her blood heat in her veins.

Natalie sighed, trying to dismiss her instant reaction to him. "I've kissed you twenty times. What's so important about *that* kiss?"

"It's The One. The most important kiss of all. Nothing can compare to it, I assure you. But I'll make you a deal," he offered.

"A deal? Does it allow me to skip the Christmas

party? I'll gladly spend that whole night naked in your bed if you'll let me skip the stupid party."

Colin's lips curled up in a smile that dashed her hopes of that negotiation. "While that sounds incredibly tempting, no. You're going to that party with me. But, if you promise to come and not give me grief about it the entire time, I'll let you open this box." He picked up the silver-wrapped box with the snowflake hologram bow and shook it tantalizingly at her.

Considering she was pretty much stuck going to the party anyway, she might as well agree and finally soothe her curiosity about that package. "Okay," Natalie conceded. "I will go with you to the party, and I will not bellyache about it."

"Excellent. Here you go."

Natalie took the box from Colin's hand, shaking it to listen for any telltale clues. No such luck. She'd just have to open it. Peeling away at a corner, she pulled back the wrapping to expose a white gift box. Lifting the lid, she found a Swarovski-crystal-covered case for her tablet.

This wasn't some cheap knockoff they sold at the flea markets. Natalie had done enough weddings to recognize real Swarovski crystal when she saw it. She'd seen covers like these in the hands of Paris Hilton and other celebrities. Out of curiosity, she'd looked it up online once and found far too many zeroes at the end to even consider it. It was impossibly sparkly, each crystal catching the flickering candlelight of the restaurant, and it twinkled like thousands of diamonds in her hands. It cast a reflection on the ceiling like stars overhead.

"Do you like it?" Colin asked.

"Yes, I love it. I've always wanted one, but I don't

think I ever told anyone that. What made you think to buy me something like this?"

"Well," Colin explained, "whenever I see you at the chapel, you've got your iPad in your hands. It's like a third arm you can't live without. It seemed a little boring though. I thought a girl that drove a little red sports car might like a little bling in her life. Besides, jewelry seemed…predictable."

Natalie shook her head. "I'm pretty certain that a fling doesn't call for gifts, much less jewelry. This is too much, really. What is this for?"

"It's your Christmas present. I thought you could make good use of it at your upcoming weddings so I wanted to give it to you early. Besides, we're not supposed to make it to Christmas, so I thought if I was going to give you something, the sooner the better."

"It's perfect," Natalie said. Even as she ran her fingertips over the shining stones, she felt guilty. Not just because he'd bought her a gift, but because Colin had given it to her early because she was too flaky to stick with a relationship for two more weeks. She shouldn't feel bad, though. They'd agreed to the arrangement. It had even been his suggestion, and yet she found herself already dreading this coming to an end. "But you shouldn't have done it. It's too much money."

Colin only shrugged at her complaints. "What is the point of earning all this money if I don't do anything with it? I wanted to buy you something and this is what I came up with. End of discussion."

"I haven't gotten you anything," she argued. And she hadn't. She hadn't bought a Christmas gift in years and she was adamant about not receiving one. Every year she had to remind people she was on the naughty list, so no gifts. It had worked so far. Then Colin came in and started busting down every wall she had, one at a time. Soon, if she wasn't careful, she'd be completely exposed.

Colin reached across the table and took her hand. "You've given me plenty without you even knowing it. The last year has been really hard for me with the divorce and everything else. For the first time since I found out about Shane, I'm excited for what each day holds. That's all because of you."

"That may have been the most amazing bread pudding I've ever had," Natalie said as they stepped out of the restaurant and back into the mingling flow of holiday shoppers.

"It was excellent, I have to admit." He wasn't entirely sure where he wanted to take Natalie next, but he knew he didn't want to rush home. Not because he didn't want to make love to her again, but because he wanted her to take in some of the holiday ambience. This was a shopping center in December, but it wasn't the day-after-Thanksgiving crush. There was rarely a riot over a sale at the Louis Vuitton.

He also wanted to simply spend time with Natalie. He'd meant what he said in the restaurant earlier. For the past year, he'd been going through the motions, trying to figure out what his life was supposed to be like now that he wasn't a husband or a father any longer. It had been easy to focus on work, to center all this attention on expanding Russell Landscaping into Chattanooga and Knoxville.

It wasn't until his sister announced her engagement that he'd snapped out of his fog. Pam may not have been the right woman for him, but there was someone out there who could make him happy. He'd started dating again, unsuccessfully, but he was out there. And then he'd spied Natalie at the engagement party and his heart had nearly stilled in his chest from the shock of how beautiful she'd become.

How had the quiet teenager with the dark braid, the braces and the always-serious expression grown up into such a beauty? The timing was terrible, but Colin had known that he would do whatever he had to do to have Natalie in his life again.

Of course, at the time, Colin hadn't known about her pessimistic stance on love and marriage. That had been like a dousing of ice water. It was cruel for the universe to bring him into contact with such a smart, beautiful, talented woman, then make it impossible for them to have any kind of chance of being together. She even hated Christmas. That was a smack in the face of everything he held dear.

Their night together after the bridal shop had just been a chance to release the unbearable pressure building up. He had been dismayed to wake the next morning and find he wanted Natalie more than ever. Continuing to see each other casually until the wedding was a good idea in theory, but it was prolonging the torture in practice. This date, this night together, would probably do more harm than good in the end. But he couldn't stop himself.

Colin knew he was playing with fire. He hadn't gone into this thinking any of it would happen the way it had, or that he could somehow change Natalie's mind. At least about love and marriage. His determination to help her find her Christmas spirit had made slow progress, but progress nonetheless. He could already see cracks in that facade after only a week of trying.

He could see a similar weakness when she was around him. Her mouth was saying one thing while her body was saying another. When she'd stepped out in that wedding gown, it was like nothing existed but her. As much as she built up her theories about biology interfering in relationships, he could tell she was comfortable around him. Happy. Passionate. If they could both be convinced to take whatever this was beyond the wedding, there would be more between them than just sex.

But would what she was willing to give him be enough to make him happy? Companionship and passion seemed nice, but without love in the mix, it would grow tired, or worse, she might stray, like Pam. Without the commitment of love and marriage, there was no glue to hold two people together. It didn't matter how alluring or wonderful Natalie seemed, she would never be the woman he wanted and needed. But for now, for tonight, none of that mattered. They'd had a nice dinner and he had a bet to win. Reaching out, he took her hand. "How about a stroll to walk some of that dinner off?" he asked.

"I probably need to."

They walked together through the outdoor mall, passing a trio of musicians playing Christmas carols. Farther up ahead, Colin could spy the giant Christmas tree that the mayor had lit the week before. The whole place was decorated. There were white twinkle lights in all the bushes and wrapped around each light post. Near the fountain was a fifteen-foot gold reindeer with a wreath of holly and a cluster of oversize ornaments around his neck.

"The lights are pretty," Natalie admitted as they neared the big tree. "It reminds me of the tree in Rockefeller Center."

"Now why would a Grinch go see the tree in New York?" he asked.

"I was there on business," she insisted. "I went down to see the ice skaters and there it was. It's pretty hard to miss."

They approached the black wrought iron railing that surrounded and protected the tree. It, too, was wrapped in lighted garland and big velvet bows. Colin rested his elbows on the railing and looked up at the big tree. "I think our tree is nicer."

Natalie cozied up beside him and studied the tree more closely. "I think you're right. This tree is kind of impersonal. Ours had a special something."

"Maybe we need hot cider," he suggested.

"No," Natalie groaned, pushing away from the railing. "There is no room left in me for anything, even hot cider."

She reached for his hand and he took hers as they started back to the other end of the shopping center where they'd left his car.

"Thank you for bringing me here tonight," she said. "I've never seen this place decorated for the holidays. It's pretty. And not as crowded and chaotic as I was expecting it to be."

"I'm glad you think so," Colin said with a chuckle. "If you'd have been miserable, it could've set me back days."

"No," Natalie said, coming to a stop. "It's perfect. A great first date, I have to say."

"It's not over yet." As they paused, Colin noticed a decorative sprig of mistletoe hanging from a wire overhead. He couldn't have planned this better if he'd tried. "Uh-oh," he said.

Natalie's eyes grew wide. "What? What's wrong?"

Colin pointed up and Natalie's gaze followed. He took a step closer to her, wrapping his arms around her waist. "That's mistletoe up there. I guess I'm going to have to kiss you."

"Sounds like a hardship," she said. "Christmas is such a burdensome holiday. Shop, eat, decorate, make out... I don't know how you people stand it every year with all these demands on your time."

"Am I wrong or does it sound like you're coming around to Team Christmas?"

Natalie wrapped her arms around his neck and entwined her fingers at his collar. "I wouldn't say I'm that far gone yet. A lot hinges on this kiss, though. I've never been kissed under the mistletoe, so I can't understate how critical this moment is to you potentially winning this bet."

"No pressure," Colin said with a smile. Dipping his head, he pressed his lips to hers. Her mouth was soft and yielding to him. She tasted like the buttery bourbon sauce from the bread pudding and the coffee they'd finished their meal with. He felt her melt into him, his fingertips pressing greedily into her supple curves.

Every time he kissed Natalie, it was like kissing her for the first time. There was a nervous excitement in his chest, tempered by a fierce need in his gut. Combined, it urged him to touch, taste and revel in every sweet inch of her.

As they pulled apart, Colin felt the cold kiss of ice against his skin. Opening his eyes, he saw a flurry of snowflakes falling around them. "It's snowing!" he said in surprise. Nashville did get cold weather, but snow was an unusual and exciting event. "How's that for your first kiss under the mistletoe? I kiss you and it starts to snow."

"Wow, it really is snowing." Natalie took a step back, tipping her face up to the sky. She held out her arms, letting the snowflakes blanket her dark hair and speckle her black coat. She spun around, grinning, until she fell, dizzy, back into Colin's arms. "I guess I haven't been paying enough attention to the weatherman," she admitted when she opened her eyes.

"I'm not sure snow was in the forecast. It must be a little Christmas magic at work." Colin looked around as the other shoppers quickly made their way back to their cars. Not everyone appreciated the shift in the weather. In the South, snow typically ended up turning icy and the roads would get bad pretty quickly. They all had to make an emergency run to the grocery store for milk, bread and toilet paper in case they lost power.

He wasn't worried about any of that. Colin just wanted to be right here, right now, with a flushed and carefree Natalie in his arms. She'd worn her hair down tonight for the first time and it looked like dark silk falling over her shoulders and down her back. The cold had made her cheeks and the tip of her nose pink, accentuating the pale porcelain of her complexion.

But most enticing of all was the light of happiness in her eyes. It was the authentic smile he'd been so desperate to lure out of her. The combination threatened to knock the wind out of him every time he looked at her.

"When I picked you up for our date tonight, I didn't think you could get more beautiful," he admitted. Colin brushed a snowflake from her cheek. "I was wrong. Right this moment, you are the most beautiful woman I've ever laid eyes on."

Natalie tried to avoid his gaze and ignore his compliment. He wasn't sure why she was so uncomfortable hearing the truth. She was beautiful and she needed to believe it.

Instead, with a dismissive shake of her head, she said, "Flattery won't help you win the bet, Colin."

"I'm not trying to win a bet," he said, surprising even himself. "I'm trying to win you."

Nine

"You're here!" Amelia nearly shrieked when she spied Natalie and Colin come through the front door of the sprawling mansion in Belle Meade she and Tyler had bought earlier that year. "I didn't believe it when he said you'd agreed to come."

"It's not a big deal," Natalie muttered as she slipped out of her jacket. "You just saw me this morning."

Amelia took both their coats to hang them in the hall closet. "It's not about seeing you, it's about seeing you at my Christmas party. That's a pretty big deal, considering you've never bothered to come before."

"You always held it at your cramped apartment before," Natalie argued, although Colin doubted that the setting had anything to do with it.

"Whatever," Amelia said dismissively. "The important thing is that both of you are here. Come in. Everyone is in the kitchen, of course. Thousands of square feet and everyone congregates there."

Colin took Natalie's hand and led her away from the nearest exit into the house. It was a massive home, large even by his standards, though it looked as if Amelia and her husband were still trying to accumulate enough furniture to fill it up. They had the place beautifully decorated for the holidays, though. A cluster of multiple-sized Christmas trees with lights sat by the front window like a small indoor forest. A decorated tree that had to be at least fourteen feet tall stood in the two-story family room. Any smaller and it would've been dwarfed by the grand size of the house. The banisters were wrapped with garland and ribbon. There was even holiday music playing in the background. Colin was pleased to drag Natalie to a proper holiday gathering.

"Everyone, this is another of my friends and coworkers, Natalie, and her date, Colin. He owns Russell Landscaping."

A few welcomes and hellos sounded from the crowd of about twenty-five people milling through the kitchen, dining room and keeping room area. He recognized a few of them—the wedding photographer, Bree, and Gretchen, the decorator. Bree was hanging on the arm of a dark-headed guy in a black cashmere sweater. Gretchen was alone despite the huge diamond on her finger. He wasn't sure what that was about.

"What would you like to drink?" Amelia asked, rattling off a long list of options.

"I also have a nice microbrew from a place downtown," Tyler offered, holding up a chilled bottle he pulled from the refrigerator.

"Perfect," Colin said, taking it from his hand. Natalie opted for a white wine that Amelia poured for her.

"Help yourself to something to eat. There's plenty, of course," Amelia said, gesturing to the grand buffet table along the wall.

Plenty was an understatement. The caterer in her had gone wild. He and Natalie perused the table, taking in all their options. There were chafing dishes with hot hors d'oeuvres like barbecued meatballs, chicken wings and fried vegetable eggrolls, platters of cold cheeses, finger sandwiches, crudités, dips and crackers, and more desserts than he could identify.

"She's gone overboard," Natalie said. "This is enough to feed a hundred wedding guests. She's just no good at cooking for small numbers. You'd think being pregnant would slow her down, but she's like a machine in the kitchen."

After surveying everything, they each made a plate and moved over to a sitting area with a low coffee table. They ate and chatted with folks as they milled around. Eventually Gretchen approached with her own plate and sat down with them.

"I'm sorry Julian couldn't be here with you tonight," Natalie said.

Gretchen just smiled and shrugged. "It's okay. He's almost done refilming some scenes the director wanted to change and then he'll be home. We'll have a great first Christmas together even though he missed this."

"Your fiancé is in the movie business?" Colin asked.

Gretchen nodded. "Yes, he's an actor. You've probably heard of him. Julian Cooper?"

Colin hesitated midbite. "Really?"

"I know, right?" Gretchen said. "Not who you'd expect me to be with."

"That's not what I meant," he countered. "I'm sure he's very lucky to have you. I've just never met anyone famous before. Feels odd to be one degree of separation from an action hero."

Gretchen smiled, obviously bolstered by his compliment. "You're also officially four degrees from Kevin Bacon."

Colin laughed and lifted his drink to take another sip.

"Excuse me, did I hear Amelia say you own Russell Landscaping?" the man beside him asked.

Colin turned his attention to his right. "Yes." He held out his hand to shake with the man, turning on his bright, businessman charm. "I'm Colin Russell."

"I'm in the construction business with Bree's father," he explained. "I'd love to talk to you about landscaping at our latest project. We're breaking ground on an apartment complex in the spring and looking for a company to handle that for us."

On cue, Colin pulled out his wallet and handed the man his business card. He lost himself in work discussions, realizing after about ten minutes that both Natalie and Gretchen had disappeared.

"Give me a call and we'll set something up," Colin concluded. "I'm going to hunt down my date."

Getting up, Colin carried his empty plate into the kitchen and got a fresh drink. Amelia was buzzing around with Bree helping her, but the others weren't in there. He wandered back into the living room toward the entry hall. Maybe they'd gone to the restroom as a pair, the way women tended to do.

He'd almost reached the entry when he heard Gretchen's voice. Still cloaked in the dark shadows of the room lit only with Christmas lights, he stopped and listened.

"All right, spill," Gretchen said.

Colin heard a hushing sound and some footsteps across the tile floor of the hallway. "Are you crazy?" Natalie asked in a harsh whisper. "Someone is going to hear you. What if Colin heard you?"

"Come on, Natalie. He's all tied up in talk about shrubs and mulch. It's perfectly safe. Tell me the truth. Bree and I have twenty bucks wagered on your answer."

"You're betting on my love life?"

Colin chuckled at Natalie's outrage. He liked her friends.

"Not exactly. We're betting on your emotional depth. That's probably worse. See, Bree thinks you're a shallow pool and believes your big talk when you go on about love not being real and blah, blah."

"And you?" Natalie asked.

"I think you've changed since you met Colin. You've bebopped around the office for the last week like you're on cloud nine. You've been texting him all the time. You haven't been as cranky. You were even humming a Christmas carol this morning."

"So, I'm in a good mood."

"Natalie, you even forgot about a bridal appointment on your calendar tomorrow morning. Your mind isn't on your work, and I think it's because you've realized you were wrong."

Colin held his breath. He was curious to hear what Natalie was going to say but worried he was going to get caught listening in. He leaned against the wall, casually sipping his beer as though he were just waiting for Natalie's return. Even then, he strained to catch the conversation over the holiday music.

"Wrong about what?"

"Wrong about love. You are in love with Colin. Admit it."

Colin's eyes widened. Would his skeptical Natalie really say such a thing? If she did, it could change everything.

"I am not," she insisted, but her voice wasn't very convincing.

Gretchen seemed to agree. "That's a load of crap. I get that you haven't been in love before, and until recently, neither had I. But when it hits you, you know it. And it's not biology or hormones or anything else. It's love. And you, sister, have fallen into it."

"I don't know, Gretchen. This is all new to me. I'm not sure I would call this love."

"Is he the first thing you think about in the morning and the last thing you think of at night? Is he the person you can't wait to share good news with? Does your busy workday suddenly drag on for hours when you know you'll get to see him that night?"

"Yes. Yes, yes and yes," Natalie said almost groaning. "What am I going to do?"

That wasn't exactly the reaction Colin was hoping for when a woman declared her love for him. Yes, she loved him, but she was miserable about it. Considering this was skeptical Natalie, he supposed that shouldn't surprise him. She'd go down kicking and screaming.

"Just go with it," Gretchen encouraged. "Love is awesome."

That was enough for him. Colin was about to cut it too close if he loitered here any longer. He scooted silently across the plush living room carpeting toward the kitchen to get something to nibble on and wait for Natalie's return. While he tried to look calm on the outside, he was anything but.

Could it be true? Was Natalie really in love with him? It had only been a few short weeks, but they'd technically known each other for years. Stranger things had happened. If he was honest with himself, he was having feelings for her as well. He could've answered yes to all of Gretchen's questions. Was that love? He was as clueless as Natalie there. He'd loved his parents, his son, but his attempts to fall in love with a woman had failed.

He felt more deeply for Natalie than he had for any other woman, even Pam. He was mature enough to admit that whole marriage had been about Shane, not about love.

Love. Was that what this was?

It could be. It felt different, somehow. Despite everything going on in his life, he was preoccupied with the brunette who had challenged him at every turn. She was like quicksand, drawing him in deeper the more he struggled against her. Colin had gone into this fling keeping his heart in check, or at least he'd tried to. Natalie wasn't the kind of woman he could settle down with and he knew that. But after spending time with her, he knew this couldn't be just a fling, either. He wanted more, and if Natalie was honest with herself, he was certain she wanted more, too. It was just a matter of convincing her not to run the moment her emotions got too serious or complicated. She might believe in love now, but he got the feeling that getting Natalie to believe in the beauty and power of a good marriage would be the challenge of a lifetime.

Colin popped a chocolate mint petit four into his mouth, looking up in time to see Natalie and Gretchen stroll back into the room. Natalie looked a little pale from their revealing discussion, her ashen color enhanced by her black dress.

No, Natalie might be in love with him, but she was anything but happy about it.

"You've been awfully quiet tonight," Colin said as they pulled into her driveway. "You've hardly said a thing since we left Amelia and Tyler's place."

Natalie shrugged it off, although she felt anything but cavalier about the thoughts racing through her head. "I'm just a little distracted tonight," she said. To soothe his concerns, she leaned in and kissed him. "I'm sorry. Would you like to come in?"

"I would," he said with a smile.

They got out of the car and went into her townhouse. Natalie didn't normally feel self-conscious about her place, but after being at Colin's and Amelia's, her little two-story home felt a bit shabby. Or maybe she was just an emotional live wire after everything that happened at the party.

"Nice place," Colin said as he pulled the door shut behind him.

"Thanks. It's nothing fancy, but it suits me." She led him through the ground floor, absentmindedly prattling on about different features. Mentally, she was freaking out, and had been since Gretchen cornered her at the party. Yes, she'd been quiet. She'd been analyzing every moment of the past two weeks. Was it possible that *she* was the one to break their casual arrangement and fall in love with Colin? Surely it hadn't been long enough for something like that to happen. They'd only been out a few times together.

Then again, Gretchen and Julian fell in love in a week. Bree and Ian fell in love again over a long weekend trapped in a cabin. Amelia had given Tyler thirty days to fall in love and they hadn't needed that long.

So it *was* possible. But was it smart?

Her brain told her no. Love equals heartache. But she couldn't stop herself from sinking further into the warm sensation of love. Colin made it so easy by being everything she never knew she always wanted. She wished he hadn't been so charming and thoughtful so it would be easier to fight.

But even if she *was* in love, it didn't change anything. It didn't mean she wanted to get married. Marriages seemed to ruin good relationships. Maybe it was marriage, not love, that was the real problem.

As Natalie turned to look at him, she realized he had an expectant expression on his face. "What?" she asked.

"I just complimented you on your large collection of classic country vinyl albums," he said, gesturing toward the shelf with her stereo and turntable.

Natalie glanced over at her albums and nodded. "My father bought a lot of them for me," she said. "We used to go to thrift stores looking for old records on Saturday afternoons."

"I mentioned it twice before you heard a word I said." Colin chuckled softly. "You're on another planet tonight, aren't you?"

"I am. I'm sorry." Natalie racked her brain for a way to distract him. She certainly wasn't going to tell him how she was feeling. Running her gaze over his sharply tailored suit, she decided to fall back on her earlier distraction tactic—seduction. She wrapped her arms around his waist and looked up at him. "Have I told you just how handsome you look tonight?"

He smiled, all traces of concern disappearing as he looked down at her adoringly. "Not in the last hour or so."

"Well, you do," she said, slipping her hands into his back pockets to grab two solid handfuls of him. "It's enough to make a girl want to throw the bet so she can experience that amazing kiss you've promised."

Colin shook his head. "There's no throwing the bet. You either shed your humbug ways or you don't. Either way, I'm not giving up until you've been converted. I don't care how long it takes."

"Even after I've won?" she asked.

"You bet. I think Christmas in Buenos Aires will be lovely, and I'll see to it that it is."

Natalie laughed. "You're inviting yourself to my vacation prize? I don't recall asking for company."

"I don't recall asking permission. I am paying for the trip, after all."

Natalie twisted her lips in thought. She was both thrilled and terrified by the idea of Colin still being in her life a year from now. She was so confused about all of this, she didn't know what to do. "So if I win the bet, will I ever get this infamous kiss? I don't want to miss out on it."

Colin narrowed his gaze at her. "How about this? How about I give you a little taste of how amazing it will be right now? That should be enough to tide you over until I've won."

She certainly couldn't turn down an offer like that, especially knowing that his talented mouth and hands would distract her from everything else she was worried about. "All right," she agreed. "Lay one on me."

Colin shook his head at her. "Before I do that, I think we'd better adjourn to the bedroom."

"Why is that?" Natalie asked. "It's just a kiss."

"You say that, but this won't be an ordinary kiss. You'll be glad we waited until we're in there, I promise."

"Okay." She wasn't sure if he could deliver on the hype, but she was looking forward to finding out. Taking his hand, she led him up the stairs and down the hallway to her master bedroom.

Her bedroom had been what sold her on the townhouse. The master was spacious with large windows that let in the morning light. Even filled with her furniture, there was plenty of room to move around. "All right," she said, standing beside the bed with her hands on her hips. "Let's get a sampling of this infamous kiss of yours."

Colin moved closer and Natalie couldn't help but tense up. She didn't know what to expect. This wasn't even *the* kiss and she was nervous with anticipation.

"You look like I'm about to eat you alive," he said with an amused smile.

"Sorry," she said, trying to shake the tension out of her arms.

"That's okay." He stopped in front of her, just shy of touching. Instead of leaning in to kiss her, he turned her around and undid the zipper of her dress. He eased it off her shoulders, letting it pool to the floor.

"What are you doing?" she asked, curiously. What kind of kiss required her to be naked?

Leaning in, Colin growled in her ear, "I'm about to eat you alive."

Natalie gasped at the harsh intensity of his words, even as a thrill of need ran through her body. Before she could respond, he unclasped her bra and pulled her panties to the floor. Completely naked, she turned around to complain about the unfairness, but found he was busily ridding himself of his clothing as well. In a few moments, it was all tossed aside and he pulled her close.

"When is the kissing going to start?" she asked.

"You ask too many questions. This isn't a wedding you're in charge of. There are no schedules, tablets and earpieces tonight. Go with it."

"Yes, sir," Natalie said with a sheepish smile. Admittedly, she had trouble letting go and not knowing every aspect of the plan. She didn't think she had anything to worry about here, so she tried to turn off her brain and just let Colin take the lead. That was the whole point tonight, anyway.

His fingers delved into her hair as he leaned in for the kiss. Natalie braced herself for the earth-shattering impact, but at first at least, it was just a kiss. He coaxed her mouth open, letting his tongue slide along hers. His fingers massaged the nape of her neck as he tasted and nibbled at her.

Then she felt him start to pull away. His lips left hers, but technically, they never lost contact with her skin. He planted kisses along the line of her jaw, the hollow of her ear and down her throat. He crouched lower, nipping at her collarbone and placing a searing kiss between her breasts. He tasted each nipple, then continued down her soft belly until he was on his knees in front of her.

He placed a searing kiss at her hipbone, then the soft skin just above the cropped dark curls of her sex. Natalie gripped Colin's shoulders for support as his fingers slid between her thighs. She gasped softly as he stroked the wet heat that ached for him.

With his mouth still trailing across her thigh, Colin gently parted her with his fingers. His tongue immediately sought out her sensitive core, wrenching a desperate cry from Natalie's throat. He braced her hips with his hands as her knees threatened to give out beneath her.

She wasn't sure how much of this she could take. Standing up added a level of tension she hadn't expected. "Colin," she gasped, amazed by how her cries were growing more desperate with every second that passed.

She was on the edge, and it was clear that he intended to push her over it. Gripping her hip with one hand, he used the other to dip a finger inside her. The combination was explosive and Natalie couldn't hold back any longer. She threw her head back and cried out, her body thrashing against him with the power of her orgasm.

When it was over, Natalie slid to her knees in front of him. She lay her head on his shoulder, gasping and clinging to his biceps with both hands. She was so out of it, it took her a moment to realize Colin had picked her up. He helped her stand, then carried her to the bed only a few feet away.

"That," she panted as reason came back to her, "was one hell of a kiss."

"And that wasn't even the winning kiss," Colin said as he covered her body with his own.

"I can't even imagine it, then. It seems odd that your prize would be more a reward for me than for you."

He slipped inside her, making her overstimulated nerves spark with new sensation. "I assure you I enjoyed every second of it now, and I'll enjoy every second of it when I've won."

For that, Natalie had no response. She could only lift her hips to meet his forward advance. Clinging to him, she buried her face in his neck. His movements were slow, but forceful, a slow burn that would eventually consume everything it touched. She didn't resist the fire; she gave in to it.

She was tired of fighting. She had spent her whole life trying to protect herself from the pain and disappointment of love. She'd fought her urges for companionship, suppressed her jealousy as each of her friends found a great love she was certain she would never have.

And yet, here she was. Despite all the fighting and worrying, she had simply been overpowered. Gretchen was right. Natalie was in love.

"Oh Natalie," Colin groaned in her ear.

She loved that sound. She wanted to hear it again and again. Her name on his lips was better than a symphony orchestra.

Placing her hand against his cheek, she guided his mouth back to hers. That connection seemed to light a fire in him. Their lips still touching, he moved harder and faster than before, sweeping them both up in a massive wave of pleasure. Natalie didn't fight the currents, she just held on to the man in her arms, knowing she was safe there.

She never wanted to let go. But could she dare to hold on?

Ten

"I can't believe we're almost done with the house," Natalie said. "You've worked wonders on it."

Colin smiled. "I'm pretty pleased with the results."

"Seems a shame you can't keep it after all the work you've put in. You don't appear to care much for your own house. This place suits you more."

That was probably true, but he didn't need this place. "I can always buy another house. I'd like to see Lily and Frankie raise their family here."

"What is left for us to do?" Natalie asked as she looked around.

"I have to clean out my parents' office. I left that for last because there's so much paperwork to go through. I need to figure out what should be kept. I'm hoping we can shred most of it, but I really have no idea what they had stored away in all those drawers."

"Let's do it, then."

They walked up the stairs together and Colin opened the door to the small, dusty room he'd avoided the longest. Turning on the overhead light illuminated the big old oak desk on the far wall. It had two large file drawers, one on each side, housing any number of documents and files they'd thought were important to keep. It took up most of the space like a large man in a small dressing room.

Colin had lots of memories of his dad going over invoices at this desk long before Russell Landscaping could afford their own offices, much less their own office building in the city. This was where his mother wrote checks to pay the bills and managed correspondence. She hadn't been a big fan of email, always penning handwritten letters to friends and family.

There was also a large bookshelf on one wall with all his father's books. His dad had always been a big reader. He loved to curl up in his chair by the fireplace and read in the evenings. Volumes of books lined the shelves, and Colin dreaded going through them. As much as he felt the urge, he didn't need to keep them all, just a couple of his father's favorites.

"I'll take the shelves if you want to start on the drawers," Colin suggested. "We can throw out all the office supplies."

They each started their tasks. Natalie filled a wastebin with dried-up pens, markers and old, brittle rubber bands. After that, she started sorting through the file drawers.

Colin easily found his father's favorite book—*Treasure Island*. His father had read, and reread, that book twenty times. It was his favorite, as evidenced by the worn binding and fraying edges. He set that book aside.

It would go on Colin's shelf until he passed it on to his children. Other volumes weren't quite as important.

Colin quickly built up a stack of books to keep, then another to donate. He scooped up a handful for charity and turned, noticing Natalie sitting stone still in the office chair. The expression on her face was one of utter devastation.

"Natalie?" he asked. "What is it?"

Looking up at him, she bit at her lip. "It's…um." She stopped, shuffling through the papers. "I started going through the filing drawers. It looks like your mother actually filed for divorce."

Colin's breath caught in his lungs. He set the books down on the desk before he dropped them. "What? You must be reading it wrong."

Natalie handed over the folder. "I don't think so. It looks like your mother filed two years before their accident."

Colin flipped through the paperwork, coming to the same conclusion despite how much it pained him. His parents didn't divorce. What was this about? Leaning back onto the desk, he tried to make sense of it all.

"It looks like she started the process, but they didn't go through with it." Somehow that still didn't make him feel much better.

"I'm sorry to hear they were in a bad place," Natalie said. "I never noticed anything wrong as a kid, but in my experience, there's no perfect marriage. Everyone has problems, despite how they might look from the outside."

Colin set down the pages and frowned. "Of course there's no perfect marriage. Just because I want to marry and have a family someday doesn't mean I think it's going to be a walk in the park. You have to work at it every day because love is a choice. But it's a choice worth making. And judging by this paperwork, it's worth fighting to keep it."

"How do you get that? I always thought your parents had a good relationship. If even they filed for divorce at one point, I don't see that as a positive sign."

"What's positive is the fact that they *didn't* get a divorce. Things got ugly, but they decided not to give up. That makes me hopeful, not disappointed. If my mother could go as far as filing for divorce and they managed to put the pieces back together, that means there's hope for any marriage."

Judging by the look on Natalie's face, he could tell she wasn't convinced. She was so jaded by other people's relationship failures that she couldn't fathom two people actually loving each other enough to fight through the tough times.

That worried him. Despite what he'd overheard at Amelia's Christmas party, he didn't feel that confident that Natalie would stay in his life. She might love him, but she was still a flight risk. When this wedding was over, the two of them might be over, too. That was the thought that kept his feelings in check when they were together.

"You know what?" he said. "Let's just put all these files in a box and I'll go through them later. I think clearing the room out is time better spent."

Natalie just nodded and started unloading files from the desk drawer into the file boxes he'd bought. They worked silently together until the room was empty of personal items, and then they hauled the boxes downstairs and into his truck.

The mood for the night had been spoiled and he hated that. His parents' near-divorce was hanging over his head, opening his eyes to things he'd never considered. It seemed strange to drink some wine and go on like he didn't know the truth.

And yet, it made him feel emboldened, too. He'd gone into this whole situation with Natalie consciously holding back. It was defensive, to keep himself from getting in too deep and getting hurt, but it also occurred to him that it might be a self-fulfilling prophecy. If he didn't give all of himself to Natalie, she wouldn't ever do the same.

If he wanted to keep Natalie in his life, he had to fight for her and be bold. His parents fought to stay together, and he was willing to do the same. But what would give her the confidence to believe in him and their relationship? She was so determined to think of marriage as a mistake that most people struggled to get out of. How could he convince her that he was in this for the long haul and she shouldn't be afraid to love him with all she had?

There was only one thing he could think of, and it was a major risk. But, as his father told him once, no risk, no reward. That philosophy had helped him build the family landscaping business into a multimillion-dollar operation across the Southeast. He had no doubt it would succeed. If he could pull it off, there was no way Natalie could turn her nose up at it.

Just like his Christmas bet, he intended to get everything that he wanted and make it into something Natalie wanted, too. He knew exactly what he needed to do. The timing couldn't be more perfect.

"What are you doing Wednesday night?" he asked.

* * *

Natalie looked out the window at the twinkling Christmas lights up ahead and knew exactly where they were. "Are you taking me to the Opryland Hotel?" Natalie asked.

"Actually, no, we're going someplace else."

Sitting back in her seat, she watched as Colin slowed and pulled into the parking area for the Grand Ole Opry. At that moment, she perked up, her mind spinning as she tried to figure out what day it was. It was the sixteenth. Blake Wright's concert was here tonight. But it was sold out…

"Colin?" she asked.

"Yes?"

"Did you…? Are we…?" She was so excited she couldn't even form the words. Why else would they be here if he hadn't managed to get tickets to the show?

"Yes, I did and yes, we are," he answered, pulling into a parking space.

She almost couldn't believe it. "There were no tickets left. They sold out in ten minutes. I know—I called."

Colin nodded as he turned off the car and faced her. "You're absolutely right. There were no seats left."

Natalie narrowed her gaze at him. "So, what? We're just going to lurk by the back door to see if we can get a glimpse of him?" She was willing to do that, of course, but it didn't seem like Colin's style.

"Something like that. Come on."

They got out of the car and he took her hand, leading her away from the crowd at the entrance and around the building toward the back. The door they were headed for said Private Entry in big red letters, and a very large man in a tight T-shirt stood watch. Colin didn't seem to care. He marched right up to him and pulled two tickets out of his jacket.

No, wait. Natalie looked closer. They weren't tickets. They were *backstage passes*. The security guard looked them over and checked the list on his clipboard.

"Welcome, Mr. Russell. So glad to have you joining us tonight." The mountain of a man stepped aside and let Natalie and Colin go into the sacred backstage of the famous concert hall.

She waited until the door shut before she lost her cool. "Are you kidding me? Backstage? We're going backstage at a Blake Wright concert? This is the Grand Ole Opry! Do you know how many amazing artists have walked where we are right now?"

Colin wasn't left with much time to answer her questions, so he just smiled and let her freak out. Passes in hand, they walked through the preconcert chaos until they located the stage manager.

"Looks like our special guests are here," the man said. "Welcome, folks. We've got two designated seats for you right over here." He indicated two chairs just off the curtained stage area. They were going to be watching the show from the wings, literally sitting unseen on the stage itself.

Natalie was so excited, she could barely sit down. Colin had to hold her hand to keep her from popping right up out of her seat. "Please tell me how you managed this," she said at last.

"Well, you know who does all the landscaping for Gaylord properties?"

She had no idea. "You?" she guessed.

"That is correct. Russell Landscaping has the contract to design and maintain all the outdoor spaces including the hotel and the concert venue. I called up a friend here and they set this up for me. Since there weren't any seats left, we had to get a little creative."

Natalie could hardly believe it. "This is amazing. I can't believe you did all this. I mean, you already gave me my Christmas present. What is this for?"

Colin shrugged. "Because I could. You told me how your dad used to take you and how much you liked Blake, so I thought it would be a nice gesture."

"Well, I'm glad I dressed appropriately," she said, looking over her off-the-shoulder red silk top and skinny jeans with cowboy boots. "You just said we were going someplace to listen to country music. I was thinking maybe a bar downtown."

"Well, I would've given away the surprise if I'd said anything else."

Natalie could only shake her head. As the opening act brushed past them to go out onstage, she muffled her squeal of delight in Colin's coat sleeve.

When Blake and his band finally took the stage, it took everything she had not to jump up and down. She tried to play it cool, since she was here because of Colin's business connections, but it was very hard. Natalie could hold her composure during any kind of wedding crisis, but this was too much.

It was not just a great concert, but there were so many memories centered around this place. Her parents had been house poor, putting everything they had into a nice home for their family at the expense of everything else. They didn't have the latest gadgets or the coolest clothes, but she went to a good school and had everything she truly needed.

But once a year, around her birthday, her dad always

took her out for what he called a Daddy-Daughter date. She'd grown up listening to his favorite country music, and starting on her fifth birthday, he took her to a show at the Opry. It didn't matter who it was or that they had the worst seats in the house. It was more about sharing something with her father.

That tradition had fallen to the wayside after the divorce, and it had broken Natalie's heart. She hadn't stepped foot back into this concert hall since the last time her daddy brought her here.

And now, here she was, backstage. She didn't talk to her father very often, but she couldn't wait to tell him about this. He'd be amazed. Maybe it would even inspire him to take another trip here with her for old times' sake.

Glancing over at Colin, she realized he looked a little anxious and not at all like he was having a good time. He was stiff, clutching his knees and not so much as tapping his toes to the music. "You don't like country music, do you?" she asked.

"Oh no," he argued. "It's fine. I'm just tired."

Natalie didn't worry too much about it, focusing on the amazing show. About halfway through, Blake started introducing the next song.

"The song I'm going to play next was one of my biggest hits," he said. "It was my first real love song, written about my wife. I want to dedicate this song tonight to a very special lady. Natalie Sharpe, please come out onto the stage."

Natalie's heart stopped in her chest. Colin tried to pull her up out of her seat, but it took a moment for her to connect everything. "Me?" she asked, but he gave her a little shove and suddenly, she was onstage where everyone could see her.

"There she is," Blake said. "Come on out here, sugar."

Natalie walked stiffly over to where Blake was standing. Under her feet were the very boards of the original stage. The lights were shining on her, the crowd cheering. She thought she might pass out.

"Are you enjoying the show?" he asked.

"Absolutely. You're awesome," she said.

Blake laughed. "Well, thank you. Do you know who else is awesome? Colin Russell. Colin, why don't you come on out here, too?"

Natalie turned and watched Colin walk out onstage. What the heck was going on? Her life had suddenly become very surreal. It was one thing for Colin to arrange for her to get to go out onstage with her idol. Both of them onstage changed everything.

Blake slapped Colin on the back. "Now, Colin tells me he has something he wants to ask you."

The whole crowed started cheering louder. The blood rushed into Natalie's ears, drowning out everything but her heart's rapid thump. She barely had time to react, her body moving like it was caught in molasses. She looked over at Colin just in time to see him slip down onto one knee. *Oh dear, sweet Jesus.* He wasn't. He couldn't be. This was not happening.

"Natalie," Colin began, "I've known you since we were teenagers. When you came back into my life, I knew you were someone special. The more time we spend together, the more I realize that I want to spend all my time with you, for the rest of my life. I love you, Natalie Sharpe. Will you marry me?"

Now Natalie was certain she was going to pass out.

She could feel the whole concert hall start to spin. Her chest grew tight, her cheeks burned. What was he thinking? All these people were watching. Blake was watching…

Colin held up the ring. It was beautiful—a large oval diamond set in platinum with a pear-shaped diamond flanking it on each side. The cut and clarity were amazing. The stone glittered with the lights on the stage, beckoning her to reach out and take it. All she had to do was say yes, and he would slip it on her finger.

And then what? They'd get married and last a few years at best? Then they'd get divorced and spend months squabbling in court? In the end, she'd become a bitter divorcée and sell this same beautiful ring in a ranting ad on Craigslist.

Yes, she loved him, but why did they have to get married? He was ruining everything they'd built together by changing their whole relationship dynamic. Love or no, she couldn't do it. She just couldn't get the words out. All she knew was that she had to get out of here. Avoiding his gaze, Natalie shook her head. "No. I'm sorry, I can't," she said, before turning and running off the stage.

As she ran, she was only aware of an eerie silence. The entire concert hall had quieted. The crew backstage all stood around in stunned confusion. Apparently no one had expected her to reject his proposal.

"Natalie!" she heard Colin yell, but she couldn't stop. She weaved in and out of people and equipment, desperately searching for the side door where they'd come in. Just as she found it, she heard the music start playing again. Life went on for everyone else, just as her life started to unravel.

Bursting through the doors, she took in a huge gulp of cool air that she desperately needed. The security guard watched her curiously as she bent over and planted her hands on her knees for support.

Marriage? He'd proposed marriage! He'd taken a perfectly wonderful evening and ruined it with those silly romantic notions. Why did he do that?

"Natalie?" Colin said as he came out the door behind her a moment later.

She turned around to face him, not sure what to say. She felt the prickle of tears start to sting her eyes. "What were you thinking?" she asked. "You know how I feel about marriage!"

"I was thinking that you loved me and wanted to be with me," he replied, his own face reddening with emotion.

"We had an agreement, Colin. We were not going to fall in love. This was supposed to be fun and easy."

"That's how it started, but it changed. For both of us. Tell me you love me, Natalie. Don't lie about it, not now."

She took a deep breath, trying to get the words out of her mouth for the first time. "I do love you," she said. "But that doesn't change my answer. I don't want to get married. That just ruins everything that we have going so perfectly right now. I've told you before I don't believe in marriage. Proposing out of the blue makes me think you don't listen to me at all. If you did, you never would've done something like...like..."

"Something so romantic and thoughtful?" he suggested. "Something so perfect and special to commemorate the moment so you'd never forget it? Something that a woman that truly loved me could never turn down?"

"Something so public!" she shouted instead. "Did you think that you could twist my arm into accepting your proposal by having four thousand witnesses? You proposed to me onstage in front of Blake Wright! All those people watching us." She shook her head, still in disbelief that the night had taken such a drastic turn. "That whole thing is probably going to end up on the internet and go viral."

Colin's hands curled into controlled fists at his sides. She could see the ring box still in one hand. "Is that what you think I was doing with all of this? I couldn't possibly have been trying to craft the perfect moment to start our lives together. Obviously, I was just *coercing you* into marrying me, because that worked out so well for me the first time."

It was perfect. It had been perfect. And if she was any other woman, it would've been the kind of story she would've told her grandchildren about. But she couldn't pull the trigger. This was too much, too soon. She'd just come to terms with loving him; she wasn't ready to sign her life away to this man. They might have known each other since they were kids, but how much did they really know about each other?

"You hardly know me, and yet you want to change me. If you really loved me, Colin, you wouldn't force me into something I don't want to do. You would understand that I need time for a step this big, and that I might never want to make that leap."

He ran his hand through his hair in incredulity. "Yes, I'm such a horrible person for inviting you to be a part of my family and to let me love you forever. What a bastard I am!"

Natalie stopped, his beautiful, yet rage-filled words

sending a tear spilling down her cheek. There was no stopping the tears now, and she hated that. She hated to cry more than anything else. How had this perfect night gone so wrong? "You can do all that without a marriage."

"But why would I want to? It doesn't make any sense, Natalie. Why can't you make that commitment to me? You know, I always thought you were such a strong woman. So in control, so self-assured. But in reality, you're a damn coward."

"What?" she asked through her tears.

"You heard me. You hide behind this big philosophical cover story about love and marriage being this forced social paradigm and whatever other crap you've recited because you're afraid of getting hurt. You're afraid to give in and let someone love you, then have it not work out."

Natalie didn't know what to say to that. It was true. She'd justified her own fears in her mind with all the statistics and academic findings she could spew. But the truth was that she used it all to keep men away. She'd done a hell of a job this time. She didn't want to lose Colin entirely, though. Couldn't they just go back to before he proposed? Pretend like tonight never happened?

"I might be scared to take the leap, but what if I'm right? What if I'd said yes and we had this big wedding and four kids and one day, we wake up and hate each other?"

"And what if we don't? What if we do all of that and we're actually happy together for the rest of our lives? Did you ever consider that option while you were wringing your hands?"

Did she dare consider it? Her mom considered it over

and over just to fail. Time had turned her into a bitter woman constantly searching for something to complete her. Natalie wouldn't let herself become like that. "I'm sorry, Colin. I just can't take that chance."

Colin stuffed his hands in his pockets, his posture stiff and unyielding. "Don't be sorry. If you don't want to marry me, that's fine. It doesn't matter what your reasoning is. But I'm done with the two of us. One marriage to a reluctant bride is enough for me. Come on, I'll drive you home."

"I think I should take a cab. That would be easier on us both."

She saw the shimmer of tears in his eyes for just a moment before he turned and walked away. Natalie could only stand and watch as he got into his car and drove away.

As his taillights disappeared into the distance, Natalie felt her heart start to crumble in her chest. She'd been so afraid to love and be loved that she had driven Colin away and made her fears a reality.

With one simple *no*, Natalie had ruined everything.

Eleven

Colin avoided going to the chapel for as long as he could. He didn't want to see Natalie. He didn't want to spend most of the evening with her, pretending everything was fine for the benefit of his sister and her fiancé. Like any injured animal, he wanted to stay in his den and lick his wounds alone.

The worst part was that he knew he'd done this to himself. Natalie had been very clear on the fact that she never wanted to get married and yet, he'd proposed to her anyway. He'd thought perhaps it was some sort of defense mechanism, insisting she didn't want it so people wouldn't pity her for not having it.

Overhearing her confession to Gretchen of being in love with him had given him a false hope. Somehow, he'd believed that offering her his heart and a lifetime commitment would not only show her he was serious, but that she had nothing to fear. That hadn't panned out at all.

What was wrong with him? Why was he so attracted to women who didn't want the same things he wanted? It was like he was subconsciously setting himself up for failure. Maybe *he* was the one who was really afraid of being hurt, so he chose women he could never really have. What a mess.

Pulling his truck into the parking lot of the chapel, he parked but didn't get out. The rehearsal was supposed to start in twenty minutes. No need to rush in just because there was no sense in going all the way home first.

Glancing out the window, he looked around at the other cars. He spotted Natalie's sports car, plus a handful of other vehicles he didn't recognize. There were no motorcycles, though. And no little hatchback. Where were Lily and Frankie?

Reaching for his phone, he dialed his sister's number. "Hello?" she shouted over a dull roar of noise around her.

"Lily, where are you?"

"We're stuck in the Vegas airport. Our flight got cancelled because of bad weather in Denver. We've been changed to a new flight, but it's not leaving until tomorrow morning."

"Tomorrow morning? You're going to miss the rehearsal and the dinner." Colin knew the weather wasn't Lily's fault, but things like this always seemed to happen when she was involved. Who booked a flight that connected through Denver in the winter, anyway?

"I know, Colin!" she snapped. "We're not going to make it in time for your choreographed circus. That's why I called Natalie first and told her. She said she'd handle things tonight and go over the details with us tomorrow afternoon before the service. We're doing what we can. It isn't the end of the world."

Nothing was ever a big deal to Lily. She said Colin was wrapped too tight and needed to loosen up, but he would counter that she needed to take some things—like her wedding day—more seriously.

"Just cancel the rehearsal dinner reservations," she continued. "It was only the wedding party and Frankie's parents, anyway."

That he could do. Thank goodness they hadn't opted for the big catered dinner with out-of-town guests. "Fine. You promise you'll be back tomorrow?"

"I can't control the weather, Colin. We'll get back as soon as we can."

Colin hung up the phone, a feeling of dread pooling in his gut. He was beginning to think this entire thing was a mistake. Lily didn't want this wedding, and he'd twisted her arm. If he hadn't done that, he wouldn't have made such a calculated error with Natalie. Lily would be happily courthouse married. He wouldn't have learned the truth about his parents' marriage yet. There also wouldn't be an extremely expensive diamond engagement ring in his coat pocket.

He needed to take it back to the jeweler, but he hadn't had the heart to do it. He'd return it on Monday when all of this was over. That would close the book on this whole misguided adventure and then, maybe, he could move on.

With a sigh, he opened the door and slipped out of the truck. After talking to Lily, he knew he needed to get inside and see what needed to be done to compensate for the absence of the engaged couple.

Inside the chapel, things were hopping. The doors to the reception hall were propped open for vendors to come in and out with decorations. He could see Gretchen and the photographer, Bree, putting out place settings on the tables. A produce truck was unloading crates of fruits and vegetables into the kitchen.

Natalie was in the center of the chaos, as always. She was setting out name cards shaped like snowflakes on a table in the crossroads of the chapel entrance. A large white tree was on the table in front of her, dripping with crystals, pearls and twinkle lights. She was stringing silver ribbon through each name card and then hanging it from a branch on the tree, creating a sparkling blizzard effect.

She reached for another, hesitating as she noticed Colin standing a few feet away. "Have you spoken with your sister?" she asked, very cold and professional once again.

"Yes. Will we still have a rehearsal?"

"Yes." Natalie set down a snowflake and turned toward him. "It's not just for the benefit of the bride and groom. It helps the pastor, the musicians and the rest of the wedding party. They only have a best man and maid of honor, so it might be a short rehearsal, but it's still needed to get everyone else comfortable with the flow."

"Are the others here?"

"We're just waiting on the maid of honor."

"What about the parts for the bride and groom in the ceremony?"

"We'll have to get someone to stand in for them both. I've had to do this before—it's not a big deal. I had a bride get food poisoning, and she missed everything leading up to the ceremony. It all turned out fine."

"Okay." Her confidence made him feel better despite the anxious tension in his shoulders. "I'll stand in for Frankie, if you need me to. I'm not in the wedding party, so I don't have anything else to do."

Natalie smiled politely and reached for her paper snowflake again. "Thanks for volunteering. You can go into the chapel and wait with the others if you like. We'll begin momentarily."

Even though he was angry with her, he couldn't stand to see the blank, detached expression on her face when she looked at him. He wanted to see those dark brown eyes filled with love, or even just the light of passion or laughter. He wanted to reach out and shake her until she showed any kind of emotion. Anger, fear, he didn't care. She had been so afraid to feel anything before they met. He worried that after their blowup, she'd completely retreat into herself. He might not be the one who got to love her for the rest of her life, but someone should.

Natalie would have to let someone, however, and he had no control over that.

He wanted to say something to her. Anything. But he didn't want to start another fight here. Instead, he nodded and disappeared into the chapel to wait with the others. That was the best thing to do if they were going to get through all this without more turmoil than they already had.

The maid of honor walked in a few minutes later with Natalie on her heels. She had her headset on and her stiff, purposeful walk had returned.

"Okay, everyone, I'm going to go over this once, quickly, then we will walk through the whole ceremony so everyone gets a feel for their roles and how it will all go."

Colin stood with his arms crossed over his chest as she handed out instructions to the string quartet in the corner, the ushers and the wedding party.

"Colin is our stand-in groom today. After you escort in your parents, you and the best man are going to follow the pastor in and wait at the front of the church for the ceremony to start. Everyone ready?"

All the people in the chapel, excepting the musicians, went out into the hall. Colin and the best man, Steve, followed Pastor Greene into the chapel, taking their places on the front platform. The string quartet played a soothing melody that sounded familiar, but he didn't know the name. At the back of the room, Natalie gave a cue to the pastor before slipping into the vestibule. He asked everyone to rise. The musicians transitioned to a different song, playing louder to announce the coming of the bridal party.

The doors opened and the maid of honor made her way down the aisle. She moved to the opposite side of the landing and waited for the doors to open a final time. The music built a sense of anticipation that made Colin anxious to see what was about to happen, even as a stand-in groom for a rehearsal.

The doors of the chapel swung open, and standing there holding a bouquet of silk flowers, was Natalie. His chest tightened as she walked down the aisle toward him. She was wearing a burgundy silk blouse and a black pencil skirt instead of a white gown, but it didn't matter. The moment was all too real to Colin.

But with every step she took, reality sunk in even more. This wasn't their rehearsal and they weren't getting married. She had turned him down, flat, in front of a couple thousand people and a country music star.

The sentimental feelings quickly dissipated, the muscles in his neck and shoulders tightening with irritation and anger.

Natalie avoided his gaze as she approached the platform. She looked only at the pastor. Her full lips were thin and pressed hard into a line of displeasure. Neither of them seemed very happy to have to go through all this so soon after their blowup.

This was going to be an interesting rehearsal.

Natalie wished there was someone else to fill in for Lily, but there just wasn't. Everyone else was preparing for tomorrow and Bree was capturing everything—including her awkward moments with Colin—on camera. All she could do was man up, grab the dummy bouquet and march down the aisle so they could get through this.

"Frankie will take Lily's hand and help her up onto the platform," the pastor explained. "Lily will pass her bouquet to the maid of honor to hold, then I will read the welcome passages about marriage."

Natalie took Colin's hand, ignoring the thrill that ran up her arm as they touched. She clenched her teeth as she handed off the bouquet and listened to the pastor go through his spiel. They had opted for the traditional, nondenominational Christian service, passing on any long biblical passages. Colin had insisted that Lily didn't want to stand up here for a drawn-out religious service. She wanted to get married and then cue the party.

"When I finish, Frankie and Lily will turn to face each other and hold hands while they recite the vows."

This was the part Natalie was dreading. Turning to Colin, she took the other hand he offered. It was awkward to stare at his chest, so she forced her chin up to meet his eyes. The initial contact was like a punch to her stomach. There wasn't a hint of warmth in those golden eyes. He hated her, and she understood that. She had thrown his love in his face. She didn't know what else to do. Say yes? Dive headfirst into the fantasy of marriage like everyone else? She could see now how easy it was to get swept up into it. The current was strong.

Even now, as they stood on the altar together, she felt her body start to relax and her resistance fade. Colin repeated Frankie's vows, the words of love and trust making Natalie's chest ache. His expression softened as he spoke, slipping a pretend ring onto her finger.

When it was her turn to recite Lily's vows, the anxiety was gone. She felt a sense of peace standing here with Colin, as though that was where they were truly meant to be. She loved him. She was scared, but she loved him and had loved him since she was fifteen years old. She'd never felt this way for anyone else because of that. Her heart was already taken, so why would she have any desire to love or marry another man?

She wanted to marry Colin. There was no question of it now. Why did she have to have this revelation two days too late?

She felt her hands start to tremble in his as her voice began to shake as well. Colin narrowed his gaze at her, squeezing her hands tighter to calm the tremble. She was glad to have an imaginary ring, because she was certain she would've dropped any real jewelry trying to put it on his finger.

Natalie felt tears form in her eyes as the pastor talked about their holy vows. She wanted to interrupt the rehearsal, to blurt out right then and there that she was wrong. She was sorry for letting her fears get in the way. And most important, that she very desperately wanted to marry him.

"I'll pronounce them man and wife, then instruct Frankie to kiss the bride," the pastor explained. "They'll kiss, holding together long enough for the photographer to get a good shot. Then Lily will get her bouquet and the couple will turn out to face the congregation. I'll announce them as Mr. and Mrs. Frank Watson, and then you'll exit the chapel."

The musicians started playing the exit song. Colin offered his arm and she took it. They stepped down the stairs and along the aisle to the back of the chapel.

When they walked through the doorway, he immediately pulled away from her. She instantly missed the warmth and nearness of his touch, but she knew the moment had passed. The Colin standing beside her now hated her once again.

She recovered by returning to her professional duties. She waited until the maid of honor and best man came out of the chapel behind them, then she returned to the doorway, clapping. "Great job everyone. Now, at this point, the bridal party will be escorted away so the guests can move into the reception hall, then we'll bring you back into the chapel to take pictures. Does anyone have any questions?"

Everyone shook their heads. It was a small wedding and not particularly complicated aside from the absence of the bride and groom. "Great. Let's make sure everyone is here at the chapel by three tomorrow. We'll do some pictures with Bree before the ceremony. If anything happens, you all have my cell phone number."

People started scattering from the room, Colin

amongst them. "Colin?" she called out to him before she lost her nerve.

He stopped and turned back to face her. "Yes?"

"Can I talk to you for a minute?"

"About what?" She'd never seen him so stiff and unfriendly. It was even worse than it had been before the rehearsal. "Everything for the wedding is set, isn't it?"

"Yes, of course."

"Then we have nothing to talk about."

His abrupt shutdown rattled her. "I, I mean, could you please just give me two minutes to talk about what happened at the concert?"

He shook his head, his jaw so tight it was like stone. "I think you said all you needed to say on that stage, don't you?"

She had said a lot, but she had said all the wrong things. "No. Please, Colin. You don't understand how much I—"

He held up his hand to silence her. "Natalie, stop. You don't want to marry me. That's fine. I'm through with trying to convince unwilling women to be my wife. But like I said that night, I'm done. I don't want to discuss it ever again. Let's just forget it ever happened so we can get through this wedding without any more drama, okay?"

Before she could answer, Colin turned and disappeared from the chapel. Natalie heard the chime as he opened the front door and headed for his truck.

With every step he took, she felt her heart sink further into her stomach. Her knees threatened to give out from under her, forcing her to sit down in one of the rear pews. She held it together long enough for the musicians to leave, but once she was alone, she completely came undone.

It had been a long time since Natalie cried—good and cried. She got teary at the occasional commercial or news article. She'd shed a tear with Amelia when she lost her first baby in the spring and a few at the concert the other night. But nothing like this. Not since… she paused in her tears to think. Not since her father left Christmas day.

She dropped her face into her hands, trying not to ugly sob so loudly that it echoed through the chapel. There were a lot of people going in and out of the building today, but she didn't want anyone to see her in such a wretched state.

"Natalie?" a voice called from behind her, as if on cue.

She straightened to attention, wiping her eyes and cheeks without smearing her mascara. "Yes?" she replied without turning around to expose her red, puffy face. "What do you need?"

Natalie sensed the presence move closer until she noticed Gretchen standing at the entrance of the pew beside her. "I need you to scoot over and tell me what the hell is going on."

She complied, knowing there was no way out of this now. Gretchen settled into the seat, politely keeping her gaze trained on the front of the chapel. She didn't say a word, waiting for Natalie to spill her guts on her own time.

"I like Christmas," Natalie confessed. "I like the lights and the food and the music. My holiday humbug days are behind me."

"What? That's why you're crying?"

"Yes. No. Yes and no. I'm crying because I've finally found my Christmas spirit and it doesn't matter. None of it matters because Colin and I are over."

Gretchen groaned in disappointment. "What happened? You seemed pretty enamored with him a few days ago."

"He...proposed. Onstage at the Blake Wright concert. In front of everyone."

"Well, I could see how a lifetime promise of love and devotion in front of thousands of witnesses could ruin a relationship."

Natalie noted her friend's flat tone. "I panicked. And I said no. And I didn't do it well. I said some pretty ugly things to him."

Gretchen put her arm around Natalie's shoulder. "Why are you fighting this so hard? What are you afraid of, Natalie?"

"I'm afraid..." She took a deep breath. "I'm afraid that I'm going to let myself fall for the fantasy and he's going to leave."

"The fantasy?" Gretchen questioned.

"Love. Marriage."

"How can you still see it as a fantasy when you know you're in love with him?"

"Because I can't be certain it's real. This could just be a biological attachment to ensure the care of my nonexistent offspring. And even if it is real, I can't be sure it will last."

"You can't be certain of anything in life, Natalie. Maybe it's biology, maybe it's not. But by pushing Colin away, you're guaranteeing that you're going to lose him. It doesn't matter if your feelings will last now."

"I know," Natalie said with a sigh. "I realized that

today when we were standing on the altar during the rehearsal. Up there, holding his hands and looking into his eyes, I realized that I want to be with Colin. I want to marry him. He's worth the risk. But it's too late. I've ruined everything. He won't even speak to me about anything but Lily's wedding."

"I think he might just need a little time. You've both got a lot on your minds with the wedding. They're so stressful. But once that's done, I say reach out to him. Put your heart on the line the way he did. Take the risk. If he says no, you haven't lost anything. But if you can get him to listen to how you feel, you can gain everything."

Natalie nodded and dried the last of her tears. Gretchen was right. How had she become a relationship expert so quickly?

She knew what she had to do now. She had to hand her heart to Colin on a silver platter and pray he didn't crush it.

Twelve

Colin was trying to keep his mind occupied. Just a few more hours and all this would be over. He could give the keys to the house to his sister, pay the bill for the wedding and walk out of this place like he'd never fallen in love with Natalie Sharpe.

Sure, it would be that easy.

He was busying himself by greeting guests as they came into the chapel. He assisted the ushers in handing out programs, hugging and kissing friends and family as they came in. A lot of folks had shown up for Lily's big day and he was pleased. They had sent out a lot of email invitations, but in the rush, he wasn't sure who had accepted until they walked in the door.

He was very surprised to see Natalie's mother and father walk into the chapel. They had big smiles on their faces as they chatted and made their way over to him.

Perhaps time and distance had healed their wounds, even if Natalie's remained fresh.

"Mr. Sharpe," Colin said, shaking the man's hand.

"How are you, son?"

"Doing well," he lied. "So glad you could make it for Lily and Frankie's big day."

He hugged Natalie's mother and the usher escorted them all down the aisle to their seats. Casually, he glanced at his watch. It was getting close to time. He'd expected to see Frankie by now, but every bearded, tattooed guy that caught his eye was just a guest of the groom.

Glancing across the foyer, he spotted Natalie and instantly knew that something was wrong. She looked decidedly flustered and he didn't expect that of her, even after everything that happened last night. She looked very put-together, as usual, in a light gray linen suit with her headset on and her crystal-encrusted tablet clutched to her chest, but there was an anxiety lining her dark eyes.

As much as he didn't want to talk to her, he made his way through the crowd of arriving wedding guests to where she was standing. "What's the matter?"

Taking him by the elbow, she led him into the hallway near her office where they were out of the guests' earshot. "They're not here yet."

"They who?"

"Your sister and her fiancé. The flight they were supposed to be on landed four hours ago, I checked, but I haven't heard a word from either of them. I've got a hair and makeup crew twiddling their thumbs. The wedding starts in thirty minutes and I've got no couple to marry."

An icy-cold fear started rushing through his veins. He'd worried about this almost from the moment he'd insisted that Lily have a formal wedding. It didn't surprise him at all. She'd given in to his request far too easily. He should've known she'd do something like this when the opportunity arose. "I'm sure they're on their way," he said, trying to soothe her nerves even as his lit up with panic. "This has to happen all the time, right?"

"No. It's *never* happened. I have had grooms bail, brides bail, but never both of them together. You've got to track her down. Now. She's not answering my calls."

"Okay. I'll try calling her right now." He stepped away from her office and went down the hall to the far corner where the sounds of the crowd wouldn't interfere. As he was about to raise the phone to his ear, it vibrated and chimed in his hand. When he looked down, it was like someone had kicked him in the stomach. The air was completely knocked out of him.

It was a photo text from his sister. She and Frankie were standing under the Chapel of Love sign, sporting wedding rings. They were wearing jeans. She had a little veil on her head and a carnation bouquet in her hand. "Guess what? We decided to stay in Vegas and elope! Sorry about the plans."

Sorry about the plans. His chest started to tighten. Sorry about the plans? There were two hundred people in the chapel, a staff in the kitchen preparing the dinner. There were *ten thousand dollars'* worth of flowers decorating the ballroom. That was just the ballroom! But the bride and groom decided to elope in Vegas. So sorry.

When he was finally able to look up from his phone, he caught Natalie's eye from across the hall. She looked the way he felt, with a distraught expression on her face. She held up her own phone to display the same picture he was looking at.

They moved quickly toward each other, meeting in the middle. "What do we do?"

Natalie took a deep breath. "Well, obviously there isn't going to be a wedding, so we can send the preacher home. The food and band are already paid for, and there's no sense in it all going to waste. So if I were you, I'd lie and tell them that Lily and Frankie got stuck in Vegas because of bad weather and decided to elope. Invite them to celebrate at the reception, have dinner, eat the cake and send everyone home."

Colin dropped his face into his hands. How had this week turned into such a disaster? His proposal to Natalie couldn't have gone worse. His sister was a no-show for her own wedding. He was feeling like he wanted to just walk out the door and lock himself in his bedroom until the New Year.

He supposed her suggestion was sensible. There was no point in wasting all that food. "I guess that's what we'll have to do, then. What a mess. I'm going to kill her when she gets home. I mean it."

"There is one other option," she said in a voice so small he almost didn't hear it.

Colin looked up to see Natalie nervously chewing at her lip. "What other option?"

She looked at him for a moment, a determined tilt to her chin that hadn't been there before. "This is going to sound crazy, but hear me out, okay?"

"At this point, I'm open to anything."

"I'm sorry, Colin. I'm sorry about the way I reacted to your proposal. I know I hurt you and I didn't intend to. But you were right, I was just scared. My whole life I've seen relationships fall apart and I told myself I'd never put myself through that. And then I fell in love with you anyway. I didn't know what to do. When you proposed, the moment was so perfect and I just panicked. I ruined it all and I can never tell you just how sorry I am. I would go back in time and change it if I could, but I can't."

Colin had certainly not been expecting this right now. With everything else going on, he wasn't entirely sure he was emotionally capable of handling her apology. "Natalie, can we talk about this later? I understand you want to get this off your chest, but we're in the middle of a crisis here."

"And I'm trying to fix it," she countered. "Do you love me, Colin?"

He looked down at her heart-shaped face, her brow furrowed in worry. The headset lined her cheek, the microphone hovering right at the corner of her full, pink lips. Of course he loved her. That was what hurt the most. They loved each other, but for some reason, everything had gone wrong and he didn't understand why. Although he didn't want to admit it, he figured it couldn't hurt at this point.

"Yes, I love you, Natalie. That's why I proposed to you. I wanted to start a life with you and I thought you wanted the same thing."

"I didn't know what I wanted, but now I do. I do want to start a life with you."

Colin barely had a chance to process Natalie's words before she dropped down onto one knee in front of him. "Natalie, what are you doing?"

"I love you, Colin. There's nothing I want more than to marry you and build a life together. I'm sorry that I ruined your grand proposal, but I have another one for you. Will you marry me?"

Colin looked around, trying to see if anyone was watching the bizarre scene in front of him. "Are you proposing to me?"

Natalie took his hand and held it tightly in her own. "Yes. I want to marry you, Colin. Right now."

He stiffened, then dropped down on his own knee, so they could discuss this eye to eye. "You want to get married right now?"

She smiled wide. "Why not? We've got a chapel full of your family just a few feet away. My parents are even here. The wedding gown fits me. Not to mention that we've got a big, beautiful reception waiting that you and I planned together. It's exactly the wedding I would choose if we were going to get married any other day. It's going to go to waste if we don't use it, so why not today?"

Colin's heart started racing in his chest. Would they really go through with this? "Natalie, are you sure? I can't bear to have another wife change her mind and walk out of my life. If we get married today, we're getting married forever. Are you okay with that?"

She reached out and cupped his face, holding his cheeks in her hands. "I am very okay with that. You're not getting rid of me, mister."

"Okay, then yes, I will marry you," he said with a grin. He leaned forward to kiss her, the mouthpiece of her headset getting in the way.

"Oops," Natalie said, lifting it up. "Just as well," she noted as she leaned back. "I think we need to save our next kiss for the one at the altar, don't you?"

It was entirely possible that Natalie had lost her mind. She wasn't just getting married, she was getting married on a whim. It was crazy. It was so unlike her.

And she'd never been more excited in her life.

She wanted this more than anything, and getting married quickly was the only thing that would keep her from sabotaging herself.

Natalie rushed toward the bridal suite, reaching out to grab Gretchen's arm and drag her down the hallway with her.

"Where are we going?" she asked. "I'm supposed to be fetching something for Bree."

She kept going. "Don't worry about Bree. I need you to help me get ready."

"Help you get ready to do what?"

"To marry Colin."

A sudden resistant weight stopped her forward progress and jerked her back. "Would you like to repeat that, please?"

Natalie sighed and turned toward her. "The bride and groom aren't coming. Colin and I are getting married instead. I need you to help me get dressed."

Gretchen's jaw dropped, but she followed her willingly to the bridal suite in a state of shock. The hair and makeup crew were loitering there, waiting for the missing bride.

"Change of plans, ladies," Natalie announced, pulling off her headset and tugging the band from her ponytail. "I'm the bride now. I need the best, fastest work you can do."

She settled down in the chair and the team quickly went to work. A soft knock came a few minutes later and Bree slipped in with her camera. "Are we ready to take some pictures of the bride getting read—?" Bree stopped short when she saw Natalie in the chair. "What's going on?"

"Natalie is getting married." Gretchen held up the cell phone picture of their wayward couple. "You're taking pictures of her and Colin instead."

Bree took a deep breath and started nervously adjusting the lens on her camera. "Well, okay then. You might want to give Amelia a heads-up in the meantime. She'll have a fit if she's in the kitchen and misses the ceremony."

Gretchen nodded and slipped out. Within about twenty minutes, Natalie was completely transformed. Her ponytail was brushed out, straightened and wrapped into a French twist. She was painted with classic cat eyes, dark lashes and rosy cheeks. They opted for a nude lip with a touch of sparkle.

By the time Gretchen returned, Natalie was ready to slip into the dress. "Colin has spoken to the pastor, so he's on board. I brought your dad out of the chapel to walk you down the aisle. He's waiting outside."

Perfect. That was an important detail she hadn't considered in her rash proposal. Thank goodness her parents were both here. She'd never hear the end of it if either of them had missed her wedding.

"Let's get you in this gown," Gretchen said.

It took a few minutes to get Natalie laced and buttoned into her wedding dress. The hairdresser positioned the veil in her hair and turned her toward the full-length mirror to look at herself.

Her heart stuttered in her chest when she saw her reflection. She made for a beautiful bride. And this time, unlike at the bridal salon, she was really going to be the bride. This was suddenly her day, and her gown. She was so happy they'd chosen this dress. Any other one just wouldn't have suited her.

"Wow, honey," Gretchen said. "You look amazing. Do you have heels?"

Natalie looked down at her sensible black flats and shook her head. That was one thing she didn't have. "I guess I'll just go barefoot," she replied, kicking out of her shoes.

Gretchen picked up the bridal bouquet that was waiting in a vase on the side table. She handed it over to Natalie with a touch of glassy tears in her eyes. "I can't believe this is happening. I'm so happy for you and Colin."

Natalie took a deep breath and nodded. "I can't believe it either, really. But let's make it happen before reality sets in and I launch into a panic attack. Go tell everyone the bride is ready and cue the musicians."

Gretchen disappeared and Natalie waited a few moments until she knew the doors to the chapel were closed. She stepped out to find her father, looking dumbfounded, on the bench outside. "Hi, Daddy."

He shot up from his seat, freezing as he saw her in her dress. "You look amazing. I'm not sure what's going on, but you look more beautiful than any bride I've ever seen in my life."

Natalie leaned in to hug him. "It's a long story, but I'm glad you're here."

The music grew louder, cueing up the bride. Natalie nearly reached for her headset before she remembered she was the bride this time. "Let's go get married, Daddy."

They walked to the doors and waited for them to swing open. The chapel was filled with people, all of them standing at the bride's arrival. It was hard for her to focus on any of them, though. Her eyes instantly went to the front of the chapel.

Colin stood there in his tuxedo, looking as handsome as ever. There wasn't a touch of nervousness on his face as he watched her walk down the aisle. There was nothing but adoration and love on his face. Looking into his eyes, she felt her own anxiety slip away. It was just like at the rehearsal. Everything faded away but the two of them.

Before she knew it, they'd walked the long aisle and were standing at the front of the chapel. Her father gave her a hug and a kiss on the cheek before passing her hand off to the waiting Colin. "Take care of my girl," he warned his future son-in-law before taking his seat.

They stepped up onto the raised platform together and waited for the pastor to start the ceremony.

"Dearly beloved, we gather here today to celebrate the blessed union of Frank and Lily."

Colin cleared his throat, interrupting the pastor as a rumble of voices traveled through the chapel. "Colin and Natalie," he corrected in a whisper.

The pastor's eyes widened in panic when he realized his mistake. Natalie had worked with this pastor before and knew that he had the names typed into his text. "Oh yes, so sorry. To celebrate the blessed union of *Colin and Natalie*."

The pastor continued on, but all Natalie could hear was the beating of her own heart. All she could feel was Colin's warm hand enveloping hers. When the pastor prompted them to turn and face each other, they did, and Natalie felt a sense of peace in Colin's gaze. He smiled at her, brushing his thumbs across the backs of her hands in a soothing motion.

"Are you okay?" he whispered.

Natalie nodded. She had never been better.

"Do you, Colin Edward Russell, take Natalie Lynn Sharpe to be your lawfully wedded wife? Will you love and respect her? Will you be honest with her? Will you stand by her through whatever may come until your days on this Earth come to an end?"

"I will."

"And do you, Natalie Lynn Sharpe, take Colin Edward Russell to be your lawfully wedded husband? Will you love and respect him? Will you be honest with him? Will you stand by him through whatever may come until your days on this Earth come to an end?"

She took a deep breath, a momentary flash of panic lighting in Colin's eyes. "I will," she said with a grin.

"Fra-*Colin*," the pastor stuttered. "What token do you give of the vows you have made?"

"A ring," Colin replied, pulling the same ring box from his coat pocket that he'd presented her with on the stage Wednesday night.

"You had the ring with you?" Natalie whispered.

"I was mad, but I hadn't given up on you yet." Colin opened the box and settled the exquisite diamond ring over the tip of her finger.

"Repeat after me. I give you this ring as a token of my vow." He paused, allowing Colin to respond. "With all that I am and all that I have, I honor you, and with this ring, I thee wed."

"...and with this ring, I thee wed," Colin repeated, slipping the ring onto her finger and squeezing her hand reassuringly.

"Natalie," the pastor asked, "what token do you give of the vows you have made?"

In an instant, Natalie's blood ran cold. She'd planned every moment, every aspect of this wedding. Everything but the rings. She had no ring. "I don't have anything," she whispered to the pastor.

The pastor hesitated, looking around the room for an answer to the problem as though there would be rings dangling from the ceiling on threads. This was probably the most stressful ceremony he'd ever done.

Even though she was the bride, Natalie was still a problem solver. She turned to the pews and the faces looking up at them. "Does anyone have a man's ring we can borrow for the ceremony?"

"I have a ring," a man said, getting up from Frankie's side of the chapel.

He was obviously a friend of Frankie's. They both shared a common love of bushy beards, tattoos and bow ties with matching suspenders. He jogged up the aisle, slipping a ring off his finger and handing it to Natalie.

"Thank you," she said. "We'll give it back as soon as we get a replacement."

"That's okay, you can keep it."

He returned to his seat and Natalie looked down at the ring in her hand. It was a heavy silver band with a skull centered on it. There were glittering red stones in the eye sockets. Natalie bit her lip to keep from laughing. A ring was a ring and that was what she needed. There was no being picky right now. She placed it on the tip of Colin's finger and repeated after the pastor.

It wasn't until the ring was firmly seated on his finger that Colin looked down. He snorted in a short burst of laughter and shook his head. Skulls must not be his thing.

The pastor didn't notice. He was probably just happy

they had rings and it was time to wrap up the ceremony. "Colin and Natalie, as you have both affirmed your love for each other and have made a promise to each other to live in this union, I challenge you both to remember to cherish each other, to respect each other's thoughts and ideas, and most important, to forgive each other. May you live each day in love, always being there to give love, comfort and refuge in the good times and the bad.

"As Colin and Natalie have now exchanged vows and rings, and pledged their love and faith for each other, it is my pleasure and honor to pronounce them Man and Wife. You may kiss the bride."

"This is the part I've been waiting for," Colin said with a wide smile. He took a step forward, cradling her cheeks in his hands and lifting her lips to his own.

"Wait," Natalie whispered just before their lips touched. "I need to tell you something."

Colin hesitated, his eyes wide with panic. She realized then that he thought she was changing her mind. "You won," she said quickly.

"Won what?" he asked.

"You won the bet," she admitted with a smile. "Merry Christmas, Mr. Russell. It's time to claim your prize."

"That I will. Merry Christmas, Mrs. Russell."

The kiss was soft and tender, holding the promise of a lifetime together and a thousand more kisses to come. It sent a thrill through her whole body, both from his touch and from the knowledge that they were now husband and wife. He had promised her a life-changing kiss and that's what he had delivered in more ways than one.

"I love you," he whispered as he pulled away, careful not to smear her lipstick before they took pictures.

She could barely hear him over the applause of the

crowd, but she would know the sound of those words coming from his lips anywhere. "I love you," she said.

"Please turn and face your family and friends," the pastor said, and they complied. "I am pleased to present for the first time, Mr. and Mrs. Colin Russell."

They stepped down the stairs together as man and wife while the crowd cheered. Hand in hand, they went down the aisle as their guests showered them with tiny bits of glittery white-and-silver confetti that looked like snow falling down on them.

They stepped through the doorway into the lobby. Waiting for them was Gretchen. She had picked up Natalie's headset, stepping in as wedding planner. "Congratulations." She held out a tray of champagne to them both and escorted them to the bridal suite to wait while the guests moved to the reception hall.

Alone in the suite, Colin wrapped one arm around her waist and pulled her tight against him. "You're all mine now," he growled into her ear.

"And you're all mine. For this Christmas and every one to follow."

Epilogue

One year later, Christmas Eve

Natalie slowly made her way through the renovated kitchen carrying the glazed Christmas ham. She intended to put it on the dining room table, but Colin was quick to intercept her and snatch the platter from her hands.

"What are you doing? You don't need to be carrying heavy things."

Natalie sighed and planted her hands on her hips. Being seven months pregnant was certainly a bigger challenge than she'd expected it to be, but she was making do. "I'm just pregnant. I'm perfectly capable of doing a lot of things."

Colin put the plate on the table and turned around. "I know you are. You're capable of amazing things, my wife." He kissed her on the lips. "I'd just much rather you enjoy yourself and your friends instead of being in the kitchen."

"Okay," she agreed, "but you come with me. All the food is out and we're ready to eat."

Hand in hand, they walked into the great room in what had once been the childhood home of Lily and Colin. When Frankie and Lily had returned from Vegas, Colin had still wanted to give them the house despite everything, but Lily hadn't wanted it. Just like the wedding, she was happy with the simple apartment and less hassle.

Instead, after they got married, Colin and Natalie took up residence there. She was all too happy to call the old house her home. He sold the supermodern mansion and she sold her townhouse. After a few renovations to update some things to their liking, they moved into the house. It was where she'd had her happiest childhood memories and once she found out she was pregnant, she wanted her child to have those kinds of memories in this home, too.

The rest of the From This Moment business partners and their spouses were loitering around the seating area, warming themselves by the fireplace. Newlyweds Bree and Ian were snuggling on the couch with glasses of wine. They'd finally tied the knot in October—oddly enough, the first of the group to get engaged and the last to wed.

Gretchen was feeding a chocolate *petit four* to Julian as they stood at the front window admiring the extensive Christmas lights display Colin had put together outside. They had married in the spring in a small chapel in Tuscany, fulfilling Gretchen's dream of seeing Italy at last.

"The food is ready," Natalie announced from the entryway.

Amelia was the first to get up from her seat by the fire. "I wish you would've let me help you with that. There's no need for you to manage the whole dinner by yourself. I know what it's like to cook at seven months pregnant."

"I'm fine. You're always doing the cooking. I wanted to do it. Besides, you've got baby Hope to worry about."

Amelia gestured over her shoulder to her husband Tyler. He was standing by the Christmas tree, letting their six-month-old look at the lights and shiny ornaments. "Not really. He's hardly put her down since the day she was born."

"Still. I'm fine. I might be out of practice when it comes to Christmas, but I can still manage cooking dinner."

"Okay, but we're doing the dishes," Amelia argued.

"Absolutely," Gretchen chimed in. "You're not lifting a single fork."

"I won't fight you on that. I hate doing the dishes."

The crowd all migrated into the dining room in a chaotic rumble of conversation and laughter. They took their places around the table, with Tyler slipping Hope into her high chair.

It was hard for Natalie to believe how much their lives had all changed in the past two years. They had all found amazing men and fallen madly in love. Each of them had married, and soon, there would be two babies playing in the new chapel nursery. It was enough to make her start tearing up at the dinner table.

Damn hormones.

"I'd like to thank everyone for joining us tonight for Christmas Eve dinner. The holidays are times to be spent with friends and family and I know how important all of you are to Natalie, and to me." Colin raised his glass to the group. "Merry Christmas, everyone."

The four couples sitting around the table each raised their glasses to toast a festive holiday season. "Merry Christmas," they all cheered.

* * * * *

LET'S TALK
Romance

For exclusive extracts, competitions
and special offers, find us online:

f facebook.com/millsandboon

🐦 @MillsandBoon

📷 @MillsandBoonUK

Get in touch on 01413 063232

For all the latest titles coming soon, visit
millsandboon.co.uk/nextmonth